THE SPIRIT OF NAGASAKI

A NOVEL

Alan Devey is the Author of one previous novel, a romantic comedy called Wallfloweresque, and the Co-Creator of satirical webzine Home Defence (www.homedefenceuk.com).

Published in 2009 via Lulu.com

ISBN: 978-0-557-03439-0

Cover design by Chris Perry.

To my mother and to my father, who kept me away from religion back when I was most susceptible.

"I had to add, though, that I knew a single word that proved our democratic government was capable of committing obscene, gleefully rabid and racist, yahooistic murders of unarmed men, women and children, murders wholly devoid of military common sense. I said the word, it was a foreign word, that word was *Nagasaki*."

- Kurt Vonnegut, *Timequake*

Chapter One

Ely McCluskey became aware of the smoke first, a sight that made him stop weeding and stare, stare northwards and up into the air. Great swathes of acrid mess, the colour of ash, seemed to drift on the wind, float from that land owned by the religious fruitcakes and over the hill. Across the field from Ely his son paused in their work to glance from the billowing clouds of greyness to his father and back again. Danny waited to see if some non-verbal signal from the old man would let him know how to proceed. Sure enough, after a minute of motionless deliberation, Ely abandoned his work and set off, walking with purpose to the adjacent road where his truck was parked. Without needing a gesture, Danny moved from his position to join him, across the ploughed soil.

The rattle of the truck's diesel engine broke the quiet of morning as Ely sped down lanes he had traversed his whole life. Beside him Danny pulled out a battered mobile phone and checked the power level, just for something to do. It seemed the device would need recharging later that day. He only used the phone to inform his mother when they were coming for meals or to meet up with friends at the local pub, but like most kids his age Danny became anxious if the device wasn't constantly to hand. Ely's son was seventeen, a ruddy, noiseless type, one of nature's farmhands, lacking the intelligence or wherewithal to escape his family heritage. Pretty soon Ely would have to get used to thinking of his only child as a man, something he would have to force himself to do. Danny remained very much a boy.

They approached the source of the smoke, a haze that enveloped the whole horizon, blocking out the blue sky this chilly January day. The only fumes Ely had seen rising from the fruitcakes' land before were thin plumes, a sight you would associate with burning compost heaps or a campfire. This was something else altogether, a vision on a par with those fires when foot and mouth had infected the country. That was a time of great emotion in rural parts, Ely forced to stand aside as the army came to execute healthy livestock with bolt guns, throwing the cadavers onto a great, burning pyre, like something medieval and unreal.

Danny swung down from the vehicle as it ground to a halt, a gate barring the strangers' territory from the rest of this area. On the metal struts a sign warned anyone who wasn't affiliated with S.O.N. they were trespassing and would be dealt with accordingly. Normally Ely wouldn't have opened this gate for love nor money, not wishing to go anywhere near those weirdos, the source of so many strange rumours passing through local circles. Who could tell what they might do if you ventured onto their property? The entrance had been secured with a large padlock and heavy metal chain when Ely drove past before, but this time there was no such anchor. Danny simply had to push the gate with all his might, allow them the freedom to drive on.

Negotiating his way up this unfamiliar lane, Ely was assailed by another sense-memory relating to the bad days of a viral disease that decimated his industry. The man swept strands of thinning white hair back over his head. Ely had hoped he would never again experience that sensation, the feeling of being engulfed by the smell of burning flesh. He struggled to pull a worn handkerchief from his pocket to cover his nose and mouth, looking across to the boy whose face remained impassive. The man wondered if that worry and fear he felt was beginning to show on his features, he hoped not. The driver motioned to the object in Danny's hand and told the boy to dial 999, request all three services. The boy did so in his usual gruff manner, advising the telephonist to send vehicles to a field off the Old Skelton Way. By the time he had finished the call their truck was within sight of the structures making up the large farm. The outbuildings and farmhouse remained untouched, what looked like converted animal enclosures and greenhouses unaffected by the fire, but beyond them the source of the smoke grew obvious. The huge barn was ablaze.

Ely parked his truck beside the farmhouse and grabbed whatever items might prove useful from the compartments, indicating that Danny should do the same. They took tools, bandages and a bottle of water before Ely switched the engine off. It was at this point, as the coughs of the cantankerous old vehicle faded away, that a high-pitched wail grew audible across the yard. One banshee-like call, a pained scream. Danny raced after his father around the farmhouse wall, the two of them confronted with the vision Ely most feared.

This barn was enormous, perhaps fifty metres by a hundred. Flames and roiling smoke spilled from its window-slits and rose up the outside walls before dispersing into the air. Sections of the roof were wooden and alight, adding to the choking fumes that came from the construction. The scent of fuel, perhaps petrol or kerosene, hung heavy near them, mixing with the gut-wrenching odour of scorched meat. A smell that, along with the intermittent moaning, told Ely there were dozens of people inside, and all of them were dying.

The older man motioned for his son to stay well back. With the claw of his hammer, Ely began to prise away the nails that secured planks of wood over the barn doors. Danny did what he was told, staying back and marvelling, not for the first time, at how a lifetime of working the land kept his father strong and sprightly, even as he approached sixty. The cries from beyond the door continued as Ely, sweating with the heat and exertion, used a foot against the wall as leverage, the nails loosening without too much difficulty, some no more that half an inch into the thick wood. One piece of timber came free and fell to the mud-streaked tarmac beneath his feet, then another, then a third, Ely had to turn away every thirty seconds or so and raise the dirty cloth to his face, attempting to breathe oxygen through the material. When the fifth and final two by four came free, Ely paused before reaching for that handle, halfway up the eight-foot entrance. The door came ajar inch by inch, waves of smoke billowing out towards Danny with each tug his father gave.

Heart-pounding from the effort and nauseated by the sickly tang of roasted flesh, Ely took a step away from the barn, bent over and emptied the contents of his stomach on the ground. Behind him Danny could only watch in horrified fascination, the scene inside becoming terribly vivid through the vapoury gloom.

Inside charred remains littered the floor. Two corpses, blackened and smoking, were entwined in each others' arms. Around the pair tens of others lay face down or kneeling, many still alight, human forms gradually becoming unrecognizable the further he looked. Danny continued to stare into this charnel house, unable to turn away until a horrific sight jolted him. Emerging from the shadows came a smoking figure, wraithlike in its forward motion, feral noises issuing from somewhere deep in the throat. The boy took a step backwards, fighting his instinct to run and squinting to get a better look. This ghoulish being was a woman, that much was clear from her swollen belly and clothing, material that burned terribly. Much of this female was on fire, her hair, her arms, her chest and back. Danny's next reaction was to rush towards her and help, but the damage was far too advanced for his efforts to do any good. Instead the boy went on watching, eyes fixed and mouth open, as the flames licked at the woman, melting the flesh of her belly and freeing the foetus there. This unborn child flopped disgustingly from her body, hit the ground and sizzled into a puddle of blood and viscera on the tarmac. Then nothing but a red stain. Yet for a split second the child was recognizably human, four tiny limbs and a face, that face which held a clear expression, turning from confusion to terror in an instant. Danny felt his legs give out and collapsed to the ground, forcing his eyes away. The blackened shell that remained, all that was left of the melted thing's mother, crumpled like wet cardboard.

When the retching ceased Ely gathered his remaining strength to see if there was anything he could do for the victims. Though beams and sections of the barn still smoked the structure looked solid enough. The man took a glance inside, a look that told him they were too late. Afterwards, and for the rest of his life, Ely would remember those dead in their prone positions, night-black and virtually shapeless. There were tens of corpses, some with flames licking at what was once their skin, others just heaps of mangled remains, like piles of soot or carbon sculptures. At that moment Ely didn't take much of it in because a smouldering hand had enclosed his ankle when he stepped into the barn. Ely was not someone who allowed himself to feel abject fear, saw it as undignified in a man, but during those seconds his heart leapt into his mouth, and the urge to flee overwhelmed the farmer. With all his remaining resources Ely fought off this compulsion and looked down at the thing that held him.

Somehow the man was still alive. Ely knew it was a man because of his hands, otherwise it would have been difficult to tell. His body was a charred mass, one hundred per cent burns, all black except for those piercing blue eyes that implored Ely to bend down and listen to what the shrivelled lips were trying to say. He did so, catching the words "stop" and "get" but little else, the man relinquishing his grip on Ely and dying then, dying right there in front of him. His last utterances in the world were drowned out by the sirens of emergency vehicles.

Ely struggled to pull himself together, they would have to meet those authorities who arrived with their professionalism, their questions and procedures. Outside the barn another cadaver lay face down on the tarmac,

Danny crouched beside it, a soft whimpering coming from the boy as he clutched at himself, head resting on both arms. Danny's pathetic noise joined the varying pitches of police cars, ambulances and fire engines, all racing each other down the country lanes and tracks, hurrying after that unmissable beacon of distant smoke. Local cars pulled aside allowing the vehicles to pass, the drivers changing destinations in a second, electing to turn where the roads were wide enough, switch directions and follow the sirens to this incident. These motorists, overcome with curiosity in this quiet county where little of any consequence occurred, would later regret this action. Naive rubberneckers soon went back, forced away by the stomach-turning stink of the scene, while nearby, inside those dozen farmhouses that formed an erratic border around the smoke-shrouded countryside, this same smell made drool drip from the mouths of sheepdogs, the animals salivating uncontrollably.

Jon

> "Writing for a penny a word is ridiculous. If a man really wants to make a
> million dollars, the best way would be to start his own religion."
>
> - L. Ron Hubbard

He struggled to keep up with her, across the verdant plains stretching out
toward the coastline they came upon, heather and lush greenery scratching at
the half inch of skin where his slacks rode above the ankle. She was faster than
him, this woman called Rebecka he knew so well, fitter and more purposeful as
she strode onwards. It was a legacy of the decade that separated their ages, time
no amount of visits to the gym or changes of diet could claw back. Jon stopped
to breathe deeply as the figure ahead turned and beckoned him onwards. He
resumed the journey at a swift trot, jumping clear of thistles and flowers he was
in too good a mood to crush. Soon Jon caught up with her, wondering again at
the magnificence of this woman. Rebecka interlaced her fingers through his and
pulled him on with a slight smile, towards a descent that led to the beach. She
was an inch or so taller than Jon's five-eight, with dark hair and coal-black eyes,
a striking contrast to his piercing blue. In another lifetime they would have had
many children thought Jon, all with compelling features that demanded the
world's attention. That was a different reality though, in this one circumstances
had conspired against them. Only in recent years had he given up on quixotic
ideas of rescuing Rebecka from the work she had tolerated for so long. A
lifestyle Jon, despite his proclivities, could never hope to fully understand, why
she kept at it or what it meant to her. Over the past months Jon had finally
come to terms with this state of affairs, convinced himself to be satisfied with
the close friendship he was determined to continue nurturing.

    The splashing hub of imminent sea wafted to their ears through the
windless summer air. Within a few hundred yards the pair found themselves at
the cliff edge and once more Jon grew certain the West Country was the most
beautiful place in England, perhaps on earth. Beside him Rebecka took in the
foamy brilliance of the ocean and the picture-perfect greenery to either side with
an exultant sigh. Before Jon had time to try and articulate the things he felt her
grabbing at his hand and he was forced to follow, the strength of this woman

never failing to surprise him, Rebecka immensely powerful for one so slim. She led him to the stone steps that stretched part-way to the inlet, their apparent destination. Where the stairway ended the pair were forced to hop across great grey rocks to reach the sand, Jon feeling exhilarated and wicked, like a schoolboy playing truant.

They set down on a flat section of the dry sand, the only others enjoying this bay a red-headed girl and stocky guy in bathing suits over to the other side. Rebecka looked out on the sea and Jon found his sunglasses, putting them on so she wouldn't know he was staring. The woman was so beautiful, propped up there on her elbows, long legs stretching out to the tide, the only sign of her advancing years those crows' feet spreading across from the edge of each eye. But he suspected she wasn't untouched by ageing inside. On each of his recent phone calls Rebecka sounded despondent, uninterested in her life or his words. A cliché perhaps, but her voice was that of a woman who badly needed a holiday.

Despite his optimism through the concoction of this trip, Jon was still surprised when she agreed to come. Being able to afford this kind of getaway was one of the advantages of his position, an affordable indulgence on the director's wage that was no more than he deserved after twenty-eight years of ten-hour days. He had accrued nearly three decades of good impressions from the right people, valid contributions in several meetings a day, a steady reputation for diligence that saw him rise up the corporate ladder with ease. So it was a rare perk of his existence to bring Rebecka here, tell his wife the next week would be taken up with some vital business trip, then drive this woman to their guest house and give back some of that pleasure she had lost over the months. He'd seen Rebecka smile more over the past two days than during the ten times they had met previously, his trysts with the woman becoming less and less frequent in recent years. Despite this drift away she still crept into his mind in bored moments, the first thing he thought of in the morning and his mind's last memory at night, ever-present in Jon's head as she had been for fifteen years.

Jon Foulkes rented separate rooms at the bed and breakfast because he wasn't optimistic enough to believe anything physical might happen. Neither did he wish to give Rebecka a reason to remonstrate with him, something she would surely do if he tried anything so hackneyed as a seduction. It was more than eight years now since she had last made love to him, and none of the exorbitant sums he offered since then proved enough to make Rebecka change her mind. Jon wasn't downhearted any more, he reckoned she had lost a taste for the act of sex rather than any individual man, but it had become increasingly difficult to remain close friends, what with his schedule and her role. Jon began to lose his desire for the other girls in her house, feeling mercantile and inappropriate, something he had started to experience in his conscience as the unfaithfulness it was. When their encounters became infrequent hope ebbed away from Jon, cynicism that led him to consider turning his career part-time, contriving to spend more time in social clubs, wine bars, gymnasiums. Meanwhile Rebecka's mindset seemed to take a parallel turn for the worse, her role in the house bringing with it many problems, both from the silly girls who lived there and the punters who frequented it. Now these complications were far away for them both, at least temporarily. The woman lay back on the sand, sunlight glinting off her aquiline nose, hundreds of miles from a grey northern city whose very name summoned up twin spectres of tedium and drudgery. A rush of fatigue overtook Jon. The man decided to lay back and rest his eyes as well.

Jon awoke as Rebecka raised herself. She had turned from the sea and was staring at a formation of rocks across the inlet, her gaze unwavering and intent as the woman looked to this glistening, black configuration.

"What is it, what do you see?" The question was asked in the voice of a lover. Rebecka responded with a low whisper.

"There, before the base of the cliff." A finger pointed. "Can you make it out? See what those stones look like."

Jon squinted at the rocks she indicated, much eroded and haphazardly arranged by nature, formed into the general shape of a person. Before he could mention the strangeness of such a sight Rebecka had risen and walked towards this grouping, slow and deliberate across the sand. With some effort Jon got up to follow her, joints clicking as he did so. The formation was near the young couple who did not look up, engaged as they were in the sharing of a cigarette. Standing beside Rebecka, Jon was struck by the resemblance of the main rock to some kind of human being. The odds of this occurring naturally must have been astronomical.

"It is she," Rebecka gripped his arm forcefully. "But she has turned her back on us. She has turned her back on the whole world."

Jon felt his blood run cold. "Who?"

"Holy Mary, mother of God."

He looked again, this time making out the shape of a female figure reversed amid the rocks. How Rebecka knew, with a voice and touch that transmitted nothing but certainty, that this arrangement was a manifestation of the Biblical virgin, Jon couldn't comprehend. He was about to ask when the woman's hand clenched, fixing the flesh below his shoulder in a painfully tight grasp.

Jon turned his head. Guttural noises had begun to come from somewhere deep in Rebecka's throat, unearthly grunts and rhythmic growls mixed with sharp yelps, cries of a kind Jon had never heard a human make. The woman's eyes rolled up into her head, only the whites remaining visible, and the upper section of her body began to shake spasmodically. The flesh of Rebecka's face and neck had found the most nauseating shade of grey. Jon longed to escape her arm, run and get help, but despite the panic deep inside him, Jon could not free himself, such was her vice-like grip.

Startled by these eerie noises, the young couple arrived at Jon's side, the stocky guy evidently wishing to help in some way, although one look at Rebecka's abnormal appearance warned him off grabbing her or trying to calm the woman down. The pair remained several feet away from this unpredictable creature instead, addressing their questions to Jon.

"What's happening to her?" The guy asked.

"She saw the Virgin Mary in those rocks over there." Jon fought the words out through the pain in his arm and no little horror at the course events were taking. "Then this happened."

"Looks like some kind of trance." The redhead had to shout above the groans. "Has she experienced anything strange like this before?"

"I don't know."

Behind them two more tourists walked around the outcrop that separated the bay from the rest of the beach, a middle-aged couple sauntering across the wet sand as the young girl spoke with her boyfriend.

"I think she's receiving some kind of message."

"Really?" The guy wasn't convinced. "Do you really believe that Joanne?"

Joanne said, "I've told you not to mock people."

Rebecka gave out a sequence of shrieks that caused Jon's heart to skip, the woman rocking so far back he feared she was going to pull them both down onto the sand. All feeling was gone from his left hand now, the circulation cut off. It was to be minutes more before Rebecka finally relinquished her hold, time in which the middle-aged pair hurried across to witness the cause of this commotion. Beside them the teenage girl dropped to her knees to make a silent prayer, something that embarrassed her boyfriend who, like Jon, was at a loss how to proceed.

The reverie ended as suddenly as it had begun, Rebecka's dark eyes returning to their natural position as her cries ceased. She fell to the sand and Jon was released, staggering back a couple of steps, out of breath and clutching at his sore arm. The inlet became quiet again, a silence broken only by the occasional squawk of a gull passing overhead. The oldest man, a fellow in shorts and roughly the shape of a bowling pin, rushed over to an unconscious Rebecka and tried to rouse her with exhortations and light slaps to the face. Jon and the younger man gathered to help but all three took a step back when the woman's eyes flicked open, glaring at them like a betrayed hypnotist. Unsteadily, but refusing the hands that offered help, Rebecka rose and walked towards Joanne who remained on her knees, mouth forming the words of an invocation. The girl looked up at this older woman as Rebecka placed a hand on her forehead, raising Joanne to her feet as though operating the strings of a puppet. Once the girl was fully upright Rebecka relinquished her touch and turned to address the quintet in a voice both clear and strong.

"I have been told what to do." She said.

After that moment Rebecka spoke of many things to her astounded company. Joanne sat cross-legged before the woman, Jon standing beside her, both hanging on every word. The other couple watched from a respectable distance as Joanne's boyfriend, whose name turned out to be Stuart, looked on

10

in frustration. Rebecka talked for more than an hour without stopping, attempting to convey the magnitude of her experience in words that sometimes faltered, sometimes rose, powerful like entreaties. Mary had appeared to her, as real and lifelike as those figure who sat before Rebecka now, the Virgin there to relay a message from God. He was unhappy she said. More than unhappy, He was sickened. Sickened by the religions that took His name as a starting point but neglected the teachings of His son, sickened by those who chose to manipulate the Bible for their sinful ends. Soon a day would come when the Lord once again returned to mend his creations, cleanse this land of false idols and excesses. But God would not be the wise and caring deity He was without giving His flock the chance to escape their fate through unselfish acts and pious living. To that end, one person had been chosen to free the God-fearing from this broken and flawed world; a woman Mary called *The Goddess Rebecka.*

This Goddess would enable those who followed her to find salvation through the teachings of Jesus, within a new way that would exclude no one. Such was the weakness of existing religions, their outdated prejudices, the many forms of bias, a favouring of the rich over the poor; the educated over the lost. This was not the way Jesus taught us to behave two thousand years ago. The Goddess must welcome anyone who would contribute to her new way of worship, refugees from a spiritless world rotten with addiction and bigotry. Because salvation is most important for those who possess nothing, those our culture ignores except to exploit. The young and disenfranchised, the disaffected minorities, the silenced and alone. All would be welcome, freed and put back in touch with their bodies, flesh created in God's image but neglected or forgotten in the rush of everyday life. They would be freed to reclaim their place in the natural world, a family of love and liberation only she could bear from now on.

Rebecka had asked the apparition how it was possible she, one woman, could find the strength to achieve all this, to which the Virgin Mary spoke again in her unearthly tones, like a thousand bells tinkling across the sky.

"You are not alone my Goddess. Look around and the means will become clear. Like the rest of His flock, you have lost the ability to see what is important, thus you have betrayed your true potential. Now I flood your life with truth, restoring magic to the lives of others before it is too late, saving followers with imagination and belief. Humanity cannot continue along its current path. Very soon our Lord will return to restore His world to its former glories. Only those who have learned the lessons of humankind's past tragedies can escape. Only those who use this knowledge to live by the teachings of Jesus can avoid being held to account. Simply by saving others with empathy and love, by relearning equality and tolerance, you may transcend corruption and false paths in order to save yourselves. God has chosen to work through you Rebecka. This time the story begins with a woman of woman born."

Jon banged another metal peg into that soft earth beneath the grass. A field overlooking the inlet wasn't the ideal place to pitch a tent, too overgrown and exposed, but doubtless this hadn't been a consideration when Rebecka gave out the instructions. This request came after all her talk had ended, after she had spoken in vague terms of a glimpse into the apocalypse granted by her vision. She maintained those present at the start were the privileged ones, avatars of this new way of worship that would enrapture so many, just as she had been caught up in the rapture that day. It was at this point two things happened, breaking the stillness of the scene. First Rebecka rose from the rock on which she was seated and placed a hand on Jon's forehead, whereupon he felt a flood of inner peace, the like of which he had never experienced before, only hearing of such tranquillity when addicts described receiving their fix. Bending down to whisper in his ear, Rebecka told Jon to collect her belongings from the guest house and purchase five Bibles and a dozen candles. At the same time Stuart came over to Joanne, the girl younger than Jon had first thought, maybe eighteen or nineteen. He forcibly demanded she accompany him away from "all this crap". When Joanne refused, Stuart attempted to pull her up by the arm. Finding the girl tensed against him, Stuart was reduced to inchoate threats, how he would call "her father" or "the police". These warnings were abruptly silenced when Rebecka turned her furious gaze on him. Jon last saw Stuart stumbling across the beach, hands desperately trying to extract his mobile phone from a pocket.

Whatever garbled message Stuart communicated to the authorities he hadn't convinced them, there were no officers or police cars intruding on the coastal setting when Jon returned from his expedition a couple of hours later.

Along with the requested goods he had stocked up on provisions and found a camping shop where Jon bought the largest tent he could find, a twelve-berth he was ordered to fix into the ground along with a two-man teepee. Jon knew these would come in useful, Rebecka said earlier she would not be leaving this scene until further guidance arrived.

The middle-aged couple left after that initial speech in a typically British manner, preferring to ignore events they couldn't fully explain. Evidently they or Stuart had got through to the local television station because, despite the lack of police, Jon was forced to park far back along the road when he returned, behind a white van bearing the logo of West Country TV.

Down on the beach the report was getting started, Joanne watching with fascination as Rebecka allowed small amounts of make-up to be applied to her face. A thirty-something blonde briefed the Goddess on her role while sound people and cameramen adjusted their equipment.

"I think we have enough background information on your story Miss Marsden. Now, when I ask a question, speak clearly and look at me. The mike will pick up whatever you say."

"I understand." There was none of the upbeat sureness that had characterized her earlier speech, Rebecka looked suspicious of this whole procedure. Still she had accepted the situation, probably interpreting this interview as God's will, another outcome written in advance. Jon set his bag down and sat beside Joanne on the beach to watch the action, the girl smiling up at him as he touched her arm.

"What will be the central message of your religion?" Asked the interviewer.

"The message we shall put across is that it's not too late, though soon it will be." That voice was back again, sure and deep. "Now is the time to return to the true lessons of the Bible, those taught by Jesus Christ our Lord. Thanks to the will of God I have been chosen to show this path to anyone who comes looking." Rebecka turned her head so she faced the camera, much to the distress of the blonde who motioned for the interviewee to turn back, a signal that garnered no response.

"This is a spiritual movement, it exists for anyone who feels they should give up all that clutters their life. In return I will create the world anew inside the collective mind of my followers, a world of love and hope, free from the hypocrisy and anxiety of our days." Rebecka's dark eyes bore their way into the lens. "You will require more than vague faith and good intentions in this new world. Traditional churches and their antiquated teachings cannot hope to understand the state of our planet." At this point her voice grew in volume, booming across the cliffs. "For all who spend their days in pursuit of wealth, who would rather stare at screens than the wonders of our earth, who feel out of place and unhappy, confused and lost. For all of you, forget what has gone before and join me here. We are creating new heavens and a new earth, everything from your past will be forgotten."

The call to arms was simple and breathtaking, a testament to Rebecka's considerable magnetism. Jon checked the guy ropes of the smaller tent, saddened to ponder how her words would become diluted in the context of the television piece. Undoubtedly much of the story would be lost, too intense for an escapism-seeking audience, this world-altering incident reduced to a final story on the regional news, one piece of quirky local colour, edited to depict Rebecka as some kind of wacky eccentric.

Jon placed his mallet beside a patch of heather, unzipped the flap and moved inside the tent, breathless but pleased. Even if you disregarded her story, and Jon did not for he had been there, the change in Rebecka was inexplicable. How had this woman suddenly been granted the erudition of a gifted public speaker, a talent she had never shown in all the years Jon had known her? The only possible explanation was the one given, and it wasn't just her delivery but the message as well, a message that struck a chord deep inside him.

Dusk approached now, enveloping the coastal landscape like a grey-haired uncle embracing you at twilight. Jon thought of his home life, how small a role Susan had played in his existence recently, how simple it would be to leave her and the lifestyle she was associated with far behind. Jon wasn't concerned about what might happen; his wife could only accept the decision. She had no choice but to realise they all had parts to play in Rebecka's grand plan. Something had happened this day, down in the cove where, even now, Joanne and the Goddess lit candles and meditated together, and although Jon possessed neither the mental resources nor the imagination to understand exactly what it was, Rebecka's vision gave him a chance to aid her in this task, to see events through with his newly-named Goddess.

He could hardly have suspected it then, but that first evening in the church would be the high point of the experience for Jon. Guiding that fine woman and her first female acolyte up the darkened steps to their new quarters, staring at the candlelit splendour of her face as she embellished their manifesto, talking of a return to the numinous beauty of God's world, restoring silent mystery to lives where everything has been explained, diminished by some expert or scientific theory. Then she kissed him on the cheek, a whisper of thanks in Jon's ear before retiring to sleep in the larger tent with the girl. It was to be the last time she would touch him.

By the afternoon of the next day they had begun to make their way to the bay and surrounding area, the curious and hopeful, those who found something in Rebecka's mission statement, however much it had been warped by the television producers. Some were travellers, intending to pass through but so enthralled by the story of what was taking place they pitched down right there. Others came with nothing, hitching south and walking the final miles to learn about God's plan and themselves. These wanderers found kindred spirits at the site, young people without jobs or the desire to take up a career, drifters and dropouts, the scions of middle class empires who had rejected the cash-conscious way of life. Rebecka found places in the tents for those without the means of shelter, took them aside one by one to find out about their backgrounds and brief them on her vision, assure each individual they would have a purpose very soon, a role in the church set aside just for them.

As the week ended the fields above the inlet took on the appearance of a commune. A dozen or more tents dotted the heather, youngsters descending the steps to bathe in the cool sea. People smiled and smoked and talked and fell laughing into each others' arms as the Goddess oversaw it all, sometimes receiving individuals in her quarters but mostly spending the days alone, studying her Bible and thinking. On those rare occasions when she sought out Jon's company it was only to instruct him on supplies. Apart from basic foodstuffs, each of the new arrivals was allowed one additional item per day, and Jon would be accompanied by a couple of girls as he drove to the nearby village, collecting tobacco and chocolate, wine and snacks. He didn't mind the expense, being able to help made him feel good. Even seeing so little of Rebecka seemed perfectly understandable. She was preoccupied with recent events and the shared future, forever musing. Jon's days came to be filled by others, youngsters using him as a source of advice, an elder statesman to be grilled on aspects of life, a kind of surrogate father. He wasn't sure how useful his advice was on subjects as diverse as families, love, or the failings of the world at large, but it didn't seem to matter. Like most teenagers, these kids just wanted someone to absorb their words and respond when they talked. Jon Foulkes was more than capable of filling that post. As the evenings drew in one of the girls might fall asleep with her head in his lap, or grab Jon by the hand and lead him to the sea where they took moonlit swims without the burden of clothing. The man felt his libido stirring once more. Resurgent desire, amorous inclinations he had feared were lost to history.

Unfortunately this idyllic state of affairs couldn't continue. At the end of the week his allotted time for the business trip would be up. Much to his chagrin, Jon was forced to make the journey north. He left as day broke over the ocean, the first one to rise, a man stopping for a moment to stare at the impromptu campsite, tents of every shape and size with confused folks inside them all. All except the largest, where great conviction dwelled.

Seated in his Peugeot, Jon experienced the outside world for the first time in days, days that seemed like months, he had travelled so far within himself. The radio was full of sombre talk, wars and escalating tensions, suicide bombers and spree killings, endless terrorist activity. The Western world was intervening with a bludgeon, forcing countries into taking sides on the Middle East, on China, on Africa and Eastern Europe.

By the time Jon reached his detached house Susan had left for her weekly stint at the playgroup, one day a week looking after infants that might have sated her desire to mother, a need that had never been satisfied by children of her own. Or maybe these Mondays only served to increase her yearning, Jon had never been able to work it out. He phoned colleagues and superiors at work, using his influence to successfully negotiate an extended leave of absence. Then Jon threw the remainder of his casual clothes into a suitcase and was almost out the door before he remembered the note. The letter apologized for

16

his absence without explaining it, contained words imploring Susan not to worry without telling her why, sentences assuring her he'd be in touch but not mentioning when. Jon left the envelope beside the telephone where she couldn't fail to see it then locked up and leapt into his car, tuning the radio to a classical music station this time.

The dashboard clock was showing well past midnight when Jon got back to the coast, exhausted but elated. From the road he could hear singing, saw the orange light of wood-fires that had come to characterize nights at the gathering. Yet something felt different as he walked across the scrub toward camp, and for the first time the unmistakable scent of marijuana hung in the air. As Jon approached his tent Joanne gave up her place around the blazing fire and skipped over to the largest structure, pulling at the canvas.

"Goddess, goddess - he's back."

Joanne looked over at Jon and after a few seconds a man emerged from the tent, followed by Rebecka. In the moonlight Jon saw this person was much older than most of the arrivals, probably in his late thirties and tall, over six feet. Both figures approached Jon. The man offered his hand.

"Hello there, good to meet you."

"Jon, this is Douglas. He came here today to help us."

Douglas smiled at Rebecka. "The moment I heard about the Goddess here I had to see this for myself. After witnessing Rebecka on television I was convinced of her veracity." Jon nodded unsurely as Douglas continued. Rebecka was standing awfully close to him. "After all, who could argue with conviction like that?"

Jon pulled three folding chairs from inside his tent, careful to avoid the dozing form of a teenage girl passed out in his sleeping bag.

"Why don't we take a seat?" He said.

"Douglas asked me to show him the place of my vision." Rebecka was struggling to bury an aspect of her voice as she sat, some undertow of childlike excitement. "And while we were there I had another one."

"It really was quite something." Douglas took Rebecka's hand in his. Jon felt a cold shiver run up his spine. "Tell him what you saw Goddess."

"I was granted a glimpse into the future Jon. I saw the three of us running a church the like of which had never been seen before, one that understood how to save the people of this century. I saw a faith rescue hundreds of God's children from the unhappiness of their lives."

The two of them waited for a response.

"Sounds possible." Jon said softly.

"Possible? It's more than possible! Look around you Jon." Douglas cast a hand across the surrounding acres, a gesture that took in the kids singing half-remembered hymns. "This is already happening, and it's we three who can make sure the potential is effectively channelled."

Up close Jon could make out the man's features more clearly. Douglas possessed the symmetrical features and square jaw of a matinee idol, a jutting end to his face that contrasted wildly with Jon's own weak chin, tapering off unhappily into the flabby jowls no amount of working out could remove. This man's hair was exceptionally black, perhaps unnaturally so, leading Jon to suspect he died the follicles. Douglas was dressed smarter than anyone else in the field, adding to the general air of authority about him, an air that made Foulkes chary, unnerved.

The man went on. "This afternoon the Goddess and myself set ourselves down with two copies of the good book and the task of interpreting her revelations. I think you will be amazed by the understandings we gleaned."

"I get it now Jon, so much more clearly than I did." Rebecka and Douglas looked at each other as she spoke, glances of respect and a hint of something else. "These are unsure times we find ourselves in and the young are the most vulnerable. They do not have a bedrock of faith to guide them through frightening times."

Douglas cut in. "But what we have here Jon, what we three possess that could be so unique, is a certainty. One offered by God Himself. The way forward is here. Though long and hard and fraught with pitfalls, it is correct. That way shown to the Goddess."

"I feel blessed, like Abraham when our Lord led him into casting everything aside. For a life he could not predict in a land he did not know."

"We haven't had time to work out all the tenets of this faith, I've only been here a matter of hours." A wry grin from the man. "But what we do possess are foundations from God to build our intricacies upon. These intricacies will form a gateway to the spiritual experience for searchers who have come to us. Those and many others yet to find the Goddess. There's will be a life suffused with Godly alternatives to the world's venality, a way of entering into the simple joys of both this life and the next, joys forgotten in the ridiculous rush of society."

"Douglas knows of what he speaks." Her hand rested in his. "For years he has studied our modern culture, how it corrupts and distorts, replaces belief and meaning with false deities."

"Do you know what I've discovered Jon? What people really want despite all the frivolous distractions they surround themselves with every day?" Douglas didn't wait for an answer. "The only thing our brothers and sisters genuinely wish to know, the only thing we all need to be sure of, is that God loves us."

The warm night air carried the laughter of youngsters across the field. Some had risen from their places around the fire and begun to dance, eyes shut and arms outstretched, as if feeling the wind. When Jon spoke he tried to keep the irritation out of his voice, retain that equanimity he knew was essential to the new spirit of cooperation.

"Fine, I'm familiar with what you say and I think you're right." He paused. "On most of the points anyway. What I need to know is this." The duo fixed their eyes on Jon. "What do we do next?"

Douglas said, "Well Jon, we can't stay here. As refreshing as I find this little gathering, somebody owns the land. Whether it's the National Trust, the council, or some other body, they're sure to intervene soon. When they do it will cause the kind of negative publicity we need to avoid."

"The church requires a base." Rebecka was level-headed again, typically persuasive in her tones. "Probably more than one, otherwise we will have nowhere to recruit."

"I have property, a house on Cornish land where Rebecka can move to, at least for a while. I'm only too happy to give this place up for whatever purpose the church can find."

"However, we cannot ask Douglas to open his doors to strangers."

"Besides, the farm is somewhat isolated." Douglas paused, as if reflecting on this. "No, we would need somewhere closer to what is laughably

19

called *civilization* in order to operate effectively."

"Which is why I'm asking you to lease us a property in central London." Rebecka looked Jon over. Perhaps she thought he appeared strangely bereft of enthusiasm, but it was mainly fatigue and shock taking its toll. Jon was attempting to take everything in, not be unsettled by the propensity of these two to pick up the conversation where the other had left off, a habit he and Rebecka never managed.

"If it's the money that concerns you, just think of it as a loan." The man eyed Jon with concern. "I foresee the church generating it's own revenue streams with no little immediacy."

Jon spoke wearily, "I can't say I have a problem with cash flow." He yawned. "I'm just exceptionally tired, it's been a long day."

"It has for us all, long but revelatory." Douglas turned his smile to the admiring face of Rebecka.

"Yes, well, if you'll excuse me. I shall discuss this with you further in the morning." Jon rose and folded his chair, a question occurring to him as he did so. "Oh, one last thing."

"Yes my brother, what is it?"

"Do we have a name yet?" Jon addressed his query to Rebecka. The Goddess answered without hesitation.

"We were christened by my vision today." Behind them wood crackled on the fire. "From this day forth our church will be known as *The Spirit Of Nagasaki.*"

The Spirit Of Nagasaki. S.O.N. in acronym form. An appropriate abbreviation for a faith based on lessons from the Son of God. Yet Jon felt the monicker was somewhat off-putting. A name Rebecka and Douglas had meant to remind the human race of its disastrous history, a history this new faith would enable them to move away from, ended up conveying a message more redolent of past horrors than the optimism their church ascended from, that brightening future her vision showed them all. But what the Goddess wanted, the Goddess got. If the apparitions appearing to her said The Spirit Of Nagasaki, then The Spirit Of Nagasaki it was to be. Jon guessed he had spent too much time listening to PR executives, all exhorting the values of positive messages behind the brand. What the movement was called mattered little, as long as it's tenets were in place. This wasn't about marketing; it was about showing people the way. They weren't pushing some universal product. Those for whom God willed it would be saved.

What was more upsetting to Foulkes was the way Douglas had ingratiated himself within the movement straight away. The man undeniably had something, a compelling personality and comprehension of the people around him, something that made you eager to win his approval, whatever your age or status. Jon didn't mind that, had fought against the tendency to subordination when introduced to Douglas himself, saw now how his leadership abilities could only be assets to their cause. No, it was the way Rebecka regarded Douglas that irritated Jon. She looked to him with a sense of wonder, wonder approaching awe, and it seemed inappropriate. After all, wasn't she the one our Lord had chosen to commence His work? She should admire no one. Then there was the way he had gone into detail on the financial aspects of the church, matters that seemed crass when there were many other important aspects to think about. Rebecka hadn't mentioned money since her vision, and to Jon it wasn't an issue. He possessed the necessary credit, to be used in whatever way she deemed fit, end of story. The woman understood this implicitly, devoted her time to the significant questions instead. And that suit Douglas wore? That apparently hand-tailored and irrelevant status symbol? How out of touch did he wish to seem? Most of the people who stuck around did so to escape those who wore suits, Jon certainly had. But it would be petty and counterproductive of him to mention these errors, so Foulkes held his tongue and proceeded to do what was necessary, both for Rebecka and himself.

A couple of weeks later Jon was speeding east, covering the two hundred miles from the wilds of Cornwall to England's capital. Behind the wheel he smoked and tapped a finger in time to a recently purchased Mozart CD. The man was heading to his office on the top floor of a terraced property in Soho, a dilapidated dosshouse until recently when Jon had leased it for virtually nothing via a contact made in the housing department of Westminster council. Employing various workers and handymen, Jon managed to make the place liveable inside a week. The kids who started out sleeping on the floor had moved furniture in, painted the walls, unpacked their belongings and soon each of the rooms began to fill to capacity.

Jon was returning to this, his new home, after an initial visit to Elliott's farm, a nascent paradise in the Cornish heartland surrounded by breathtaking countryside and little else. Douglas and Rebecka were the only residents beyond a couple of friends, or perhaps they were employees. This duo of associates, surly and unsmiling men Douglas didn't bother to introduce, lounged around the farmhouse as the owner detailed progression in Rebecka's plan, the woman sat at his side all the while.

Their operation would start with two-tiers, Jon running the lower one in London, assisted by frequent visits from Douglas. Those who came for enlightenment and the receiving of Jesus were to be welcomed into the fold for a trial period, during which time they would be taught lessons, both from the Bible and Rebecka. Miscreants after a free lunch or shelter could quickly be cast out, but those Jon recognized as having something to offer S.O.N., some strength, allure or conviction, riches of one kind or another, might perhaps be inducted into the second level. This upper tier was the rural way, a lifestyle closer to God and far away from metropolitan distractions. Those who made it into the Cornish surroundings would be the select, allowed to inhabit land which, in honour of the fresh theology, Douglas had christened *Newtopia*. More than followers, these were *disciples*, and as disciples of the Goddess they must forsake all worldly goods, sell their belongings and pass subsequent monies on to the church. For doesn't the Bible say, we must not pile up our treasures on the earth?

Upon arrival each disciple would undergo a planned initiation, time alone with the Goddess to confirm the individual was devoted to her above all else, Rebecka deducing which function would best suit her recruit. If the acolyte loved the Goddess above the world and its pleasures, above family and their own well-being, then they would gain the blessing of Jesus and be welcomed into the fold.

"But remember Jon," Douglas emphasized. "Only the most promising subjects can be put forward for Newtopia. We shall require documentary evidence, personal history, assertions of loyalty in their own hand, before myself and the Goddess will even consider them for this honoured place. To recreate

Eden the select few must prostrate themselves before the glory of our Lord."

Rebecka raised her leather-bound Bible and read from its pages.

"*As He says in Luke, If anyone comes to me and does not hate his father and mother, his wife and children, his brothers and sisters - yes, even his own life - he cannot be my disciple.*" She closed the volume. "Jesus demands all our love Jon. There is no room for belief in anything but his teachings."

"In return we bring those who pass these tests to His love, both in this life and the next. Our love for Jesus is mutual my brother, he wishes us to succeed."

Smiling beatifically, Douglas handed Jon a batch of documents and shook the man's hand as Rebecka remained solemn, barely acknowledging his departure. It riled Jon, a prickliness he felt under his skin as the car motored along, how this self-contained woman had no words of gratitude for a partner who worked twelve hour days to make sure the ground-level administration of S.O.N. fell into place. The paperwork alone was an enormous chore that could only increase, Jon was running extensive background checks on everyone who attempted to come to the house. Now he was being asked to collate files on each acolyte, observe their individual strengths and shortcomings. All this along with his role as leader of the house, a guide for the weak and confused.

Would it work? A system that prioritized a remote farm, far away from the past lives of these kids? Jon couldn't be sure. Taking in the lost wasn't financially viable, sooner or later the funds would run out, and what then? Granted, some of the new recruits had passed savings onto Jon as he confirmed there was a place for them in the church, a form of thanks for this corner of a happy house, but these donations would run out too. That wasn't the real problem though, Jon's faith in the movement had sustained him this far and it wasn't about to let him down now. God would grant them what they needed. No, what got him was those kids he lived with holding Rebecka up as some mythical figure, free of human weakness, without flaws. There she was in Newtopia, uninterested in how he struggled, too immersed in her happy little nest with Douglas, shacked up away from reality.

Outside the Peugeot a truck flashed its lights at Jon's car for no apparent reason, adding to his agitation. Whenever Rebecka was spoken of around his *filtration base*, the talk came in tones so hushed and reverent he found it ridiculous. Those who had found S.O.N. in the days following Rebecka's vision were often pressed to speak of her, pressurized by room-mates into giving up secrets about this heavenly female, the conduit of divine inspiration. Jon turned to glance at the pile of paper on his passenger seat and gave a sigh. Here were more of her words for them to fall hungrily upon, lessons regarding the evils of capitalism and a globalized world, an outlook that failed to apportion blame for past indiscretions or condemn specific sinners, boasting instead of Rebecka's ability to turn the susceptible towards the light.

The traffic was typically thick as Jon drove through greater London, a daytime bustle that played on his nerves. There were almost fifty closely-typed pages to add to her existing manifesto, meditations on the Bible and related thoughts which Jon would have to find time to work into the overall message he'd been constructing for *thespiritofnagasaki.com*, furthering Rebecka's theology through electronic means. Thankfully a natural hierarchy had begun to form during these early days in the base, a set-up where a corpulent devotee in his early thirties called Simon had taken it upon himself to ease Jon's burden, become the ever-listening ear and focus of spiritual matters. Simon was mature, analytical, and in possession of a better than working knowledge of the Bible, so he quickly became Jon's right-hand man. The checks Jon ran through the Internet revealed one or two unfortunate incidents in the man's past, but Simon was sincere in his regret and besides, they needed the help.

Jon parked his car outside the terraced house, passed Soho denizens and tourists walking nearby, people who stepped into chic eateries for dinner and drinks. Simon wasn't the only helper Foulkes had been lucky enough to enlist since establishing the town house. A terrifically sweet twenty-year-old named Jane now acted as his personal assistant and more, a business degree dropout who set herself the task of organizing Jon's schedule, typing up his notes, fielding phone calls and offering a different kind of succour come nightfall. The man opened the front door, glimpsing her flexible form in his mind's eye. This sight provided Jon with a shiver of erotic anticipation. The chants of the devout drifted from within, sing-song hollers of divine worship. Jon strolled down the hallway towards these sounds, feeling upbeat for the first time that day. In the front room Simon led a dozen or so people through the late afternoon rite of worship, a time for followers of the S.O.N. way to praise

24

Jesus in whatever words came to them, eyes closed and hands shaking in the air, music on voices that skittered between the melodious and atonal. Spotting Jon looking from the doorway, Simon gave a smile and beckoned him in. The older man refused, content as he was to observe. This was faith, pure and true, the untarnished glow of youngsters. Jane was the stand out, her lithe form and smooth movements, this girl shaking her rich hair to the rhythm of voices. Not for the first time since this church had begun, Jon felt all petty vexations humbled away from his heart, destroyed by the unity and passion before his eyes. Followers of the Goddess cried and laughed, sang and hummed, placed hands on each other and hollered out in unmitigated joy at the love of Jesus coursing through their bodies. Jon couldn't help but be delighted along with them, this communal joy welcoming him back to his empire, making the man feel he belonged.

Chapter Two

Where the hell was he going? Joe Sweeney popped another pellet of gum into his mouth and chewed at it ferociously. The woman in the post office he had stopped at half an hour ago insisted on repeating the directions until they were memorized rather than writing the route down, so by the third time she recited her admixture of lefts, rights and straight aheads, the sentences began to blend in with one another, her shrewish colleague squinting through the window at Joe's vehicle the whole time. In fact, all the locals were fascinated by the big black car, ceasing their journeys down the narrow streets to peer, then hurrying away as the owner returned. Maybe this was the source of that hostility Sweeney sensed around him. The powerful machine was like a badge of officialdom. These country folk probably thought he was someone from the council. Joe couldn't help the size or shape of his car, the Met provided it, while the nature of his work meant that Sweeney was no stranger to suspicious looks. Joe ignored them and drove on, hoping he could remember enough of the route to find his way to the farm.

Unfortunately the place he was looking for wasn't close enough to a named settlement for the signposts to help, and he grew confused by winding lanes and leafy junctions, crossroads overshadowed by canopies of oaks and birch trees. Joe punched in the number of his contact on the site but the reception was sporadic and he couldn't reach the Chief Inspector. Sweeney knew this assignment hadn't been what he needed, right from the second an early morning phone call demanded he arrive at New Scotland Yard for the 8am briefing. Apparently the HQ had to be seen to do something. The head of the Critical Incident Division was reliably informed that the natives down there were less than accomplished, needed an experienced officer to give them guidance, show the bumpkins how to proceed. Someone with a bit of media savvy was required in Cornwall to ensure the news blackout continued, at least until everyone was sure what had taken place. As the assistant to the Major Enquiry Team divulged with a chortle, none of the hicks down there could be trusted to gather the evidence correctly, never having dealt with anything like this before.

And he thought Joe had? Admittedly, Sweeney had long made his living dealing with incidents anyone else would have found unusual, for eight years since being placed in the post of Special Investigator, a floating role from where he slotted into whatever team the heads of New Scotland Yard decided upon. In those eight long years Joe had tackled the aftermath of a dozen preventable catastrophes, reconstructed flashpoints all across this green and pleasant land, from corporate killings that would never be prosecuted to mind-boggling conspiracies of murder, every case strikingly beyond the pale. But this? A bunch of religious nuts who had suddenly elected to top themselves? What role Joe might play in this episode was difficult to determine. They were dead now, probably living it up in a better world than this. Him being sent out to the middle of nowhere in order to piece it together was not what Joe needed right now.

Sweeney stopped the car at the side of a lane, the section of verge unobscured by branches, and tried his mobile again. This time the signal got through and a soft Devonian burr advised Joe how to proceed. The site turned out to be fairly close, and the rest of his journey wouldn't last more than a couple of miles. Joe jotted down the Inspector's directions and started up the engine, rubbing at both eye sockets in an effort to gain some clarity. He was running on too little sleep after the war of attrition Lillian had waged on him the night before. In some ways it was a relief to have his wife talking to him again, but unfortunately she didn't have a good word to say. Lillian had never been a verbose character, always happy to exist on the fringes of a conversation rather than actively participating, and this was a major part of her allure for Joe in his younger days, tiring of those frenetic girls who loved the sound of their own voices. But lately the quietness had been nunlike in its sweeping intensity, her silence only interrupted by single syllable responses to Joe when a nod or shake of the head wouldn't suffice. Sweeney had longed to hear her voice again but would have preferred it if the hush was broken by happier circumstances than last night's recriminations. The revelations from their daughter were preying on the minds of both parents, that much was obvious. There was an atmosphere, a feeling something was likely to give. When the argument came it wasn't like the old days, times when their differing points of view gave way to compromise, decisions allowing the couple to move forward together. Instead Lillian became accusatory and bitter, alleging that Joe had degenerated into an empty vessel over the past decade, a container for blank nothingness where once there existed a fond and loving man. Who could wonder at their child's present situation when you saw the example that had been set for her?

Taken aback by her vitriol, Joe tried to steer his wife back to the here and now, what they could do to resolve Sarah's problems, but Lillian was just getting started. She ridiculed the suggestion he might act differently, told Joe to give up on the idea of changing because she knew him too well. He had lost whatever it was she once loved. Emotionally hysterical by now, Lillian ranted about how unhappy she was every day, and when he attempted to interject, advise her there was medicine they could prescribe for that sort of thing, she just laughed and continued her raging speech, becoming even more shrill. How could drugs give them back the man her husband used to be? Bring peace to the daughter who couldn't walk outside their door without fucking up? Restore the looks and the hope and the endless possibilities of Lillian's youth? Joe gave up at this point, searched the house until he found a blanket instead, his wife's words continuing to resound through the walls. Another hour elapsed before she finally talked herself out, the noises quieting to a regular sob, by which time he had settled on the sofa, intending to grab a few hours kip, Joe dreaming of ravens and funerals and women from his past.

The nightmares were broken by the ungodly ring of a telephone beside his head, the sun outside just beginning a morning ascent over the patio. Then it was coffee and chewing gum all the way here, no time for apologies or more harsh words.

The track was pitted and strewn with stones, sections of it forcing Sweeney to progress in first gear, an action that led to revs of complaint from the unhappy engine. As the lane ascended scenery on either side began to open out, affording spectacular views of the Cornish landscape. In the distance green fields plunged into wide valleys, like something from a watercolour. Animals dotted far-off plains, the white speech bubbles of sheep grazing across their expanses.

Set against these sights was the scene Joe parked before. Police and white-coated individuals strutted between the scattered outbuildings of a farm, conversing with each other and harrying others. Several men wore surgical masks over their faces. A uniformed officer with a neatly trimmed moustache

28

came to greet Sweeney as he struggled to escape the driver's door.

"Chief Inspector Dickson sir." The officer extended his hand.

"Joe Sweeney." They shook, a smell of burning hung over the area. "How are things progressing here?"

"There were between twenty and thirty individuals in the barn when the fire started, that much has been established." Dickson continued looking Sweeney up and down, as if one glance wasn't enough for him. "It's going to be a while before we can identify any of them."

From the look on his face, Joe could tell the Inspector had expected someone quite different. No surprises there, they usually did. Tell someone from the regions that a *Special Investigator* is coming to assist them and they envisage a high-flying big shot, someone ready to tear in and expose small-town techniques for the outdated mannerisms they were. In all likelihood Gordon Dickson had never been to New Scotland Yard, but he still saw those who worked there as models of integrity and efficacy, the cream of Britain's crop rushing to complete twice the work his underlings could achieve in half the time. Instead here was the Inspector, confronted by this shambling man, at the back end of his fifties and failing to wear the age well, unkempt grey hair strewn across a partially-exposed pate and bloodshot eyes, something in the face suggesting a preoccupation with faraway matters. Joe knew how he must look, particularly to someone as wet behind the ears as this Inspector, but first impressions weren't his priority. Dickson could react any way he wanted, at least he hadn't jovially remarked on Sweeney's surname as most of the younger officers did, asking if Joe used to work in the flying squad, grinning unpleasantly and thinking they were the first to make this remark.

The Chief Inspector said, "Let me give you an understanding of the layout we we've been confronted with. As you can see, this is the farmhouse we're currently using as a base of operations." Sweeney took another glance at the free-standing structure, one hulking mass of weather-beaten brickwork. "We'll come back here after you've seen the farm. There are witnesses you'll want to talk to." They stepped away from the eroded building. "Over here are two greenhouses."

Joe followed the Inspector a hundred yards across a field of earth, the rich soil still partially frozen by frosts from a few nights before. There were two glass structures here, massive hothouses perhaps three hundred feet in length. Utterly empty now, that tinted glass concealing the interior hid only space. Whatever used to grow in these places had been uprooted, all equipment removed or destroyed prior to the fire. Behind the second construction was a small pile of charred remnants. Sweeney sifted through this with his fingertips, stalks and pieces of stem mixed with ashes and the occasional blackened leaf.

"We're not sure what type of plant-life was cultivated here." Dickson looked down at Sweeney who brushed his hands together.

"Get someone to take that away and analyse it when you have a moment." Joe rubbed the remaining ash on his trousers as the Inspector made notes in a pocketbook. "It's probably not important, but we'd do well to make sure."

"Yes sir."

Dickson strode toward the other buildings, Joe hurrying to keep pace. On the right the fire-damaged barn remained the centre of activity, assembled forces charged with collecting tiny pieces of bone that littered the interior. Sweeney looked the other way, at the figure by his side. The Chief Inspector was a clean-cut man, even down to his immaculately groomed facial hair. Joe wouldn't have put him at much past thirty with Dickson possessing the eager industriousness that ensures regular promotion, unavoidably lost by urban recruits within a year or two of London's creeping disillusion. Most likely the West Country generally threw up little more for Gordon's detecting faculties than domestic disputes or the periodic appearance of a dead vagrant.

"We think some of them slept in here." Dickson indicated a five-foot high stone building with makeshift walls of corrugated iron at the front and back. "It used to be a sty or henhouse, something for keeping animals secure. They must have converted it into a more general shelter. There's a similar structure adjacent to this one, at the back."

Bending double to enter the place, Joe made out dirty mattresses stretching to the end of the outhouse, maybe twelve or fourteen of them laid on the floor. There appeared to be no way of heating this place. Attempting to sleep here during winter must have been unpleasant, a test of resolve to say the least.

Back in the harsh daylight and blinking like a newborn, Sweeney followed the Inspector to that final farm building, the stench of burnt matter growing stronger as the men approached the barn. Inside forensic experts used torches and protective gloves to sift through the ash for pieces of skeleton or anything else that might come to light, particles and fragments to eventually be relayed to a coroner.

Dickson said, "I advise the use of a mask if you intend to go in there sir."

With a shake of his head, Sweeney moved around the barn's exterior, coughing into a tissue as he went. At the rear Joe found something he had first spotted from across the field, a patch of earth approximately four feet by eight a different shade to the rest of the ground. Sweeney shifted some of the soil with his shoe, confirmed it was looser than the other earth. In the distance a sparrowhawk rode the wind's faint updraughts, swooping and gliding as if the action had no point or purpose, flight just for the hell of it. Dickson stood behind Joe's shoulder and spoke hospitably as the older man watched this bird of prey.

"Time for a drink I should say."

Tea was served in the farmhouse kitchen, a room empty save for the equipment the constabulary had brought with them. Sweeney sat on his own and drank, the Chief Inspector departing to track down the witnesses, leaving Joe with his thoughts, something the man was less than grateful for as his mind turned inexorably to Sarah. Joe opened his jar of pills and swallowed one capsule with a mouthful of the warm, sweet brew. There were only a dozen or so blood pressure tablets left and Sweeney had no idea how easy it was to get prescriptions around here. Joe replaced the lid and thought of his daughter the way she used to be. Once he had thanked God for blessing them with a beautiful baby girl, less pressure for a father than that man who sired boys. But Sweeney didn't think like that any more. Since puberty Sarah had presented her parents with an ever-increasing succession of worries and she wasn't about to stop any time soon. During adolescence the girl took to staying out all night, grew skinny and irritable, existing on a diet of alcohol and whatever else she imbibed, convincing herself it was all one extended good time. Older boys with battered cars began to pull up outside the Sweeney residence come evening, honking loudly until Sarah abandoned the bathroom and ran outside to join them, these hefty men happy to go out with a teenager, looking to exploit her naivety.

She dropped out of college, vanished for days at a time, returning only to provoke her normally serene mother into high-pitched shouting matches, the two women competing with each other in a force of emotion through arguments that only ever ended with slammed doors. Lillian asked where they had gone wrong while Joe stayed in the background, trying to get his daughter to take notice whenever he could. Sweeney knew the daughter would come home eventually, and when she did Sarah would need both of them, as soon as she grew out of this particularly acute phase of mood swings and rebellion.

His prediction proved horribly accurate. Sarah had arrived back at the family home a couple of months ago with her latest boyfriend in tow; a typically Neanderthal twenty-something called Clark. She proceeded to set them down in the lounge to begin her story. The tale took in a recent ear infection and the antibiotics she had been prescribed for the ailment, medicine that counteracted the morning-after pills she was taking as a matter of course and led to a late period, a miscarriage, and now a pregnancy. All the way through Sarah cast herself as the victim. Shouldn't someone out there have advised her this could happen? Spoken to a young girl of those women who had been caught out in the past? Someone? Her doctor or the clinic or the sex educators at school or someone?

They undoubtedly had Joe remembered thinking at the time. Or at least tried to, but it wasn't just her parents Sarah refused to hear. In fact, he doubted she had listened to anyone over thirty in years. So that was the long and the short of it the girl said, in six months time Joe and Lil would have a grandchild, and anything they did now could hardly alter that fact. The pair had discussed it among themselves and decided to go ahead with the birth.

Much to everyone's surprise Lillian didn't fly off the handle. Instead she embraced her daughter, saltwater staining the girl's shoulder, and gave up exhortations of love and support. At the same time Clark swore on his life to stay with Sarah, hold down his recently acquired job in the construction trade, provide for his girl and their new baby. He knew his past record wasn't good *Mr. Sweeney*, but he had turned the corner now, felt ready to settle down at last.

So yes, the kid's father was feeling proud and chivalrous and honourable, believing he could get his act together, make this life they had fallen into work for a young family inhabiting that small flat he rented. But how would he feel two or five or ten years down the line? Who could say how long Clark would stick around for? Not that these were Joe's main worries. In many ways she'd be better off without him. No, what Sweeney couldn't shake from his head was the vision of Sarah that was always conjured up now when he thought of her. The girl shuffling indoors to admit her pregnancy after many days away, a gaunt and fragile thing who, at seventeen years old, couldn't have weighed more than seven stone.

The kitchen door opened and Dickson led the way for two other men, the elder of this pair removing his flat cap as they arrived, both of their heads bowed.

"Special Investigator Sweeney, this is Ely and Danny McCluskey. They were the first ones on the scene yesterday."

"Please, take a seat." Joe pointed to the wooden chairs on the other side of the kitchen table. Ely smoothed a few strands of hair over the crown of his head while the boy kept his gaze on the floor. The kid looked disorientated and scared, maybe a bit simple as well. One glance told him these were ordinary folk who had suffered some misfortune, stumbled across unmentionable horrors in the course of their daily toil.

At the Inspector's prompting Ely relayed events from the previous day in the halting voice of one unused to conversation. His thick Cornish brogue meant that Sweeney had to make the man repeat himself several times, something that caused embarrassment for them all.

When the farmer was done Joe pondered his story for a minute or so, fingers linked behind his head.

"Do you have any opinions on the way this investigation has been conducted so far Mr. McCluskey?"

"You're barking up the wrong tree if you think they killed theyselves sir." It came out *zur*. "That barn door was nailed shut and them people wanted to get out. I'm just sorry I couldn't do more to help 'em."

"You did more than anybody could have reasonably expected Ely." It was the Inspector's reassuring voice. Sweeney leant back in his chair.

"Just one more question Mr. McCluskey, then you and Danny are free to go." At the mention of his name the boy moved slightly without looking up. "You said you *knew of* the people who used to live here without actually talking to them."

"That's right sir, bunch of fruitcakes they were. I sometimes saw 'em coming or going but they din't never speak to the likes of me."

"I wonder whether you could make a rough guess at how many people would have been living on the farm at any one time."

"Hard to say." Ely thought about it, his hand touching the white strands on his head. "There were a lot of 'em though, you'd see 'em workin' the fields most days. I'd say at least forty. Maybe fifty sometime. But there were a lot of toing and froing, like I say."

Joe extended an arm. "Thank you Mr. McCluskey, I won't take up any more of your time." Ely shook the hand. "If we require your assistance in future one of my colleagues will be in touch."

The pair stood to leave with more thank yous from Dickson and a muttered goodbye from Ely. When they were gone Sweeney pulled out his pouch of tobacco and began to roll a cigarette. The Inspector took a chair facing him and jotted something in his pocketbook while Sweeney lit the roll-up and inhaled deeply, eyes following the expelled smoke.

"I'd all but given these up."

Dickson wasn't interested. "What do we do next sir? I've been instructed to have all the manpower you need at your constant disposal."

Sweeney watched the white curlicues rise from the lit tip of his cigarette. He disliked being harried in his work, particularly when enjoying a smoke. Only his second of the day as it happened. Joe deliberately took another long drag before offering Dickson his answer.

"Gather three of your strongest men and make sure they've got good shovels." He stubbed out the roll-up. "It's time to start digging."

Bree & Josh

"The only freedom left is the freedom to starve."
- Richey Edwards, *The Manic Street Preachers*

Greg told his life story again, excerpts from the past caught by those who came and went in the kitchen as dinner was prepared. A small chap, whose utter devotion to this phase of life gave him the wide-eyed certainty of a zealot, Greg previously existed as an advertising lackey and an environmental extremist before wending his way to Newtopia and he had a tendency to bend one's ear about the route. Josh had heard versions of these tales several times before, but he didn't mind listening again. His friend was self-deprecating and witty and besides, there was little else to break the monotony of potato peeling.

The talker explained how much he enjoyed this life in Cornwall, how he'd come to hate London after living there for years. A city of the sleepless where he, Greg the insomniac, fitted in only too well, blending with the others who endeavoured to catch a few minutes shut-eye on the tube as he travelled to the agency of a morning. Every passenger deprived of the recommended nightly hours by all manner of prerogatives; the longest working weeks in Europe, too many social opportunities for the taking, noise enfolding Greg as he lay awake, sounds which split the night, from planes to trains to on-edge neighbours, incessant arguments and raucous parties that combined with never-ending construction work to disturb his restful hours. It didn't suit him, became too much, and Greg was about ready to crack when a chance encounter with an old school friend sporting dreadlocks led him to quit the marketing career, move into a squat in Bow and start a new life as an animal rights activist. His days were spent organizing raids on testing laboratories, picketing the offices of cosmetics companies, sabotaging fox hunts with false scents and roadblocks, the feeling of revolution and togetherness.

During one of the anti-hunting trips imaginative idealism got the better of several comrades. Once the chase was over they returned to the kennels and released the dogs, ushering tracker hounds into a battered transit van with the haste and conviction of outlaws.

Only when the canines were back in the squat did it become obvious they were pack animals. These twenty dogs would not be tamed. They ripped the second-hand sofa to pieces, crapped on the carpets, pissed in the beds. Worse, when someone arrived at the front door, be it resident returning home or casual caller, the beagles would rise from their positions around the house and descend as one upon this figure, growls and barks swelling to a cacophony that invariably awakened whoever was trying to nap between missions. The last straw came when the dogs almost savaged the mother of one girl, a gentle lady who had only dropped by to see how her daughter was doing and deliver some home-made jam. The bloke who opened the door had to thump one of the onrushing dogs with his hand to prevent it from jumping for the middle-aged woman's throat, at which point she turned an unhealthy shade of white and refused the offer of admittance.

That afternoon the same activist who instigated the animals' liberation returned from the outside world with two dozen burlap sacks, a ball of twine, and a vial of potassium chloride his ex-girlfriend had smuggled out of the veterinary surgery where she worked. While Greg held the beagles down the guy injected each dog with the lethal substance, a third activist tying them up in the bags. As the creature's hearts stopped, their eyelids flickering shut for the final time, Greg came to realise he no longer wanted a part of this naive idealism, struck by the carnage, all these dead dogs not worth the few foxes they might save. Fighting for the increased ethical rights of animals suddenly seemed like a hopelessly dated way of life, like Victorian thinking or free love. At that moment he experienced utter despair inside, a spirit-turning emptiness.

Greg remained blank as the heavy sacks were tossed into the collective's van and driven to Tower Bridge, each bundle passed through the arms of three young men, dumped into the Thames with a far-off splash.

It was while engaged in this gruesome task the vacuum inside Greg came to be filled with a kind of light, the sensation of God asserting Himself, levering His presence into Greg's soul. He refused the lift back, walked for miles in the city that night, trying to figure out what this wash of meaning and fulfilment could mean, a wave that had unexpectedly turned his heart. By the time Greg's tired feet dragged him back to Bow, the only possible explanation was clear. The Lord had made Himself known, answered a prayer Greg didn't even realise he was making, showing him the future in an instant.

Before Greg could explain to Josh how this moment of revelation had spurred him on, ending with his life in S.O.N. and a place in the farmhouse, they were interrupted by the appearance of Bree. She twirled into the kitchen with a flourish, kissed Josh on the cheek and held to his arm while describing her day. Any outsider to their relationship would have classed the girl as exceptionally thin, perhaps even unwell, but to Josh, who had known and loved Bree through all the drawn-out years of her illness, the girl was fleshy and well-covered, positively bursting with health. She was certainly gleeful that afternoon, skipping around her boyfriend in that theatrical way she had, radiant with happiness at the way her life was progressing. So what if they saw less of each other than during the bad old days? This was just a symptom of their new-found faith and well-being, mutual trust returning to their lives. Both Josh and Bree had individual responsibilities now, commitments to the religion that had cured her. To shirk these tasks was out of the question. That the couple no longer spent every day and all night together was a small sacrifice to pay for life, two strong hearts beating in unison. Like the Bible said, love *was* as strong as death, and that love, both for the Goddess and for each other, had got them where they were today.

Bree bid goodbye to her boyfriend, the girl's bird-like frame stretching up to hug him, Greg looking on with a smile. She had to leave them to the meal, otherwise the girl was going to be late for her afternoon prayer meet. Then there was Bree's one to one with a recent arrival who might make some progress with her self-image, given enough time. The girl spun out leaving Josh to stare after her, small curves distinct against the outline of that grey smock she wore, a dopey look on his face as he watched her move away, an expression Greg remarked on with a chuckle. Josh didn't care. The contrast between Bree's physicality now and that of a year ago was amazing, too remarkable to believe.

Back then Josh would leave the office at four every weekday, unable to concentrate on the endless customer data he was supposed to be inputting, responses and figures all blending into each other. Josh walked briskly from his workplace to the flat they shared, always hoping she'd eaten something while he was away. Bree and Josh moved in together after university because it made financial sense, both families giving the union their unqualified blessing, the devotion these young people felt for each other obvious whenever they were together. The girl was smart and ambitious although she often felt tired, standing at five foot four but seeming tinier. Josh soon noticed she was always on a diet, a habit Bree blamed on her mother when questioned. Mrs. Moore had never been happy with her shape and Bree appeared to have inherited this dissatisfaction. Hers was a strange relationship with food, she would talk of dishes and ingredients as much as anyone else, then recoil from snacks and nibbles when offered, as if the bite-size portions were alive and malevolent, like bugs.

Josh hadn't been unduly worried at first. Bree was accomplished in her studies, eventually gaining a first class degree in tourism, and she applied for jobs after graduation with stalwart optimism. Taking temporary employment to pay the rent, Josh began to make work friends for the first time, his mind becoming absorbed with their obsessions through office hours as he failed to notice Bree's worsening condition. Meanwhile his girlfriend failed miserably at her interviews, became apathetic and listless, their lovemaking grinding to a halt. Bree lost interest in the world, often staying indoors for days at a time. When she did go out, usually to accompany Josh on a shopping expedition, preparations for the trip would take anything up to an hour, an inexplicable level of disorganization for a girl who was once so systematic, Bree packing and repacking her handbag, checking her pockets and appearance a dozen times.

Here was a person who had charmed her man with a quick mind and good heart, Bree's magnanimous love of those around her captivating his soul, the way she looked beyond peoples' differences and faults to a common humanity. And this tender young woman was falling apart.

Her obsessive fascination with food, that stuff of life, the new enemy, continued to grow. The simple act of giving Bree an apple became tinged with emotions as sweeping and diverse as pleasure and terror, recrimination and regret. She would stare in wonderment at the green object until Josh could stand it no longer, ended the exhaustive rumination by removing the fruit from her grasp and holding Bree in his arms once more.

She was down to six stone nine pounds now, bones visible through her skin on those rare occasions when she gave him a glimpse of bare flesh, ribs protruding and skin waxy, like an embalmed corpse.

Josh unlocked the communal door to their block of flats and climbed the stairs. Inside his home she was balled up on the couch, daytime game shows blaring from the TV, a glamour magazine open at her feet. The girl offered a weak *hello* from the depths of her baggy jumper, worn today to conceal that emaciated shape beneath. Josh kissed her forehead and moved to the kitchen where today's notes were stuck around the surfaces. Post-its arrayed on cupboard doors bearing messages intended to sustain her resolve.

Go Without!
No!
You Fat Bitch!

He tore up the squares of paper and took a swig from a milk carton. Each morning Josh set out a selection of breakfast things in the vain hope Bree would get some nutrition inside her. Then he took a handful of prepared statements from a drawer in the spare room, despatches meant to inspire her throughout the long day that stretched ahead.

Bacon For Breakfast - Yum!
Be Well Today Girl.
I Love You.

Bree had usually replaced them with negative tidings of her own by his return, breaking Josh's heart in daily increments.

So the game went on, a particular duel within the more general sport that drove Josh to his wits' end. The contest saw the lovers on opposite sides of a divide, battling against each other, no trick too dirty if it achieved the desired ends. Bree would shake crumbs from the toaster to affect the appearance of breakfast consumed, hide food in her pockets when Josh wasn't looking, lie to reassure him. The endless falsehoods of the girl were somehow justified if they kept alien foodstuffs from her mouth, the sensation of fullness anathema to a body gradually retrained to associate well-being in the stomach with fat in the appearance. Meanwhile Josh became underhand against her, deliberately upping

39

the calorie quotient for every recipe he concocted while telling her otherwise, mixing in butter and cream, cajoling the girl into mouthfuls at hourly intervals, so little success that even a child's portion down the throat was cause for celebration. She was a kid again in many ways, one that had to be watched constantly, forced into action for its own good, a little baby who couldn't be trusted to survive on her own.

What haunted Josh through these days was the question of trust. If they knowingly lied to each other now, how could they be relied upon to utter the truth in future? Wouldn't the lies simply grow, until he began having affairs and she pretended not to notice? The stress was breaking this man, disrupting his sleep patterns, days loaded with the pain of fighting her will like it was the enemy and battling this disease as if he were a psychologist, the boyfriend becoming doctor and concerned parent all rolled into one. Josh knew his ultimate aim in adopting these personas, he needed to get her well again, this girl he still loved with every ounce of his being. But what was Bree's goal here? What were her actions the final solution to? Whatever would they result in? The girl could never be thin enough, that much was obvious. Yet at some level Bree remained that smart girl he fell for, however much her brain shrivelled with malnutrition, and that girl knew there was only one outcome to her behaviour. Bree's life would end in the drawn-out suicide of anorexia nervosa if something wasn't done to halt this decline. In an intellectual capacity Bree knew this, she could see outside herself, witnessed the repugnant spectacle Bree Moore was becoming. The girl refused to look in a mirror lest she see the gap growing between her legs, the rapid yellowing of every tooth.

Sometimes Bree would try to suggest solutions in a lucid manner, never accepting that a determination to eat could only arise from her own soul. At the same time, Josh continued to rack his brains for the answer, a key that must exist, out there somewhere.

Funny thought Josh, chopping vegetables now alongside Greg, funny-strange how his accomplishment in the culinary arts arising from those days of necessity allowed him to fill a vital role in Newtopia. Back in the bad old days he'd spent long hours inventing dishes that might tempt Bree's faltering appetite, her condition ensuring each day was a challenge, another struggle between his latest nutritional masterpiece and her illness. How rarely he'd won back then, with his stroganoffs and falafels, whereas nowadays the inhabitants of this new home gobbled up his recipes with grateful prayers.

Josh was glad his work in S.O.N. amounted to a straightforward role. He enjoyed the task of feeding many followers, often improvising from the plainest of supplies. This was not a man suited to the metaphysical questions behind his religion, those issues of theology and spiritual aid many spent their days on the farm grappling with. Indeed, Josh would never have envisaged faith as a way out of his predicament back then. The only resolution he'd come up with was to research the guts out of the disease, try to conquer this condition with a complete understanding, insights that might vanquish its hold on his girlfriend.

To that end Josh took to spending the early hours of Saturday morning in the local library. Before Bree even awoke, he would sit for hours in the fusty reading room, studying books and documentation, case histories and success stories. Of the latter there were few, it seemed anorexia had the highest death rate of any psychiatric condition, a fifth of sufferers expiring from this degenerative disease. Josh was shocked at the statistics. One book said a million women in the UK suffered from an eating disorder of one type or another. That was two hundred thousand potential fatalities. Two hundred thousand! This from an illness reported on irregularly, rarely spoken of except among the circles of the afflicted. Certainly Josh had little awareness of the immensity of this sickness, not until a loved one had come within anorexia's tightening grip.

The knowledge he was not alone, that there were thousands of men out there as anguished as Josh, failed to reassure him. Reading on, he learned how the disease was effectively incurable, sufferers stuck within a cloud of emotional guilt and physical hunger their whole lives, science and nurturing sometimes granting them periods of remission, but such intervals were brief. Before long the sickness took hold again, led to a cessation of the menstrual process and infertility, the unnatural growth of body hair, an impaired heartbeat, sometimes hypothermia. Then the defences of the body began to fail, fluid building up in the cavities, a victim's muscles disappearing, her teeth falling out and internal organs weakening. A collapsed lung, the failure of the kidneys, a heart which, in the end, simply gives out. This was a vision of Bree's future that flashed into Josh's mind when he was off guard, a picture jolting his faculties, like the sudden gory images in a horror film.

These weekend research trips proved counterproductive in many ways, upset Josh to such an extent he returned to Bree in a bout of hatred, loathing the way this girl was taking their future from them, knowing deep down it wasn't her fault, and hating that too. Yet Josh carried on educating himself, a masochistic strain of behaviour that felt proactive somehow, even if reading about this illness was usually disheartening.

The only thread of hope he clung to was this issue of remission. If 80% of those who suffered from an eating disorder remained alive, then logically anorexics should make up some of those, and there was no reason why Bree shouldn't be one of the four out of every five granted a reprieve. A brief search on the library's computer system brought up a list of county support groups, one gathering in a clinic nearby. After much urging the girl eventually succumbed to Josh's pleas, consented to attending for an hour each week, sixty minutes spent inside a room with a psychiatric nurse and ten other sufferers. They were female, all with huge eye sockets and languid stalks for arms, dressed in shapeless clothing and shuffling through the doors under the protective gaze of loved ones, avoided meeting anyone's gaze.

To circumvent a lengthy period of boredom in the waiting room with its uncomfortable plastic chairs and signs giving advice on venereal diseases, Josh began taking early-evening coffee across the road. He was joined in the faceless chain-shop by George; a naturally cheery man in spite of his current predicament. George was forty five and his daughter just seventeen, yet she had been displaying the symptoms of anorexia since the age of twelve, vetting the food prepared by others, constraining what was put into her stomach. This man saw the affliction as worse than the menace of *drugs* that obsessed so many parents his age. At least with heroin you could inflict cold turkey on your child George argued, keep cocaine or amphetamines away from the kid until their body no longer craved these substances. But how could a daughter be forced into doing something every fibre of her being opposed? It didn't work, none of their efforts to cure her, not even the hospital visits when things got really bad, times when his girl was fed through a tube to keep her alive. What kind of a life did Mary have on a drip? But the only alternative was taking her back, and every time she went home the unwillingness to take nourishment through her mouth kicked in, this girl relapsing with terrible inevitability.

Josh liked George, he was personable and ever hopeful despite the evidence, an ally in this perpetual fight against a malady aimed at removing their loved ones. He understood that unwholesome intimacy with death which comes from having an anorexic relative, made Josh feel he wasn't alone in this plight. George gave the younger man his phone number in case Josh went through a particularly bad patch or ever felt the need to discuss ways of combating the disorder.

So Josh experienced a twinge of sadness when he waited for George in vain one week, eventually drinking a cappuccino by himself which only led to more solitary brooding. The man didn't turn up with his daughter the next week either, nor at the session after that, Josh eventually deciding he should call in case the worst had happened, express condolences to a man he respected.

George sounded muted on his mobile and Josh broached the subject of Mary with care.

"Is your daughter okay? When you didn't show up Bree and I were worried."

"Apparently she's fine." George's voice was level. "Not that I've heard from her recently."

"No?"

"No Josh, my daughter has exchanged one kind of living death for another. She's fallen in with some group of religious types."

"Really?"

"Just upped and left one night, they call themselves the Ghost Of Hiroshima or something. It sounds like utter nonsense..." The reception flickered then returned. "...one phone call from Mary, they're supposed to have cured her which I would say is good news, but she's not allowed to stay in touch. She had to get special permission just to give us a quick ring. Apparently they're meant to renounce all those who refuse to believe in the Goddess, I ask you."

Josh's interest was piqued. He tried to remain sympathetic.

"Can't the police do anything?"

George gave a snort of disgust. "The authorities don't interfere with this sort of incident, Mary's eighteen now and they've no reason for suspecting

43

any harm will come to her. It's just unpleasant and foolish that's all. My wife says we should be grateful in some ways, from what Mary said she's taking regular meals again. But I'm not one to give up without a fight, as you well know Josh. We've found a support group for families who have lost loved ones to these cults, they're doing what they can..."

But he wasn't listening any more. When the older man finished talking Josh politely wished George all the best and hung up. The next Saturday he was straight on the Internet, and when the search engines failed to bring up a response to the name George had given, Josh did a more general trawl through minority interest faiths, his probe bringing up a wide variety of small-time religions including one entitled *The Spirit Of Nagasaki*.

The web site was bright and enticing, packed with theological information that Josh skipped for the most part. S.O.N., as the group called themselves, stressed the inclusivity of their doctrines, encouraged the curious to visit a base in Soho and see how their faith was put into action. Josh scribbled down this address and the next day found himself on a London doorstep explaining the motives behind his visit to an overweight man dabbing at his perspiring face. He was shown in to the hallway, offered a wooden stool while this Simon fellow fetched the person who "would be in the best position to advise you".

This individual turned out to be a man named Jon, tired from the overwork he mentioned repeatedly and in possession of the two bluest eyes Josh had ever seen. He ran through Bree's plight once again for this middle-aged man while followers came and went along the corridor, this house like a cluster of catacombs, all apparently inhabited. Jon advised him to come back when someone called *The Goddess Rebecka* was in town on one of her fortnightly visits. As the human inspiration for S.O.N., it was she who could offer the spiritual salvation Josh sought for his lover.

Jon sorted out a pile of documentation for Josh to study and checked the Goddess' schedule for times when she would speak with girls like Bree. The man advised Josh to read through the brochures and leaflets, pass them on to his girl, see if they couldn't find elements in the manifesto that touched them both. Josh thanked him and was gone, out into the chatter and swerve of a city that never stopped for Sunday afternoons.

That night he worked through the printed words of the religion. Whilst logical enough, the tenets merely confirmed to Josh he would never be theologically inclined. The argument of these people was undoubtedly convincing, there were indeed many faults in the modern way of life, but pleasing God in this world to sit at His side in the next remained low on Josh's priorities. Top of his list was that sickly girl who, if anything, had shed even more weight over the previous few weeks, and wasn't interested in the possibilities of this church, at least not to begin with. Hardly surprising, less and less drew her attention these days, but one pamphlet he offered did hold Bree's eye. The glossy rectangle bore a photograph of the founding Goddess astride a great river, the admiring faces of young women gazing up at her from the banks. Words spilled from this woman's mouth, great bold type asking the reader a series of questions.

How Do You See Yourself?

Does Your Body Horrify You?

Are You Constantly On A Diet?

Do You Set Aside Money Each Week For Plastic Surgery?

Are You Ashamed Of Being Seen In The Nude?

If your answer to any of these questions is 'yes' then you are one of the many society has lied to. It is a lie that puts thousands of women through unnecessary pain every year.

But help is at hand. Our Goddess can correct the destructive self-image you hold, an image that is so, so wrong. Call the number below to learn when the next in Rebecka's series of corrective symposia will take place in your area.

Josh mentioned the forthcoming visit of the Goddess and without having to be prompted a fascinated Bree demanded to go. She was sick of facing up to her state of health in ways that only served to make her feel more negative, the self-help sessions weren't doing any good as far as she could make out. He held her then, a sob catching in his throat, feeling that pathetic frailty beneath her jumper, wondering if this was their last chance.

Husbands and boyfriends were allowed to sit in on the symposium, but only at the back where they might go unnoticed. There were five women of varying ages alongside Bree in the room, all seated in a semicircle around Rebecka who spoke with compelling clarity, establishing eye contact with each of them in turn.

The Goddess wouldn't stay in this building when she came to London thought Josh, sat in the shadows like a spare part. Rebecka had arrived a short while before the talk, flanked by two large men, and she proceeded to greet some of her acolytes, many of whom asked to be touched, like a crowd of royalists reaching for the Queen. Not that the woman gave off regal airs or graces, this darkly attractive Caucasian with the lined skin. Rather she possessed the offhand manner of one who is aware of her own importance, but unwilling to let this understanding bleed into arrogant behaviour. The Goddess was striking and cold and when she spoke the words captivated them all, her assertion that the cure for every contemporary ailment could be found in the Bible if only we knew where to look.

She quoted the Word from memory, "*I say unto you. Take no thought for your life, what ye shall eat, or what ye shall drink; nor yet for your body, what ye shall put on. Is not the life more than meat, and the body than raiment?*"

"The world you live in." Rebecka went on, black eyes flicking between the women. "Has convinced you that irrelevancies are vital, impossibilities must be sought continually, strive all your lives while choosing to neglect God-given well-being and happiness. Let me speak an absolute truth that may shock you my sisters. Every negative thought you have of your body is untrue. They are lies created by a sick society that depends on your insecurity for profit, the revenue from its diet schemes and beauty products. Our flesh was created in God's image as clearly as any man's. When you starve and make your body sick because you wrongly believe it is the thing to do, you defile our Lord's handiwork."

Rebecka rose from her chair and walked behind the girls, resting a hand on each of their foreheads in turn. "I know it will be hard, the road to recovery is long. Your poor souls must cast out a lifetime of evil that has been thrust down your very throats. Is it any wonder you have been rendered sick? But God loves your form, as do I. So will the world, if you let it. Our idols should not be underweight models or the famous. God loves a woman who is strong enough to do His work. Only by eating our bread and loving ourselves will we be fit for God's tasks on this earth. It is for Him to control the functions of our bodies. One of His children cannot hope to possess that power. No sensation in woman is ever less than holy. No need can be fostered that should not be sated under His gaze. Hunger is no different from the need in our hearts for love and sex, for friendship and understanding."

The Goddess went on to talk of the oppression she had witnessed through the years, how this latest manifestation was simply the modern link in a chain of misogyny stretching back through time. From insidious myths, such as women existing as God's afterthought, to the idea they should be forever subservient to man, there were a thousand methods employed to nurture the neuroses of the fairer sex. The feminist elements in her tract made Josh feel vaguely guilty, but there was no denying the truth of Rebecka's words.

"I have seen so many like you through the years my sisters, they litter the hospitals and refuges, suffer in violence or collapse in the street. All the time your worst enemy is in here." Rebecka pointed a finger at her head. "Your attitude, your hopelessness, corrupt teachings which fill female minds with lies for all our days on earth. So many women fall, women from blessed backgrounds with love and hope to offer if only they knew how. If only they could overcome their depression and weakness, forget the gymnasium or that struggle to defeat appetites, and instead channel their immortal power into furthering the message of Jesus." She paused for a second to survey her rapt audience, the girls hanging on every word. Josh looked to the men either side of him. They too were singularly attentive. To his left Jon stood and watched, an unreadable expression on his face, a glint of something knowing in the man's azure eyes.

"We whose faith is collectively *The Spirit Of Nagasaki* will hold your hands as you walk the road to recovery. Understand me when I promise that it will not be easy. But open your hearts and minds to the Word, and I will take you there."

There was a pause and when Rebecka spoke again the tone was formal, no longer intended to inspire. "Those of you who have what it takes to join our church and make yourselves well raise your hands." Three arms went up immediately, another joining them after a few moments. "Good. I shall see each of you individually to determine suitability, both for a role in S.O.N. and our unique method of healing." The Goddess took in the four converts one by one, her gaze coming to rest on Josh's girl.

"I will begin with Bree Moore. If the rest of you would like to wait here, the one to one enlightenment will not take longer than half an hour. It is a period during which the two of us must receive total privacy."

Rebecka led a compliant Bree to the upper rooms. The space they vacated was left in silence, a noiselessness that seemed to last for aeons but was broken within a minute as partners rejoined each other. Those women who had refused the offer of the Goddess were led away by their men while others lingered, awaiting this private audience with their new mentor.

Jon took a seat next to Josh and struck up a conversation, the man more personable today, gently questioning Josh on Bree's background, his opinions of S.O.N. and their hopes for the future, reassuring the young man she was in good hands. Josh found himself revealing a good deal of his past and present, his job and studies and working life, feeling pleased that someone was interested in him after so long spent focussed on another. Before Josh knew it the better part of an hour had elapsed and Bree was back, escorted in by one of those thick-bodied helpers, a wide smile ornamenting her face.

Josh feared she might have been ordered to remain mute after her time alone with the Goddess. If so, Bree didn't observe the oath. So talkative was the girl on their return journey, descriptions of what she had undergone at a carefree volume, the couple drew consternation from other passengers. Josh couldn't have cared less. She was so lively and invigorated, as upbeat as that lovely girl he had known when they first fell in love.

Bree spoke of the deep satisfaction as Rebecka touched the skin of her forehead for the first time, the kind of welcome most people spend their whole lives looking for, a touch transmitting hope into her soul. Josh nodded and held her hand. She took for granted how much he thought of her, assumed he wouldn't be offended by these claims. Or maybe it was true , maybe he just couldn't compete with the spiritual power of this Goddess.

When they reached the loft-room, Rebecka had begun by reading the Bible, the woman pointing Bree to the Psalm of the afflicted, the statement *my heart is smitten, and withered like grass; so that I forget to eat my bread.* And wasn't that amazing? Didn't Josh see what had happened to her was the same thing that always happens when a heart has lost God? The sufferer whose *bones cleave to his skin* and whose *days are like a shadow that declineth, his skin withered.* The Lord knew, He understood the human condition, even thousands of years before she exhibited the symptoms. With humanity nothing ever changed.

Then Rebecka had raised herself and Bree instinctively copied her movement. The Goddess silently removed her clothes and the girl understood this was what she must do as well. Amazed at her lack of self-consciousness, Bree shed the attire and the pair stood before each other for several minutes, windows on the female form, the Goddess uttering soft questions she knew the answers to already, queries and statements that applied to them both.

Was she not beautiful? That which was created by God could not be imperfect.

Was her body not a cause for celebration? The woman gives life and must learn to be worshipped because of this, not least by herself.

Could she not learn to love this heaven-created flesh? Yes, affirmed Bree. Yes she could.

In that room Rebecka proved to her we were all ideal visions of the Lord and Bree understood. So when the Goddess laid both hands on her the girl was happy just to exist, happy for the first time she could remember. In that instant Rebecka cared about her, no matter how insignificant Bree Moore might have once felt, and Bree found she cared for herself as well, solicitude that existed alongside a deep and abiding love for the Goddess, this woman with the sensual touch of an angel. Rebecka assured the girl her sickness had been real and that it was not her fault. The blame lay with a disease that had almost destroyed her, a disease that would threaten no more. With the help of Jesus this girl would regain weight, return to her God-given shape. If Bree was well enough she would be allowed to commit in a few months time, the Goddess permitting her to leave life's tribulations behind and join the church.

Josh was happy for her, the situation might have left their future together more uncertain as ever, but he couldn't argue with the positivity Rebecka had instilled into his girlfriend. He didn't allow himself Bree's optimism though; there had been false dawns in the past. More dashed promises might have broken his damaged heart.

This exile of hope may have accounted for Josh's surprise when the girl began to eat. From the moment they arrived home on that revelatory Wednesday she consumed food with an ease, an omnivorous intent her lover hadn't witnessed in years. Josh abandoned his office job when Bree's weight began to drop dangerously low so now he was in the privileged position of watching a miraculous recovery from close quarters, day by heart-lifting day. There was a new purpose to Bree's existence, the expansion of her diminished stomach little by little, gaining weight pound by pound. She didn't need his supervision any more and the improvement in their life together was astonishing. His lover was an adult again, a self-governing individual, one fellow soldier in the war against disorder, and many of his usual routines were suddenly redundant. Josh could do little but sit back and watch her fly.

They took walks together in the park, gloried in kitting her out with a new wardrobe, Josh spending his savings with a thrilled abandon. He found himself with a sex life once more as they came together, Bree initiating the lovemaking more often than her tentative man, unfamiliar as he was with the erotic possibilities of her body. She spoke regularly of the future during those post-coital caresses, kept her focus on a larger purpose within S.O.N.

"I won't fail again my dear." Bree promised, running a finger down his chest. "There's a goal now, an aim in life. You see, I get it, I totally get it Josh, and so few do. With God's help I can follow in Rebecka's footsteps and give girls like me a chance to live."

Josh responded to these declarations with silence. He thought of peers, people working fifty hour weeks to afford a piece of property that housed a relationship far flimsier than theirs. Eventually the young man relented, a glimpse into the future awaiting him without the girl convincing Josh he had to make a decision. Confronted with the choice between a painful break-up or ambivalent assimilation into a new faith he found the second option more inviting.

Ladling vegetable stew onto metal dishes for those followers who had since become his second family, Josh reflected how different the reality of living close to the Goddess was from everything he'd thought. Despite a lack of heartfelt belief, S.O.N. gave Josh something not altogether different from what it provided for Bree. A support network, reassurance, shared goals, the feeling of operating as a vital cog in this machine designed for unconventional purposes. Whatever the reason, Josh found himself enjoying this life, particularly after the pair of them proved their dedication and received the honour of Newtopia, bussed away from the cramped relentlessness of London. The change in life soon proved worthwhile, but at the time joining up was one long succession of hassles for something he wasn't a hundred per cent behind. Foremost among these problems was explaining their decision to shocked families. Fortunately Josh's parents were mainly okay, wishing them both well as their son stored some of those belongings he was loath to sell around the house. Josh assured his folks they would write regularly, and an instinctive understanding of his current happiness along with glimpses into Bree's new found vitality did enough to convince. The Moore family proved less pliant. Bree's mother had previously affected a noisy thankfulness to the church for making her daughter well again, but now she argued with ostentatious despair against her single-minded offspring. This spindly chain-smoker in her mid-fifties didn't trust what she called; *that cult*. She disliked the way Bree, in that focussed way of hers, resolved to give every penny she owned to S.O.N. upon joining. Mrs Moore knew what people got up to in those places, oh yes. Child abuse and sick perversion and unnatural behaviour and why couldn't she just go back to acting like that good Catholic girl they raised her to be? Josh and Mr Moore, a beleaguered man with a face the colour of dust, looked at one another uneasily as Bree countered by calling her mother's lifestyle 'Godless' and 'bourgeois'. The girl vowed to take what was hers from the house, because to pile up worldly goods was an affront in the eyes of God. Then they wouldn't see her again, she was leaving town with Josh to start a new life servicing a faith that had saved her. They would help those in need and refuse to avert their eyes from suffering as her parents had done with Bree. Mr. Moore intervened then to calm the situation, Josh helping his girl collect her things, attempt to silence Bree and then get the hell out of that opulent property, deep in the heart of suburbia.

The sun shone down on Newtopia as dozens of disciples set themselves at the long wooden benches to receive the food Greg hurried to deliver, some observing grace, others tucking straight in. Josh continued to spoon out portions as he watched the scene through a kitchen window. What a relief to never communicate with the lapsed and atheistic again, forget those outsiders who could never comprehend. He went outside to eat in brilliant daylight then. Life on the farm wasn't perfect, their schedules could be frustrating and disconnected and hard at times, when the responsibilities piled up and the pressure to treat strangers as brothers made Josh uncomfortable. But Bree was happy, this girl who took the last space next to him and that plate he'd brought out especially for her, and Bree being happy made him happy. She loved this place as Josh loved her. The cooperative life suited them pretty well.

Opposite Greg launched into another tall story from his time on the fringes of extremism, tales of frightening meat-workers with white powder in envelopes, one butcher cottoning on to the fake anthrax and who posted it, running from his shop to chase Greg with a large cleaver and a bloodthirsty holler. Bree giggled and tucked into the stew, her hip touching Josh's leg, the noise of hungry people filling their bellies all around them in the warm summer air.

Chapter Three

The digger's claw pulled swathes of loose earth from the ground, stopping at intervals whenever a voice called out. Then the men in white would pitch in, reach over the side or climb into the hole, use their fingers to brush dirt from the found object. Sometimes a belonging was uncovered, some trinket, soft toy or article of clothing, but more often it bore the sickly flesh-colour of a corpse.

Joe stood ten yards from the grave, smoking hard. He had seen sixteen of the dead pulled from that space in the ground already. The workers were twelve feet down now and these grisly discoveries showed no sign of ending. The victims had been interred two at a time, side by side in parallel trenches, each pair a few inches of earth above the last.

When a limb appeared the officers in coveralls would carefully extract the body, hefting the remains onto a nearby vehicle that was equipped with a canvas stretcher. Under Dickson's supervision each of the dead was driven across the field, deposited on sheets of tarpaulin in the front yard, another section of plastic laid over the top to save their dignity.

Sweeney breathed out slowly, watching grey clouds stream over the horizon. The Chief Inspector was coordinating this operation pretty well, even if Dickson had looked like he might vomit when that first corpse, a boyish-looking female who couldn't have been more than twenty, was lifted into the daylight. Dickson's face drained of colour then and he turned away as Joe took in the girl's strangely peaceful features, trying not to dwell on the mousy hair and skinny frame that reminded him of his own daughter. By the time Sweeney flung a blood pressure tablet into his mouth the Inspector had composed himself, was back and ready to issue orders, unwilling to show weakness in front of his men. Pride could be a useful emotion in testing times.

Hard to credit these blemished cadavers once had personalities of their own, characters that would have been expressed naturally less than a week ago. All of the dead possessed names and histories, a network of lives somehow mixed up in this murderous religion, families around the country praying for loved ones who would never return. Only framed photographs from years gone by remained for parents and siblings to cradle. Another body, that of a man with light hair, was hauled from the ground. His limbs were set askance, face formed in that now-familiar rictus grin, features somehow benign, even in violent death, the outward expression of some willingness to give in. The sight and stench overpowered Joe's daydreams. He stumbled over to the corpse, grateful that however dank and disgusting this investigation proved, it contained less horror than the task for those informing relatives.

The dead man possessed that same pattern of bruises to the neck as the others Joe had seen, a collection of grey-blue marks consistent with strangulation. So that farmer was right, the suicide theory could be discounted. Sweeney followed the vehicle across to the farmhouse where the cadaver was laid out and covered. He checked the hands and faces of a few of the dead and found them the same, no damage consistent with a struggle. Hell, some were even smiling, beneficence in their expressions, as if those last moments in the world had been happy ones. This evidence was highly unusual, most of the corpses Joe had seen possessed faces caught somewhere between horror and fear. The murdered almost always went to their deaths unwillingly, terrified by events concluding their tenuous grip on mortality, spirits fighting the onset of darkness to the bitter end.

A seventeenth body was transported over to the yard where Sweeney stood, an area that was rapidly becoming full of shapes under tarpaulin. Joe left Dickson's team and took a stroll down the lane toward the edge of the grounds, cadging a cigarette from the Sergeant who was posted on the property's entrance, a man with instructions to keep out press and civilians while the exhumations were taking place. Wilson was his name, a man close to Joe in age and height but with a vaguely officious manner that meant these monotonous duties suited him.

"How are they getting on?" Wilson offered up his packet.

Cupping his hands, Joe lit the cigarette. "Still coming."

"Hard to credit it." Wilson shook his head slowly. "You know Mr. Sweeney, I'm a religious man myself." He put a match to his own cigarette. "I often wonder how a loving God can sit back and watch what goes on in His world."

"Just because it goes on doesn't mean He condones it Sergeant."

"No, I suppose you're right. Evil has always been done in His name and it always will be." Beside them birds chirruped through the trees. Wilson looked up as a magpie flew toward its makeshift nest. When the Sergeant spoke again it was to himself.

"*Come all. Behold the works of the Lord my people, what desolation he hath made in the earth.*"

Sweeney returned to the scene to find the work over, solid earth near the macabre discovery left undisturbed. There were two dozen corpses beside the main building, twenty two adults and a couple of male children, bodies which had been put into the ground as two piles of twelve, stacked neatly in the earth. A regimented, almost ritualistic, burial.

Officers continued to place the belongings they found beside the dead into plastic bags, sealing away watches, hairbrushes, pens and plastic novelties with due care and attention. Dickson approached Joe, a bottle of water in one hand, the other mopping at his brow.

"Investigator Sweeney, we've been looking for you."

"A brief reconnoitre." Sweeney spoke loudly as the Inspector blew his nose, wiping at the moustache underneath. "Have we a place to store them?"

"I've arranged for the village hall in Shelton to be used. The nearest police station is there, about six miles that way." Dickson pointed northwards, over the hill. "We've enough equipment there to improvise a mortuary. This can be sealed off until someone comes forward to identify the dead."

"Shelton?" Looking behind Dickson, Joe could see a pale arm protruding from one of the plastic sheets. "Good, we'll need a base for communication purposes."

An officer pushed the limb back under its cover with a foot. Removing his face mask, the man hawked a gob of phlegm into a nearby flower bed.

The idyll and humanity of Shelton could not have been more of a contrast with the sights they left behind. This was a village populated by three hundred isolated souls, although you could have been forgiven for believing there to be far fewer this January weekday.

Young mothers pushed prams along uneven pavements and one or two clusters of old women huddled conspiratorially to discuss local gossip, some of which undoubtedly took in those official-looking vehicles parked along the high street. Joe wasn't concerned, none of those biddies would investigate the goings-on or alert anyone but their bridge circle. There were plenty of Devonian police lurking around the village hall to dissuade the casually curious.

Beside the Shelton station a small library could be seen, while a short walk up the road was the guest house Sweeney had booked himself into until this thing was settled. The village also boasted several shops, a post office, and one poky chemist wherein a languid woman with a bubble perm informed him they were out of his tablets but some should be delivered "any day now".

Sweeney killed his roll-up in the police station's only ashtray and pulled out some tobacco to make another. This building had three distinct sections, none more spacious than that farmhouse kitchen the investigation had recently vacated. Around the front desk and reception area officers from Exeter fluttered like moths, setting up their base of operations, Shelton's usual issues of local vandalism and lost pets forgotten while paperwork was studied and phone calls made. Through the wall to Sweeney's left lay a holding room, one eight foot cell whose previous occupants were likely to have been a succession of drunks. Finally there was Joe's temporary office that looked like a meeting or interrogation room, or maybe it was just where the Shelton police took their tea breaks, Sweeney didn't have the faintest idea. At least there was a table for him to work at, upon which Joe spread the documentation Dickson's boys had been able to dig up so far, colourful booklets and detailed sheets retrieved from the cult's London headquarters, bases they had hurriedly abandoned a couple of months previously and were currently being combed by New Scotland Yard. Next to these pamphlets lay downloads from that Internet site, *thespiritofnagasaki.com*, still running until the technical guys in London closed it down.

Joe had glanced briefly at all of this, but in the light of what happened the relevance of the religion's promises, its doctrines and theology, escaped him. None of the crap before Sweeney told him why some sixty innocent people were dead. For the average murder there was a motive, suspects who had the opportunity, logic behind the act. With terrorist acts Joe could always find a warped reasoning, the sense of injustice that rose from the violence, discover who had reason to hate the victims so he was never far from the perpetrators. Sweeney had never dealt with genocide, prayed he never would, but he knew there was always a corrupt regime or bloodthirsty movement close by. But premeditated mass murder? The wiping out of a nascent faith? From where did the purpose or means come? What about survivors? Executioners? Witnesses?

He lit another roll-up and realized he was settled in now. The repellent sights exorcized domestic troubles from Joe's mind. Sweeney no longer doubted the wisdom of being placed in the thick of this incident, old worries long since replaced with fresh doubts. Misgivings like how the hell his acting bosses at the critical incident division expected Joe Sweeney to make any progress. The Devon and Cornwall police couldn't keep this quiet forever, even with the victims' families sworn to secrecy for the good of the investigation, news of these deaths would leak out eventually. All of which meant time was against him, the clock was ticking.

Noises from the corridor broke his reverie. Several sets of heavy footsteps passed the door, followed by Sergeant Wilson who stuck his head in. Breathless with achievement, he informed the Special Investigator they had a suspect.

The man inside the cell resembled the Saturday night doorman at a provincial nightclub. At least he would have done, but for the wildly unkempt hair and aura of day-old sweat that hung around him. The captive was a powerfully built individual with a mottled complexion and one recently blackened eye. The man kept his vision away from the officials as Joe talked to Wilson outside the barred door.

"We found him about half a mile west of the farmhouse, just sitting there on a rock. He was staring into a stream and chucking pebble into it. No idea how long he'd been there. He didn't move or pay any attention when we called so it wasn't difficult to sneak up on him."

"Do we know his name?"

"No identification on the suspect sir and he hasn't said much. Called himself Stoker at one point, that much we know."

Joe studied the fellow before him. Stoker's clothes were virtually rags, mud-splattered and ripped, like he'd been living outdoors for a month.

"So the only information you got in return for that black eye was his surname?"

Stoker looked up for the first time. The man's face was dirty as the rest of him and his lower lip looked as if it had recently been split. Beside Sweeney the Sergeant had gone an unhealthy shade of crimson.

"You have to understand sir, the lads have seen some terrible things over the past few days."

"I suspect this gentleman has experienced far worse." Joe raised his voice. "Stoker!" The captive turned. "Mr. Stoker, my name's Joe. You need to tell me what happened." Stoker looked to the floor.

"It's no good sir."

Sweeney rapped at the bars with a knuckle. "Open this door."

"Are you sure that's wise Mr. Sweeney? He's a big fellow."

"Yes, I can see that." Joe turned to Wilson. "Let me ask you a question Sergeant. Did he put up a struggle when you brought him in?"

"No sir, he was placid all the way."

"And yet you still beat him up?"

"That wasn't me sir, I intervened to stop it as soon as I could."

"I believe you Sergeant." Joe checked his watch, he felt like time was being wasted. "My point is this, I believe it's safe for me to enter and I do so at my own risk. Now please unlock the door."

Under Wilson's concerned gaze Joe went into the cell. He sat on the metal bench beside the stocky man who failed to acknowledge his presence. When Sweeney spoke it was in his reassuring voice.

"Don't worry Mr. Stoker, no one's going to hurt you." No response. "But we do require your story. All we have at the moment are a great many dead people and you."

A full minute passed. The captive's body odour mixed with the more general stench of the pen, a smell of disinfected surfaces. "If you fail to explain matters we're going to have to assume the worst about you Mr. Stoker."

"The name's Stoker." It was a small noise for such a big man, words barely getting out.

"I know that, what I need..."

"No, no." The man silenced Joe. "You're calling me *Mr. Stoker*. My name's not Mr. Stoker. It's *Stoker*, just Stoker."

"What I need to know, *Stoker*." Joe kept his frustration hidden. "Is if you were at the farm when the killing took place."

"I was always at Newtopia."

"Good, that's good Stoker." Did he sound as patronizing as he felt? Joe couldn't help himself, it felt like he was communicating with a small child. "Now, tell me everything that went on. Did you have anything to do with what happened?"

The captive looked into Joe's eyes for the first time. Sweeney was struck by the expression on the man's face, a domestic animal trying to make sense of a situation far beyond its comprehension, like a dog trapped by earthquakes. Stoker made one more statement before lapsing back into silence.

"Everybody had something to do with what happened, we all did." The man stroked his brow with a grimy hand. "I was just a follower, carrying out God's word. It was her who had the vision and him what had the power."

Ruth

"It wasn't barbarous communism that sent a chill down our spines. It was the deteriorating fabric of civilization everywhere. Drugged normality. Faster and faster cars. Illiterates of the imagination."

- Winston Harris, *Jonestown*

She didn't think it possible the conference centre would become full, there were a hundred chairs set out on the lower tier alone, probably another fifty above. From the research she'd undertaken so far all indicated towards a small-time operation, perhaps a future threat, but little to be concerned about at present. Maybe a thousand words of forewarning would be appropriate, or a short article in one of the supplements.

Locating herself in a row at the back, the woman was far enough away from the stage for that notepad and Dictaphone to go unnoticed yet close enough to get a decent view. A raised podium with two microphones was being set up at the front. There were no backdrops or complicated affectations, nothing gaudy that might lead one to believe a performance was about to take place. This setting could have been waiting for a political speech or public announcement. Yet the atmosphere around the auditorium was of an audience expecting to be entertained, as if anticipating a show or concert of some kind. All manner of individuals took their seats close to Ruth Schwitz; the young and untidy; the middle-aged and garrulous; a surprisingly high percentage of minorities. Quite a preponderance of females too, Ruth estimated the percentages in her head and came out with sixty-forty in favour of her sex, most of them younger than Ruth's thirty-two years. Many were of university or college age, although some women could only have been in their forties and beyond, the wide hips and greying hair of those who took the *Daily Class* every morning.

This newspaper was behind Ruth's attendance today. A recent e-mail from Sandi Hunt, the single-minded editrix, had dictated a change of policy. The *Class* was quietly dropping it's flagship campaign, the naming and shaming of paedophiles for the good of the British public and its vulnerable children, in favour of a search for new outrages in immoral works of art, drug-taking authority figures and questionable religious sects. Ruth suspected the decision to cease publishing lists of sex offenders' addresses on the front page was not one Sandi took willingly. Pressure had been exerted from every section of the liberal media after several of these men's homes were torched by angry mobs, perverts forced to hide out, fearing for their lives. As the editor declared, it would have been interesting to know how these left-wing softies reacted to the knowledge paedophiles were living in their neighbourhood, watching their children. All those bleeding hearts with their statistics, lies and damned lies, how a kid was a thousand times more likely to be killed or abused by a member of his own family than the random sicko in the street. The percentage of paedophiles they claimed weren't repeat offenders, the victories of therapy. Yet even Sandi had to concede things were getting out of hand, when a group of the most easily influenced *Class* readers took it upon themselves to beat a small-town paediatrician to within an inch of his life.

So that was that. The newly crowned editor's first crusade ended within a few weeks, bellicose bastions of society shouted down by a London intelligentsia who accused the *Class* of whipping up violence and hatred. Those liberals refused to condone a paper they saw as *shaming* the degenerates too far, some paedos responding to the vilification with clinical depression or even suicide. Hunt's position wasn't great, and if she continued pursuing every Humbert Humbert in Britain until they were all either dead or forced into seclusion, it would have become even more untenable. No matter that large sections of the public wanted these deviants persecuted and demonized, the paper had to stop.

An immediate change of emphasis was required, to save both the reputation of the *Daily Class* and Sandi's credibility in charge. Reporters were sent to hunt down stories that featured the tabloid's favourite themes, the intriguing whiff of corruption and lax morality, as salacious as possible. This lack of rectitude could then be explored and condemned in print, middle England grateful once again crusaders like Ms. Hunt were out there to expose the ethically questionable, users and filth discredited, removed from posts of responsibility and ostracized.

When she came across the religious group calling themselves *The Spirit Of Nagasaki* on the Internet Ruth thought she might have hit the jackpot.

Circulars around the office of the press association revealed several staff had received worried letters or concerned phone calls, communications from families who had lost a member, relatives absorbed by this growing cult. The story held a potentially ideal combination for the *Class*. The web site stressed a belief in personal and sexual freedoms along with the rejection of regular society. If Ruth could infiltrate this group's procedures and meetings, uncover financial mismanagement or the abuse of its devotees in some way, she was within touching distance of another promotion. Images of a potential front page flashed through her head, a grainy photograph showing some cowed religious type under the legend **EVIL CULT LEADER HAD SEX WITH CHILD, 9**. Anything along those lines would be beautiful.

A few days of steady investigation later and here she was, waiting patiently in a large amphitheatre outside Epping for the brainwash to begin, her mind still captivated by prospective headlines. The lead story was a goal Ruth had nurtured ever since she joined the *Daily Class* six years before, her ambition becoming stronger on becoming the youngest senior reporter in the paper's history. That was last September, when diligent work and her wholesale adoption of the paper's world view quickly brought positive results. Her appearance may have helped too, Ruth Schwitz had dyed blonde hair and gracefully long limbs on the kind of unobtrusive face and body that tended to inspire neither great attraction nor ambivalence. It proved a useful combination when pursuing interviews from the kind of middle class folks easily impressed by fashion-spread style, expensive perfume, big-city sass.

The reporter rarely mentioned her life before the age of twenty five, that year when she completed her M.A. and began the job on which she'd worked such long hours ever since. This was a woman whose occupation overshadowed her social and romantic lives. Ruth wasn't the kind of girl for whom a career was something to be avoided through housewifery and child-rearing. In many ways the *Class* was her life now, both intellectually and in terms of power exercised. She had memorized the tabloid's philosophy to an almost obsessive degree whilst keeping her own, milder views, separate. Miss Schwitz could always be relied upon to instinctively understand the tabloid's stance on big news stories:

War? Unfortunate, but necessary.

Traditions? The bedrock of a civilized society, there to be preserved.

Progress? Unnecessary and undesirable. Can only lead to a collapse in security.

Morals? The only things protecting Great Britain from anarchy.

These were the commandments of those lengthy shifts she took in the beating heart of the paper, so much of her time taken up with producing copy that when Ruth was away from the office for more than a week she found herself yearning for the publication. A deep-rooted desire to return, back into the pressurized thrust of a salary-inspired schedule, that pacey, engine room mentality placing a news office at the centre of the world.

Maybe it was a result of this overwhelming dedication that Ruth tended to fall in with men who shared her unerring commitment to work. She currently held a mortgage on a discreet flat in Enfield with her boyfriend of four years, a man Ruth felt she really ought to get around to marrying at some point. Jake was a banker and borderline workaholic, the nature of his career taking him all over Europe in business class. While glad to share her space with a like-minded soul who, in his favour, was both generous and charming, a great friend and fairly accomplished in bed, Ruth sometimes found herself wondering if they shouldn't see more of each other. One of the reasons the pair weren't yet wed was her tendency to see Jake for one night every other weekend, a frustrating period when one of them was often too shattered for *quality time* with the other. The couple probably spent longer talking on their mobiles than in person, warning each other well in advance if they had to meet up for some financial transaction or family commitment that required the presence of them both.

The rear section of this level was packed and the front seats filling now as Ruth checked her make up on a compact mirror. There really were a great many girls here, a sight that seemed to discredit the statistic she had discovered in the course of her recent studies. Perhaps it was another lie; the bulletin that said if current trends continued, in twenty years the number of young people attending church services would have dwindled away to nothing. Well they had certainly flocked here in their droves, these young women in their tight tops and denim. The brunette in the chair to her left caught Ruth giving her a curious look and responded with the white beam of a smile. No doubt the paper would be heartened to learn youngsters remained who sought meaning in life beyond alcohol or drug abuse, sex before marriage or criminal acts. She just hoped what was uncovered here wasn't about to contradict the big story, that copy already written in her head, one or two gaps left to be filled by forthcoming observation.

Ruth was leaning across to ask the brunette what had brought her there this evening when her words were interrupted by a sudden absence of light. A collective gasp in the darkness was followed by the lush swell of gospel music, this instrumental wash acting as a calmative while a succession of spotlights lit the stage. Into the glare strode a profoundly handsome man with black hair, clad entirely in dark clothes, save for the square of perfect white below his neck. The figure walked across to the podium and raised both hands to acknowledge cheers of support from the crowd. Although Ruth was struck by his good looks, the confidence with which he worked the audience, it was the aural force of the man that made the reporter's desire take hold, a need that spread from her stomach upwards. His voice was husky, assured and clear, all-encompassing like honesty, while the words he uttered made sense to Ruth, right from the start.

"Good evening everybody, so glad you could make it." A few cheers. "I can't begin to tell you how much this means to me, all of you taking the important first step and coming here today. Let us hope by the end of my demonstration this will mean a great deal to you too." The man surveyed his crowd. "I see some familiar faces among us this evening, but many more friends I have not met. This is all to the good. For the uninitiated out there, my name is the Reverend Douglas Elliott, and it is my privilege to give back today what has been lost. Do our first timers know why they came this evening?" No response. "Well then, let me explain. I know your reasons for attending my brothers and sisters. It is all part of the search. Everyone here is a true seeker!" Cries of agreement. Douglas extracted a microphone from its stand and began to prowl the stage.

"What is it I am looking for, you ask. Well my friends, let me ask you to think back a second, not to yesterday or even last week, but all the way to your childhood. Those carefree days when everything seemed possible and grown-ups promised you the world. Do you remember those times?" Affirmative calls. "You could have become anything imaginable. How many here wanted to be an astronaut?" Several dozen hands shot up. "An inventor?" About twenty. "The Prime Minister?" Five or six.

"Oh yes, brothers and sisters. We were hopeful and happy and then we grew up and what did we find? An adult life with responsibilities that took away our freedoms. Suddenly we had to spend the week in a stifling job just to survive, were expected to cook like chefs every evening, brave the emptiness of culture at weekends, leave the television on at all times, as if it could fend off loneliness." Douglas moved from right to left, studying the faces before him. "And can anyone tell me what this life leaves us lacking?" A few shouts from the front of the auditorium Ruth couldn't understand. From the Reverend's exaggerated body language she could tell the suggestions were to his liking, Douglas cupping a hand to his ear as these responses continued.

"In a way each of you is right, but those who said *friends* are most correct. Our race has forgotten that human beings need companions in order to justify ourselves. I'm here to help you reject the sham of singularity, all the pretending that says we can do without an extended family of sympathetic souls, allies who will hold out a hand in times of need, love us unconditionally and absolutely, support our frailties with care and attention. To the lie we can do without friends I say NO MORE!" The audience responded to his shout with an echo. "NO MORE! We are all family here, and though we may not know it, we share the same goal. The only true purpose in this world of our Lord is to look upon each other as equals, to love what we see there. If our race learned anything from the Son of God all those years ago it was to respond to love and selflessness in kind, a lesson most have forgotten." Douglas was out of breath, face falling downwards as his words rushed into the microphone. It took several seconds for the man to cease his panting and look back at the audience. When he did the figure on stage looked directly at Ruth. He held her gaze, a stare boring into the journalist's soul, making Ruth feel faint, unsteady on her chair.

"Why have so many forgotten these lessons my friends? I will tell you, it is because the organizations that took the Son's name to follow in His wake have failed us. The old churches still preach abstinence while all around is indulgence, speak of yesterday's values when we exist today, lecture intolerance even as Jesus stood for understanding. Believe it brothers and sisters. Listen to the Word and we are told how the crippled and malformed were welcomed into

His temple. Were Jesus amongst us today he would take in those cast out through no fault of their own, for Christ came to earth in the name of the hated and victimized, the addicts and the bastards, the sick and the lost, those who needed God's love the most." Under the artificial light sweat glistened on the man's forehead.

"We have all seen them, have we not? Every Sunday they come to old-fashioned sermons in their expensive cars, the white and affluent, those who spend weekdays ignoring the broken littering the streets around them. They would condemn those who live in deprived neighbourhoods, shrink away from difference. They arrive on the Sabbath to pray for themselves, believing a few hours can reserve their place in God's eternal kingdom. Let me tell you something my friends, the rich are living a lie!" Cheers and clapping. "Transcendence cannot be gained in instalments my friends, you cannot find it in astrology or feng shui, and giving out the occasional prayer is not enough. Spirituality isn't intravenous, the word of God must be adopted as a way of life, a means of fulfilment and joy in this world without thought of the next. For only our Lord can determine the fate of his children when the time comes, and believe me when I say this, the wealthy and selfish are already lost." More whoops of agreement. Douglas set the microphone back in its stand and wiped his face before continuing.

"The Son taught us we must keep our thoughts on the world above, the higher hopes of mankind, not these things that lie upon the earth. What you and I share is a healthy distaste for the world around us, its lies and corruption, the relentless pursuit of money that leaves so many of our kin impoverished and exploited." Ruth felt his eyes on her again. Were these comments directed at the paper? No, they couldn't be. He had no way into her soul. These words were just a trick, weren't they? A rehearsed attempt to fool the gullible. And yet, and yet. The ring of truth in every pronunciation, the certainty in his powerful voice. The clarification of her vague feelings, feelings she had never allowed herself to explore before. It was all there in Ruth's mind, as explicit as his speech.

"What if I told you that the alternatives on offer were as soulless as materialism? There is no redemption to be found in the brief rides of Godless sin or the lurid colour our world promises, the superficial kaleidoscope we are taught to long for. The overloading of beleaguered brains with accumulated sensation will only lead to a life of alienation, the unavoidable onset of sadness, a creeping boredom as your days are irretrievably wasted." A croaky quality in the man's voice was cured by a mouthful of water. "People say things have got better, that we live longer and have more than any of those who came before. But do these times of plenty make us happy?" Cries of *NO!* "Of course not my friends. You have eyes, the same as I. You see the downhearted and lost, those who rely on chemicals to give them a reason to live, an addiction to pills or sex or coffee or television that allows loved ones to forget the emptiness of hollow lives. Today the human race possesses more means of communication than its forefathers, and yet we say less than they ever did, opening our mouths to allow out little of worth. We despatch e-mails and text messages and voicemail, all watering down real emotions and hiding our true selves. We send electronically regards that ought to be made in person, that always were in the past. For how can we truly express love without looking into the eyes of another?"

The Reverend cast his gaze across the audience, as if trying to catch the eyes of everyone in turn. When his glance fell upon her, Ruth experienced that same butterfly nausea she had last felt when called into the editor's office for promotion. The reporter swallowed some saliva and tried to concentrate on how these events were unfolding, unaware of the notepad and pen that now fell from her hand to the floor.

"I'm aware everyone before me has a story to tell, you wouldn't be here otherwise." Douglas stepped to the side of the podium, taking the mike with him. "So I'm going to call a few of you up here to tell your unique stories for us all. I will leave it up to the Lord to decide who should provide our inspiration today."

The man dropped to his knees and began to emit a deep humming noise, eyes screwed shut before a crowd who looked on, agog and wondering. After ten seconds or so the drone began to take the form of recognizable words. Douglas seemed to have trouble spitting the name out, as if his mouth were unused to the process of making syllables all of a sudden. Then the words "*LYNN TURNER!*" and his finger picking out a woman part-way along the fourth row. She was one of the middle-aged types Ruth had stereotyped as *Class* readers earlier on, saggy and way past the menopause, her beige cardigan stretched tight across a gravity-stricken chest. The applause and yells of encouragement swelled to an overwhelming level as the woman rose and, with agility surprising for one of such bulk, skipped up the steps. Once onstage Douglas embraced Lynn and handed her the second microphone.

"OhmyGod! OhmyGod!" She was flushed with excitement, peering out at friends and using a chubby hand to fan her face.

"Welcome Lynn, so glad you could be here." The evangelist paused to let this woman acclimatize to her surroundings. When she had looked over the entire set he went on. "Now, I want you to tell these good people how your life has been going lately."

Lynn looked at the audience, then to Douglas. An apologetic note entered her voice. "Not too well father."

"How do you spend your days Lynn?"

"Well, since my husband died I've only myself to care for, so I have lots of time to watch television. Soaps and quiz shows mainly." She looked to Douglas who nodded, encouraging Lynn to go on. "Apart from that my hobbies are my cats, Sparky and Mickles, and my soft toy collection."

"You like chocolate as well don't you Lynn?"

She blushed. "How did you....?" Douglas raised his pupils to the sky and Lynn felt herself forced to admit the weakness. "That's my one vice father."

"The Lord tells me of a problem with your nerves."

"Yes, it's true." The woman felt shamed by her admission, Ruth could tell that even from where she was seated. "The doctor has me on diazepam, but I still worry. The house isn't safe since Fred died and I don't like to walk the streets alone. People talk behind my back, but they don't need to hide their disgust. I know I'm carrying too much weight...." She began to cry, great heaving sobs that resounded through the building. Douglas hurried to hold her, his microphone positioned behind Lynn's shoulder so it would go on picking up his voice.

"That's right my friend, let it out. Each of us knows what it's like to live without love, to look in the mirror and see only ugliness and failure." Addressing the audience now. "Lynn spends her days buying rubbish, watching rubbish, eating rubbish, and soon she feels terrible, just like millions of others. But let me tell you something brothers and sisters. All that was forgotten after I joined the church of the S.O.N. There I learned that every ailing soul can be made well, all healed with nurturing and unconditional acceptance. Each of us is strong and useful and beautiful in God's eyes, especially you Lynn. You're beautiful." The noise from the woman ended and she raised her head to look into the man's face. Lynn's voice was picked up by his mike as the other cord dangled from her fat fingers.

"Nobody ever called me beautiful before." Ruth could believe her. The moment felt fake, but if this was an act it was an exceptionally well played one. The journalist was moved in spite of herself.

Douglas nodded. "Most mortals see only the beauty of outer appearances, but our Lord allows me to see into your heart Lynn, and that heart is true. I hope you will share it with us again." He led the bulky woman to the back of the stage. "Show your appreciation for Lynn brothers and sisters!" The woman gave a shy wave and stood at the rear.

As the clapping ceased Douglas dropped down and began to hum once more, this time climaxing in an arm outstretched to the upper tier and a cry of, "*JAMES SHRYMPTON!*"

Ruth twisted her neck to witness a young man in a shirt and tie make his way down the steps unsteadily. James looked like he suffered from the British condition, reserve that made him feel out of place at uninhibited events. But this crowd wasn't letting him remain in the background.

The episode unfolded much like the previous one, although James was more reticent than Lynn, the Reverend unable to bring him to tears. The audience learned how Shrympton was unceremoniously laid off from a utility company in an act of corporate downsizing designed to maintain high bonuses for directors and maximize shareholder profits. James' supposed job for life became an irrelevant and expendable position, soon filled by a temporary employee who worked without pension or paid leave for two thirds of the young man's salary. This unfortunate experience had the trickle down effect of his fiancé calling off their marriage, the girl leaving James with bills he couldn't pay and no alternative but to move back in with his parents at the age of twenty-nine. James was broke, depressed and alone and Douglas knew exactly whose fault that was. He launched into a condemnation of corporate chairmen, the way they rewarded each other for failure and destroyed the lives of their staff, the golden handshake that always came, even if terrible acts had been presided over by the outgoing suit. But James wasn't worthless like them and an alternative world existed, life away from workstations and computer systems, a movement where all were equal under the sight of the Goddess, where nobody would be cast out. Perhaps it was time for the man to join *The Spirit Of Nagasaki*.

The story of James sounded vaguely contrived to Ruth. She began to wonder if these people on stage were plants, existing members of the cult who had agreed to take part in the show. Douglas hugged the young man, not as convincing a performer as Lynn, but probably good enough to fool most of the people here, then fell to his knees once more. As the low drone filled the air around her, Ruth remembered why she was here for the first time since Douglas took the stage, feeling vaguely annoyed at this evangelist for tricking her into feeling something that was probably fake. This was an impressive show sure, yet there couldn't be anything more than chicanery happening here, there simply couldn't. Ruth had been carried along by the electricity, much against her instincts, better judgement that now reasserted itself.

For the third time the noise stopped, the man's eyes opening and his finger picking out a member of the crowd, someone at the back this time, a name uttered into the mike.

"*RUTH SCHWITZ!*"

Then the spotlight was on her and the brunette was pushing Ruth up and forwards and her first instinct was to freeze but her legs were moving of their own accord. And as she walked up the aisle toward the open arms of that tall and attractive man the reporter felt like an actress receiving an Oscar, thoughts swimming around her head: *This is not happening, I am in a dream, soon I will be awake and back in the real world and it will be time to dress for work.*

From all around her came cheers and applause, a few people standing to urge the woman on, so caught up in the magic they had witnessed already, bodies running on instinct, their encouragement pure melodrama.

Before the curtain James and Lynn clapped politely as the evangelist grasped Ruth in his arms. She knew he could feel her trembling, shivering with confusion and fear, because Douglas whispered *Don't Worry* in her ear. The man was so overwhelming and assured, a delicious muskiness emanating from his warm body. Ruth felt both safe and turned on, despite that granite bolus of trepidation filling her stomach.

The Reverend Elliott passed Ruth a microphone, this woman confused by the many sensations that assailed her, blinking at the lights and onlookers as Douglas turned to speak to the crowd.

"Before we begin the healing process for Miss Schwitz, let me tell you something my friends, something which may shock and appal you." Twisting to his left the man looked Ruth up and down, a neutral expression on his face. "This woman is an imposter ladies and gentleman! An infiltrator, a Judas Iscariot in our midst!" Gasps from the assembled company. "This person before us is not a seeker but a member of that brainwashing group we call the media! She is a journalist with the gutter press. A low-down hack who came here today fuelled by negative energy, looking to embellish lies for her paper. Her aim is to destroy all the good work that has been done in the name of the S.O.N. and make the world think ill of us." Jeers and boos rose from the area in front of them. Ruth squinted at the lines of people and found hostile faces spitting venom, vile expressions she instinctively shrank from.

Douglas raised a hand for silence. "Wait, wait a second my friends. I say to you now, we would not be scholars of Christ's teaching if we failed to see good in everyone." The man walked over to Ruth and put a protective arm around her, the blonde woman happy to bury her face in his chest like an upset child. "*The Spirit Of Nagasaki* includes everyone. We believe all can be saved, even journalists." A few relieved chuckles around the auditorium. "Ruth, I know you believed that coming here this evening was simply another day's work, but there is more than that. God sent you to us for a reason." The reporter raised her head to gaze at the man's chiselled features. "You have been dissatisfied for such a time that you no longer even notice the sadness, is this not true?"

Ruth took a step back and put the microphone to her lips. "I-I don't know."

"Of course you don't my dear, the life you lead is killing all your hope without leaving the time to step back and realise it." He moved closer to the woman, communicating face to face now. "The Lord took me inside that pain Ruth, all those years of fast times and hard drugs in your twenties, the debt and the cravings and the need to obliterate yourself. How you forgot the present and gave not a thought for tomorrow or the people you hurt along the way.

71

What I say is true isn't it?"

"Yes." Tears beginning to roll down her cheeks. "Yes, it's all true."

"But that life could not go on forever. Hedonism will always end in a terrible shock, as the inhabitants of Sodom and Gomorrah learned to their cost. For you it was the knowledge of that child you carried, a baby whose father was unknown to you."

"I've never told anyone." Sobbing now, barely able to get the words out. "How did you know?"

"The Lord sees everything my sister. Will you never understand this? He watched as you entered the clinic and destroyed that child within your body." A collective intake of breath from the mesmerized audience.

"I-I'm sorry, I'm so sorry." Quaking as though naked and cold, the pain of this memory coursing through her.

"Don't be Ruth, don't be." Douglas held her again, embraced the woman until her shaking stopped. "It is not for God's children to condemn the actions of another. At S.O.N. we realise it is futile to try and understand the situation of others. It's not our place to inflict rules upon people, still less for us to judge."

The outpouring of emotion onstage rendered all the other attendees silent, those present utterly compelled. When Douglas relinquished his grip Ruth felt like they were the only two people in the room, perhaps the world. The man produced a handkerchief and gently wiped her eyes before speaking again.

"So Ruth, what of your life at present. Have you come any closer to that happiness you always sought?"

Looking into the eyes of this darkly handsome man, Ruth tried to utter the truth.

"I don't really know, I used to think so."

"Really?" Surprise on his face. "Happy in work that keeps love and friendship out of your life? Happy with a career based on intrusive half-truth and evil lies? Happy through days of hostility and negligence? Happy within an industry that routinely destroys the lives of the God-fearing and feels no remorse? Happy in a relationship with a man you never see? Who even now is in a Stockholm hotel with one of the three women he keeps around Europe as common-law wives?"

"What?" The colour drained from Ruth's cheeks. "That's not true, it's not."

"No? Have I not spoken the truth of your life thus far? Why should I lie now?" Ruth was moving her head from side to side, refusing to believe the evidence of her own ears. "Have you worked in a place that depends on falsehood for so long you will not accept the truth when confronted by it?"

"No, no, no...." Ruth dropped the microphone and sunk to the floor, hands freed to hide her face. Douglas knelt beside the woman and began to stroke her hair.

"Hush my child. It is sad, but sometimes God's truth must be unpleasant in order to heal. We would not wish for Him to sweeten the pill. As it says in the good book, *happy are those who know what sorrow means, for they shall be given courage and comfort.* The pain will cease my sister, and then we shall be here for you, won't we good people?"

A chorus of agreement as Douglas helped the tearful woman to her feet, Lynn and James guiding her toward the backdrop, Ruth fighting to regain her composure all the way, feeling empty and eviscerated but strangely unworried. She knew in her heart the truth about Jake now and perhaps some part of her was relieved by it. A glance into the faces of the crowd confirmed the hostility had passed, men and women projecting a warmth and empathy now, enshrouding Ruth as she struggled to remain on her feet. The woman was suffering from dizziness and disorientation, like she'd inhaled tear gas.

Douglas returned his attention to the crowd. "Once more my friends we learn the value of submission to something larger than ourselves. The love of Jesus and the philosophy of our Goddess, a world view of joy and transcendent spirituality that welcomes us into the grand plan. Simply by coming here today you have put yourselves within sight of the holy. I congratulate you on this decision, the rejection of empty modern ways, this affirmation of love for each other, this pure and honourable way forward. If anyone has not been touched by the church of S.O.N. I would ask them to leave now." No one rose from their seats. "For the rest of us, it is time to celebrate our love. I GIVE YOU - MUSIC!" A fist in the air and that gospel boom returned over the speakers, music at such a volume Douglas had to shout

73

to be heard.

"YOUR BODIES ARE THE TEMPLES OF THE HOLY SPIRIT! JESUS LIVES INSIDE ALL GOD-GIVEN FLESH! USE YOUR BODIES FOR GOD'S GLORY!"

Rows of people stood and began to dance without reserve, eyes shut and arms windmilling freely, a hundred torsos moving in time to the grandeur of this sound. Opposite the celebration Ruth took in this uplifting sight, one which let her cast out the revelations of a few minutes before for an instant, left the woman awestruck and wondering. The power of this man was undeniable, the kinetic figure in his dog collar who walked a circuit of the front row, grabbing hands and greeting the audience like old friends. Before him young and old moved to the cascading onrush of strings and soulful vocals, the notes and reverberations inspiring them all.

Yet despite the smattering of minorities this crowd was mainly white, Caucasians dancing unabashedly to gospel and chanting of their love for God. Some buried remnant of journalistic training kicked in, Ruth's mind telling her these WASPs had never before sung their hearts out, not like the proles on football terraces or workers at karaoke nights. What Ruth witnessed before her was one spectacular release, years of tension transmuted into a sweet communion, a freeing experience. Before her the faces of women were contorted in ways that suggested a sexual rapture. The male expressions less orgasmic but still in the midst of an obliterating high, this catharsis of movement and song freeing them of insecurities and inhibition.

These thoughts were interrupted by Lynn and James who each grabbed one of Ruth's hands to encourage her to sway with them, the pair forming words of praise for Jesus in time with the music. The reporter's first instinct was to resist, but after a few seconds Ruth found herself caught up in the moment, closing her eyes as she issued senseless words and deep moans, adrenalin coursing through every vein. Hers was a sense of liberty and arousal, the magnitude of it rendering Ruth's past experience tiny by comparison. Inside that suburban amphitheatre the woman shook and chanted with ever-increasing delight.

With hindsight Ruth's evening was a big adventure, comparable with those of her younger days; the release at clubs and all night raves alongside trusted girlfriends. Yet even those good times had been tainted, corrupted by predators watching intently while Ruth danced or undercut with the threat of violence, brawling fuelled by the alcohol necessary for revellers to let go.

She stretched and yawned, daylight spilling through the window onto her lithe body. In that auditorium there existed only natural highs, an environment of unquestioning acceptance where love and friendship and Godliness were given room to flourish. The emancipation Ruth felt was total, up there in the spotlight, unable to bear any malice for that man who circled each row in turn, Douglas laying his hands on those who bounced and whirled, urging them to feel the weight of the holy spirit. The evangelist dashed to surrender everyone to his touch, shouting commands as he went.

"I INVOKE THE POWER OF THE GODDESS!" And members of the audience would shudder then fall to the floor.

"FEEL HER LIGHT SHINE UPON YOU!" And the recipient of a brush to the face would stagger back as if sucker-punched.

"PRAISE GOD IN ANY LANGUAGE BUT YOUR OWN!" And the chanting became a speaking in tongues, scores of ordinary folk making haunting sounds, like experimental opera singers, dredging up ghostly utterances from the depths of their subconscious. The great room filled with incredible noise, unearthly birdsong, men and women sweating profusely as they collapsed into each other's arms.

Ruth opened her eyes to gaze in wonderment at this display, overpowered by the scene Douglas had created, that man who bounded on the stage and toward whom she instinctively moved, freeing herself from the grasp of the others who continued to moan as if hypnotized.

The show reached its conclusion, the evangelist bidding his crowd farewell, advising those who had found enlightenment to sign up for the full *Spirit Of Nagsaki* experience in the foyer. The music ceased and helpers emerged from the wings, men whose purpose was to aid those still recovering as the majority regained their composure and filed out, still trembling from the release. Problems came from those followers who grabbed at chairs, attempting to raise their bodies on unsteady legs, some slumped on the floor, repeatedly crossing themselves. Ruth watched Douglas bring James and Lynn back to reality, easing the pair into the everyday world and passing responsibility to a stocky man with unkempt hair who guided them towards the exit. In the aisles a few of the audience continued to speak alien languages while others described their vision of the Lord's appearance in a stream of babble. Several writhed on the floor as if suffering a fit; violent convulsions while mouths gibbered, individuals shaken to their senses and made to breathe deeply by the S.O.N. workers.

Ruth reached under the covers to the other side of her bed where the warmth from Thomas remained, her other hand absent-mindedly touching her nipple above the sheet. She had never seen anything like it at the time, the deliverance of regression, educated people snorting and barking like animals. She was shocked and captivated. Ruth herself would join in at future events, give herself up to the holy spirit, the need for it to emerge through human vessels, feeling both rapturous and numb as she expelled garbled tones never before heard from her lips. Ruth wandered to the bathroom and ran a tap. As enthralling as that sight was the first time, much of her attention had been focussed on Douglas. Unwilling to let the man exit without her, she followed him offstage and jogged to catch up, imploring the Reverend Elliott to take her with him, back to his world of S.O.N. because nothing in life meant anything now and it was time for her to take control and DON'T GO!

Douglas calmed her, assured Ruth that her conversion was admirable but regrettably there were processes to be observed. He wasn't the person to take new recruits through the steps. She was guided into the presence of Thomas then, a man who lived in one of the London bases and would act as her Shepherd. Thomas was older and shorter and less good looking than the evangelist but he possessed the same physical assurance, self-confidence that came from a personal relationship with God. The man explained how their church didn't require anything more from its subjects than a donation and regular attendance at prayer sessions, but Ruth was adamant. She desired a place in the structure of S.O.N., wanted to absolve herself of the past, leave present irrelevancies behind.

Over the next few weeks Thomas spent many hours in discussion with the woman, gradually becoming convinced of her devotion to the Goddess and perhaps falling a little in love with her, the teacher-pupil relationship soon turning physical. Meanwhile Ruth surreptitiously emptied her bank accounts and slipped away from her old life with its sham engagement and illusory concerns. Ruth had never been much good at goodbyes so she didn't bother with them now. Eventually Jake and *The Daily Class* would realise she wasn't coming back and by then the woman hoped to be safely ensconced in her new life. Besides, both her boss and ex-fiancé were so wrapped up in their own concerns, it would take them weeks to even grasp she was gone.

Ruth splashed some warm water on her face and dried the skin with a towel, feeling Thomas slip an arm round her bare waist as she did so, the man bristly and aroused, nuzzling at her neck with his mouth. The contentedness Ruth felt since coming to the church was like nothing she had experienced before, her world-weary reflex and cynical nature dispelled by so many who genuinely *believed*. There were worries when she first joined, how could there not be? Journalism had been Ruth's life for so long, she came to love it, but only because there was nothing else. Now she had God's love, the philosophies of the Goddess who Ruth hoped to meet in person soon, as well as the friendship and attention of twenty cohabiters who considered her an equal. There was still power in her life, to be maintained and brought to bear, but these days it was of a different kind. Her influence lay directly over people now rather than with nebulous ideals or prejudiced words, a carnal domination of the men she lived with and from whom Ruth gave or withdrew attention as she saw fit. The woman loved this lifestyle, her new ways that resulted in more sexual satisfaction than Ruth had ever known, the nightly touch of others constant and rewarding. Then her days were immersed in the lessons of Jesus and the teachings of Rebecka, explosive consummation of self that rendered the old obsessions meaningless. Ruth thrust her fingers into Thomas' thinning hair and pulled him back onto the mattress, wrapping her legs around his thighs as she did so, wordless so as not to wake the couple opposite. Thomas stroked her cheek and pushed himself closer under the covers. Another day of comfort and pleasure awaited them, of intricate theology and imminent knowledge.

Chapter Four

At the back of his makeshift office Joe watched proceedings and smoked absent-mindedly, a pile of case papers near his feet. Across from him Wilson was doing the bad-cop routine on Stoker, the captive regarding this sergeant with growing amusement and no little contempt. Behind the suspect two local policeman stood guard, both of them almost six and a half feet, tall and unmoving like great helmeted lamp-posts, ready to act should Stoker make a break for freedom. Fat chance of that thought Joe as he extinguished the roll-up. Being kept prisoner didn't seem to concern this thickset man in the slightest. Sweeney had let the eager sergeant interview this captive after his own style of questioning yielded nothing more than silence, but Wilson was outsmarted at every turn by Stoker, the suspect replying to threats and questions with a light smile and vague pronouncements, either from the Bible or his own philosophy. The interrogator was becoming increasingly frustrated. Evidently the West Country's petty crooks and small-time villains weren't this difficult to crack.

Sergeant Wilson spoke through gritted teeth. "I'm on your side Stoker, believe me, I am. There are a lot of folk round here who'd like to see you roughed up. I told them no. Give him a chance I said, we'll get the truth soon enough, no need for any of that business." It was obviously an effort to remain calm. "But you're giving me no choice pal. I don't want to give you back to the boys but if you don't tell me what happened I might have to..." Stoker looked at Wilson the way a lion might regard a persistent insect, as a minor annoyance and nothing more.

"There are dead people next door, lines of them." Wilson was suffering from a nervous tic that made the whole of his cranium twitch. This motion became particularly obvious as his head moved close to Stoker's stillness.

"Were you responsible? Why did they die?"

Stoker stared into the eyes of his questioner for long seconds. Again it appeared there would be no answer but eventually the man spoke in even tones. "*A precious thing, in the Lord's sight, is the death of those who are loyal to him.*"

"Really pal? You really believe that?" The Sergeant was blustering now, a bad sign. "God wanted all those innocent people sacrificed did He? Those women and children next door? What kind of sick, twisted, deity did you people worship anyway? Can you tell me that?" Saliva from Wilson's mouth flew at Stoker. The captive wiped his bruised face and gave Joe an unreadable look. Sweeney rose from his chair and put a hand on Wilson's shoulder.

"Calm down sergeant, it's not worth getting yourself worked up."

Wilson turned. "I'm sorry sir, there's just...."

"I know, we were all there, but this isn't working. Go and take a break, get yourself a cup of tea." Sweeney addressed the two officers. "You men, get this prisoner cleaned up and fed. I want him checked over by a doctor." The sergeant paused on his way out, watching as Joe took another look at the suspect. "And get his hair cut while you're at it."

Joe mused as Wilson left, a wronged expression on the sergeant's face. "Is there anything else I wonder?" Sweeney looked at the man. "You'll require legal representation Stoker. Do you have someone in mind, or shall we arrange a solicitor?"

The man shook his head. "I won't need anyone."

"No?"

"Lawyers are just another symptom of the malaise that afflicts your world. I want nothing to do with them."

"And if we try to beat a confession out of you?"

Defiance in the man's eyes. "It won't work."

"No, I suspect it wouldn't." Sweeney indicated that the police should take Stoker away. "Just don't complain when we doctor your statements later on."

The captive was led out and Joe sat back down, rubbing his eyes. He'd kept his mobile phone off and taken himself to bed early, but still Sweeney's sleep was troubled. Visions of that scene at the farm returned to his mind tinged by the unreality of dreams. People from Sweeney's past pulled from the ground as he watched, horrified and powerless.

After a caffeine-heavy breakfast the bubble perm disappointed him again, promising her unhappy customer his tablets would be in by the end of the week but unable to specify when, the chemist offering everything from antihistamines to aspirin as a replacement.

Joe left the office and grabbed more coffee from reception, thanking the morose sergeant for his efforts as he did so. Moving next door to the town hall, Sweeney showed his I.D. to another local officer and made his way into the old-fashioned building.

Signs pinned to notice boards advertised jumble sales and playgroups, incongruous among the foul odour of the dead, the murdered and the burnt, drifting in from the main room. The hall was dimly-lit and cold, its windows open and every curtain drawn. Trolleys bearing shapes covered by white sheets stretched from wall to wall, two noticeably shorter than the rest. Joe walked over to the pathologist, a hunched and balding man with spindly fingers that were currently exploring the face of a dead man. The expert had arrived this morning from Scotland Yard with little forewarning of what awaited him, only to be confronted with scores of bodies, some immolated beyond all recognition.

Over and above the medical man stood Dickson, the Inspector watching with curiosity as the physician examined the corpse of a young, acne-scarred male. So the head of operations had overcome his revulsion, was beginning to cope with seeing death up close. Joe greeted Dickson cordially, wishing he were similarly composed.

"Special Investigator, this is Hugh Yately, our forensic mastermind. Hugh, meet Joe Sweeney."

The man continued to inspect the cadaver, pressing its limbs as he checked for stiffness. "You'll excuse me if I don't shake hands."

Dickson smiled. "How's our man?"

"Not a great deal of help." Joe desperately wanted a cigarette but felt it wasn't appropriate, not in the current environment. "We've made him more comfortable. I'll go back and have another shot later on."

"Good, good." The Inspector scratched at the wiry hair of his moustache. "Did you let Sergeant Wilson have a try?"

"Yes, it was quite enlightening." Sweeney humoured Dickson, he knew Wilson was the Inspector's best man. "Unfortunately we failed to learn anything new. His technique wasn't right."

"Never mind, we'll get there." Dickson indicated toward the body before them. "The initial post-mortems back up your strangulation theory."

"Asphyxiated with some kind of chain or belt at a guess." Yately closed the cadaver's mouth and covered it with a sheet. "The injuries are consistent with an object at least partially metallic." The pathologist leaned on the trolley, his back unnaturally bent.

Joe addressed this misshapen man. "Is it possible these people could have killed themselves?"

"Not impossible but unlikely. There are cases of self-strangulation on record. That would explain the lack of other bruising in all but one of our corpses. But even someone in the grip of a mania would be unable to throttle themself nine times out of ten. The body has too many instinctual defences that will activate in that kind of situation." Yately lit a cigarette.

"I didn't think this was how multiple suicide happened." Relieved by the hunched man's lead, Joe placed some tobacco in a cigarette paper. "What else?"

"Well, the slow onset of decomposition combined with the continuing presence of rigor mortis would suggest the victims have been dead no more than a few days." Yately looked down at the shape and took a long drag. "In fact, I can go you one better than that. In my opinion all the bodies you retrieved from the ground died within hours of each other, perhaps even minutes."

Joe lit his roll-up and they remained silent for a while, a cloud of smoke building in the section of hall where the men stood. The quiet was broken by coughing from Dickson who excused himself and left to get some air. When he was gone Sweeney spoke again to the unflappable Yately.

"What would you say if I told you the victims were members of a religious cult?"

Yately pondered the question for a moment. "I'd say that information was essentially irrelevant Joe. Like you say, this wasn't a mass suicide." He took another drag and exhaled. "When you find a motive for what happened here, I suspect it will be one of the usual ones."

Only the two of them in his office, just as Joe had requested. Sweeney faced Stoker across the table, mugs of coffee between them. The prisoner's dark hair was closely cropped now and he'd been dressed in a new t-shirt and trousers, his flesh clean and clothes radiating freshness, much to Joe's relief. One of the captive's wide brown eyes remained swollen but Stoker was presentable at last, he no longer looked like exhibit A in a case for police brutality.

Joe took a circuitous route into the conversation, trying to build up trust with talk of Shelton and the local food, how Stoker had been treated and whether the man required anything more. It had been obvious to Joe for a while that this brawny figure seated opposite was exceptionally self-assured, believed he could evade anything the authorities threw his way, outwit these inferior policemen who bothered him. Good, thought Sweeney, let the boy believe that.

"You might have realized I don't have much in common with the other officers."

"I knew that from the start Joe." His manner was relaxed and condescending, Sweeney tried not to let the attitude annoy him.

"We're not interested in avenging those deaths Stoker, I'm old enough to have lost any belief in justice." Joe took a sip of his bitter drink. "But I'm intrigued, intrigued enough to stay here until the truth comes out. You're a smart boy Stoker, too smart to be a patsy." Nothing crossed the man's face. "I don't believe it should be your place to suffer for this crime." Still the suspect remained impassive. "Why didn't they take you with them Stoker? Why were you left behind?"

"I wasn't left behind, I stayed."

"Why on earth would you stay?"

A pause "You won't find your answers here Joe."

It was like extracting blood from a stone, or maybe trying to feed thousands from a few loaves and fishes. Sweeney sighed internally and drank the rest of his coffee, leaning back to study the suspect.

Stoker returned his gaze. "*Free among the dead, like the slain that lie in the grave, whom thou rememberest no more: and they are cut off from thy hand.*"

"Enough of that Biblical rubbish." A shadow flickered across the burly man's face. "What you should be saying is *I'm sorry. Sorry I was involved in so much death, but I was just a pawn. Let me tell you about the real culprits.* Do you get it my boy?" Joe grew louder as the words came tumbling out. "You're guilty in some way, and soon the remorse will come, and maybe you're good at concealing your conscience, maybe you've been suffering from it ever since this happened, wondering why you were allowed to survive and no one else was, maybe that's why you ran."

Stoker remained calm. "No. I'm alive, I'm still here, that's all." Defiance returned to his features. "I didn't run. I might have left, but I stayed. Perhaps you should take a look in your own backyard."

"I don't understand what you're saying."

"Think about it Joe, why hadn't your mob heard about us before this happened? Where's the background info? Ask yourself that Joe. We were around for years and we weren't hiding from anyone."

"Play games all you like." An undercurrent of anger in Sweeney's voice, he knew the weakness of lapsing into Wilson's style but failed to stifle the emotion. "There are innocent people dead thanks to you, bereaved families suffering." Joe rose from his seat and loomed over Stoker. "And all you do is play games."

"Since we're talking about Wilson, I was wondering whether you might be able to get me sample of his handwriting." An affected politeness in Stoker's voice. "You've done so much else for me, that shouldn't be a problem?"

Joe fell back into his chair. He felt tired and a long way from home and very close to retirement age. Swilling the dregs in his mug, Sweeney pulled out the jar of capsules and swallowed the last one with this lukewarm liquid, a combination that tasted ferric on his tongue. Stoker watched the Investigator's movement as Joe's thoughts left the room. He tried to think of some other way to proceed, a possible course, something that might serve to restore his optimism, even if it served no immediate purpose. Joe knew that threatening this man was useless, but they were powerless to follow any other course. Bringing this silent captive to court would be futile too; juries wouldn't convict one man on dozens of murder charges when his role was clearly accessorial. If Scotland Yard tried to charge this man the leftist media would smell scapegoating, not hesitate to tell their demographic about the injustice. No, Joe had to be patient and wait for Stoker to come out with it, his story. Gut instinct said he would eventually, they usually did, once the weight of events became too much and a guilty soul demanded unburdening. In the meantime Sweeney needed to educate himself a little. This investigation was moving forward too slowly in a muddle of inexperience and unschooled fumblings. Perhaps Shelton's library could teach him what to do, open Joe's eyes to whatever they'd missed here. Mankind's past was littered with horrific disasters and terrible tragedies, many of which initially were as inexplicable as this one. Wasn't it true we should learn from the past to avoid repeating its mistakes? Or something like that anyway.

Certainly Joe was getting nowhere with this conniving goon whose muscle-bound appearance belied a quick wit and devious nature. Sweeney collected his raincoat from a peg on the way out, leaving a baffled Stoker alone in the office.

Nolan

"You learn to build your own roads,
On today because tomorrow's ground is too uncertain for planning
And futures have a way of falling down mid-flight."
- Patricia Coyles, *Victim Of The Lockerbie Air Disaster*

The cumuli massing overhead promised rain, a mixed blessing. Showers would soften up the earth for digging and call a temporary halt to the day's work but Nolan wanted to continue. The man was proud of his fitness and intended to go on testing it. He would be sixty-one later in the year but Charlie could still do a session of outdoor work that would have broken the back of a man half his age. Nolan only suffered the adverse effects of fieldwork through an occasional pain in his hands when trying to sleep at night, nothing serious. He released two more potatoes from the ground and deposited them in one of the great circular buckets that littered the field, wincing as a plane flew over the compound, a fluffy contrail across what remained of the morning's blue sky. Then it was back to digging, the agricultural work that suited Nolan. This combined with an ability to build any kind of contraption he'd won the favour of his Shepherd and a place at Newtopia. While he found them rewarding, these long days of cooperative labour he had secured made Nolan grateful he hadn't gone to seed during the post-retirement years, a time when many with nothing to fill the days deteriorated into irretrievable disrepair.

In the distance two aides came and went between the greenhouses, connecting up hoses and watering unseen foliage. Nolan paused in his harvesting for a moment and kicked a stone across the soil, through the green flowering of potato plants. Leaning on his spade, Nolan watched a friend and disciple work the rows fifty yards to his left. Jim was a good-humoured man in his thirties whose friendliness belied an unsightly appearance. His nose had been broken in the past, and both ears were oddly misshapen, tufts of hair protruding from the holes, serving as a distraction from eyes which never opened further than half an inch. These slits always regarded others on the farm with fondness or amusement. Jim Saxon was the first resident to befriend Nolan on arrival a fortnight before, the younger man describing the layout of Newtopia, explaining work timetables for the manual labour side of operations. The man spoke from long experience, Jim having been accepted into *The Spirit Of Nagasaki* a year before. Determined to turn over a new leaf, Jim had devoted much of his meagre spare time since to educating himself. The man always had a book on theology or global affairs to hand, tomes borrowed from the well-stocked bookcases in the farmhouse.

The two men hadn't managed a second conversation until the previous night, a result of their busy schedules and the silence observed during work hours. Yesterday evening Nolan remained awake amid those who dozed all around, so Jim began whispering his story from the adjacent mattress. While the dozen other inhabitants inside that outhouse snoozed on, Nolan wrapped the blankets around him and listened to Saxon explain how his religious conversion was precipitated by necessity. In the months before coming to S.O.N. Jim's gambling debts had massed to such an extent he could see no way out. The expensive addiction, once a brief weekly escape from the stresses of two small children, had swollen, become the monkey on his back that every punter dreads. The connected men who ran the casinos and had once been so generous with their credit lines sent ex-cons to Jim's place of work for intimidatory purposes. Uncivilized by the made to measure suits they wore, these great hulking monsters waited outside the taxi rank for Jim's return at the end of his shift. In a manner unlikely to be misinterpreted, they explained how he would shortly be taking his meals through a straw if he didn't pay up, and while trapped in hospital they wouldn't hesitate to move on to Jim's family.

Options were low and falling away all the time. Jim's house was rented, and selling everything wouldn't even pay off half the money he owed, could only serve to leave his family bereft and out on the street. He considered skipping the city but couldn't bear to leave the boys behind. Then there was Joan, a forcefully attractive woman whose shrewd nature would have caught up with him sooner or later. Jim feared the wrath of his wife as much as any heavies, and giving her up was out of the question. If anything Jim's love for his wife had only grown through the eight years of their marriage, to the point where he now suffered from a debilitating uxoriousness. Thoughts of a life without her were unbearable in the extreme. For all Jim's worldliness and street-smarts, moving to some far-off place and never being able to meet another woman was his big fear, having only loneliness and a grizzled visage in the mirror for company. The failures of adulthood had killed what little dating confidence Jim might once have possessed, memories of misunderstandings and embarrassments, doomed attempts at courtship back in the eighties, testaments to Jim's amorous ineptitude that made him cringe to recall. No, this woman was Jim's eternal soul mate, so patient and encouraging throughout their marriage, producing two strapping boys fortunate to take after their mother in intellect. Jim couldn't afford to lose that love, so what was the alternative? There wasn't any, save personal injury and time in a hospital bed, a period the family might not survive unbroken.

Then that leaflet came through the door, promises of a better society existing out there within the larger world. To Jim the religion offered a refuge, not just for himself but the rest of the Saxon family as well. Joan took some persuading, there were tears shed and harsh words exchanged, the woman unwilling to accept the sudden upheavals on what appeared to be a thoughtless whim. Only when her husband finally admitted the truth of his situation did Jim's wife become convinced he had no choice but to abscond. And abscond he would, with or without her and the boys. Her husband wasn't joking. Joan was forced to take a long look at life as a single parent, the loveless nature of her future without Jim, and eventually concede the issue. His way was best, the right path for all of them.

That was the beauty of the Goddess' faith. *The Spirit Of Nagasaki* received the four of them into its fold, provided accommodation without being offended by the minuscule donation Jim made to its cause. The faith of the S.O.N. removed the Saxons from the pressure and threat of the outside world, asking only that they follow the ways of the Goddess and do her bidding in return. Before long this well-settled family came to the attention of the upper echelons, Rebecka herself visiting the London base one Saturday to marvel at the good behaviour and obedience of these two boys. She studied reports that attested to Joan's mothering technique, effective not just with her sons but other followers, the woman always ready when someone needed her. Rebecka took a private audience with the head of house, listened closely as he spoke of Jim's immersion in her teachings, learning how this acolyte with the thuggish appearance had gorged himself on *The Spirit Of Nagasaki*, educated in its doctrines to such an extent he could answer the kids' questions more knowledgeably than most of the in-house Shepherds.

The statements were so positive it wasn't long before the Saxons found themselves called from their city centre room into the agrarian community of Newtopia. The fact that his children were good for the ambience of the place undoubtedly helped. No reflection on Nolan, but single males had to be thoroughly vetted before they were allowed into the compound, and there was no shortage of women or young couples eager to sign up for the faith. Families though, they were something else entirely. Having a few kids running around put a smile on the adults' faces; they were a positive boon. The boys brought a harmony to Newtopia, an image of bourgeois respectability within the nascent society as they were parented by dozens of different teachers. Although Joan and Jim were forced to inhabit separate beds until their vows were renewed under the laws of the Goddess, it was a small price to pay for the safety and happiness they found in deepest Cornwall.

The older man was touched by this story and said so, Nolan remaining awake for a while after Jim rolled over and fell unconscious, the fellow beside him exhausted by the process of dredging up his past. Nolan knew Jim was expecting a story in return, if not the next night then sometime soon. Everybody at Newtopia had a tale to tell from life before the Goddess touched them, the circumstances they had left behind. Nothing brought residents together like the sharing of personal history.

The man resumed his digging, the sky above taking on the grayish tinge that comes before a rainstorm. Nolan had no desire to return to the past, was not yet reconciled to the origins of his faith, but he knew going back would soon become unavoidable. The memories had surfaced with increasing regularity since he came to this place. Nolan's return to the West Country meant he now lived no more than a short drive from that wife who should probably be thought of as *estranged*. As far as he knew Glenys continued to live in the cottage they had shared for over a decade, a property located just across the Devon border. That house was where Nolan saw out the nineties, a time when life consisted of little more than the Times crossword and tending a patch of garden out back, the television schedules and regular cycle rides into the country, coming back to the comfort of his moth-eaten easy chair with foam bursting from the armrests. It was a time of emptiness and contemplation, the post-retirement years, a period of recovery as a medicated Nolan picked at the foam or tried to get some sleep, and as the panic attacks dissipated the gulf between Charlie Nolan and his wife grew. Trivial irritations started to assume monstrous proportions, her tendency to read magazines in bed filling the man with an inexplicable fury. He interpreted the act as lacking respect for the wind down after the day, a time before sleep that ought to be filled with study of the most serious and weighty volumes. He would turn away and fume, then again when she was always in the way as he tried to do work around the house, yet never there with a kind word. For her part Glenys found him distant and preoccupied, a pale shadow of the thoughtful man she married. The pair drifted apart, even as they remained in the same house, sleeping in separate beds, then different rooms. Nolan took to preparing food for one and washing his clothes independently, the couple gradually becoming strangers during that decade of prosperity, never conversing or even acknowledging the presence of the other, hopelessly childless and without the mutual friends who might inspire nostalgia and fondness.

Then came the terrorist event. Nolan watched nine hours of television that cataclysmic day, flicking between channels as the terrible moments ran before his eyes again and again. In the weeks that followed this granite-etched date the world suddenly began to share Nolan's paranoia. People stared up at those ever-present planes soaring above, wondering if the flight paths weren't somehow more erratic than they used to be, changed trajectories for these machines whose steady noise and horrifying potential previously went unnoticed. Now they came to hold a malevolent influence over us all. Nolan wasn't about to get obsessed by the attack, he was only as interested as most of the world. Indeed, it wasn't 9/11 that threw him back to those buried memories. Charlie's flashbacks were precipitated by a less spectacular incident the following month, another aircraft coming down in the same beleaguered city, this plane crashing into a residential borough with earth-shaking force.

While correspondents speculated, officials reassured, and experts investigated, Nolan stared open-mouthed at those TV pictures. The plane's engine, detached from the machine it was meant to operate, lay on the forecourt of a garage like a dislocated work of art, a great metal object that remained intact after the crash. Houses underneath the glide path were doomed to destruction, fire raining from the skies onto helpless residents or unoccupied buildings. Nolan saw a local man whose mind could not process the disaster, his inability to enact the appropriate response leading him toward the flames, so overwhelmed with fear for loved ones he neglected his own safety. Suddenly Nolan couldn't hold back the recollections. In an instant he was returned to that dark night, one December evening in 1988.

Nolan remembered the scene as if it was the week before, not thirteen years ago. Charlie had spent much of the day catching up on paperwork at the border base of the Dumfries and Galloway police where he'd worked for more years than he cared to count. Not being a man to extract satisfaction from the tidy formality of clerical duties, Nolan was glad to return to the fireside warmth and enticing food-smells of his terraced house near the centre of Lockerbie, easing a tired body into his armchair just as *This Is Your Life* began, Glenys humming to herself from the kitchen. Anticipation was building for this week's celebrity, soon to be surprised by that big red book, when a strange shaking took hold of the windows, vibrations that spread through the whole house, as if the area were located on a seismic fault line. Glenys rushed through the doorway to ask her husband what was happening but Nolan was already at the window, stunned by the sight of flaming debris falling down towards his town.

In the distance the wing of a jumbo jet crashed past their eyes, a great white rhombus silhouetted against the clouds, plummeting onto townsfolk who would see only a thunderous black mass. His wife closed her eyes and prayed for their lives to be spared as Nolan watched the pieces of aircraft land on homes in a crushing onslaught. Fire burnt like a beacon in the distance, incinerating the lawns and driveways, rooftops and hedge ways, whole properties ablaze.

When the noise stopped Nolan found a torch to venture outside with and see what might be done. Certain as he could be the barrage was over, the man left Glenys on the phone to the emergency services and opened his door. Outside the picture was one of devastation and carnage. Where minutes before there existed the festive atmosphere of Christmas, a celebratory backing of carol singers and local people delivering cards, now there was only horror. No more than ten yards from Nolan's doorstep the corpse of a young woman lay in the foetal position, her body smashed, like a doll that had fallen from thirty thousand feet. Across the road elderly neighbours emerged from the garage where they had taken refuge and covered the dead girl with a blanket, stepping around those small fires that burned along the road. Nolan moved quickly toward the area where the main section of aircraft had gone down, hopping over flaming tarmac as he did so.

Charlie was beaten back before he could get close to Rosebank Crescent, the scene of the worst devastation and a road where he and Glenys had nearly bought a house in the mid-seventies. The heat and smoke stopped Nolan in his tracks. Where once there was a row of houses now only a smoking crater confronted him. Nolan's hope there might be survivors was shattered in an instant. His next thought was that he ought to seal off the place, keep adrenalized townsfolk away, those people who even now gathered behind him, ignoring requests to return to their homes. But how could even the most conscientious policeman cordon off an area that might stretch as far as the North Sea? The authorities would end up treating eight hundred square miles as a murder scene, but just then something nagged at Nolan to forget this formality, keep looking for survivors. His belief, ridiculous in the face of logic, that it might be possible to pull someone from these ruins. Turning from the geographical monstrosity before him, a furrow in the land as deep and wide as the holes they created for archaeological excavations, Nolan went on to survey the rest of the town.

Up ahead roofs were missing from buildings while other structures were entirely absent, rubble and smoke the only hint homes had once stood. To Nolan's right residents rushed to cover body parts strewn across their gardens with whatever came to hand, sheets and cloth, old rugs or canvas. The great twisted shape of a fuselage was visible through the haze, the plane having landed on what used to be a children's playground. An overpowering stink of melted metal mixed with a general smell of burning, the nagging doubt in Nolan's head that continued to demand he act. The off-duty officer took care to avoid detritus, stepping over plastic cutlery and bread rolls while moving toward the broken piece of machinery. Behind him locals stayed where they were and stared at the ruins, the distant sound of panda cars and fire engines becoming louder as Nolan reached the fuselage. He shone the torch into its partially flattened centre, Charlie's hope evaporating once more as he made out shapes through the dim light. There was no one alive inside, only the terrified expressions of fifty or more passengers, all still strapped to their seats. Lines of dead travellers filled the body of this jet, skin unnaturally white, faces panicked.

Nolan clambered over seats and metal on his return from the disaster site, the man carefully regulating his breaths all along the main street. Colleagues from Dumfries and Galloway took stock of the situation from beside his house. Nolan signalled to the men in their insulated uniforms, explained there was nothing to be done for those in the wreckage.

Back home Charlie made his wife promise she wouldn't go outside, drank a pint and a half of water and advised Glenys to phone her mother and sister, let her relatives know she was alright. Nolan returned to the chilly winter air, walking east at a steady trot, toward that rural area where he'd seen another piece of the jet come down, passing wreckage all the way. Often he would recognize pieces of humanity spread across the yards and pavements like broken mannequins, pausing in shock to stare at the body of a man fallen against a chimney breast, the corpse spreadeagled across the roof of a house like some kind of sick sculpture.

Eventually the buildings of town petered out and Nolan arrived in the grounds of Tundergarth Farm. Here the nose of the plane was separated from the rest of this craft, a hundred foot high landmark. The Maid Of The Seas had fractured in mid-air, broken into many pieces like a clay pigeon, a murderous indignity wrought upon the once proud aircraft. Tundergarth's owner, a perpetually hostile third-generation farmer who went by the name of Wilkes, was nowhere to be seen. Nolan looked at the undamaged house and saw a light burning. The man was likely sheltering in fright. This jagged cone of metal took up much of an otherwise bare field a quarter of a mile from the farmer's property and the darkness of night forced Nolan to wave his torch from left to right, approach the debris like a blind man with a cane.

The front section of the aircraft contained more grisly sights, a score of bodies that included the pilot who was slumped over what remained of the control panel. Nolan went inside to find another young woman dead at his feet, separate from the restrained corpses, balled up on the metal floor in a defensive posture, like a hedgehog fearful of a predator. He ran the light over her with unsteady hands and saw the body was unmarked, no injuries to ruin the girl's flesh or blemishes on her perfect skin. Charlie manoeuvred out of the metal cavity, staring up at the troposphere outside. The implications of this horrendous firework display had fully coalesced in Nolan's mind. There was no longer logic behind his search, no point in rushing to the next dreadful scene. All the passengers who had been travelling in this mutilated Jumbo Jet were dead, eradicated swiftly and violently, along with many of the town's residents, people Nolan knew or recognized. This Scottish settlement was decimated and big news. Even now teams from around the country were beginning to converge, picking over this tragedy before the police had time to search the wreckage.

A second beam of light broke the gloom and Nolan found himself confronted by the bewildered face of Farmer Wilkes, the man's cantankerous nature quelled by that monstrosity he was caught up in. Upon identifying officer Nolan the farmer broke into a babbled description of his evening, how he had heard the crash from inside his house, decided to come out and investigate despite the fear he felt but taken ages to get ready, excuses for the delay. Desperate to move thoughts away from his worries for those townsfolk he'd spent so many years protecting, Nolan suggested they conduct a sweep of the farmer's land to see what could be uncovered. Together they searched the acres that surrounded the twisted metal, a hunt commanding the men's attention for more than an hour. The pair found luggage and belongings, items of clothing strewn over the fields, a charred Samsonite suitcase and an intact holdall Wilkes opened, drawing Nolan's attention to the plastic-wrapped packages of white powder inside, a substance neither of the men could place. Soon after their discovery the farmer spotted a police surgeon hurrying across the fields, the man accompanied by two officers with whom Nolan was vaguely familiar. The doctor had driven up from Bradford in response to a BBC newsflash and Charlie illuminated the scene inside for him, so the surgeon could begin the awful task of pronouncing the passengers in the nose dead. The man methodically checked each pulse, as though life might prevail somewhere amid this slaughter.

The rest of that night became a sleepless blur as Nolan returned to his team, the resources of the smallest police force in Scotland stretched to their limit. The authorities offered assistance to the emergency services, tried to evacuate damaged buildings, gave comments for insistent reporters in the wearied tones of distressed men discussing the self-evident: No, it was too early to say. Yes, everyone was doing all they could. Voices were kept level, tones remaining dispassionate.

Once daylight intruded upon the site a number of unfriendly CIA operatives precipitated a change in leadership. The new imperative for Nolan and his fellow policemen was to go home and rest up, await further instructions and try to enjoy what remained of the festive period. A difficult task when the television screen was filled with speculative news reports and half the windows in his house looked out upon this ravaged town. It was a view Nolan could soon recreate with his eyes closed, the man spending hours each day staring at the damage until suddenly it was 1989 and Glenys sent him for a doctor's appointment. Nolan's GP proceeded to diagnose him as suffering from stress-related depression, prescribed medication to nullify the effects of that traumatic event.

Weeks slipped by, a time for the community to grieve for its eleven dead kin and begin to rebuild their lives. Nolan attended every local funeral as a mark of respect, an action that went against the wishes of his wife, Glenys believing their services could only put more strain on Charlie's weakened mental defences. The rest of the man's days were spent waiting to be called back to work, while at night he would wake in a cold sweat, dreams haunted by visions of dead women on rooftops, children lying in the street, the horribly skewed cadavers of men caught by trees and hedges. In this alternate world Nolan always opened the door to a tableau of corpses, a scream catching in his throat at the sight outside. People were contorted, as if occupying drill positions in preparation for a nuclear attack, only these motionless figures weren't pretending.

On other nights the unscathed girl from the nose cone would flit through his subconscious, an American woman whose child would never again see its mother. In Nolan's nightmares she rose from her protective ball as he stepped through the debris, proclaimed herself fine and walked away from his desperate grasp, across the field at Tundergarth and off to die out of sight.

Glenys would calm her husband as he started awake each night, gradually convinced they could not go on living in a place so closely linked to the horrors of that night, horrors continuing to live inside Nolan's mind. When the decision of the force was made official, confirmation they wouldn't be calling him back into service, a perplexed Nolan took the generous pension and allowed his wife to convince him that their retirement ought to be spent elsewhere, the sizeable pay-off covering the purchase of a secluded cottage outside Torminster. From Scotland to South West England was a long way for a couple in their fifties, but Glenys was certain the miles she put between Charles and Lockerbie would aid her husband's recovery. What she didn't foresee was his dissolution into boredom and inertia once they left behind friends and acquaintances for this picturesque yet unfamiliar landscape. Then came the footage from Queens, a cloud of smoke above a built-up area, businesses and homes crushed in a split second, Nolan's recovery reversed in a stroke. The man's composure was overturned by images of an aircraft falling onto the residents of Brooklyn, and suddenly Nolan couldn't breathe, pitching forward out of his chair, hitting the carpet on both knees, back in the grip of a panic attack after so many years.

Fat drops of rain began to fall around Nolan as he continued to unearth vegetables, oblivious to the many S.O.N. brothers who halted in their labours and made for cover, Jim's two sons scampering out of the farmhouse to urge their dad indoors. His nineties convalescence in England had distanced Nolan from the atrocity, both mentally and geographically. Lockerbie was far enough away for the man to detach himself from the tragedy's aftermath. Nolan found he could maintain the neutral eye and dispassionate mindset previously used when resolving neighbourhood disputes, refusing to waste his energy on anger as the investigations unfolded and information seeped into the public domain. He learned of the 215 warnings received by intelligence services in the year before the disaster, all of which predicted an attack on American Airlines in Europe, all of which were ignored. Nolan watched the Prime Minister reject pleas from the bereaved for a public inquiry, Thatcher failing to offer the balm of truth to sufferers on both sides of the Atlantic, preferring to leave her citizens in ignorance. He caught The Four Tops speaking of their brush with death on TV, relief written on their faces as the men described the fortune of a producer who kept them in the studio longer than anticipated, the quartet missing their scheduled flight on The Maid Of The Seas, speaking of the happenstance as if it were divine intervention.

When Glenys wasn't around to disapprove Nolan would research the facts. Usually it was just a couple of hours each month, enough for him to combine the long-ago evidence of his own eyes with learned conjecture and reach some conclusions. First came a realization; the man smuggling that holdall of drugs Wilkes found had travelled under a false name. Not only that, he was one of the CIA's own. The agency's appearance on the border and subsequent lack of interest in the other victims was the result of a need to protect this corrupt operative as well as the reputation of the organization that employed him. The focus of attention was not because the Central Intelligence Agency man existed as a terrorist target, he was simply a profiteering drug mule.

Occasionally Nolan would ring up the station at Dumfries and Galloway under the auspices of concern for old colleagues, subtly getting those answers that told him every officer on duty that night had been moved or sacked or prematurely retired like him. Then there was the police surgeon who had come from Bradford, that selfless gesture of Samaritanism, a man who struck Nolan as decent and likeable during the minutes he'd spent with him. The doctor's reward for examining twenty square miles inside a day and a night, working to hunt down and confirm the dead in freezing conditions, was denouncement. He was branded a rule-breaking loner by superiors and eventually sacked on the fifth anniversary of that black date for no discernible reason. Nolan saw the hands of those corrupt security services in everything, men trying to protect their own by quietly dismissing the innocent and smearing the honourable. Edifying as these deductions were for Charlie, revelations quickly become old if you have no one to share them with. It was the early part of the decade, a time when Nolan was losing his ability to communicate with Glenys, and he knew explaining these beliefs to his wife would only cause her to worry or dismiss him as wide of the mark. So Nolan sat back and continued to passively absorb the unfolding evidence, not allowing himself to be overheated by the injustices he believed were coming to light.

During Lockerbie's immediate aftermath the transport secretary had issued a brief statement. In confident words he assured everyone the killers would be brought to book, then left for his Christmas holiday in the Caribbean. Sure enough the culprits were quickly unearthed. From the available evidence it seemed certain the *Popular Front For The Liberation Of Palestine* had placed a cassette recorder containing a bomb inside the jet's hold. This extremist group were in the pay of Iran, a country seeking revenge for America's recent act of aggression, shooting down an Airbus over the Persian Gulf. To Nolan and others the theory appeared sound, the proof incontrovertible. He waited for the terrorists to be located and brought to book.

Unfortunately for those seeking justice, both Britain and the U.S. had recently sided with the Iranian government against Saddam Hussain's Iraqi regime. Soon Desert Storm was undertaken in a flush of patriotism and expensive weaponry and the West simply could not be seen to go after their new allies. Many believed the President chose to cast around for suitable scapegoats instead, eventually settling on Gadaffi's regime. Much to the surprise of the victims' families and the utter disbelief of Nolan two vaguely dishonest Libyan nationals were named for indictment. On the flimsiest of evidence one of the pair was convicted and the mourners finally had someone to blame. Yet the revenge of imprisonment felt empty somehow, a failed attempt at closure, blame that left nobody free to heal. Maybe it was all the time that had elapsed since the attack, or perhaps even the most gung-ho of the bereaved had been left with serious misgivings. Few people were satisfied by the verdict. Not Libya, not Charlie's old home town, not America and certainly not Nolan himself who felt a worm of disgust in his gut, wondering how world leaders could live with themselves. How Bush and Thatcher could sleep at night after gaining political mileage from the suffering of others. Nolan would never have called himself naive, but even with all his years on the force, only now did he fully understand what politics was all about. This manipulation of the innocent to justify the powerful in their conscienceless actions, that was politics. Meanwhile Abdelbasset Ali Mohamed Al Megrahi, whose only crime for Charlie was to be a shady foreigner associated with men the West perceived to be against them, was left to rot in jail.

Ultimately Nolan took the philosophical view, both to remain in good health and for the sake of his sanity. He managed to keep most feelings in check all the way up until that pivotal autumn of 2001, when memories triggered by the news forced their way into his consciousness. The recollections brought with them feelings of despair and long-suppressed rage, a crushing disenchantment with the world and its inhabitants, sensations that resulted in weeks of unsteadiness and depression, Glenys too far gone from the intimacy of twelve years ago to comfort him now. While his wife slept through the nights alone Nolan plumbed the depths of his being in their other bedroom, took care to disappear in the daytime, afternoons spent softly crying, away from her eyes.

By the time of that week before Christmas Glenys had left their cottage to spend the festive period with her sister, Nolan left by himself for the most soul-deadening and lonely time of year. In an effort to take his mind off the approaching anniversary of that dreadful December night and to avoid wallowing in his own misery Nolan journeyed into Torminster. He hoped the lights and decorations of town, the eagerness in the eyes of children and soothing hymns that drifted through the air, could provide the lift his spirits required. Charlie was gazing at the window display of a department store, fake snow on reindeers that pulled a sleigh of expensive perfumes, when the call came, that question from a mellifluous voice speaking into his ear.

"Excuse me sir, would you have a minute?"

Willing to let even some salesperson have a shot at him today, time being the one thing he had plenty of, Nolan turned to face the speaker. Before him Charlie saw a pretty young woman beaming out the smile of a person who wants something. She handed Nolan a leaflet and launched into her spiel, asking the man what he thought of the world around them, whether he followed a particular faith. Nolan watched this girl with the strawberry blonde hair and long scarf, unsure how to respond. Finally he replied, saying his views would take a while to explain, so why didn't they discuss this somewhere warm?

Nolan bought hot chocolate for them both, listening to the world view of this girl called Nicky as she extrapolated on *The Spirit Of Nagasaki*. She described how the Goddess who had invented the religion built a new community from scratch, a place where everyone was made to feel welcome and nobody could be overlooked or feel unloved. Nicky asked Nolan to regard her as an example. Back in the teens she had been afraid to leave the house, such was the triumph of neuroses in limiting the girl's freedom. Yet here she was, a few years later, out recruiting complete strangers. Because she felt no one should be alone, particularly not at Christmas.

Was it the message that converted Nolan? Or the beautiful girl with the button nose and fire in her eyes, the first woman to show concern for him in years? Maybe a part of this man had always longed for a daughter, someone he could buy warming drinks for and listen to as she talked of her life. Whatever the reason, Nicky's words found a home in him. The girl bore little resemblance to that commune of *weirdoes* Nolan had conjured up from those frequent mentions in sections of the West Country press. In fact, this young woman was imbued with such an irrefutable sense of what ought to be important, from friendship to family to love, that Nolan soon became convinced he could learn much from this faith.

That was where it began for him, at a table in Torminster's new chain coffee house, a few days before Christ's birthday. That was the start of a welcome into the fold that moved from London back to the southwest, a profound relationship with the tolerant ways of the Goddess, the rarely-seen figure who lived and oversaw and meditated from the top floor of the Newtopian farmhouse. Between them Nicky and Rebecka turned his life around, gave Nolan something to work with after years of superfluity, a belief some things were beyond corruption, that there existed an alternative to the degeneracy of regular society.

Surprised at his feeling of elevation after this saunter through the past, Nolan felt ready now, unafraid to let Jim inside. The man lifted his head and realized he was alone in the field, noticed the chill of rain soaking through his smock for the first time. The figure laughed to himself. Memories couldn't harm him now, at long last Charlie Nolan had a happy ending. But the unloading of his past onto Jim Saxon could come later. Right now there was urgent work to consider. More chosen ones were coming to Newtopia, soon moving from the city Douglas said, and Nolan had the responsibility of building their home, a necessity that would require the conversion of a second outhouse into another set of quarters.

Nolan wiped a combination of sweat and rainwater from his brow, using a boot to grind his spade into the muddy ground, the implement remaining upright as he walked across the field, the man heading for that main building where some sister, perhaps Nicky, perhaps another, would be waiting with a smile and a fluffy towel and a mug of hot tea. Charlie didn't know which of these comforts generated the warmest welcome, was unable to single one out as the touch he looked forward to the most.

Chapter Five

On the inside Shelton's library proved as modest as the exterior suggested, its main desk positioned beside a small children's area, walls decorated with sugar paper images, colourful recreations of spacemen and trains, dancing monkeys and smiling clowns. Opposite the enquiries a section dedicated to reference works journals could be found, many of these encyclopedias tatty, dust having accumulated on the stacks of magazines beside them. Amid the rarely studied documentation Joe sat by himself, flicking through the selection of heavy books piled on a table before him. The local assistant, a fortyish woman who held a certain dusky allure despite her lazy eye, had been most helpful. She arranged for immediate membership and agreed to rely on Joe's bosses to pay Shelton Council for charges incurred when Sweeney used the catch-all phrase *government business* to explain his presence in the village. His disclosure was rewarded with unlimited credit and an admiring glance from the librarian, a look that suggested Sweeney hadn't entirely lost the masculine charisma which made his younger days so pleasurable, no matter how battered he felt inside. The woman's hands pushed hair from eyes and rubbed at the skin of her face before she laminated Joe's membership card, the rules of the library stated clearly, her voice lowered to a conspiratorial whisper when describing the credit Joe had been given for photocopying and Internet access. These last services were located in the only section that sparkled with newness here, a partitioned room containing five shiny PCs.

So the modern world had permeated some parts of Shelton thought Joe as he shuffled around the non-fiction shelves, occasionally casting a glance at that assistant who looked away whenever he did so, the woman pretending to be absorbed by her filing. Sweeney collected volumes and periodicals that looked useful and took a desk out of the woman's sight line, putting other thoughts from his mind by rationalizing away her attention. She was simply curious, that was all. Intrigued someone other than mothers with easily bored children or retired men had entered her workplace this drab weekday.

Two hours or so into his studies, Joe averted tired eyes from the journal and gazed out the window to his right. A child's helium balloon, the shape of a dolphin and the colour of deepest lazurite, came into view then floated beyond the glass, the ribbon this inflatable had once been tethered by trailing in its wake. The texts before Sweeney described how minority religions recruited converts from all kinds of backgrounds. Yet the greater part of these disciples, certainly in the Western world, came from the educated middle-classes. Converts were searching for a life beyond the prosperity of their parents, looking for sureties during that confused period of spiritual transition known as late adolescence. These teenagers were hopeful and vulnerable. Often their only previous experience of religion was a vague undercurrent through school or during the wistfulness of Church-held events. When confronted with the message of Christ for the first time such innocents found themselves deeply touched, particularly if the revelation coincided with a crisis in their personal lives. What a religious group offered was different from obsessions with the perfect career or collection of possessions, far away from the image consciousness and subculture tribalism of their peers. Cults subsumed an incomplete personality into the wholeness of the collective, returned the lost to traditional values espoused by God. New faiths tantalized with promises, became powerful during periods of global unrest, times when the confused looked to humanity's oldest beliefs for succour. Religion prevented believers from suffering the frustration of ambiguity in uncertain times.

One of the books contained a printed list of guidelines aimed at helping parents predict when confused offspring might run off and join a cult. The chapter told of danger signs including neurotic and humourless tendencies, a detachment from the family and drastic mood swings. Such indicators paralleled a steady physical deterioration from the faith-inflicted diet, combining with hypersensitivity to criticism and an aggressive defiance when challenged. The description sounded like every teenager Joe had ever encountered, up to and including his own daughter.

Sweeney turned from the window to look at the mess of magazines and tomes strewn across the table. So the weak were most at risk and the befuddled likeliest to abandon everything and join up. Yet the victims of a cult weren't society's dimwits. These were usually smart kids, often from privileged backgrounds. Why would so many otherwise astute youngsters willingly give themselves up to reclusiveness and privation?

Joe fought the urge to go outside and smoke. It was cold out there, and

Sweeney didn't need any more coughing fits to understand his lungs were complaining at the tobacco intake of the past few days. The histories of theological movements he had pulled from the shelves taught Joe that the need for God had always been there. The human race was infinitely credulous when it came to matters of the Bible, however high the individual IQ. We no longer believed the world to be flat or witches existed only for burning, but there existed a thread of ideology stretching back thousands of years that maintained a white-bearded figure ruled from the clouds, while a scaly devil commanded fire deep in the earth. To Joe's surprise, the present strain of Christianity turned out to have been initiated by a diseased and murderous King. Henry VIII altering the doctrines to make his divorce from Catherine of Aragon legal. He could then marry Anne Boleyn and take charge of church revenues to fund his numerous wars. Joe wondered if today's C of E faithful realized their way of life had been dictated by a power-crazed bigot who ruled five hundred years before, asking himself whether Protestants were really so far from the extreme movements Shelton library yielded up, other faiths like Mormonism with its promise that followers could have their own planets by following the dictates on angel-bestowed tablets. Then there was the Russian Orthodox Church which precipitated the death of twenty thousand monks from the seventeenth century onward by altering the syntax of its liturgy. Even the West Country housed small-time kooks. A religion called the Chrisemma Foundation operated out of Totnes, its theology allowing anyone with forty pounds to visit the two leaders and worship a woman called Emma as their God.

He read on, discovering how the Moonies flourished when Japan pulled out of Korea, a cult initiated by the eponymous Reverend who claimed to have once carried a man on his back for two hundred miles. After the Nagasaki atom bomb there was a spiritual vacuum in Korea that Moon rushed to fill. Was this where the name of the S.O.N. came from? As with Moon's new market, opened after years of Shinto oppression, maybe the people of England saw *The Spirit Of Nagasaki* as a viable alternative to the discredited babble of Christianity. They had come upon this new way of finding answers to the big questions by trawling through the emptiness. The Bible as their talisman and traditional religions examples to reject.

Sweeney couldn't be sure, it was all speculation. He needed more material relating to the history of this particular faith. Joe flicked through the books one last time. So many of the famous cases of the twentieth century, from Jonestown to Heaven's Gate, had ended in a massacre. But these cults expired with willing self-destruction, those who believed a better world awaited them. There weren't any precedents for the genocide of this case. Not that other sects cared much for their followers. The testaments of the deprogrammed read like a litany of abuse and neglect. Many small-time movements were ravaged by sexually transmitted diseases, the downside of free love rampant amid polygamous communities. Even if acolytes weren't incestuously promiscuous, there was malnutrition and exhaustion to cope with, workers having little to eat and forced to work long hours at the leaders' behest, expected to overcome the temptation of food. This lack of nutrition resulted in the unpleasant symptoms of kitosis; bad breath and recurrent nausea; endless fatigue. Joe couldn't recall any of the corpses appearing undernourished, few of the dead girls were as skinny as his own daughter, and the asceticism of the S.O.N. theology didn't scream of uninhibited sexuality. He decided to get Yately to check the bodies for STDs or malnutrition anyway. Whatever results the forensic reports turned up, these details might help them see the bigger picture.

After replacing the volumes on their shelves Sweeney took the remaining journals to the photocopier and set about duplicating articles mentioning *The Spirit Of Nagasaki* by name. He raised the copy shade to its darkest level just as the librarian had advised. Joe was aware of her eyes on him as he stood over the temperamental machine, tapping a finger on the plastic shell while the bulb flashed. When he moved beyond that temporary wall to take a seat before a computer she followed him, making no attempt to hide her interest. Joe became distracted from his task, unable to focus on the retrieval of information from the Internet's disparate ocean, made nervous by that feminine figure hovering behind him.

"Can I help you at all?"

"Probably you can, yes." The librarian leant over Joe and placed a hand on the mouse, her subtle perfume cutting through the general stuffiness. She took him to a search engine via the PC's settings.

"This one's quite comprehensive, just enter a phrase or question and it'll bring up a series of links."

"Excellent, thank you." His reasoning told Joe he needed a pill and a cigarette, but simultaneously Sweeney's body demanded he ask this woman to dinner. Her ample chest brushed against his arm as she straightened up and Joe noticed the ring on her finger for the first time, a totem of marriage matching his own. Rather than ask the assistant what she had planned for the evening Sweeney let this librarian walk away. He felt too old and tired for the tawdry immediacy of an affair, and it wouldn't have done his blood pressure any good. Joe allowed himself to watch the woman as she returned to the enquiry desk. Her physique had retained the firmness of youth, and Sweeney found himself regretting his decision several times before going back to the monitor. Joe tapped the cult's name into the on-screen box wishing there were tablets you could take to control fluctuating arousal. To be hormonal at his age was undignified.

The detective spent the next hour meticulously exploring links, collecting prints of features and news reports that might aid his investigation. Night had begun to descend as Joe gathered his papers together to exit the building, thanking the librarian and giving her his mobile number. Joe knew the act was ostensibly an innocent strand of the business, but part of him hoped she would call for other reasons.

Outside he walked through dusk, caught up again by the questions his research created, wondering if these sects really did put their devotees through an endless cycle of hardship, the back-breaking work and penury so many books documented. If so, why would such large numbers submit to exploitation? Their motives couldn't be philosophical ones, surely? Nowhere in history's portrayal of cults was there mention of the joy and happiness young people ought to be feeling, that celebratory delight at being alive all kids experience. A pleasure Joe was sure he'd known once, although the man was unable to resurrect this sensation.

Sweeney shuffled up the high street's narrow walkway, approaching the light and strictures of his accommodation, one irrevocable understanding coursing through his nervous system as the man entered that guest house. A remedy winning out over all the necessities of his faltering body. Joe needed a drink

Trina

"Unto the woman he said, I will greatly multiply thy pain and thy travail; in pain thou shalt bring forth children; and thy desire shall be to thy husband, and he shall rule over thee."

- Book of Genesis 3:16

Many were the arrangements of flowers bedecking the great barn, carnations and roses and lilies, all bunched in colourful explosions around the walls and walkway. Some of the displays bore messages of goodwill from people the bride had never met, such were the side effects of celebrity. Bouquets from strangers were one of the myriad benefits the young girl had never considered when craving fame in her youth. Trina raised the veil to scratch an ear, trying to forget the pain inflicted by the corset section of this shimmering dress, a bodice that kept cutting into her skin. The discomfort was more than compensated for by the inch it took off Trina's stomach and the pertness restored to her breasts. The bride knew her body needed to look its best for the photographers.

Trina Callow had been out of the spotlight a long time. She had taken a while to access the gregarious persona she used to have for the question and answer session held at Newtopia the day before, an affectation that had once come so naturally. Fortunately the female reporter from *Welcome!* magazine was patient, understanding, even vaguely awed. She guided Trina through her first interview in a year with straightforward and fawning queries. How had she replied again? Trina struggled to recall. Not with anything revealing, that was for sure. Her guard was up and she had been too well briefed to let anything slip. The young interviewer noted the disciples working their land and the idyllic countryside as they sat outside the farmhouse, Trina describing her new lifestyle as "like reality TV without the cameras". Recollecting this sound bite made her smirk, an expression hidden by the lace. Most of the time her life at Newtopia was too good to be compared with reality, televised or otherwise. Particularly when her reality before S.O.N. was selfish obsession, years of loneliness and the tears that came with it.

The bride glanced around her at those attending the ceremony, thirty or more brothers and sisters she had come to love in the long months preceding this day. Those making up the crowd were dressed smartly for the occasion, suits and dresses obtained by the Goddess. This was the one day of the year when colourless smocks could be abandoned. Trina angled her head. There were certainly a lot of flowers decorating this barn and she was gratified the public hadn't forgotten her. While the bride readied herself that morning, Douglas arrived to inform her a honeymoon suite awaited the newly-weds, Newtopia's second most lavish bedroom now containing many wedding gifts from admirers. The Reverend spoke of a mountainous pile, forwarded commodities wrapped in shining paper. So fans remained out there, even after all this time. Ordinary people like those acolytes all around her, a public that continued to admire Trina Callow, ensuring a residue of iconic status remained in the country's collective memory.

To the right of the bride to be Josh stood amid the patient throng, a hand in Bree's and two fingers between his collar and the skin of his throat. This attire felt itchy and unnatural, Josh hadn't worn a smart shirt since quitting the office job and he disliked the unfamiliar pressure against his neck. He scratched at the nape and returned his attention to Trina. By Josh's calculations she must have been almost forty, but the bride continued to exude both star quality and a raw sensuality. Motherhood and testing times had done little to diminish her curves, a shape highlighted by that tight dress she wore for the ceremony, its white material flowing from the perfect inclines of her rear down to the floor. This body was the same one Josh had spent hours dreaming of in his teens, the boy pouring over Trina's raunchy confessions in men's magazines, drool falling onto undressed perfection highlighted by the accompanying photographs. Today her blonde hair and pearlescent skin were hidden by the wedding dress, but Josh knew what was underneath that delicate material. Those full breasts, the exquisite behind, the physical attractions of a woman who once described herself as the ultimate tease.

The memory made Josh perspire, his unrealistic fantasies. He would never stop loving that buoyant girl at his side, Bree stretching now to see more of the congregation. Bree was number one, although there would always be a place reserved in his heart for this former starlet. What drew Josh's attention to Trina was lust, unadulterated priapism, from the first time he encountered her enticing growl and come-to-bed look on a weekend pop show until this very moment. Back then he was a sexually confused young boy, yet fifteen years on Josh couldn't help imagining the imminent wedding night with him in the groom's place. How he would peel that dress off Trina, inch by inch, take the woman again and again, as if all those years of desire had to be expiated by daybreak. Josh squeezed Bree's hand as the images flowed through his mind, an involuntary movement that caused the girl to look up at him fondly. Her boyfriend seemed so enraptured by proceedings, overwhelmed by the occasion. Undoubtedly his thoughts coincided with Bree's, how they would soon be having a S.O.N. wedding too. What a fantastic party it would be, revelry celebrating the love between them. Making their union official before Rebecka and Jesus Christ.

Bree rose onto her tiptoes to study the row of bridesmaids and page boys. The Saxon children were shifting their weight from one leg to the other, boys nervously unsure of their role and what it involved. Trina's daughters appeared more relaxed, cute as bunnies in their petal-pink outfits. At eleven and eight Chastity and Niagara were the youngest of the bridesmaids. Beside them stood Beth, fulfilling the maid of honour role. The girl looked well, composed and ready, so Bree caught her eye and gave up a smile. She was proud of her success with this seventeen year old from the broken home, a child whose self-esteem had seemed damaged beyond repair when she first arrived at the church. Through the world-altering message of the Goddess and careful mothering Bree was able to turn Beth's health around. The girl could look in a mirror now without turning away, eat a full meal without regurgitation, talk of her upbringing without lapsing into tears. She had Bree to thank for that. Beth was the female mentor's first success in her Newtopian post, resolving the psychological issues of other young girls.

The bridesmaid returned Bree's smile and looked sideways, checking the others charged with attending Trina Callow. Beth hoping the Saxon boys had emptied their bladders before the ceremony began. Her gaze moved over them to rest on the oldest page boy, his handsome face like a younger version of the Reverend Elliott but classier somehow. That square jaw and commanding presence were vaguely familiar, even if Beth couldn't quite place them. Unable to recall where she might have seen Gareth prior to S.O.N., Beth knew that his broad-shouldered good looks sent shivers down her spine. She studied him in minute detail, willing Gareth to turn her way, endlessly intrigued by this male, the source of so many half-heard rumours around Newtopia. A guy so tall and dark, Beth wondered if she wasn't in the grip of her first crush. While she watched the pageboy, not quite twenty and slightly uncomfortable in his man's body, he shifted awkwardly to scan the barn. When Gareth's green eyes passed over the girl she blushed furiously, resolving to keep her concentration on the bride from then on to save further embarrassment.

The taped organ strains began, triggering Trina's thoughts which left these surroundings and transported her back to the eighties, a time of personal success and those songs she loved. All her memories prior to that decade were full of longing, hopes of fame and jet-setting fuelled by the dance routines she would meticulously copy from the TV shows. When stage school rejected her application, Siggy Callow resolved to turn his daughter into a star anyway, keep the girl away from traditional education for days at a time so she could attend singing lessons and dance classes. Siggy saw his only offspring as a way of attaining the success that had always eluded him, and by the time she passed her O-Levels, Trina knew daddy's love depended on her achievements in show business. The young girl would be rushed from geography examinations to performances at talent centres, her routines videotaped for the benefit of the experts. Siggy hawked these films around every agency in London until one of the pensive old men agreed to take her on. What finally secured Trina a place on their books was less her questionable singing ability or stumbling movement than the burgeoning carnality of her figure. Even so, Katrina was to find herself eighteen and dejected before a record company executive broke the silence, requested she try out for a girl group he was hawking around town.

In her over the top eagerness to please Trina almost blew it. She fell out of tune at one point in the cover version and became over ambitious with the accompanying moves, a fraught attempt to compensate. Luckily Trina's father had selected the outfit she wore to the session and with his usual insight into the industry Siggy chose a low-cut number showing plenty of leg. Katrina Callow's place in the three-piece was assured. She was to be the bubbly, outrageous, happy-go-lucky blonde stereotype. The high-grade tits and ass that would compliment Leila's dark good looks and the overly made-up cuteness of Cindy, together now as an act the manager christened *She-Saw*.

The girls began their assault on popular culture by taking their intricate dance routine and quartet of songs to five schools a day, sweating their guts out in assembly halls under the leering gaze of deputy headmasters, enticing prepubescent girls to climb onto their chairs and copy the *She-Saw* moves. Outside school hours or at weekends the trio were whisked to photo-shoots and interviews for teeny magazines, the publications keenly offering up this next big thing to an easily influenced readership. Official biographies were produced in which the birth-date of Cindy, the only member of the act who could sing, was brought forward by half a decade. From now on she would be closer in age to those kids who bought the records.

When the first single arrived, an anaemic and ill-judged cover of a song popularized by a legendary seventies diva, public ambivalence combined with a lack of radio play for an underwhelming chart position. In with a bullet at thirty-three before dropping off to nowhere. The group's manager redoubled his efforts. Suddenly the girls were fixtures at exclusive London clubs and industry functions, going arm in arm with million-selling stars who happened to release records through the same label. *She-Saw* switched their attention to radio interviews and television appearances, the company plugging ferociously, chain stores given more copies of the record at lower prices than any other single released in the same week. Within the space of a fortnight Trina lost all opportunity to take time out. The girl was suddenly without a spare moment to ring home and make sure her mother watched the Saturday morning show, looked on page seven of today's paper, turned on the radio *right now*, because they're playing my song!

The gamble was a big one on the record label's part. Had that second single flopped *She-Saw* would no longer have been a viable commodity, the sums they invested written off by men in downbeat meetings while the girls were left to drift away from entertainment, into early motherhood and day jobs, penury and depression. Fortunately the song they selected for this high-stakes game was the strongest composition the company's office had received in years. This single became the pinnacle of a respected male songwriter's four-decade career, a ballad of such immediate melody and unifying sentiment the public made it top five in its first week of release, an almost unheard of position for the early eighties and the highest new entry in a year.

Vindication for all concerned, relief their hard work hadn't been in vain. Sadly there was no time to relish this success, not even one day to schedule a party. A person can struggle to achieve fame for years, perhaps even longer, and its flash-flood arrival still startles, invariably takes a new celebrity by surprise. Before they knew it *She-Saw* were on the treadmill of the manufactured groups, forever pushing themselves toward the next level of exposure in the public eye, unable to stop the wheel spinning lest everything crash down, forever dodging that screeching descent into premature obscurity, what the teenage mags called *the dumper*.

So Cindy, Leila and Trina kept going, from a leap into the spotlight as instant and absolute as any of the prefabricated bands that followed, through a constant promotional schedule to plug their yet-to-be-recorded album. The girls were thrust into working weeks of sixty hours and more, time that didn't include the seemingly endless trips in economy class, travelling to and from transatlantic destinations. The places all merged into one, a single city where the permanent jet-lag and newness of it all left Trina feeling like a hologram, an impostor in her own fame.

On its second week in the chart their single climbed to number one and *She-Saw* celebrated with a glass of champagne each as they arrived in Tokyo, the alcohol making Trina feel vaguely unwell. She slunk off to bed at the first opportunity only to be awakened by a call from her father. The man sounded excited and hyperactive, telling the girl how pleased he was with her success. But this was just the first step, she would have to work doubly hard from now on to sustain this climb to the top so she'd better stop talking and get some sleep. Fighting the yawns as he wittered on, Trina could only grunt tired noises in response.

The months went by like hours, endless concerts and professional commitments that began to take their toll. Three sleep-deprived and hormonal young women inhabiting the same personal space, disagreements and cattiness as the girls finalized marketing strategies with their manager or tried on outfits designed to make them look thinner. Trina became frustrated at how many hours each day they wasted being *styled*, so much making up and scrubbing clean she didn't have time for a decent night's rest. Disagreements of both opinion and artistry left more hostility in the air, but the venting never amounted to much. Too many people were on hand to smooth ruffled feathers, and despite the continuing top ten hits none of the trio could quit. The group had to stay together if they hoped to earn any money. Due to the six figure sums invested in their singles, *She-Saw* were forced to exist on a weekly allowance no higher than the minimum wage for the first two years. The lack of recompense made little difference to Trina, she had been raised as a workaholic martyr for celebrity anyway, and there wasn't any free time in the schedule to shop, but Leila became increasingly cranky while Cindy brooded

For a frenetic eighteen-month period the girls were shuttled between studios and video shoots, public appearances and the stage. When their self-titled debut album eventually appeared the smattering of hit singles ensured substantial sales and the profits began to roll in. Trina didn't care much, she derived gratification from seeing her face on magazines and the telly, chose to let her mother and father cover the accounting side of things. The young woman wished only for the impossible now she was well off. That they could pay someone to make the days twenty per cent longer, in order for her to get some proper sleep.

Leila became the band's profligate, splashing out on ostentatious jewellery, extravagant gifts, flash cars she couldn't yet drive. Meanwhile Cindy's frustration at her lack of power over the group's music or image grew. Disillusioned and older than the others, she found herself unable to work sixteen hour days without artificial stimulation, beginning to cultivate an intimate relationship with that new drug she had encountered in the U.S. Cocaine elevated Cindy above the boredom and loneliness at the heart of her career and it made her feel damn good to boot. Soon she was spending three figure sums every week on the energy-giving substance while remaining aloof to the male hangers-on. Perhaps, as one promoter joked, so she wouldn't have to share her stash with anyone.

In fact none of them had real boyfriends, *She-Saw* were in no position to invest the time to sustain a relationship. Instead the girls chose brief affairs where they could, Trina soon learning that the attractive man in the street was either too intimidated to make the first move or proved to be the kind of money-grabbing wanker who went to the tabloids when the dating ceased. Ordinary guys always went for quick bucks in exchange for dignity-destroying accounts of kinky sex, whining about how they were wronged, feelings of being let down just because she had to leave their bed and play a show in Europe. When a second kiss and tell story about her appeared Trina wiped away the useless tears, trying not to think of her parents reading the paper over their breakfast table, and resolved to date only those who wouldn't go to the press in future, fellow celebrities and those with lives like hers. A few clean-cut types came and went, spur of the moment dalliances with timid English presenters who were driven away by the intensity of Trina's sexuality, her growing experimentation between the sheets. Then she found her man.

She-Saw were performing a single from their fourth album, *Girls Like These*, when it happened. Despite the ongoing success of the act, by then amounting to fifteen top twenty hits and almost a million album sales worldwide, they weren't the main attraction on that Saturday morning show. Instead top billing was taken by Australia's leading rock band, a growing worldwide force fronted by Terence Freeman. An unadulterated sex symbol, his wild man reputation and yen to be Jim Morrison combined with flowing locks and a propensity for leather trousers to cause a moistening in the underwear of young girls wherever they played. While his band *Succumb* pounded out a derivative guitar sound, Terence span and sang, shook his shoulder-length hair and caressed the mike, a performance that oozed eroticism for the benefit of an agog studio audience and the viewers at home.

Some complaints would have come in anyway. British viewers were quick to report any corrupting influence, but the floor manager's big mistake was to put both groups on the semicircular sofa for a post-performance chat with the programme's tomboy host. When Freeman sat next to her Trina's heart quaked, the man giving off an uninhibited masculinity and air of imminent danger, the kind of aura she had never found in uptight British guys. Before the blonde knew it she was flirting with him off-camera. A gifted and prolific temptress, Trina took her coquettishness to a new level for this desirable singer. He struck her as smart and cool, not hung up on himself, even modest when she, with characteristic boldness, queried Terence's reputation for being well-endowed, much to the horror of the hostess who remained within earshot. By the time filming switched back to them Trina was in his lap, heat between the pair there for all to see, entwined in each other's arms, the girl resolving never again to let go. Within half an hour they had consummated the attraction in his dressing room and felt ready for the next step. In those post-coital minutes before collecting their energies for a second bout, the couple began to make plans.

Immediately it became clear to friends that the pair couldn't get enough of each other, making a passionate match rarely encountered outside of steamy romance novels. Terence bought a house in London and Trina moved in, the girl convincing him to spend nine months of the year in the city with her tantalizing wiles and insatiable hunger. They screwed every which way, fucked themselves raw, remained locked together for days at a time. No use of their bodies became taboo, every touch was permissible.

Such was the frequency of these couplings it came as no surprise when probability intervened. One Friday night, two years on from that first sweaty encounter, the contraceptives failed. Having suppressed mothering instincts for years in order to forward her career, Trina found herself relieved and pleased. She was particularly delighted by the positive manner in which Terence took the news. If she had any doubt the rock star loved her it was eliminated in seconds as sudden and absolute delight overtook his face. Terence offered to make an honest woman of her but, happy as she would have been to become Mrs. Freeman, Trina deemed officializing unnecessary. They embraced and made love once more, ecstatic that an unconsciously willed wish had come true.

The record label was less happy. Trina's pregnancy disrupted the promotional duties of *She-Saw* and meant their fifth album shifted the least units of her career. Yet the group's manager was forced to admit he couldn't blame the poor figures solely on the act's lack of visibility. The eighties were petering out and *She-Saw*'s trademark brand of synth-heavy disco pop felt increasingly anachronistic in a scene stuffed with fresh dance movements and the cross-pollination of genres. When Cindy was forced into rehab on the eve of her thirtieth birthday to salve increasingly paranoid behaviour, the story proved a final indignity for the most successful girl group of the decade. Leila found herself unemployed and broke at twenty-five, setting about snaring a rich man before the allure of her celebrity wore off. Meanwhile Trina began the nineties by giving birth to the most exquisite little girl Terence had ever seen, a baby they christened Chastity in an ironic gesture the glossies lapped up.

That beautiful child, dressed today in a pink bridesmaid's outfit, suppressed a sneeze before taking the handkerchief she was offered with *thanks*. Jon returned to his position as organ music rang around the barn, watching Rebecka lead Keith by the arm along the carpeted walkway. In *The Spirit Of Nagasaki*'s variation on the ritual of marriage traditional roles were reversed, the bride waiting for her imminent husband to be given away by the Goddess. The groom took up his position beside Trina, staring ahead fixedly as Rebecka joined her aides beside the dais. Douglas stepped onto the raised platform to begin the ceremony, addressing those gathered while Trina looked into her man's eyes. His serious expression was almost comical, Keith intently focussed on his bridegroom's role in events. The man was a few years younger than his bride, a former professional footballer who had been much in demand during his glory days. As a player Keith was blessed with a natural talent for tactics and split-second decision-making. From midfield he would spray passes around with an overweening elegance, knowing exactly how to follow his manager's directions, a knack that combined with his lightning pace to make the player one of the most sought after wing backs in England. Unfortunately Keith possessed several characteristics that went against the game's culture of boisterous gracelessness and social regression. The man enjoyed music and the arts, leading a refined lifestyle with his first wife Deidre, rejecting the customs that surrounded football; booze-sodden nightclub visits and casual sex. Keith preferred fine wine, good food, articulate conversation, and he felt proud of his nonconformist refinement. So proud he wasn't afraid to detail the tendencies in an article on his way of life for a broadsheet supplement.

After the feature was published Keith found himself a victim of fallout, news of the player's intelligence and perceived effeminacy spreading rapidly among his fellow professionals and the fans. On the pitch members of the opposition would whisper *poofter* in his ear until a furious Keith struck out and was sent off, leaving the turf as the controversy burned on. Speculation on his sexuality and 'sham' marriage spread from the terraces to the gutter press. Deidre had been brought up to believe there was no smoke without fire where the weight of public opinion was concerned, and with their sex life suffering from the stress soon she was filing for divorce. Keith was distraught, his game fell apart and the man lost all hope of an international place. Then a double fracture to his right leg sidelined the player for a season, a excruciating injury that he eventually came to see as a godsend. The period of convalescence away from the field gave Keith plenty of time to reach a conclusion. Football was no longer the right career for a person like him, instead he needed to explore the spiritual side of life he'd always found so fascinating. During his recovery Keith studied various faiths and religions, but it was the philosophy of the Goddess Rebecka that really spoke to him, its emphasis on individual and collective happiness exactly what he needed to rise up from the sadness of his circumstances.

Once he was fit enough to begin training again Keith gained revenge on his club's bigotry and the homophobic chanting of its fans, unexpectedly renouncing football altogether and turning his back on the world. By this time the media had all but forgotten him and paid little attention as Keith pawned the trappings of his old life, bringing several hundred thousand pounds with him into *The Spirit Of Nagasaki*.

His story ebbed into Trina's ear after their first night of passion together in the farmhouse, Keith so different from Terence, frightened inside and needing to unburden himself of lingering worries. The ex-footballer believed he'd only been allocated a place at Newtopia due to his generous initial donation, having found little work to suit him since that move to the country. Trina soothed this new lover, her sexual skill leading Keith into the kind of utterly sated glow he had not experienced for many years. She reassured the man, telling Keith whatever he could offer was up there with the efforts of anyone else and he shouldn't fret, she at least found him special. At the end of their second night of intense lovemaking Keith politely asked Trina to marry him and after a long discussion with the Goddess on the potential benefits of such a union, she accepted.

The voice of the Reverend Elliott filled the cavernous barn. "Many waters cannot quench love, neither can the floods drown it. If a man would give all the substance of his house for love, it would be utterly contemned. Love will not be treated with contempt my brothers and sisters. Like the perfect flower, it flourishes away from the trappings of civilization. In spite of the ephemerality that overcomes the outside world, love has visited us here, here at the home of the S.O.N."

Continuing to stare at the groom, Trina tried not to compare him with Terence. Those days were gone, Keith was loyal and tender and would make both a good husband and diligent father. She fought to let something overwhelm her as those rousing words of love continued, but the main sensation felt inside was one of relief. For low-level women in *The Spirit Of Nagasaki*, females who did not possess the power of Rebecka but, like Trina, could equal her in sexuality and entrancement, the rotas and responsibilities were exhausting and occasionally distasteful. To be married and under the unequivocal ownership of another would improve her quality of life no end.

Douglas continued his speech. "What the Goddess teaches us is that we must explore our selves together. Unlock the full range of possibilities from the surface and within, gain a true understanding of body and soul. Once we children of Jesus have experienced all facets of ourselves within *The Spirit Of Nagasaki* we shall know our destiny in absolute terms, know it just as these two people uncovered their future together, a union we gather to confirm, witnessed by the Goddess Rebecka and Jesus Christ our Lord."

From the side of the walkway Nolan glanced behind Elliott to the woman he spoke of, a noble and wonderful creature whose imperious arrival in the barn imbued the atmosphere with an extra dimension of eagerness, as if all those involved wanted to give a little extra now, play their part one hundred per cent. Nolan understood this; it was the effect the dignified and beautiful Goddess had when she oversaw her faith.

Jim and Joan stood to Nolan's right and watched their sons, willing the boys to stand up straight, pick up on their cues, give a good account of the family. The two young males had conducted themselves with grace so far. Charlie saw no reason why they shouldn't continue to do their parents proud, represent the Saxons well on this big day. This afternoon Nolan felt none of the cynicism or disinterest he had suffered long ago, a sense of waste and anticlimax spoiling his enjoyment of weddings in the past. His negativity finally led Charlie to stop attending the ceremonies of friends and colleagues around 1981. An inability to issue positive comments or pass on congratulations without feeling like a fraud meant the man had refused all invitations since, but this was different from those charades. Perhaps enough time had elapsed for Nolan to enjoy youth's promise again. He felt like a changed man anyway, genuinely wishing Keith and Katrina well, a wash of hope overcoming Charlie as the ceremony continued. Good feelings for them all, those disciples who listened to the words of the Reverend Elliott as his speech approached its end.

"It is my prayer that your love for one another may grow more and more, become greater through increased knowledge and complete understanding. From this day forward we let nothing and no one come between your feelings for one another, just as nothing separates those present from the love of the Goddess."

Nothing would come between them, Trina knew that. The beauty of Newtopia lay in keeping out the pressures of the world, powers left to fester beyond the boundaries as perfect lives continued within, so unlike the array of forces that converged upon her and Terence.

After Chastity was born her newly energized mother needed to assert some independence, this requirement a matter of principle rather than finance. Terence's career might have been going from strength to strength, but Trina hadn't relied on a man since she was a kid and wasn't about to start now. But how to earn her keep? The *She-Saw* back catalogue was hardly a gold mine, even the greatest hits collections were cluttering up service station bargain bins, and much of the royalties that did arrive went straight to the men who had written the songs. Trina's agent willingly announced that she was available for work, but the offers didn't exactly flood in.

With time to burn and having missed out on both college and university, not to mention the steady transition into independence most of her regular friends enjoyed, Trina began to thirst for knowledge. To catch up she became autodidactic, scouring the shelves of major book chains for subjects that interested her, purchasing self-help guides and volumes of domesticity, novels by famous peers and reflections on parenting. Of the last there were few and a gap in the market seemed to be making itself known, particularly where publications on first-time motherhood were concerned. Browsing through her purchases as Chastity slept soundly in the cot, Trina was struck by how simple it was to get published. All a person needed was celebrity status, the ability to string a sentence together and a marketable idea underpinning the project.

While Terence was away on world tours, off recording vocals or visiting his antipodean birthplace, Katrina began scribbling away through the evenings. She began with simple tips and truisms but soon the details cohered and *How To Be A Complete Mother* readied itself, to the delight of her agent. After heavy editing the text was combined with simple diagrams and illustrative photos, eventually released via an understated publicity campaign to become something of a sleeper hit.

These sales came because women of all classes took to the author's informal prose, Trina astutely electing to tell people what they wanted to hear. She extolled readers not to waste time considering what might go wrong with the procreative process, those were worries for the medical staff. Her words concentrated on demystifying childbirth along with post-partum tips for new mums. Trina deconstructed old wives' tales, citing from experience, reassured and encouraged, avoiding the confusion of scientific terminology as she tapped into the huge market of expectant mothers. Women needed to be told birth wasn't painful, wanted to know a baby's behaviour could be easily regulated by someone with a cool head, were eager to follow the author's dos and don'ts.

Sales flew into six figures and beyond, while the publishers began to clamour for a follow up. In response Trina took a step back, tried to work out which other areas of her life had been successful. Then she bought several packets of pink felt-tip pens and three reams of paper. The result was an even bigger best-seller. *Sex And How To Enjoy It* by Trina Callow was supposed to give women access to the erotic pleasure they deserved. In it the authoress came on like a cross between a qualified therapist, the advice column of a glamour magazine, and a big sister. Once again she avoided the dryness and anatomical focus of traditional self-help books to produce a volume that was both funny and helpful. The publicity machine went into overdrive and *Sex And How To Enjoy It* soon became a *cause celebre*, England unable to ever resist middlebrow naughtiness and feeling slightly guilty because of it. Women read the book because they wanted greater satisfaction, men to gain insight into the sex life of a woman like Katrina, both genders finding the publication a powerful aphrodisiac.

Trina became a fixture on Breakfast TV and late-night discussion programmes promoting the hardback. This popularity meant she soon graduated to her own chat show on Channel Four. Here the habitual flirt managed to extract personal confessions from a respected politician and an Oscar-winning actor among others, that husky voice and saucy look in her eye that caused the conversational defences of male guests to melt away.

Terence watched his girlfriend's career flourish with pride and no little amusement. The frontman found it hilarious that Poms could still be so hung up on matters of carnality, but if Trina was able to exploit this repression then good for her. Terence supported the venture where he could, but much of the singer's time by the mid-nineties was taken up with band commitments. By this time *Succumb* resembled a six-sectioned behemoth, striding to conquer the world's stadia with the noisily destructive force of a meteorite shower. Since their early years the group had toned down the drug consumption and sexual exploits, most were fathers now and their bodies wouldn't take what felt compulsory through their twenties. Terence almost always rejected the attention of groupies and the needle's allure, his wildness manifesting itself in other ways while on tour. Freeman would take his entourage on destructive rampages through Australian cities, drunkenly drive fans home on his motorbike; balancing screechy teenage girls on the machine's front and back. He smashed up hotel rooms in frustration, became shocked by his feelings of homesickness for England of all places, climbed onto the tour bus roof when low, dropping acid as he watched the landscape go by.

Four years after Chastity another baby was born, a second love child who fell into their lives like water. They called the girl Niagara and Terence wrote a song likening his daughter to the famous cascade for *Succumb*'s album. A matter of weeks after the birth Trina posed for her most suggestive photo-shoot yet, a soon-to-be legendary set of pictures promoting the new series of *Katrina Licks 'Em*. Public interest in the photogenic pair reached an all-time high, the press becoming desperate for any story that would break their bubble, some scandal or rumour to take this perfect couple down a peg or two. Journalists began to sift through ancient history, interviewing past sexual partners and pestering Trina's ailing father. Soon they were camping outside the pair's London home, hoping for clues or ructions.

One dreary English morning Freeman exited the property to be greeted by reporters rushing at him, eager for a quote on the latest allegation, some lurid inaccuracy embellished by a cocktail bar waitress. Terence's response to the questions was typical of a hot-headed Aussie male, unused to dealing with the hostility and immoral tactics of British pressmen. He punched a photographer square in the face. The man fell from Terence's path and broke his camera. As other journalists made notes and got shots of the action the prone individual was kicked once in the stomach and then the Australian went on his way. For the paper who employed the victim it was a front page story and criminal charges were initiated.

Pressure began to build on the family, problems in court adding to other suspicions. Trina had never minded if her man strayed sexually in the past, as long as Terence brought his emotions and spirit back to her, but she was finding it difficult to avoid the details, double-page spreads in newspapers every Sunday, descriptions of druggy affairs and wild liaisons. For his part Terence became testy, failing to appreciate the irony of his woman getting jealous after he'd given up on the lust-fuelled flings. The singer hadn't slept with anyone else in months, but the past was returning to haunt him.

Gymnasiums became Trina's refuge from the world of infidelity and criminal allegations. She exercised for hours each day, experimenting with diets under the auspices of basing her next book around the subject, finding herself unable to function without a morning jog through the parks of London to calm her thoughts.

The legal proceedings ended with Terence receiving nothing more than a fine, the judge familiar with the underhand workings of Fleet Street. By the time Freeman escaped the machinations of Britain's legal system his common-law wife was virtually unrecognizable. The fleshiness of her body had been replaced with a sinewy, almost boyish, quality. The woman's breasts were flat, a once-ample behind unnoticeable. Her subsequent reappearance on television screens caused uproar. Trina used her undernourishment to promote the slimming book, displaying her physique as validation of the newly patented Katrina Callow diet. Eating disorder groups condemned her war on fat, while male fans turned their attention to new voluptuas. Angry letters arrived at the offices of her agent, women whose daughters were attempting to ape Trina's impossibly toned appearance by sticking two fingers down their throat after every meal. The laddish aspects of popular culture turned against her as well, without tits and ass those magazines had no use for her outrageous proclamations. Jokes about Trina's scrawny frame began to crop up on topical news programmes and panel-based game shows. The chat show was cancelled and the Callow name soon became symbolic of celebrity failure, a shorthand for foolishness, the spotlight she had always craved turning against her.

Trina put her failing career to one side and concentrated on looking after the girls instead, trying to give up her sessions at the gym but finding herself unable, the exercise filling some gap inside that was reluctant to be left empty. As the woman pumped weights she began to anticipate Terence's return, back from his Far Eastern gigs to remove the woes of her heart, that man who could free her days from sadness with his probing mouth and liberating caresses. They had not parted on the best of terms but both were apologetic over the phone, promising to forget petty disagreements and make up for the contretemps.

Then the call came, a ringing that woke Trina with a start in the middle of the night. Terence Freeman was dead. He had been found in a Taiwanese hotel by a maid who failed to receive a response to her knock, unlocking the door only to discover it blocked. She pushed at the barrier with all her strength, forcing a way in, only to be confronted with a dead man. Terry was slumped on the floor, a belt extending from his neck to the door handle. The corpse was naked from the waist down and its eyes protruded horribly. The appearance of Freeman's body caused the maid to vent her horror in a high-pitched scream, filling the building and going on to reverberate through Trina's skull as she lay in the darkness, trying to take in the facts this officious voice was relaying to her.

It was a shockingly tawdry death for a successful man and devoted lover, a tragedy that left thousands of rock fans in mourning, grieving Terence Freeman as if they'd known him personally. Officially the death was recorded as suicide. Among the evidence cited by an Australian coroner were rumours of discontent in his home life, the stress of a court case said to have depleted the man's mental reserves. The spectre of fame's empty gratification was invoked. Articles discussed how success proved a poor panacea for this damaged individual. Commentators speculated that Terence reached the pinnacle of his profession and found himself with nowhere to go but down.

Bullshit said Trina, b-u-l-l-SHIT! Her man had never been depressed in his life. At heart Terence was an ordinary bloke with everyday concerns who, just occasionally, expressed some intense or dark need. Bearing these proclivities in mind, Trina chose to believe the alternate theory some had concocted; Terence was certainly the type to indulge in sex games. While investigating the possibilities a British documentary crew discovered nails above the beds at several hotels Freeman had stayed in. According to the psychologists these pieces of metal hammered into the walls were a sure sign the deceased engaged in auto-erotic asphyxiation, an extreme form of pleasure whereby the individual times self-strangulation to synchronize with ejaculation in order to gain a particularly powerful climax. The release is strongest if orgasm coincides with a blackout, but when a subject is alone and unconscious they are unable to ease the pressure on their windpipe. If the restraint isn't loosened oxygen can't get through and the only possible result is the permanent blackness of death.

It seemed Terence Freeman, a man whose private life was constantly drawn to the edges of the permissible, had finally taken his physical indulgence too far. He met an ignominious end in that rented room, leather trousers around his ankles, head slumped forward, long black hair falling across a still-youthful face.

After hearing the news Trina replaced the receiver and didn't speak to anyone for eleven days.

A single tear rolled down her cheek as the bride haltingly agreed to her vows and tried to look to the future. Caught up in the emotion of the moment, Bree saw salt-water hit the carpet and felt her own tears begin to flow. Soon Beth was crying too, a struggle to compose herself as she took the handkerchief Jon offered. Foulkes predicted such accessories would prove useful today. Weddings were emotive occasions at the best of times, but within the heightened environs of Newtopia young women found themselves particularly overwhelmed. This farm was a place where every emotion became magnified by the closeness of their extended family and the power of their project. Passions were swollen to a level many times that of the outside world, leaving the current ceremony particularly gut-wrenching for the more highly-strung. Jon noticed the turbulent atmosphere every time he came down here, and he wasn't sure it was healthy, hoping the allusions Douglas made to shutting down operations in the capital were just talk. There wasn't room for the whole community on this farm, and Jon was sure plenty of city-dwelling converts would reject the 'honour' of a move to this isolated compound.

He looked at Rebecka and felt the twinge inside that would always be there, the Goddess towering over everyone with the force of her presence. That smarmy Reverend on his platform was no match for her power, Rebecka's domination both pitiless and democratic. Although Jon looked to her for guidance and strength, he didn't share the belief in divine infallibility that prevailed among her followers. Jon wasn't sure the Goddess had been wise to let Trina retain her celebrity status inside their movement. The bride would gain a minor amount of publicity for this event, but S.O.N. was a faith that rejected the media in all its multifarious forms, Rebecka denouncing it repeatedly in her philosophy. The money *Welcome!* paid for nuptial insights would come in useful. Not enough people of independent means were being pulled into *The Spirit Of Nagasaki* to keep the coffers overflowing, but was it wise for a religious leader to contradict herself? At least those photographers had been kept out of the buildings, left outside during the ceremony under the watchful eye of that Jones character. Foulkes hoped *Welcome!* was no more than a benevolent publicity rag for all their sakes, and the impression its contributors gave of never possessing an opinion wasn't some kind of clever act.

Douglas went on extracting promises from the couple with his interpretation of marriage morality, derived from Bible study and the thoughts of Rebecka. To Jon the man looked oily and insincere up there, fluttering his hands over the disciples as if casting out negative energies, like some ridiculous new age therapist. On arrival yesterday Jon had been given a brief tour of the amendments to Newtopia since his first visit, a journey that took in new outdoor quarters and the lucrative plant-life of twin greenhouses among other sights. He ended up in the chambers of the Goddess, where they discussed matters pertaining to the running of S.O.N., a nasty realization overcoming Jon as he talked. From her manner and the way the pair retired yesterday it was clear that Douglas and Rebecka were sharing a bed. The envy Jon experienced combined with a vague disgust at this couple, fellow founders who were supposed to be above such weaknesses as mixing business matters with jumping each other's bones. He hadn't taken kindly to her aides either, *Elliott's stooges* as Jon came to think of them, men whom he was forced to share a room with overnight. They were surly individuals who went by the names Stoker and Jones. When the duo weren't silent they treated him with indifference, if not outright disdain. Back in London everyone knew Jon was respected and important to the organization, but out here he felt extraneous to requirements, lower in the hierarchy despite its supposed equality, like a politician abroad.

Jon made an effort to regain his composure for the imminent celebrations, not wishing to be red-faced for this glorifying of the newly-weds. It was an effort though, the words of the Reverend stuck in his ears like wax.

"My heart is filled with warmth as I pronounce you man and wife. Let The Song Of Soloman guide our celebrations as all present are glad and rejoice in thee. We shall remember thy love more than wine, the upright shall love thee and thou shall love them. I say to you Keith, you who have found her whom your soul loveth, hold Katrina and kiss her and do not let her go."

A spontaneous cheer erupted, ringing through the barn as the groom raised Trina's veil and tentatively put his lips to her damp cheek. The pair moved through the throng, page boys and bridesmaids trailing in their wake, confetti forming a paper blizzard above the couple, flakes falling to the floor and catching the liquid that fell from female faces. The tears of Trina apparently down to the charged occasion and her place at the centre of attention, Douglas uttering words that moved her deeply. Inside the bride was back with her lost love, thinking how she'd never walked down an aisle with Terence, the painful torture of regret.

In the months after his death Trina lost her appetite for exercise and success, finding herself ambivalent to obsessions that once filled the days. No longer interested in parenting or the entertainment industry, the woman let Niagara and Chastity live with her mother and hit rock bottom. She took up smoking and gained weight, kept herself inside behind closed doors, staying up all night to watch old movies, searching for some kind of truth in the output of a Hollywood that had long since vanished. Joan Crawford melodramas and cigarettes temporarily salved the pain, but there were few sights or sounds that failed to remind Trina of Terence. Every accent came from Australia, all music cried *Succumb*, the entire flat felt like a shrine to his memory. Even when she grew strong enough for a return to the world there was no relief from this funk. Trina felt awkward in social situations. She no longer had a taste for the attention, would fake a pathetic and half-hearted variation on the old wild girl act whenever the cameras turned on her. Soon every journey beyond her front door came to be lubricated by alcohol, an inebriated Trina briefly losing herself in affairs with younger men or pointless shopping expeditions, always returning to the site of her loneliness and a growing collection of pharmaceuticals that cluttered up the bathroom cabinet.

Friends rallied to drag her out of the rut, restore some of that old Katrina Callow whose generosity and thirst for life they missed terribly. Holidays were suggested, then psychiatry. Relocation, Buddhism, yoga, crystals, holistic therapy and finally *The Spirit Of Nagasaki*. Her old band-mate Cindy came to visit her for the first time since rehab with details of the new faith, a sect that forgave the mistakes of her past, returned the ex-singer's taste for the world with its community and message.

Initially Trina treated the theology with the suspicion she held for all religions, until Rebecka's interpretation of the Bible permeated these barriers. The leader's belief in our ability to live away from the distractions of civilization was persuasive, as was her method of curing ills through love and cooperation. The Goddess believed we were all waiting to join loved ones in the kingdom of Jesus, a future Trina desperately wanted to share. She straightened out enough to accompany Cindy to prayer meets and soon found herself able to do without the prescription drugs, relying instead on the regular fix of love from the church. The girls returned to her cleaned-up life, Chastity and Niagara flooding Trina with affection, making the mother see that concentrating on her own pain was selfish. With her life back together, Trina came to identify more and more with the Goddess, learned of Rebecka's visions and became driven to follow them, seeing many parallels between celebrity and the formation of this religion. Both paths involved leaving real life behind to become more than yourself. A figurehead for others who would gather in the shadow to seek your suddenly valued opinion. The two callings shared the pressure of constantly being on call as well as a need to keep striving for humanity, inspired by the understanding what you have is unique and needs to be shared with regular people.

When Trina informed the head of the London household how much capital she could donate in exchange for three places at the project the man with crystal clear eyes stared at her for long seconds before muttering that he would have to consult the Goddess personally. The accrual of her inheritance, royalties from the books and potential income through selling the flat had given her a more than generous total. In response to Trina's pledge Chastity, Niagara and their mother were driven directly to Newtopia, welcomed effusively and granted a private audience with Rebecka. This was to be the first of many head to head meetings between the two women, chats when they discussed Trina's mental health and connections, how best the faith could use her talents. It was during one of these heart-to-hearts a few days before that the decision was made to contact the sycophants at *Welcome!* magazine, those leeches on the body of celebrity for whom the happy couple agreed to pose.

Outside the barn a brisk autumn breeze blew around the pageboys and bridesmaids standing to the side of the newly-weds, Rebecka and Douglas positioned behind them. This last pair refused to smile on command as the earnest man with the camera requested changes in posture and slight movements to the left or right. From his vantage point behind the crew Jon watched proceedings uneasily, the other wedding guests hurrying back and forth around him, chairs and benches moved inside for the coming festivities.

Trina faked another joyous expression and felt grateful for the strapping holding in her stomach, one arm clutching at the girls while the other stretched around Keith's waist as the flash blinded them once again. With some effort the bride had quelled her tears in time for these photos, concentrating instead on the fine life Newtopia could provide for her family. Sometimes Trina became vaguely nostalgic for those glory days of ubiquity, times when she would thrill to a glimpse of herself on television, revel in the endless pampering from stylists, adore her role as a fantasy object for millions. Yet it was never difficult to pull the flip side from her memory, the low that proved too much, the simple life a satisfying solution for harassment and stress. In fact the only difficulties for a woman like Trina on this farm stemmed from her own character, that propensity to flirt with anyone when she was in the grip of happiness. Within the libertarian environment of S.O.N. this inclination tended

127

to result in males requesting instant gratification, becoming disgruntled if their arousal was shunned. Trina quickly learnt to quell her teasing but by then it was too late, so was she. This delay was longer than the typical fluctuations of female hormones, a blip that could only mean one thing. The seed inside her was evolving and ownerless, its father could be any of Newtopia's handsome males, or even one of the less attractive men she had rewarded for the outstanding work in the name of the Goddess.

The bride held her husband tighter. He was so honest and uncomplicated, so good with the girls. Niagara and Chastity saw this man as their father and Trina didn't doubt Keith would take care of the coming brother or sister, love this baby dearly, particularly if he believed it to be his own. A role in *The Spirit Of Nagasaki* had presented itself to Keith after all. He would become a positive paternal influence, responsible for the education and safety of her children, their children. She knew her husband would serve the faith well in his new calling.

The final photograph was taken, equipment packed away and Douglas moved to escort the magazine troupe back to their vehicles, gregarious and friendly towards these folk from *Welcome!*, a contrast with the studied blankness of Jones who joined Stoker outside the barn. The gaggle of maids accompanied Trina to her quarters, off to assist in changing the bride's attire. Keith ambled over to the watching man, the groom radiating an air of jubilation Jon found faintly distasteful. They exchanged a few strained pleasantries as flowers and sections of confetti-speckled carpet were removed from the barn, in their place arriving furniture and trays of food. Evening was encroaching on the scene by the time Douglas deemed this reception ready, word sent round to those in the farmhouse and outbuildings.

Inside the barn snacks that had been hand-prepared by Josh, Joan and others lined the tables of one side. Up front a bench held stereo equipment hired for the night, Greg sorting through a pile of compact discs behind the decks. To his right a second row of tables offered home-made wine, these bottles purchased by Douglas through a Cornish contact. Decorative paintings were pinned to the walls, colours daubed on linen by the S.O.N. children, images meant to represent life in Newtopia that were sometimes little more than impressionist smudges.

Towards the centre of the barn chairs circled a dance floor, on which some of the younger followers moved as Greg played the first tune. A familiar guitar riff rang out, the selected track a version of Nirvana's most famous song that Jon Foulkes had downloaded from an evangelical web site. In this Biblical reading the clean vocals of a choir replaced Cobain's gruff voice.

> *"I'm inspired, I've aflatus*
> *Two thousand years, some hiatus*
> *Evolutionary theorists, come debate us*
> *God's the man, he did create us*
> *We're his fish, watch him come bait us."*

Douglas gave Greg a thumbs up from the side and helped himself to a glass of red, recommending the wine to a nearby disciple. The Goddess entered with her helpers, Trina sauntering behind her in a flowing black dress. The bride was lifted off her feet by Keith and carried onto the floor as Jon watched from the entrance. Rebecka and the oldest page boy sat away from the dancers, deep in discussion while the untidy figure of Stoker lurked close by. Jones came to get a drink, Douglas thanking the aide for nursemaiding the *Welcome!* team, having to shout over the *Halle, halle, hallelujahs* of the song's chorus. He received a grunt of reply from the blank-faced man who took a bottle and disappeared. Douglas had been worried the reporters would explore the compound, maybe peer into one of the greenhouses and recognize the plants within, but the impenetrably sullen Jones prevented this from happening with his thorough and unthreatening eye. For that Douglas was grateful.

The Reverend Elliott drained his glass and felt the warm buzz of alcohol enshrouding him for the first time in months, telling himself that good work had been done today. He was justified in a little pleasure at the end of it. Douglas poured more wine, eyes flickering over the seats where Rebecka spoke to Gareth, the boy looking up in awe at the Goddess whose mouth was far too close to his for Elliott's liking. He took another gulp of wine and studied the kid's features. Gareth's appearance certainly implied blue blood, those distinct lines in his face, the squareness of that jaw, the way he held himself, a sure posture almost hiding the insecurities of adolescence. Everything about Gareth suggested a particular bloodline, coveted genes asserting themselves, his mother supplying the good looks and his father the imperial bearing. Yet however superior the breeding, Gareth deferred to the Goddess, followed the notation of her voice, nodding along with a misty edge in his eyes. This was an expression Douglas recognized. Rebecka's actions were well known to him. The behaviour of a seductress casting her spell, the dominant female laying claim to a male from within her tribe.

Douglas finished his drink and turned for a refill, almost knocking over a glass as he went. So he called himself *Gareth* this boy, the seducible. Yet the shape of his face, the regal phrenology, his manner and accent of the privileged, it all hinted at a different name. Over the past weeks Rebecka had responded cagily to questions of the boy's past, Douglas wanting to know where the boy came from, his reasons for joining. According to her Gareth was the son of a former client from the north who saw S.O.N. as an escape from his unhappy teenhood, that was all she would say. No explanation of his installation at Newtopia rather than the filtration bases, no justification behind this preferential treatment as pageboy and paramour, little evidence Gareth's contribution to the movement deserved such reward.

The teenager clammed up every time Douglas tried to talk to him, which only added to the man's suspicions, leeriness fuelled by the whispered rumours among low-level followers. Douglas cast aside an empty bottle and went back to the dance floor. The Newtopian grapevine was nonsense to some extent; no way the heir to the throne could extricate himself from his family, give up all official duties and make it into *The Spirit Of Nagasaki* without the media on his tail. Elliott drank on and saw Trina dance close to her husband, that figure-hugging number highlighting the woman's body, off-limits now and bulging slightly at the stomach. The Saxon and Callow children jumped and hopped around the couple and he watched them move for a while, feeling muzzy and dissatisfied. When Douglas became bored he looked to the chairs again. The Goddess was gone and the boy had vanished with her. Elliott felt something give inside him and took another mouthful of wine. The Reverend knew exactly where she had taken him and for what purpose. Tonight the possibilities of the physical form would be unlocked for *Gareth*. He'd have the spiritual aspects of his own sexuality awakened, even as the rejected figure of

Douglas looked for a new room to sleep in. The man felt like dashing an empty glass to the ground but regained his calm, exchanging it for a full one instead.

Seeing the expression on the Reverend's face, Jon decided to walk over to him, Foulkes suppressing a grin as he closed in. When Elliott offered him some wine Jon refused, made knowing small talk about Rebecka and the set-up instead, studying the taller man's face all the while. Douglas wore a mask of alcohol-fuelled disgust and fogged frustration, making Jon glad he'd eschewed the intoxicant, seeing once more why drink was usually banned from this faith.

In the reptile brain-cone of Douglas several base instincts were making themselves felt. He scanned the dance floor and tried to ignore the niggly pitter-patter of Jon's voice. That bridesmaid he wanted was there, strutting her stuff beside the children and adults, not really belonging to either group. What was her name? Elizabeth, that was it. A tiny little thing, on the threshold of womanhood. Douglas finished his fourth drink (or was it his fifth?), excused himself from Jon's smug demeanour and strode to join the revelry.

Greg teed up another Internet discovery on the stereo as Douglas caught Beth's eye and began dancing towards her, experiencing a rare sense of liberation. The girl blushed under artificial light, attempting to bring her movements in time with the gangling jerks of the Reverend's body.

Nearby Bree noticed the pair and felt a rush of happiness for the reticent Beth. To be chosen by such a figure on this night of nights, it was an honour indeed.

Douglas felt the wine coursing through him as he thrust and lurched, span the girl round by her hand and hollered along to a chorus he didn't really know.

Holy spirit, bring your fire! Holy spirit, bring your fire! Touch us with revival fire!

He wasn't the only one. Encouraged by this extravagance Nolan danced tentatively with Nicky as Jim and Joan sang along to this rewritten song from their youth. Josh tracked back and forth to Bree, almost bumping into Keith as the groom clutched a dizzy Trina in his arms, the youngest pageboys scampering after giggly bridesmaids down by their legs.

Chapter Six

Joe used the remote control to turn on the television and flicked through every channel in turn. Home video japes, cookery shows, a Charles Bronson movie. Sweeney poured himself another measure of whisky, added some partially melted ice from one of the trays before switching the set off again. Various statements and reports from officers affiliated with Scotland Yard or the Devon and Cornwall force had arrived at the guest house earlier in the day. The dispatch rider's brown envelope came via the landlady who mercifully left it sealed, a look of disappointment when her excitement at the official package found no mirror in her guest's fatigued face. That pile of closely typed papers sat beside photocopies on Joe's dresser, much of the information there unenlightening. Official records of the cult's financial dealings, the usual complaints from families whose offspring had run off to join the church, all along the lines of "she was too smart to get involved with something like that" and "what do you mean you can't do anything?" One or two depositions that might prove useful, nothing more.

The feature in *Welcome!* magazine from October the previous year was spread across Joe's lap. On this scanned copy a gathering of S.O.N. luminaries posed before the still-standing barn in a mockery of traditional wedding photographs. The caption listed the bride as ex-pop star/presenter Trina Callow while the smiling groom was a former professional footballer called Keith Burton. Three bridesmaids and a duo of pageboys gathered around the happy couple. At the back of this composition stood the two leading lights of *The Spirit Of Nagasaki*, named here as the Goddess Rebecka Marsden and Reverend Douglas Elliott. The woman called Rebecka, that same one who founded the movement and invented much of its dictates, looked opaque and dusky, a face shadowed further by the indistinct manner the light fell on her. Yet Joe could still make out an exceptionally attractive woman through the gloom, her strong features set in a kind of hardened beauty, the female leader serious through this festive day. The magazine's accompanying article made only passing references to Rebecka's faith, the text concentrating instead on romance, a tale wherein the Callow woman found true love "at last" with the man of her dreams in unlikely surroundings. There was a brief paragraph, enclosed by Joe's red circle, where

Trina spoke of her conversion away from show business as "like reaching the top of a wall and finding a whole new world on the other side". Apart from that Sweeney found little, the newly-weds adopting this faith's party line, effusive in their praise for the new lifestyle. This was an existence that came across as one of simple kindness; loving contact with like-minded souls in a spirit of equanimity. The one they called *The Goddess* was variously described as "inspirational" and "a seer", apparently possessed the ability to turn lives around with her mixture of philosophy and heavenly visions, a combination that set many on the path to salvation.

Sweeney drank from his glass and plucked the top document off a pile. This focus on the positives contrasted wildly with the information Special Branch had dug up on Rebecka Marsden. Up until a few years ago the woman had overseen the running of a profitable brothel in one of Liverpool's seedier districts. She was on the police files up there thanks to several convictions for soliciting, having been picked up half a dozen times during the seventies and eighties. Pressure from Scotland Yard resulted in the taking of a statement from one woman who worked in Marsden's house, now existing as a single mother on the Toxteth estate. In the profanity-strewn invective of the just-surviving classes, Angela portrayed the madam as a fiercely clued-up woman who only the foolish dared to cross. The witness told how, despite this overweening power, Rebecka was successful in organizational roles because of her empathy. She had been there all the way, from lowly streetwalker up to house madam, so the woman understood the girls, was able to defuse most of the situations they found themselves in. Perverts, violent men, those who tried to get away without paying. No troublemakers came back to the brothel after Rebecka had dealt with them. The girls respected their madam, she listened to personal problems, helped resolve issues wherever she could, as if it were all part of the job. Rebecka dispensed advice on every aspect of the sex trade, worked with troubled girls where a younger woman might have left the naive to suffer.

Against these positives Angela made it clear her former boss was not a woman to exude warmth or friendliness. While working the house Angela heard many stories of the mercilessness with which Rebecka dispatched misbehaving tricks. The girls understood it would be a mistake to exploit Marsden. This was not a woman with a soft side. Rebecka prized loyalty above all else, and professional betrayal or breaches of house regulations were dealt with instantly, the whores in question finding themselves out in the street and on their own. That said, Angela was quick to emphasize there was no illogical enmity to Marsden's rule. Hard but fair was the conclusion of this witness, although Angela's observance of the rules meant she never felt the ruthlessness of Rebecka, that implacable side all the girls knew existed and which, Angela supposed, was what got her up there above them in the first place.

Joe cast the statement aside and turned on his mobile. There was voicemail waiting but he checked the last calling number rather than listen and, sure enough, it was the home phone. Sweeney finished his drink, decided he didn't need to hear Lillian's voice at that moment and flicked the phone off. The device beeped before going black.

The documents were enabling Sweeney to put together a hypothesis on the cult's history. Essays from the church detailed how the Marsden woman was the initial catalyst, undergoing some kind of faked enlightenment on a beach. With the aid of Elliott this *Goddess* built a whole world view out of her visions, convinced gullible folk she was the earthly conduit for larger forces. By giving themselves and their money to this *Spirit Of Nagasaki* potential recruits could become like her, open up to the larger mysteries of this faith.

Soon evangelical meets were being held where Elliott used techniques similar to hypnosis, employing eye contact and constant suggestion to break down the wills of the vulnerable. Often those attending the gatherings reported 'miracles' of revelation and healing, moments that were more likely the fruit of research and well-worn parlour tricks on the part of the headlining act.

As the church evolved London's desperate people continued to swell its ranks, while the most favoured were shipped out to partake of a new, supposedly perfect, way of life on the farm. Somewhere along the way Stoker got involved with the dirtier side of the operation, that hands-on fire-fighting every cult had to deal with, and found himself embroiled in those pivotal changes to the regime that would eventually engulf it.

So truth and blame still rested on the shoulders of a man called Stoker, the key to this case and a prisoner who had to confess the next day, otherwise the investigation would be legally bound to make a decision. Either charge the captive, or let him go.

Joe rolled a cigarette to help him think. He had originally accepted the much-vaunted role of Special Investigator because detective work made good use of what abilities he possessed. Come the extraordinary crime, however inexplicable or outlandish, Sweeney's faculties would come to bear logically and with gradual understanding. Some policemen had an affinity with people of every background, many could coordinate operations involving hundreds of officers, others made their mark with physicality or firearms, while a few poor bastards showed a particular aptitude for paperwork. Joe had taken decades to work out his forte was deductive reasoning, a fact that initially led to uncertainty in the role, but now made him smile at the irony. Since taking up the post the Special Investigator had experienced nothing but professional success. His was an instinctive attraction to important evidence, a satisfaction in piecing events together with an elegance that had come to be Joe's trademark. He felt most alive when approaching the dendrite core of a case, a time to shut out the world as reasoning coalesced. This ability to immerse himself meant Sweeney thrived on the work, even when it was unpleasant or saddening. Joe had few illusions about his mess of a personal life, but the job was a haven, its own reward. He just wished his body didn't ache so much.

The whisky was easing this pain a little, Sweeney pouring another two fingers and picked over the sheath of forensic reports, financial statements and witnesses testifying. That foliage outside the greenhouse had been identified as the stems of a hemp plant, evidence which suggested drug cultivation and usage. That would certainly explain the coloured glass and deracination inside. Meanwhile several offshore accounts under the name Douglas Elliott had been emptied and shut down a few weeks into the new year, along with those registered to mainland banks under S.O.N. The withdrawals looked to have been six figure sums or higher if Sweeney's maths was correct. Cash someone currently held in their possession.

According to the followers whose membership of the cult was limited to a subscription for prayer meetings, they had arrived for the weekly healing sessions in December only to be turned away. No reasons were given, but before long most of the London members had relocated, moving to join the rest of the movement in Cornwall. It was almost as if the organization had shut up shop, inexplicably winding down operations when the religion was at its strongest. The last entry on *The Spirit Of Nagasaki* web site came in the final week of November and gave no indication why the faith might refuse new recruits or retreat toward insularity. That final posting simply gloated over the movement's success, describing doubled numbers over the past year, the church spreading its spirituality with Elliott's countrywide sessions and endless canvassing. The upbeat facts of this report, the cold scent of overarching victory that rose from the words, it reminded Joe of companies who increase shareholder dividends by ruthlessly cutting their workforces as the financial year ends. The tone of a fearful organization approaching its end was entirely absent. Whatever happened to trigger the reorganization and subsequent carnage must have been sudden and unexpected.

Joe exhaled a billow of smoke and killed his roll-up. He was drowsy and a little drink-fugged by now. Whether this could be translated into sleep, or if cult-related facts would swirl around his head for hours, was impossible to predict. He flicked through the final few papers. Identifying victims progressed slowly, mostly from the cross-referencing of medical or dental records. The decision to keep these deaths quiet meant families had to be contacted one at a time, brought out to see those bodies that were recognizable. Thus far none of the genetic material matched the Liverpool files on Rebecka Marsden and Sweeney suspected none of it would. The DNA process had turned up one or two interesting results though, it confirmed one of the corpses belonged to a man who had previously spent years in prison for a crime he didn't commit. A fellow whose life Joe couldn't help but feel was doubly unfortunate, a luckless man who went by the name of Peter Bell.

Pete

"Religion is the sigh of the oppressed creature, the heart of a heartless world
and the soul of soulless condition."

- Karl Marx

The voice of his Shepherd cut through the darkness, filling the minds of this
dozen acolytes gathered for the ten ayem prayer meet.

"You before me, you who are the body of Christ and individually
members of it, you have come to praise the Lord through your love of the
Goddess, a prayer which comes not from your mouth but your whole body."

Pete could feel the displacement of air to either side of him as members
of the church began to sway. He remained still, let the beneficence enter his
soul as it always did, that warm kiss of support the house gave out to Peter, ever
since he fell into the embrace of these new friends.

"Let us express relief at the lives we lead, for we did seek the Lord's
help and he answered. Each of us is free from fear, ready to live out our days in
happiness and laughter."

From the solitary call of one voice the room began to fill with noise,
becoming as tumultuous as some Babel, followers giving out high-pitched
chortles or shrieking guffaws. Pete forced himself to laugh, a low choke that
resembled a cry of outrage. The noise didn't come easily. What Pete experienced
at these gatherings wasn't so much mirth as utter contentment, a repose he had
never known before life in S.O.N.

"Sweet Jesus, see us as we pine and faint with longing for the Lord's
temple. Our beings cry out with joy for the living Goddess. The spirit moves us
to worship in other languages, each child unique in his dance for Christ."

Around this front room men and women began to cavort and flail with
their eyes closed, unfamiliar sounds emanating from antediluvian selves. Beside
Pete an overweight woman sang tunelessly and whirled in circles, hands
knocking his side as her body rotated. Lynn Turner had experienced the Holy
Spirit many times before. These trances always made the woman unaware of her
surroundings. Repetitive movements from Lynn's body lowered the carbon
dioxide levels in her alkaline blood. Hyperventilating and exultant, she praised

137

Jesus for taking her beyond the flesh once more, breath coming in short gasps within this higher state.

Simon had to shout above the noise. "That's it my brothers and sisters! Feel our Lord move you, go deeper to get closer!"

Pete kept his movements small scale, feeling the remaining tension leave his limbs and allowing all thought to vanish from his head under the welter of sound and kinesis enclosing the group. His was a sweet release, comparable to the first sense of holiness that had touched him, a blessing Pete understood instinctively back then and knew now. The floor under his feet shook as several followers felt God call them upwards, raising themselves closer to heaven for a second before landing back on the balls of their feet. Pete felt equal and valued inside this movement, like a thriving plant in the Lord's verdant garden, the human equivalent of a blooming flower. No petty concerns held sway over him at this moment, there were no changes in mood or situation for the buds of this enclave, simply love and existence, a sweet mercy beyond the self-consciousness of man.

The cries reached their peak, dances speeding to frenzy. Pete was thrust back into his temporal form, one of the first to open his eyes thanks to a euphoric man who clutched at his shoulder for support. Before them Simon Thistlewood shuffled from side to side, dark patches of sweat emerging through his clothes. The leader in this prayer hummed with atonality, a look of intense concentration on his face. All around attendees returned to the world of men. Some eased themselves back into the room, others collapsed suddenly on the carpet, gasping at the renewal of piety. Pete experienced his usual centring of self, feeling ready to tackle the rest of this day after a visitation from Jesus. Simon ceased his movement now, eyes flicking open.

"My friends, we have been reborn this morning. The soul of Christ has travelled inside us and He shall return for the rest of our lives. Until our next meeting, may the Goddess guide your way and *The Spirit Of Nagasaki* remain with you always."

Several followers cried *Amen* and the group dispersed. Those who inhabited the house hurried to their corners and the tasks of the day while the part-timers went back to their secular world, stepping out into the cold air and fumes of North London. As usual Pete chatted briefly with Simon, failing to notice that red rash on his neck or the ailing look in Thistlewood's eyes. The portly man had been Pete's Shepherd from the start and the closeness of their mentor-pupil relationship remained, fostered by a shared love of pop music. The pair discussed theological matters and the chord sequence they had been working on together for a few minutes, Pete's head inclined downwards, cut short by Simon experiencing a bad bout of coughing and departing for a glass of water.

Pete took the stairs two at a time. This was his day to clean the communal areas and past experience told him these tasks needed several hours if they were to be completed properly. Peter Bell was a wiry man in his forties with darkish, stubbled skin, and a broken front tooth, the lower section of enamel lost in a childhood scrap. That morning he felt imbued with an indestructible faith, enthusiasm to help him fly through the most unedifying of chores. Duties awaiting him included the disinfecting of a toilet more than thirty people shared and acres of floor space to vacuum, so Pete pulled cleaning products out from beneath the bathroom sink. Belief was a marvellous asset, it filled him with both confidence and purpose, removing the sadness from his days, making the man feel he was at the pinnacle of his life. Pete was gladdened, freer than he had ever been, more so even than the day he got out.

No one was waiting that blustery spring afternoon as the great gates of Wormwood Scrubs clanged shut behind him. Pete hadn't expected anybody to be there, much of his family had lost interest in the diminishing returns of loving him, even before the conviction. Walking the short distance to a payphone, he studied the instructions carefully and used one of the coins they had given him to call Paddy. The Irishman promised to be there as quickly as the traffic would allow and Pete chose to remain inside the call box in the meantime, the enclosed space protection from a biting wind. Cars passed at speed but no other pedestrians could be seen. Only roads and houses, residential areas before him and the shape of Wormwood looming to the rear. He looked left and right, believing he could see for miles, a trick of perspective after twelve years with walls blocking out his vision. To most people the landscape of East Acton would be of little interest, just another identikit section of dense urbanity, but Pete was struggling to take in its alien geography.

He was still staring into the middle distance that struck him as overly vivid when Paddy pulled up, beckoning through the windscreen of his rusty Ford. The Irishman began to speak as soon as Pete climbed into his car, the talk a mixture of businesslike manner and underlying excitement while the passenger struggled with his seat belt. Paddy said there was a bed waiting in the flat he shared with Johnny Swift. It wasn't much but that would give Pete a home while he sorted out a place of his own.

The restraint finally clicked into place as Paddy turned the car into a side road, wind whooshing around their vehicle, returning out to drive back the way he'd come. The Irishman was sorry there wasn't much of a welcoming committee, but at least Pete was free now. That was the main thing. Paddy spoke from experience when he said Pete didn't want a lot of publicity, it only got in the way. Hundreds of jubilant supporters ended up making you feel worse. The passenger mumbled a reply and glanced across. Paddy McDonall was deep into middle age, gaunter nowadays but fit and well, his compact form evidence of the excellent condition he had kept himself in while locked up. For the thirty-five years since being convicted of terrorist attacks he had nothing to do with, Paddy had been on a crusade to right the wrongs of the British justice system. After gaining his freedom the Irishman went on to help other innocents by whatever means he could, organizing letter-writing campaigns and persuading lawyers to help, initiating marches and protests. Pete was exceptionally grateful to this Irishman who had been through it all and fought his way out. Without his selflessness the situation of former prisoner Bell would have been nigh on impossible. The authorities had given him forty-six pounds and a one-day travel pass that morning, then sent Pete on his way. Presumably this was the foundation on which he was supposed to start a new life. In the absence of Paddy, Pete would have been left destitute and alone.

They passed the tower blocks of inner city London, men and women of various ethnic groups lining the streets. Pete was a product of miscegenation himself, a white mother and Afro-Caribbean father leaving him neither one thing nor the other. He gazed at the people flashing past this vehicle. They rushed by as if in fast-forward. Everything else seemed too quick as well. Perhaps Pete's mind had been slowed by the past twelve years, maybe now his perceptions ran at half the world's pace. The rapidity of life in this third millennia left Pete punch-drunk, as if his metabolism had quickened to keep up, this internal velocity combining with the many colours to render him nauseous and disturbed. After the greyness of Wormwood Scrubs those gaudy shopfronts and bright signs were like an overexposed photograph. Pete blinked repeatedly to adjust his eyes to the garishness, Paddy glancing over with a smile, apparently reading his mind.

"A wee bit weird huh?"

"A bit."

McDonall grinned. "Aye, but don't worry son, you'll adjust so you will. Look at me, I'm right as rain."

The car stopped at a junction and Pete watched a few spots of rain fall on the spattered dirt of the windows. Twelve years on and the world was at once completely different and exactly the same as he remembered it. Pete scratched at the coarse skin of his cheek and decided he would probably fit into South London as well as anywhere. Lambeth was well away from that place where, thousands of days ago, he'd been was picked up by the coppers. Those police who asked him to provide an alibi for Tuesday night of the week before.

As Pete told them back then, the truth was that he couldn't remember. Like so many evenings in the lessened hopelessness of his late twenties, Pete had spent that Tuesday drunk and lost. He recalled the sun setting over the house of some friends, a taxi ride to the unfamiliar pub and that hoped-for lock-in. From there the others left to find a club and Pete, unaware of where he was or how to get home, wandered strange parts of Manchester during the small hours, unnoticed by others who hurried home along the streets. At about this time, with Pete an hour or more from the canal, a girl was raped beside that waterway and thrown into the murky water. Meanwhile Pete's feet hurt and he was getting nowhere that he recognized. Huddling under his jacket, the man slept in a stairwell for a while, waking with the dawn to catch an early bus back to his digs.

Days later one of Pete's dodgier acquaintances who had also attended the lock-in was arrested for the umpteenth time, on this occasion for shoplifting and assaulting the angry greengrocer who came after him. In return for leniency the criminal offered up a name in connection with the inexplicable murder that continued to vex the force. The thief was aware Peter Bell would be unable to confirm his whereabouts at the time of the girl's death, and his statement backed up Pete's physical similarity to a man seen in the area at the time. He was brought into custody, and when the armed robber sharing Pete's cell told the officer on guard he had received a tearful confession the coppers didn't even need Bell to admit his guilt. In return for a few convincing minutes in the witness box the robber drew a greatly reduced sentence while Peter went down for life.

Paddy's car pulled into a street of run-down houses, rubbish overflowing from wheelie bins, litter strewn across every other front yard. They went up the stairs to a second floor flat where Pete was introduced to Johnny, both men grunting incomprehensible greetings and keeping their eyes down on the tatty rugs. Swift's two decade stretch had been spent mainly in solitary confinement and the strain took a toll, Johnny haggard and withdrawn now, uneasy around strangers after so long without human contact. His refusal to admit a horrific multiple murder he had no part in resulted in a form of torture that was never far from Johnny's nightmares.

The main bedroom had been cleared for the new arrival, Paddy giving up his bed for the couch, believing the released man's need to be greater than his own. When Pete tried to refuse the offer a combination of Paddy's insistence and his own inarticulacy defeated him. Instead Paddy went to the fridge to get two beers and a soft drink for himself. Because if Pete's release wasn't a cause for celebration, he didn't know what was.

They drank lager and watched TV late into the night, Paddy keeping up a running dialogue with the screen as he avoided the alcohol that fuelled his violent streak. The Irishman explained references and aspects of the world he knew would be lost on Pete, the two drinkers transfixed in taciturn fascination. When they turned in Paddy found himself unable to sleep, memories of flinching in the cameras' glare when he made lead story on the news a decade before. An ongoing toast to victory with friends and well-wishers. The look on the faces of innocent brothers and sisters released with him. This numbing assault from the media and the world outside prison flooded back to Paddy all-too clearly. The ex-con had embraced loved ones back then, blissfully unaware his experiences inside would mark him forever. What Paddy underwent meant he couldn't fit back into the normal world. He had nothing in common with those who didn't know what unjust incarceration was like. More than the lack of compensation or lost time, this absence of shared ground was the bitterest pill to swallow.

Getting up the morning after his release the Irishman didn't feel hungover or vindicated but displaced and empty, sadder than he'd ever been in his life.

Pete was awake at six the next day, that prison-set internal clock rousing him, effective as any alarm. Sitting up quickly the man took several seconds to comprehend his surroundings. He was alone. There were no iron bars, no guards ordering him to stand behind the cell door. Beyond the curtains lurked space and traffic, people hurrying to work with umbrellas raised against the drizzle, all the overwhelming implications of freedom. Pete sat on the edge of the bed with his head in his hands for more than an hour.

Johnny had prepared a fried breakfast Pete chewed on numbly before taking himself off to the benefits office. After fifty minutes in a hard plastic chair feeling the effects of his morning coffee dissipate Pete was called across by a harried man in a grey and blue tie who repeatedly asked him to speak up. The claimant was informed his Jobseeker's Allowance could be collected after four weeks unless he found work in the intervening period that would nullify the agreement. The Housing Association were less helpful. No 'Peter Bell' existed as far as the social services were concerned, and since he was without a national insurance number or formal identification, Pete found himself ineligible for accommodation.

He had wanted to buy gifts for the others, some ingredients for a good meal, daffodils to brighten up the flat. But without additional funds Pete had less than two pounds a day to live on for the next month. Yet to return empty-handed, offering only bad news, appearing ungrateful and maybe even rude, that wasn't the impression he wanted to convey. Pete could manage to purchase some basic provisions for the cupboards at least.

He walked into the great supermarket, as spacious and cool as an aircraft hangar, collecting a plastic basket and moving down the aisles methodically. Everything seemed overpriced or ridiculous, a ten-minute walk from one side of the shop to the other, from something called *Sunny Delight* to whatever the hell *Snack Pots* were. Eventually Pete managed to gather up a few essentials, scanning the displays for that affordable blue and white packaging, and went up to one of the seventy checkouts.

That afternoon Paddy exchanged writing paper and stamps for the produce, helped Pete draw up a list of everyone who had assisted in his case and worked on a template note of thanks. The resulting letters exuded a sense of positivity their author certainly didn't feel, not after the fruitlessness of his morning, but Pete hid his melancholy. The ex-con had taught himself to write gracefully during the years inside to articulate his protestations of innocence. While he was incarcerated Pete would fire off a dozen missives a day, pleas to men with influence or gratitude for those who expressed an interest in his well-being, people experiencing reservations about the prosecution's case. Pete was more thankful than he could say for their responses down the years, powerful figures in the media and legal system who picked up the baton of his innocence and ran with it. He owed it to these men and women to be appreciative of his freedom, those people who kept his appeals before the judges, ensured Peter Bell wouldn't be left to rot. His allies deserved to believe they had a hand in Pete's prosperity and happiness.

Pete ran a dust cloth across the bookshelf. The S.O.N. house was quieter now, followers diligently going about their tasks this afternoon, out spreading the word or gathering food, talking with Shepherds and reading up on the visions of Rebecka. It would be many months after his release before Pete finally got his happy ending, but he was here now, no debts or hankering for the past while under this roof. Pete's home was the third filtration base *The Spirit Of Nagasaki* ran out of London, a house that contained three large dormitories alongside two smaller ones. In each of the main living areas lay eight beds with three in the subsections. On the ground floor came that prayer and activity room when inhabitants congregated for worship and readings, while behind the kitchen a small plot of land could be found. There followers grew vegetables, green beans and cabbage, lettuce and tomatoes. Overlooking the garden was an attic space, home to the leader of the household, Simon Thistlewood at present, this man promoted following supportive work and assiduous Shepherding in the first base. Despite his elevated status Simon still chose to mentor the occasional new recruit, helping out whenever an arrival particularly interested him.

The bed was neat but Pete checked around and underneath once more, just to be absolutely sure. There was anything up to thirty devotees living in this house at any point and each follower had their own small section. These living spaces contained a single bed with a shelf above it for books and necessary equipment, as well as a small chest of drawers. Beyond that the rooms were free of distraction and had to be kept immaculate at all times, Simon warning his flock that Jon or the Goddess might visit without prior notice. These leaders would be quick to dismiss the untidy.

Pete stepped back to admire his handiwork. The room sparkled satisfyingly with his corner by far the neatest. He took a Bible down from the shelf and lay back to continue reading the story of Lot. The only others in the bedroom were that attractive blonde and the man whose bed she sat on, talking with him in a voice so low Pete could barely hear her. He had observed Ruth's desirability over the past months with an eunuch's detachment, as if it were irrelevant to him. Occasionally someone from the male dorms would quietly spend the night with a female acolyte, but Pete found his sexual energy was entirely absent these days. The libido had channelled itself into the work of the Goddess, toward the living of an unselfish and Christlike existence, so that Pete would take his place in the next world come the time. Although he watched the closeness of the pair opposite with offhand interest, nothing approaching envy pricked at the man's heart. Since his acceptance into the house, Pete was no longer troubled by such urges. He failed to experience arousal on waking for the first time in his life.

What Pete felt instead through these days was a personal power, authority that came from rising above the needs of his body which combined now with a flash of annoyance at his inability to recall the name of that man across the way. Pete ought to have known, the guy had only been introduced to everyone recently, and he did try to keep the names of all his housemates committed to memory, despite the high turnover. He had noticed from television how acquaintances felt good if you called them by their God-given monickers, like they had made an impression. Pete endeavoured to give others this happiness as they came and went, were asked to leave the church or passed unspoken tests of behaviour and ability, winning a place at S.O.N.'s Cornish Eden. For Pete it was worth spending time on this mnemonic trick rather than using *brother*, *sister* or *friend*. These were Pete's family, feeling more at ease with them than he did in the company of blood relatives.

The last time Pete visited his aunt and mother in their cluttered Manchester terrace was a few weeks after his release. The man had felt like an intruder then, sitting down silently in the lounge, sipping at tea from a cup that wasn't their best china, hot liquid burning his tongue as he forced it down. The greying women didn't ask about his experiences inside or Pete's life since, showed no emotion or tenderness for their relative, chattering amongst themselves instead; endless talk of neighbourhood issues. Once or twice they turned to Pete and inquired whether he remembered old Mrs. Something or Mr. Whatever, to which the man would reply with an affirmative grunt, agreement taking the women off on another thread of old-lady gossip. After twenty minutes of this sapping babble Pete was ready to make his excuses, kissing them both on the cheek as he pretended to go and catch a train. Then he took a walk through the old neighbourhood, picking out the changes and staring at decay beside regeneration, wondering if he should look up old friends or past haunts. In the end he decided against it. There wasn't anyone around, not after all this time. By this point in the day Pete found himself keen to escape the city he had grown up in. Manchester affected him differently now, the place seemed forbidding and unkind, a backdrop to past injustice.

He returned to the station and boarded the express for London. Paddy had bought him the ticket and called it a loan, but Pete only saw more added to the rising figure he owed the Irishman. He missed only having to pay off a debt to 'society', feeling the pressures of emancipation keenly. In fact Pete had come to realise how many aspects of prison suited him over the days since his release. The rigid timetable that eliminated confusion or indecision, the campaign for justice absorbing his time and assuaging the boredom, a lack of romantic frustration or guilt. The prisoner lost that which had occupied much of his life when they let him go, Pete's return to the world teaching him there was little here for a freed man who had never been guilty. The probation service didn't possess a framework to aid the innocent, offered no counselling or rehabilitation, and Pete had to overcome his inner demons to try and find a job on his own. Paddy offered help, suggesting connections and arranging meets with contacts, but Pete had never been an artisan and he appeared sullen or disinterested at interview, felt there was nothing he could offer. The first words a prospective boss saw on Peter Bell's record were *twelve years imprisoned* in big black letters and so he remained broke and alone, with no means of paying back Paddy or moving out.

To escape that flat where he taxed the Irishman's already limited resources, Pete took to walking the streets for much of the day. He would stroll for hours and watch the workers bustle along, remaining out on the fringes, the only Londoners who talked him the sober homeless or disenfranchised. Pete listened to these lost individuals and sometimes bought them cups of tea, feeling a connection with outcasts, men whose histories were often as depressing as his. Tales of unhappy backgrounds, redundancy and bereavement, a downward plummet in life until you wake up one morning shivering in a doorway. The timetable of the days included beggary beside cashpoints or playing a battered harmonica for swarming commuters, an effort to get enough currency for a square meal the only commitment.

One Saturday morning Pete found himself cast as the keeper of one vagrant's prized possession. This man wasn't an alcoholic or substance abuser, simply unlucky. His mother had just died and the man needed to travel light, hitching up-country for the funeral. Pete looked at the guitar he'd been entrusted with as the homeless man slapped him on the back and left in a hurry. The instrument was missing a string and badly scratched but still a gateway into his past. Thinking back on those teenage years when he learned a few classic songs while working on compositions of his own, playing amongst friends and busking for change, Pete recalled rising out of his painful introversion through the performance. Was it possible he could reach people this way again? Fingers unused to making chords moved along the fretboard, plucking at the instrument as Pete tried to get it roughly in tune. The hand movements felt natural and right.

Encouraged both by the display of friendship that left him the acoustic and a rediscovered knack for the guitar, Pete bartered with a grubby tout for a travel card and entered the underground network. For the remainder of that Saturday he rode the Jubilee Line, tentatively strumming at first but soon encouraged to play songs drawn from his hobby of twenty years before. Pete tackled ballads of hope and religion, uptempo numbers about infatuation and outrage, songs of love and protest that had lain hidden in him all those years behind bars, set aside by his misery.

The uninvited troubadour stuck to the end of trains, his singing voice croaky with disuse at first but warming to the task, Pete eventually finding his gruff range. Those who wished to listen through the journeys would step into the carriage where he played, while the more reserved and those busy yakking moved down the platform a few metres before boarding. The network employees were forced to be circumspect in their response to this singer; Pete had a pass and played not for donations but to feel like part of the world again. There wasn't any rule that prevented customers playing music for reasons of altruism, and only a couple of the more jobsworth workers asked him to leave. At which point Pete would visit the nearest public toilet for a drink of water and wander to the next station on the line.

Hours went by and his audience became drunker, Pete's renditions beginning to receive compliments and applause. The uncertain recital of *Stand By Me* requested by a fat man with a ponytail was particularly successful, Pete's version ending with much of the carriage hollering along. Then a classic Dylan composition earned Pete a kiss on the cheek from a pretty young woman who would end the night being berated by her boyfriend. These moments brought a flush to Pete's face as he finished the songs, this performer-audience relationship so much easier than one-to-one interaction. At midnight the musician left the evening's final train and ascended the station steps feeling happier than any day since the one when his barrister told Pete he was going to be free.

Much of that overturned sentence had been spent on the Isle of Wight, so when the screws confirmed Pete was being transferred to the mainland he couldn't help but wonder, even if he didn't dare hope. During the early part of the decade in Parkhurst Pete had met Patrick McDonall, serving his twenty-fourth year in on the basis of dubious forensic evidence. The prosecution maintained Paddy was responsible for handling a number of explosives used to blow up pubs, his nationality and boisterous reputation doing the rest.

Paddy instinctively recognized Pete's innocence, the two of them luminescent, beacons among the dull resignation of other cons. They took to eating and exercising together, McDonall doing most of the verbal, talk of how he was fitted up, victimized as an Irishman in England during the seventies, that most hated of minorities within a fearful time. Politicized and pathologically unable to give up, Paddy was someone an innocent man could look up to. Pete took his lead from the Irishman, dragging himself from a morass of self-pity and learning to read and write effectively while he concentrated on the facts of his case. This diligent research amused some of the guards, those screws who advised him to give up all hope, but Pete didn't listen.

His case wasn't like Paddy's, not a question of state prejudice or police malpractice so much as a foolish man in the wrong place at the wrong time. One of those inconspicuous miscarriages of justice that would have resulted in a swift execution and closed file back in the days of capital punishment. Despite the lack of scandal Pete was confident he could generate a few headlines through his situation and worked every day publicizing the mistake, making progress as he enlisted the sympathetic and intelligent with the help of Paddy's contact list.

At the end of their first year together the men made a pact. Whoever got out first would continue to campaign for the other, tireless until death or incapacitation put a stop to their efforts. Each thought they would remain in the longest, but within nine months the weight of public opinion had turned the law Lords in Paddy's favour. Pete was left both happy and sad, overjoyed at the release of a friend but mourning the loss of his only ally in Parkhurst. But the Irishman was as good as his word, remaining in England to ask the awkward questions, telling the truth people didn't want to hear, refusing to rest until Pete and Johnny and all the innocent men like them were exonerated.

Unbeknownst to Pete while he sat composing letters in his cell, the slow convergence of two separate developments would finally turn his fortune. The first of these was called the Criminal Cases Review Commission, a board put in place by the new government who had quickly realized British justice would never be perfect. Unlike the previous incumbents, these centre-left leaders saw that errors had been made in the legal process and took action to identify them. Parallel to this committee came scientific advances in the field of DNA testing, proving that the traces of semen in the victim's underwear didn't come from Peter Bell. And if Pete didn't rape her, the chances of him being the killer were minute. Slowly, very slowly, these forensic findings were referred to the commission. After months of torpid cogitation his conviction was finally overturned, resulted in a brief mention during national news broadcasts to an indifferent public. The first Pete heard of this pardon was the call from his lawyer, a message that was followed by an official and extremely brief speech from the governor within the restricted confines of his office. Before Pete could come to terms with the concept of freedom he was standing outside Wormwood Scrubs in all the clothes he owned, wondering what kind of a life was in store for him.

Pete waited a long time for that phone to ring. For apologies from the judge, the police, the government, the jury, anyone. Contrition that never came. No one was willing to express regret or even say sorry. These things happened, it couldn't be helped. Best to accept the result and get on with your life.

The smell of boiling vegetables wafted up the stairs as more followers returned to their rooms for the communal enterprise of evening. Once individual work was complete everyone came together for dinner, this meal followed by music and collective prayer. The activity room emptied when group sessions were over, every day ending with more study and readings from the philosophies of the Goddess.

Two men younger than Pete came into the room and rested on their beds, followers discussing potential work to improve the guttering on the house. Pete turned to one of the marked chapters in his Bible, a highlighted passage describing the Easter death of Christ, a story he had come to derive comfort from over the months. While he was at school Pete never understood why we called the date of Jesus' murder *Good* Friday. With all the hate and pain at that time, the crown of thorns and merciless crucifixion, surely religious folk ought to remember this day as *Black* Friday? *Tragic* Friday. No said his Shepherd, Pete wasn't reading the story correctly. The suffering and murderous rage Christ endured gave man his redemption. Pete of all people should see that good comes from hurt. Without his imprisonment and soul-searching he would not have found *The Spirit Of Nagasaki*. Simon asserted that pain strengthens the spirit, creating a need for the balm of the Lord in our lives. Jesus knew this and He welcomed the injustice, because in its wake we would all be saved. If He had not died on the cross then Pete and millions like him would never have found salvation. The Shepherd explained the Lord's work is ultimately beneficial to our lives, whether it comes as a lack of intervention in the death of His son, or simply allowing one of his flock to be wrongly imprisoned. However unjust these actions might seem in the short-term, Pete should learn to trust in His mysterious ways. They all must.

Pete slammed the Bible shut and swung off the mattress, overcome by a need to communicate with the Lord. Dropping to his knees, the man placed his hands together on the blanket and made a silent prayer, thanking God for His mercy and promising to continue the movement's work in the name of the Goddess. Then Pete rose and stretched, went out to the upstairs bathroom, strains of Simon's guitar floating down from the attic room. Pete smiled to himself as he locked the door, gladness resonating in his soul.

That Sunday afternoon when he returned the homeless guy's acoustic Pete would never have believed there could be such hope in his future. He considered making an offer for that instrument that had served so well in helping transcend the world, made him popular and thrilled that Saturday, but Pete knew negotiation would be unfair. The shabby guitar was all that man had, Pete couldn't be responsible for stealing his livelihood so soon after his mother had been taken. Besides, Pete would have to borrow money for a transaction like that, and he was unwilling to cadge off Paddy again.

Feeling more alone and withdrawn than ever after his brief sojourn under the gaze of others, Pete walked the pathways of London for hours, changing direction at random, images of the past filling his head.

When he rose out of that waking dream Pete found himself outside the prison he had left many months before, the great turrets of Wormwood's entrance rising into the cobalt sky before him. Sitting himself on the kerb, Pete tried to figure out why his feet had brought him back here, coming to understand that prison was the only place he had found to belong. It was no use fighting the feelings any more, Pete admitted it to himself then and there, his dearest wish was to be back inside. Some personalities weren't cut out for liberty and the associated problems of free will. A minority of men found settled purpose while institutionalized, and Peter Bell was one of those men. He stood up and took another long glance at the buildings of the Scrubs, a look distinguished by longing. Drastic action was called for if he wanted a cell in there.

Pete turned on his heels and left Du Cane Road, racing back to the inner city. No longer would Paddy have to worry himself over Pete's disappearances, his lack of progress fitting in with the world, the absence of hope in the skinny man's day-to-day life. All these concerns the Irishman had expressed were unnecessary. Pete was going back to what he knew.

His feet were worse than painful by the time Pete hopped a bus bound for the city centre, both trainers ragged and split at the soles. The man hardly noticed, for the first time in his life Pete was too busy working out how to be a criminal.

The bus honked at unaware drivers through the streets of Kensington, Pete reclining on the worn seat as desirable residences flashed by on either side. He didn't want to hurt people or ruin anyone's day, wondering if he should smash the glass front of a global chain-shop instead, like those protestors he'd seen on the news. The man dismissed the act as small potatoes. Government buildings were the best targets for vandalism, those authorities that had destroyed much of his life. Now was the time to take revenge, and after he was caught Pete would refuse to express remorse. Disappointed by the plaintiff's failed rehabilitation, angered by the irrationality of his actions, his trial judge would be left with no choice but to hand out a harsh sentence.

Impatient to begin this new career of premeditated misdemeanour, Pete cursed the great red vehicle as it progressed haltingly, plush homes giving way to the financial district. He had found the solution; inarticulate acts of victimless violence against the state were well within Pete's reach. The passenger looked forward to throwing road signs through the windows of the powerful.

By the time Pete disembarked near Whitehall he should have been rested and ready, but a rush of blood was making the man dizzy and he had to grip the vehicle's rail before pausing in the street. As the pounding in his head cleared Pete noticed a strange sight through that spring evening. Across the road several young women were approaching passers-by, attempting to initiate conversation like market researchers, yet possessing none of the appurtenances of that role, no clipboards or pens. Each girl seemed limited to a specific section of road, only leaving her territory if the person responding was in a hurry, chose to carry on their conversation over pedestrian crossings and around turnings. Pete was puzzled by this behaviour. He guessed the young women belonged to a syndicate of some kind, possibly charitable, but they were targeting the pavement's misfits rather than the smartly dressed commuters. These girls would ignore men in suits who wandered to the station from post-work drinking sessions, block the path of some unwashed young man with dirt on his jeans or a single mother pushing her pram. One girl, a willowy brunette in a pale cotton dress, stopped a mean looking drunk, at which point Pete sucked on his broken tooth. He assessed the traffic and jogged across the road, sidestepping taxis as they sped by. The old man swigged from a can of Special Brew, failing to understand whatever it was the girl said to him. Knowing only that something was in his way, the drunk flung out an arm to clear his path. With an agile swerve the girl dodged the graceless limb and let the man continue on his way, hand moving briefly to her chest as she watched him go. Pete reached the girl a few seconds later, the fear on her face replaced by a look of concern as she watched the drunkard shuffle off.

"You alright?" Pete forced himself to look her in the eye as he said it.

The girl formed a smile, she looked about seventeen. "Yes I am, not so sure about him." The drunk finished his can and flung it over a fence into the nearby park.

"Don't worry about that." Pete appraised the girl through twilight. She had a gentle smile and hairpins the shape of flowers. "What you doing out here alone? It's night, there's danger about."

"Thank you for your concern sir, but I'm not alone." She waved at another young female who appeared on the main street out of a side road. "My sisters are with me always, we're here tonight spreading the good word."

"The good word?"

The girl beamed. "The word of the Goddess. You see sir, we're all members of a faith known as *The Spirit Of Nagasaki*." She cast an arm about her.

"This is how we tell everyone the good news, God has chosen us to embark on a new way of life, so we might survive the hopeless capitalist world."

"That's, er..." Pete failed to understand her point, knowing only that he'd walked into a strange situation. "Whatever you say, all I saw was young girls out late talking to strangers. The way I see it, that's asking for trouble."

"Don't be silly, our brothers are watching out for us." She pointed to a minibus driving along the road towards them. On its chassis the letters *S.O.N.* were painted in various colours. The girl patted Pete's hand, this touch like an electrical charge to him. "You don't look so good sir, if I may say."

Pete watched the vehicle disappear then stared down at himself. The shoes on his feet were falling apart and his clothes looked crumpled, like used tissues. He touched his face, bristled and wet with sweat. Pete hadn't been eating or sleeping, in all likelihood he was drawn and ailing as well. This was Pete's first moment of physical self-consciousness in days and he mumbled an excuse, ashamed.

"I just got out of prison."

"Really, my God. What did you do sir, if I might be so bold?"

"Nothing, I was innocent." He watched civil servants conglomerate under a nearby bus shelter. "And my name's Pete, not sir."

The grey eyes of the girl shone brightly through dusk's gloom. "Let me guess Pete, you've been finding it difficult since you were released, am I right?"

"A bit."

"We at *The Spirit Of Nagasaki* can help you, really we can." She tugged at the cuff of Pete's frayed shirt, leading him to the roadside. "Our van circles every couple of minutes, I'll flag it down for you." The girl went on talking while they waited, Pete's attention flicking between the traffic and her pretty face.

"Our aim is to save the lost, prevent this sadness, and we always achieve our aims. We are like a big family in our house with the Goddess as our mother and all her children caring for one another. I can tell there's a lot going on inside of you Peter, and the faith of the S.O.N. needs it all. Here they are now, look."

She extended a thumb as if hitching a lift. The minibus pulled to a halt before them and the girl slid open the decorated door, ushering Pete inside.

"One for you guys Simon, take good care of him okay? Pete needs the help of the Goddess." A man holding a guitar nodded to her. The girl established eye contact with Pete after he clambered in and sat. "I'll see you soon okay? Count on it."

The door slammed shut and she reclaimed her position, the vehicle's engine kicking into life for another circuit of the block.

Inside that van Pete forgot his criminal intentions, distracted by the relaxed talk of these people, the first unqualified friendliness from strangers he had encountered since his conviction. Simon Thistlewood made a quick assessment of the arrival's personality from his gestures and demeanour. Satisfied, the man handed over sandwiches and bottled water before explaining a little of the history of S.O.N., the visions they looked to for guidance, this faith's relevance and their rejection of the economic. Their religion favoured the true message of Jesus, his humanity and inclusiveness. Each of the passengers explained a little about himself as Pete ate and drank, the man filling with well-being, genuinely at ease by the time Simon gently coerced him into reciprocating. Pete brought his story up to date with a description of his current dissatisfaction, the illegal acts his unhappiness was leading towards. Simon responded with appreciations for the Lord, praise for Jesus, thanking the Goddess they had caught Peter in time. Because here was an alternative to being sent back to prison. In exchange for hard work and honesty, *The Spirit Of Nagasaki* offered men like Pete acceptance and support, freedom from guilt combined with a new perspective on the world. A roof over his head and food in his belly.

From his satchel Simon produced a copy of Rebecka's theology and a beautifully embossed Bible, both of which he gifted Pete on the condition they were read carefully, beginning with the good book's story of Job. Pete was overwhelmed by the gesture, promised to study these teachings with care and reach a decision about his future. Then Pete raised the nerve to ask about Simon's guitar and a conversation began with the men discovering a shared fondness for sixties singer-songwriters and acoustic folk. Thistlewood offered his instrument and an emboldened Pete played *Blowin' In The Wind*, the quintet singing along, their voices drifting from the vehicle and out into the warm

155

evening air.

Over the following days Pete lost his urge to wander the city, staying indoors to study instead, Paddy's flat becoming the scene of miraculous enlightenments and profound understandings. Pete found the words of Rebecka easy enough to comprehend, her straightforward language and priorities of love and community immediately casting their spell. In a way the words recalled those religious types who ran the Parkhurst courses, sessions Pete had always been too busy with his campaign to attend. That's what he had told them anyway. Really it was the sight of a group of hardened criminals, murderers and rapists among them, waving their arms in the air as if at a concert or some outdoor party, something that made Pete nervous. The evangelists who visited his prison preached a similar message of salvation to S.O.N. but they were less revolutionary in their aims, just a bunch of hypocrites in the end. The enthusiasm of those meetings led preachers to declare that violent captives could get into heaven, but they maintained few illusions outside this time, unlike the Goddess. Her philosophy was one of egalitarianism and forgiveness.

Pete found the Biblical stories less easy although he persevered and was soon rewarded with the words of a kindred spirit. In the sufferings of Job there were a hundred parallels with Pete's existence. That humble and honourable life thwarted by his creator, the constant churning inside an incorruptible man, the innocent victim wishing the day he was born would perish and himself along with it. This devout figure wished his anguish could be placed on the scales, Job believed his sorrow outweighed the sand of the seas, and in these desperate proclamations Pete recognized the self-pity of his own life, the dwelling in exaggerated misery that satisfied some perverse aspect of his being. Pete saw how he had been as desperate as Job, horribly undone in the weeks since his release. Yet the Bible taught him no man was so lost he could not be found. In order for Pete to be rescued *The Spirit Of Nagasaki* must accept his first prayer.

When he telephoned the North London house, all nerves and hesitance, a cheerful Simon announced they had been waiting for his call, even had a bed ready. His destiny was set. Pete collected together a few frayed possessions and told Paddy he had both work and a place to stay back in Manchester. Pete hated to lie but knew he couldn't speak the truth. His ex-Catholic friend would try to talk him out of this longed-for conversion, Paddy's views on religion irretrievably darkened by the history of his troubled homeland. That last night in the flat they had drinks together and watched TV for what would prove to be the last time, kicking over old times as the alcohol worked its magic. A sober Paddy was pleased for his friend, Pete more upbeat and gregarious than the Irishman had ever seen him. Whatever this work was he mentioned only reluctantly, the prospect was making his friend eat regularly and take pride in his appearance for once, so it could only be for the best.

The next morning, clear-headed and infused with a sense of pious urgency, Pete caught a bus to the North of the city and met the other followers, every man and woman in his new home geniality personified. Pete's Shepherding would be provided by Simon himself, and the pair spent many a long day in that attic room, learning each other's foibles and discussing the intent of the Lord. Pete came to understand how Job could say *though he slay me, yet will I trust in him*, even after all God put him through. How the man kept his faith and was rewarded in the next world.

Although he soon settled into the peace of a man who had found his fate, initially Pete was somewhat overcome by the power of the place, that new clarity disinfecting his mind. The ex-con's perceptions, unencumbered by primal needs or the encroaching world, led wild thoughts to overwhelm him. Emotions whirled through Pete's head, elation and a sense of power that derived from the love of others, a war between these positives and the aggression that encircled him, furious at himself for missing the point for so long. In the midst of these emotions Pete was struck with a dangerous belief, fostered by this new openness, thinking that he could connect with anyone. The man had to physically stop himself from sharing his happiness with random people in the street, uptight pedestrians who would only have questioned his sanity.

Simon began to monitor Pete's actions, these outbursts of pure joy and erratic approaches. The Shepherd had seen spiritual rebirths go awry before. Often the chaos of awakened faith would unhinge a man or lead to uncontrollable impulses. Some heard the voice of God, became panicked by their mind unravelling before it could be rebuilt by the Goddess. To his credit Pete showed more restraint than many, governing these unprecedented energy levels, channelling his power into a desire for knowledge and an ever-growing workload. Throughout those weeks of induction Simon remained close by, and when the exchange of dialogue veered onto a fanatical tangent he would steer conversation towards pop music or his own experiences, pass the guitar to Pete and observe his protégé play some sixties songs. These musical sessions defused the tension that was created by Pete's vociferousness, the pupil recognizing afterwards how kind and tolerant the Shepherd had been with him, the pair becoming friends and brothers in the way of the S.O.N..

Such was the growing closeness of the pair and the willingness with which Pete scoured his soul for the Lord, Simon often found himself wishing to reciprocate, something he had never done with an acolyte before, fearful as he was of the consequences. One evening, after a particularly powerful exegesis on the pain of Jesus, the Shepherd took a deep breath and spoke freely at last.

Back in the secular world Simon's younger days had been tormented by denial and frustration. As a kid he never experienced the kind of crushes all his classmates talked about, and when Thistlewood made it to adulthood the truth about his sexuality finally dawned on the young man. He was gay, gay and unattractive. Simon's weight problems meant the men he wanted most never returned his lust. Unable to find an outlet for these desires in suburban England, Simon suppressed his homosexuality and complied with the wishes of his parents, working his way upwards from junior employee to head of branch operations at a recruitment agency. The substantial salary was nice, but Simon didn't have any use for it, his wages piling up in high-interest accounts until late one night, deep in the self-loathing of the sexually-frustrated insomniac, he underwent a dark Epiphany. All that spare money Simon was making, it could cure the crippling suppression that ate away at his insides, release years of accumulated pressure.

As he turned thirty Simon began commuting into London and paying for sex, decoding the personals in gay magazines then picking up punks and hustlers off the streets once he knew where to look. These stickily mercantile exchanges satisfied him for a while, but without noticing it Simon's interest soon gravitated toward the youngest boys who were selling themselves in this spiral of nightly deception. His mistake was to get too ambitious, reaching beyond the world of male prostitution, the illicit thrill of turning a straight lad so enticing. From the window of his Mercedes Thistlewood would spot a likely boy and stop in the street beside him, offer a ride in his impressive car or a day out with the promise of gifts and spending money. The third teenager to accept this ploy looked older than his years and had a butch way about him that Simon liked. But after it was over the boy was silent all the way back to his house, must have regretted the act immediately. Perhaps he became angry when thinking of the older man and what he'd done, those presents meaning little in his mire of self-disgust. Whatever the truth, that sixteen year old's fury won out over his embarrassment and the police were called. Simon lost his job, his family, his freedom. He was inside for three months, a sentence long enough to see what Pete had gone through, understanding how those places broke a man.

Upon completion of his time the name *Simon Thistlewood* was placed on the sex offenders' register indefinitely and the man tried to piece his life back together. Simon ignored the witch-hunts that had begun to formulate through the press as best he could and took each day as it came. He was coping okay until one weekend, months after the release, when Simon picked up a tabloid newspaper for the TV guide and found a list of sexually aberrant individuals and their home towns on the front page. The Shepherd knew that Pete had gone through terrible things, but did he have any idea what it felt like to have a lynch mob marching down his street? Had he seen contorted faces congregate outside, calling for his head and threatening to smoke him out? Did Pete ever know such vicious prejudice he feared for his life on a daily basis?

Tears formed in his eyes as Simon described how he took solace in prayer when facing the prospect of death, trapped and afraid in his rented room. Thistlewood had no idea why he turned to God, had always assumed the deity wasn't there for people like him, but the man persisted in this reflex, talking at length to a Lord he had never needed before. Then Simon climbed out of a back window and fled the baying hordes, ran and lost himself in the oddities of London. One desolate night he was referred to Jon Foulkes who listened to this terrified man, advising Simon his prayers had been answered. Jon gave Simon an opportunity at S.O.N., a room away from the anonymous hostel he was stuck in and a *tabula rasa*. Now here he was, in the midst of a new life, running one of the filtration bases and giving hope to others who'd got lost in the city.

Simon wiped his face and went on, describing how Rebecka's lesson; that sexual urge was merely a fuel for creation, had been revelatory for him.

Ever since this education Simon's unnatural desire had evaporated along with all lustful thought. He was granted redemption from sin by the Lord, and in return Simon found it in his heart to forgive the woman called Ruth who was living in his house, a female who had once been a prime engineer of that braying mob in her previous life. God forced Simon to overcome feelings of anger when the female journalist looked for a welcome under his roof, and with the Lord's help he succeeded. Unbeknownst to the Schwitz woman her immediate superior in the faith had once suffered at her hand, yet held no animosity towards her. Simon hoped Peter could find similar forgiveness for his Shepherd's shameful past. Because Simon had come to think of him as more than a student and follower, saw Pete as a true friend.

Pete looked at this flabby man before him, an individual who had undoubtedly made mistakes but never refused to listen. The ex-con embraced Simon unreservedly. His crying ceased, and when they separated Pete grinned conspiratorially before collecting the guitar. Simon hurried to follow his friend who called the house residents to their activity room for songs of joy and devotion, strumming the acoustic furiously while the Shepherd encouraged his flock to holler their lungs out. Glancing up from the instrument at his brothers and sisters, Pete saw how he surpassed himself in moments like these, became as one with the others in the body of this church, a union that relinquished past torments for the healing power of music.

He flushed and flipped the bolt on the door. Those first weeks of education as he worked towards the honour of baptism were some of Pete's favourite times in the church. He memorized the ethics of the Goddess in hopeful preparation and came to understand she shared his distrust for a planet that had grown faster and less friendly, both of them believing this world was unkind and complicated, beyond the grasp of humans. Although England had become more prosperous during the eighties and nineties, those times when Pete was either fucked up or locked up, Rebecka saw through this success with her razor sharp perceptions. Recognition resounded through Pete's heart when he read her conclusion. These days of plentiful leisure time and increasing ways of keeping us entertained only serve to isolate the individual. This obsession with protecting what we have and avoiding all danger reduces our society to a state of hermitic lockdown. Today scared Englanders choose home entertainment units and long-term security over friendship or adventure, and Rebecka understood all the fear and paranoia that cut a swathe through the present day. Yes, thought Pete, she knows my world. Her prophecies will undoubtedly come to be respected by everyone as the years go by, the lessons of this modern sister to Christ.

In his spare time Pete poured these revelations into a handwritten diary that his Shepherd would take away to study, feeling closer to the Goddess whenever he wrote out opinions and hopes. When his reparations for the twelve lost years finally came through Pete took this chance and gave something back, posting a cheque to Paddy before donating the rest of his money directly to *The Spirit Of Nagasaki*. Soon Pete was out in the minibus himself, helping to bring the word to men he would previously have crossed the street to avoid, empowered by the wondrous regime of Rebecka.

Not long after Simon's confession that day Pete had been waiting for finally came. Follower Peter Bell was baptized inside one of the halls that usually held the shows under the steady gaze of his Shepherd and Jon Foulkes. As his body was immersed in the great tank of water, the Reverend Elliott formally announced that this moment was a turning point in Pete's life. Few were chosen to enter the kingdom of the Lord, but Peter Bell was one of the deserving ones. Heaven would be his, as long as Pete treated his brothers and sisters as equals, worshipped the Goddess unreservedly, followed her bidding and renounced the chattels of the world. Upon the cessation of a life lived by these strictures, Peter would be accepted into the next world, taking his place at the side of Christ.

After drying himself vigorously Pete felt renewed and privileged, his flesh tingling as he shook hands with the Reverend and vowed to work hard until the coming of the prophecy. This baptism meant Pete could never be cast out of S.O.N., would be held in esteem within the movement and allowed to fulfil the role of Shepherd should the household ever call upon him. So when the believer who was waiting to enter the bathroom told Pete that Simon wished to see him as he left, the man wondered if he was to receive his first brother or sister for instruction.

Pete knocked on the door of the attic room and entered, whereupon

Simon put down the guitar and shook his hand, the man permanently pale and sweaty these days, Thistlewood having lost a few pounds but not looking any better for it, his jowly face set in a grim expression.

"Hello Peter, take a seat won't you?"

"Good afternoon my friend." Pete didn't let the man's despondent tone destroy his joviality. "What can I do for you today?"

Simon sighed. "You need to listen carefully to me Peter. I'm seeing the household one by one and I would ask you not to breath a word of what I have to say until everyone has been told."

"Okay."

"The time has arrived for us to make a choice my brother. Those who have studied the words of the Goddess knew this moment would come, but I find myself surprised our time has arrived so quickly."

Pete felt his stomach flip. "Go on."

"Earlier today she issued an edict." Outside the window leaves were being blown from the trees. "The faithful have been summoned to Cornwall. Our bus will make several trips out West tomorrow, as many as it takes to get us all down there." The crisp shapes fluttered down, landing on parked cars. "We shall not be returning to London."

"Remind me what they call it?"

"The community is known as Newtopia. I spoke with Jon this morning and he has given an assurance that space will be found for every devout soul who wishes to move."

The eminent citadel of Newtopia had been spoken of many times within Pete's earshot. To be accepted into this West Country Eden was perhaps the greatest honour the church could bestow. Now they were all going to live there. Pete's heart pounded in his chest.

"So what is the choice you say we have to make?"

"The decision is one for every city-based follower." Simon looked into the eyes of his friend who noticed again how loosely the flesh hung from Thistlewood's face. "You may join us in Cornwall, or return to your life outside *The Spirit Of Nagasaki,* keeping within the ways of the Goddess *in absentia* if you wish. That is the choice."

Pete turned away from his Shepherd, thoughts of the few he knew outside the church filling his head. A vision of returning to Paddy's hospitality came then, a life with no way to earn his keep, the rest of his days spent sitting around a draughty flat. He remembered those men on the streets, filthy tramps forever victimized or threatened, moved along by the police like unwanted cattle, suffering sideways glances from a contemptuous public. Pete wondered what Cornwall was like. Smiling, he looked up at Simon.

"That's no choice." He said.

Chapter Seven

"Let's understand each other this morning. You and I are alone in here. We won't be interrupted by the Sergeant or the Inspector or anyone else. Refreshments and food will arrive when I request them and there are cigarettes should you need to smoke. No listening devices have been fitted inside this room because our conversation is purely for my benefit." A pause. "Tell me you understand by answering me before we start. Do you see a tape recorder in here?"

"I suppose not."

"No Stoker, you do not. That's because what you say won't escape these four walls. I'm with you today because there has been enough skirting around the subject of your confinement. If you wish to respond you may speak without fear of repercussion, but for the moment your words are unnecessary. All I require this morning is that you listen."

"What if I do this?" The prisoner placed both hands over his ears in a half-hearted motion. Sweeney forced a mirthless smile and kept it on his face through the silence that followed until Stoker let his arms return to the table. The eyes of the captive were brown and red today, bloodshot areas obscuring the whiteness. Evidently sleep wasn't coming easily for Stoker and he seemed dispirited, as if yesterday's capacity for tomfoolery had been drained from him, the previous gesture one last grasp at levity, facetiousness that was doomed to failure.

By contrast Joe felt at his best since arriving in the west. He had woken only briefly in the night to find himself surrounded by ashtrays and scattered papers, one half-empty whisky bottle and an ice cube tray with tepid water in two of the plastic compartments. After braving the toilet Sweeney had undressed and fallen asleep once more, finally achieving some hours of rest. Come morning the permed female assistant was delighted to inform Joe that the pharmacy had taken delivery of a batch of Lotrel, the latest thing for what she called *hypertension*. She twittered on about the drug not matching his prescription exactly, how she would bend the rules for him because the pills were very effective with fewer side effects, just a little light-headedness so he probably shouldn't stand up too quickly while taking it.

Sweeney paid his money and studied the label that described the contents as a mixture of whatever Benazepril was and something called Amlodipine. The print also warned against mixing the drug with alcohol, although it didn't describe what would happen if he did or how these effects might differ from the general problem of drunkenness.

Joe took the packet from his trouser pocket and pulled out a cigarette, Stoker shook his head to refuse the offer, watching every movement of the Investigator with wide eyes, like a tamed canine.

"That was a nasty trick you pulled earlier."

Sweeney lit his cigarette. "I thought you might be able to shed some light on the ones we haven't been able to identify."

"I only ever knew their first names!" The smoke rose above Stoker as he leaned forward, voice emotional. "And what about the burnt ones? How in God's name was I meant to recognize them?"

"No." Joe took a drag and held it for a couple of seconds. "I suppose you wouldn't have been able to help there."

Stoker folded his arms and slumped back. After his trip to the chemist's Joe had arrived at the station with an urgent request for one of the officers. The policeman collected one photograph of each corpse that remained nameless and placed them in an envelope, the package slid under the door of the holding cell. Sweeney spent the next couple of hours sorting through paperwork, getting up to speed on recent developments as he drank coffee. He told Dickson of his plan for the day when the Chief Inspector arrived, Joe explaining the prisoner would be brought to his office for 11.30. From that point the two of them were not to be disturbed under any circumstances.

Sweeney waited for the other man to glance back at him. "We contacted your mother."

A brief silence as Stoker scratched his nose and Sweeney stubbed out the dog-end. He knew this woman was the only relative his prisoner had contacted over the past year. Eventually the captive spoke in a flat voice.

"How is she?"

"Not great, soldiering on." Joe bent down to collect a statement from the file that lay on the floor. "Suffers from all sorts of illnesses according to what she says here, although some of that might be the usual grousing. Elderly ladies like to go on when they think someone is listening." The smile returned to Sweeney's mouth while his eyes hinted at other sentiments. "You know what us old folks are like. Won't stop talking about our problems." Stoker grunted. "Don't worry though, we let her know you're alright. Informed Valerie her little boy was *helping us with our inquiries*." Joe brought the rest of the paperwork up from underneath the table. "Why didn't you go to her after the fire?"

Two policemen moved along the corridor outside, laughing about last night's football results.

"I didn't think about it. I don't remember thinking about anything." The brown eyes glazed over. "I couldn't even summon up the will to get away when the pigs arrived." Stoker rubbed at the sockets with his hands. "Can we get some drinks in here?"

"In a minute." Sweeney leafed through the papers. "Tell me about the drugs."

"Drugs?" The prisoner seemed genuinely surprised. "What drugs? I've never taken drugs in my life."

"Those hemp plants you grew in the greenhouses."

Stoker laughed, a repeated *ha* sound from deep in his throat, the noise free of jollity. "You really want to know about the pot?"

When he returned the cigarettes to his pocket Joe hit the 'on' button of the Dictaphone concealed there. "Yes Stoker, tell me what you did with the marijuana. You don't expect me to believe nobody smoked it?"

The younger man looked Joe square in the face. "We had a grant for those plants, that was where the money for the lighting and heaters came from." Stoker interlaced fingers behind his head, elbows protruding. "The funding came from a government initiative, the one they set up a while back. You must remember it Joe, a scheme to investigate whether marijuana had medical benefits."

"Is that right?" Sweeney struggled to give nothing away.

"This Home Office scientist used to come down and check our crop every month, ask him if you don't believe me. The bloke's name was Alderon." Stoker stretched both arms to the ceiling and yawned loudly. "Think about it Joe, Newtopia was the ideal site to grow a batch of reefer away from prying eyes. That farm was well out of the way. How better to avoid scandal than by contracting the cultivation out? Alderon and his boys hardly needed to use any public money if a bunch of us grew it for tax breaks."

Raising his body slowly as advised, Joe opened the door far enough to poke his head out and called for coffee. Once delivered they sipped the drinks in silence, Sweeney lighting another cigarette. Joe had lost his train of thought during the last exchange and it was taking a while to get this morning back on course. The caffeine helped though, it brought some life back into both of them, the captive finishing his mug first and pouring another.

"Ever get a chance to read the bible Joe? You should, you really should. I had time on my hands for a while there and the strange thing is parts of it are still relevant, whatever's going on in your life. I'd flick through the New Testament, somewhere like Galatians say, and I'd find a quote like; *a man is not justified by observing the law, but by faith in Jesus Christ,* and I'd think: *All Fucking Right!* Why didn't they teach us that at school, instead of the usual crap about Virgin births and Frankincense?"

The prisoner's loud monologue dissipated into the atmosphere. Sweeney was never going to respond in the same way. Instead the Investigator took another mouthful of coffee before speaking in a level voice.

"You'll be interested to hear I've engaged in all manner of enlightening research since I saw you last." Joe moved the papers before him into their file. "I'm going to try and get what happened straight in my head by thinking out loud, so you'll have to forgive me if anything comes across a bit confused." Opposite him Stoker ran a hand through his closely cropped hair. "Do feel free to stop me if I get things wrong." Stoker shrugged. The Investigator put his file down and began.

"Essentially the facts as I see them are these. Approximately eighteen months ago a new faith started up. Not so much New Age as a cult of personality, a spin on the old ways that offered an alternative to organized religion. Soon the cult's combination of anti-materialism and showmanship attracted young followers, both to its houses in London and the head of operations in Cornwall where you worked." Sweeney pointed a finger at Stoker who remained impassive. "Unlike everyone else in the cooperative you received a wage and were not required to believe in its doctrines. While you may not have observed the rules, like everyone else you took some kind of personal inspiration from the church and looked up to Rebecka Marsden, the former prostitute who served as the religion's leader and its guiding presence." Joe stubbed the butt out in an ashtray and again offered the prisoner a cigarette, this time Stoker took one. "Due to an event or events unknown, after about fifteen months the movement decided to end the residency in London and a selection of followers moved out here. Things began to go wrong when they arrived. There was overcrowding and friction, maybe a bit of paranoia crept in as well, but the group stuck with it because by that time most of them couldn't remember any other kind of life." Joe moved his paperwork onto the floor and fixed Stoker with an icy glare.

"One minute everyone was working together peacefully. The next: BANG!" Sweeney shouted the last word, slapping his right hand against the palm of his left. The combination of threatening movement and sudden noise caused Stoker to lurch. "All of a sudden *everybody's dead.*"

Joe stood up and leaned over the table, kicking his chair away as he did so. The piece of furniture flew back and crashed against the wall. The cigarette between Stoker's fingers fell to the floor. The age difference between these two men was never as pronounced as it was at that moment. Sweeney loomed over his adversary with the authority of experience and all the menace of a feared headmaster about to administer the cane. Beneath him Stoker appeared younger than his twenty-eight years and scared, like the rebellious kid who has crossed the wrong man and loses his perpetual smirk in the terror of the situation.

"All you've ever done in your life is harm people. The only thing you got out of all that wickedness was a little bit of money you'll never be able to spend." Joe hissed while keeping his head level, ten inches or so from Stoker's face. "Rebecka killed everyone, she betrayed those who loved and trusted her, including you. She bent your will to her needs my friend, and she made you guilty of murder."

"You, knuh, know Joe." Stoker was trying to keep up the pretence of cool but a stammer gave him away. "Jesus thought anger was as bad as m-murder."

"Maybe his words got twisted." The captive tried to recoil from Sweeney's breath, stale from the coffee and cigarettes, but Joe simply leaned closer. "I won't do that to *you* Stoker, no way. You've got to live with this for the rest of your days, and that's bad enough without me fabricating your statement." Joe trod on the lit cigarette that had rolled beside his shoe. "Tell me where Rebecka went after you lit the fire."

"I didn't light no fires." He was lying, Sweeney could see it.

"What did you do then pal? Force them all in the barn? Dig the pits?" The voice of the interrogator remained sibilant and cold. "Was it you who nailed the door shut Stoker? Eh?"

Stoker's head fell to rest in his arms and the man began to sob. Joe looked down at him with unmitigated contempt for long seconds. Then Sweeney moved to pick up his chair, returned to sit across from the prisoner who directed a muffled proclamation his way.

"I didn't love Rebecka." Gasp. Sniff. "Not really."

Sweeney tipped what remained of the coffee into his mug. The fluid in the pot was no longer hot and all the milk had gone, but what was there would suffice. Joe stirred two sugars into the black liquid and watched the head before him convulse.

"I spoke to the father of a girl called Jane Spencer before I came here today." Joe took a sip. "You would only have known her by her first name though wouldn't you Stoker, just like you said?" The captive continued to sputter. "Lovely young woman by all accounts, idealistic and caring. Wanted to live a worthwhile life did Jane. She was one of the first we pulled from the ground."

Another cigarette was lit. Joe knew his lungs would complain later, but keeping the mind ticking over was more important. "Jane's father told me she had grown into the sweetest girl her family had ever known. He said she wasn't interested in making money or owning things, wanted to do her bit for the world instead. Jane thought she could improve the lives of those less fortunate than her, really believed there was good in everyone." Sweeney shook his head and exhaled a smoke ring. "How wrong she was."

Wiping his nose on a sleeve, Stoker lifted his head to stare at the Investigator, a lack of comprehension in his watery eyes.

"The Spencers are a very close family. Even after Jane moved out she used to phone several times a week. They care about each other a great deal." Joe took another drag. "The year before last she told her parents about a job she'd landed, doing administrative work for a religion. Not only did Jane love the responsibility, she got to be involved with people who dedicated themselves to others. Her mum and dad were delighted for the girl, if a bit surprised. She'd never expressed any interest in God before you see." The man opposite was looking at Joe strangely, as if trying to recognize an acquaintance he hadn't seen for decades. "The parents didn't let this bother them though, they trusted Jane's judgement and the communication kept coming." Somewhere in the station there was the faint sound of voices.

"Jane must have been allowed to keep her mobile for work purposes. She kept in touch with her family secretly. I know people in the cult weren't allowed personal calls. *He that loveth his father or mother more than me is not worthy of me*, am I right?" Sweeney didn't wait for an answer. "Her father blames himself, thinks he should have had suspicions earlier. I told him, it's always easy with hindsight." Joe shook his head. "The parents began to wonder about her lifestyle when Jane wouldn't allow them to visit her house. The only places they could meet were out of the way restaurants or coffee houses. Soon these get-togethers tailed off. Jane made excuses whenever she was invited to the family home. Too much work; she was coming down with something, it was the busiest time and the bosses needed her there. By November she had severed contact altogether, wasn't responding to e-mails and her mobile had stopped working. The couple were worried, this wasn't like Jane at all. They hired a Private Investigator who managed to locate her on your farm. He took some long-range photographs from the edge of the land. They showed the girl looking okay. That was all he could do."

Joe killed his smoke. "The initial relief at their daughter's well-being gave way to other fears. She might have been physically fit, but Jane seemed to have fallen in with some kind of sect. Her parents sought expert help, they persuaded members of a deprogramming group to go out and try to bring the girl back, but the men were turned away before they could get near her. Mrs. Spencer's mental health deteriorated, while her husband tried to keep himself strong enough for both of them. He spent the days thinking, wondering what they could try next, if his energies would be best utilized through some kind of campaign or pressure group. The man was still pondering his next move when we rang."

170

Stoker seemed to be registering his surroundings again, the man's face set in an unnatural grimace, his eyes clear. Joe offered a cigarette but the prisoner remained motionless.

"Of course, Jane's background isn't unique. There are scores of tragic families behind your cult, just like there were at Jonestown or Heaven's Gate, not to mention other tragedies, Hiroshima or *Nagasaki*." Sweeney's gaze remained fixed on the abnormal expression before him. "Jane's mother probably wasn't the only one who had to be taken into care when the officer told her what had happened, not the sole bereaved parent hospitalized because she wouldn't stop screaming." The Investigator drained his cup. "Jane's father is just as distraught as his wife but he hides it better. Mr. Spencer might be able to go on functioning, for a while at least. Neither of them will ever recover of course, I've seen it before. You don't go back to the person you were before the death of your only child. Jane's parents can't suppress the mental images of their baby girl's fate. How she was slowly throttled, subjected to so much pain, dying like an animal...."

"Stop."

"...before being kicked into that hole like so much rubbish. Who's to say she was dead even then? Maybe there was some life left in their daughter..."

"Stop Joe, please."

"...maybe Jane woke up with the cold flesh of dead friends above and below her. Perhaps she revived briefly, only to choke on the earth in her lungs, suffer a fatal shock from the terror..."

"Come on Joe, don't do this."

"...maybe her eyes flicked open, and for a second Jane had no idea where she was, and when the situation sank in she used the last of her air to scream, a scream those who heard it won't ever forget..."

"STOP, STOP! I'll tell you what you want to know, alright? Just shut up for Christ's sake!" There was a desperate edge to the suspect's voice. "You have no idea what it was like to be part of what happened, to see every action you're forced into taking and know it isn't right but have no power to stop yourself. You haven't got a clue old man." Joe continued to stare at Stoker until the younger of the two men looked away, his voice quieter as he resumed the protest.

"But I'll tell you everything you want Joe you bastard, everything I can remember. And it doesn't matter to me what you think's relevant, get it? I'm going to tell it all, so you had better get us some food because we're going to be a while."

Stoker reached over to collect the packet of cigarettes.

"If I start down that road it all comes out, and you have to take down every word."

He lit a match.

"You want to hear my story Joe? Well make sure you listen right from the beginning, because otherwise you'll never understand."

Stoker

"In earlier times, when bears were more common, perhaps masculinity served a particular function, but for centuries now, men clearly served no useful purpose."

- Michel Houellebecq, *Atomised*

The plants came up to his chest, many of them reaching a height of five feet and that left a few inches of growth for the coming month. The stench from these lusty-green hemp bushes overpowered people at first, sickly-sweet and resinous, but a man soon got used to their scent, just like he acclimatized to the retina-searing light and tropical heat. Sweat drenched Stoker's vest as he moved through the foliage with a hose, taking aim at each burgeoning shrub then holding the stream there for long seconds. Every marijuana plant required several gallons of water a day to keep its THC levels high so Jones and Stoker usually took one stretch of watering each, alternating responsibility over the morning and afternoon shifts. Unfortunately Jones had recently been summoned to help the old guy wire up the new P.A. system, so Stoker was left to tend the crop by himself this Saturday. Annoyed at this delineation he left the jet on each tree for double the regular time so it wouldn't be necessary for him to return to this oppressive atmosphere after lunch.

Stoker turned the nozzle and the supply eased off, walking along the next row. At least there was space to manoeuvre since they had uprooted and destroyed all the male plants at the start of November. Before this weeding, selections that ensured a wealth of female shrubs remained and halved the foliage density, Stoker could barely turn around without becoming engulfed by greenery. He turned on the flow once more and tried to distinguish aspects of the outside world through the tinted glass. Above Stoker thousand watt bulbs were fitted eight feet up, a position from where they provided the plants with essential light. It wasn't just the thirst for moisture that took up Stoker's time. These crops had to be examined for pests and sprayed with insect repellent when necessary. Then there was the constant monitoring of temperature, a chore that involved replacing gas canisters on an almost daily basis, fuel for the heaters lining glass walls that kept the interior stifling at all times.

Quite apart from all this came the largest part of the undertaking. This would arrive at the end of December as the crop became ready. The work of Jones and Stoker involved redigging two hundred holes as soon as each batch was harvested and maintaining the shoots for the better part of six months when the next set of seeds were planted. Soon the time to reap this marijuana would be upon them once more, a discarding of the stalks and stems as they gathered the greenery together, all the flowers and leaves and seeds, a lucrative concoction.

The output of the other greenhouse would go directly into crates, to be collected by the public health department working out of the Home Office. From what Douglas had revealed to Stoker and Jones it seemed the scientists were converting this drug into some kind of syrup, for experimentation on the severely disabled. To provide resources for legitimate research was the wholly legal purpose of that other structure. But this greenhouse, the less obtrusive one that officially held nothing more than tomatoes and courgettes, was where the private initiative went on. Soon the hundred or so plants before Stoker would be hung upside down and repeatedly shaken to extract the resin. After this black substance was released the men packed it in plastic containers and transferred the boxes to their truck as the rest of the compound slept. At daybreak Jones and Stoker would embark on the twelve hour round trip to meet the latter's London contact. This dealer, whose name Stoker didn't want to know, then confirmed their opinion of the product's weight and quality before passing the appropriate amount of cash over to Jones. After this psychoactive substance left their hands it was compacted and cut up, eventually distributed in small blocks to friends of friends around the city, but by this time there was no link back to the church.

Stoker's original qualms regarding his part in this trade were alleviated as the other half of their output was purchased by government sources. As Jones was quick to observe at the start, if they produced hashish for smart people on both sides of the law, who was to say which group ensured this drug got to those who needed it most? Despite never experiencing a need to get high himself, Stoker was still part of that generation who came of age in the nineties and he'd known plenty of decent people who used pot to relieve insomnia or depression or the comedown from less benign drugs. While Stoker made a point of avoiding drug dealers and their world of profit making wherever possible, not least because he wanted to avoid his father's mistakes, at Newtopia there seemed little in the way of danger. The authorities wouldn't arrest them for cultivation here, not when half their product was destined for officially sanctioned purposes.

Stoker pumped another gallon of water into the sodden ground beneath the last plant and shut off the supply. He coiled the hosepipe around an arm and wiped at his skin with a piece of rag, mentally preparing himself for the drop in temperature all the while. Although this final day of November wasn't particularly cold for Cornwall, the contrast between that wind hitting his damp attire and his former confines made the man shiver. In the distance members of S.O.N. circled the farmhouse and outbuildings, going about their daily business or looking for something to occupy the time. Stoker picked up the smock he had dropped outside the greenhouse and put it on over his vest and jeans, knowing someone would reproach him for improper attire if this uniform were left off. The man tried to avoid having followers moan at him but there were so many rules in this place he often fell victim to unwitting lapses; minuscule oversights in ceremony or etiquette whereupon one of Rebecka's disciples would buzz at Stoker for the lack of dedication implied by his mistakes. Luckily enough both he and Jones only had to obey the superficial formalities. As employees of Douglas, the two men were not required to pass tests of belief, often leaving Newtopia for rest breaks or reasons that pertained to the business side. After padlocking the door Stoker did a lap of the greenhouse and detached the hose from the farm's outside tap. Near the side of the barn he could make out a football game in progress and wandered over for a closer look.

Sides of three faced off on the damp grass, one team captained by Josh while the other featured Keith, back with the lads after his honeymoon and gesturing now for Stoker to join them. The man refused, shouting that his involvement would make the sides unequal, choosing instead to recline his compact frame against the side of the barn for a cigarette. Before him men in their twenties and thirties passed and tackled and scored and swapped positions with abandon, one side with the sleeves of their smocks rolled up as they belted a battered sphere through the air.

Stoker suspected part of their pleasure came from escaping that overcrowded farmhouse. So many additional followers had arrived over the past two days that space was now at a premium. Many of the ground-level acolytes found themselves with their first spare time since joining thanks to the inadequate number of tasks. Typical that none of these bored types were allowed to help Stoker in his work. The man did try to convince Douglas, honestly believing he could out-argue any assistant who asked awkward questions about S.O.N.'s profitable cultivation of the weed. After all, didn't God give us the plants and seeds for our use? But the response to his request for more help was an emphatic and unwavering no.

Brushing shaggy hair from his eyes, Stoker shook his lighter to make it work. Every time he mentioned the uneven workload on the compound Douglas or the Goddess or whoever reminded Stoker that he was being paid while the believers only got food and shelter for their efforts. It was a sound argument as far as it went, but after almost eighteen months in the organization's employ Stoker was champing at the bit to get out and enjoy some of that money he'd accrued. Weeks had passed since he last got away for a night in one of the nearby towns, and Stoker really needed to unwind. Unlike Jones he was still a young man.

The ex-professional footballer ran rings around his opponents before firing a low shot past their goalkeeper. Stoker applauded Keith and savoured his smoke as thoughts returned him to the kickabouts of his childhood days. Back then Stoker suffered acutely from the enforced absences of his father, so that when the man turned over a new leaf on release his son was eager for guidance; how to cope with his imminent manhood. By then Stoker's father was a reformed criminal, no longer that face on the London gangland scene he'd been for much of the sixties and seventies, a former contemporary of the Krays. His associations combined with the acts of extortion had made the old man a focus of police interest down the years, and when the coppers finally found a witness with enough bottle to send him away the eight year stretch gave Stoker Snr a chance to reconsider his priorities. He came out a changed man, one who'd spent long nights realizing his son would grow up without a father if he wasn't careful, the boy forming an instinctive hatred for his detained dad. His son was ten when the father came back and he man wasted no time in providing Stoker with his morality of masculine existence. This code derived partly from his underworld lifestyle (don't rat on your friends, when it's business trust no one) combined with lessons he had learned in the penal system; go straight my boy, because life's too short to spend in a cell.

Stoker paid attention and matured, soon outdoing that scarred patriarch in quick-wittedness, but his was an intelligence unsuited to the conventions of school. By adolescence Stoker's teachers saw the boy wasn't cut out for differential equations or studying the use of metaphor, so when Stoker moved into the world at sixteen only manual labour awaited. His father watched the teenager drift through factory work for a while before placing a call with an old associate. Taking his son aside one evening, the old man talked of his own mistakes, those authority figures he lacked throughout his life, a lack of influence that resulted in his gravitation toward illegality. Stoker was fully grown now and shared many of his proud dad's characteristics; the forceful physique and inner strength. Now was the time for him to undertake an important transition, make a mark on this world, decide what he should do with the rest of his life. A friend of a friend in the security trade had arranged for Stoker to be included on the next training course for potential bodyguards they ran out of East London. If the boy agreed to participate he could live rent-free for the duration of this month-long scheme, and by the end Stoker would have mastered a trade. While the man didn't want to pressure his son into anything, this was a career that could make use of his natural attributes; the brawn inherited from his side and that common sense he must have got from his mother. Stoker agreed without hesitation. He was bored of shifting crates for a living, and the kid wouldn't have extinguished that glimmer in his father's eye for anything.

During the first session a wired but unsure Stoker ran into Glenn Jones, forty-one years old with indistinct tattoos and a shaved head. Glenn sat next to Stoker at lunchtime, advised the younger man to call him 'Jonesy' between complaining about the food. Jones was opinionated and friendly, gabbling away on his muddy past that had taken in many lines of work, including a spell in the military.

"And let me tell you something lad, this guy we got 'ere." Meaning the tutor who had earlier been outlining the theories that underpinned their course and would instruct them for the rest of the month. "He finks 'e's a squadron leader, all that barking out commands and orderin' blokes around. Wouldn't last five minutes in my old regiment. I've seen cunts like that all over the place since I got out the forces and they get my goat. Don't let 'em worry you Stoker ol' son." The man grinned, his irregular teeth an unbecoming shade of brown, then shovelled down the lumpy mashed potato he had expressed such distaste for a few minutes previously.

Stoker warmed to Jones, despite his strange stories and tendency to repeat himself. None of those other simian males even passed the time of day so it was a relief to listen to a voice apart from the authoritarian bark of their instructor. He was disappointed when Jones eventually had enough, failing to return after several days of steadily growing anger, the trainer picking him out for what Glenn perceived as unfair and demeaning treatment. From then on Stoker found the course dull, having to keep an image of his delighted father near the front of his mind for those times when his commitment wavered.

Come the end and Stoker was lighter on his feet and fleeter in movement, knew the dangers that accompanied fame and how to identify them, had become proficient at disarming an assailant, shaped by the course into the skilled protector of a paying client. Like most of the hopefuls Stoker breezed through the tests of simulated danger, using his body as an effective human shield and powering enemies of the dummy client into submission. Where he differed from these burly men, some of whose sausage-like fingers could barely hold a pen, was in the way Stoker breezed through the written examination. To the limitless pride of his father, the young man gained a certificate of commendation, the highest accolade the instructor could bestow. This was followed by a personal recommendation to one of the capital's largest bodyguard agencies and that teacher who had appeared so antisocial informing Stoker he held more promise than any of the men tutored there over the past five years.

Before he had time to catch his breath Stoker turned twenty and was much in demand, first as a junior for crews requiring multiple security men and then, with more and more positive references, on a one-to-one basis. Where the rich and famous found themselves unable to use trusted lieutenants, stymied for reasons as varied as visa difficulties or family emergencies the erudite woman at the agency would call Stoker up and ask him to step in. Soon the bodyguard was accompanying European dignitaries on their visits to Downing Street, shadowing American actors as they emerged into the flashbulb shock of film premieres, waiting outside studios as award-winning singers recorded their promotional slots at the BBC.

His mother was thrilled and pleased, Valerie familiar with many of those celebrities her son protected, scanning the gossip magazines for references to foreign glamour that would be coming to her neighbourhood. In her excitement Val came to see her son as a vital adjunct to these worthy and stylish individuals. Alongside their regular discussions about medical symptoms, she would expound at length to ageing friends on the sensibilities of the rich and famous, faking insider knowledge. Yes, agreed Stoker when he returned to the family home from that flat he'd taken in West Ham, he supposed it must be exciting and fun, he was glad for himself as well. These were the tacit pleasantries of the acquiescent son. In truth Stoker wasn't particularly reflective, he possessed few opinions either way. There was enough money to pay for his favourite luxuries, all the cars and designer clothes he wanted, so the bodyguard assumed he was happy.

Six years into his career and Stoker was charged with minding a Brixton-based client, one of the leading lights in the capital's burgeoning two-step scene. This vocalist was visiting a central London club for its grand opening, arriving in a limousine bedecked by more jewellery than the bodyguard had ever seen, even on a woman. The black man, several inches shorter than his minder's five-nine frame, was constantly checking his hair and outfit, and beside him Stoker experienced the first of what were to be many realizations over the course of the night. The world was here to reinforce this guy's image, and Stoker was part of that conspiracy. One burly guard laid on by the record company to help maintain a choreographed sense of danger. From the heavily policed live appearances to the profane albums with their endless boasts of lyrical proficiency, prowess with the *laydeez* and his mastery of guns, it was all a front, at right angles to reality. Stoker had heard this man's singles cluttering up the airwaves, with their overdubbed shoot-outs and murders of supporting characters. M.C. Tiger hardly seemed to care that he came from a country where such weapons were illegal, where contact with those *glocks* he claimed to collect would result in a lengthy prison sentence.

Stoker was still thinking about the pretence of his client's life when he stepped out of the limousine and checked around for anyone who might be out to get this idiot. The only guns Philip, as his parents knew him, would ever encounter were the ones he used when paintballing. This star would have soon redefined his relationship with Gatling if he spent some time in an American slum, wouldn't last five minutes in the company Stoker's father used to run with. Not without soiling his underwear.

The bodyguard slipped his dark glasses on and observed the squealing pubescent girls of every hue trying to attract Tiger's attention from behind a stretch of metal barriers. Looking patently ridiculous in a huge fake-fur coat and purple pantaloons, the star coolly refused to acknowledge his fans, sauntering past those friends of the famous who made up the queue. Some of the celebrity groupies had been waiting for hours to get in and Stoker wondered, not for the first time, at the priorities of his fellow humans. For reasons he couldn't discern Stoker had recently begun to spend portions of time contemplating existence, finding a satisfaction in turning his mind onto recent events and feelings, even if the conclusions he reached weren't always positive. When Stoker's first long-term relationship ended a few weeks ago, Tasmin increasingly frustrated at her boyfriend's indifference to commitment and unwillingness to *emote*, he had taken to leaving the television off and spending evenings in a Vodka-induced reverie. Part of the inspiration came from the bubbling sorrow of a recent bereavement, but there was growing dissatisfaction in the work of his days to contend with as well. After more than half a decade Stoker was experiencing what most people undergo earlier, the questioning of values that comes when the novelty of a sought after career wears off. He had seen it happen in others but never before paused long enough to realise the appeal of being an escort to the stars could end up as just another form of repetitive drudgery.

Before the entrance to the club Philip tapped his silver-plated cane against the steps impatiently as the doorman checked his lists for an 'M.C. Tiger'. Beside this bouncer stood another man with folded arms and a neutral expression, strands of murky colouration extending his the shirt collar up the veins of his neck. Stoker removed his sunglasses for a better look and his suspicions were confirmed. Glenn Jones gave a nod that told the other man he

180

was remembered before allowing minder and client into the building.

Once in the club those high-pitched cries from young girls were replaced by a piledriving beat from the obscure bootleg spun by a superstar DJ in his booth. Philip passed his accoutrements to Stoker and entered the throng, greeting clubbers he recognized as well as the women who were sluttish enough for his tastes. The escort checked that great fluffball of a jacket in the cloakroom and went to get a soft drink. Around him women with thigh-high boots and cowboy hats mingled beside men in Saville Row suits and gold cufflinks. Stoker felt neither lust nor envy, leaning against the bar he twirled the cane as if it were a worthless baton. In the final weeks of his father's life the cancer had spread all through the old man's system, as pervasive as blood. Stoker Snr. could barely speak, but when the words did come not a breath was wasted. The patient gave thanks to his wife for her love, expressed pride at his son's success, told the pair not to be sad, he had experienced a good enough life. A few days before his death the man stopped talking altogether and his round-the-clock nursing soon became superfluous. The fight left the flesh along with his spirit, to be redeemed or lost. After his coffin was lowered into the ground Stoker stayed at the graveside and picked up a spade, the son burying his father himself, water pouring from him in the heat of the day.

From his vantage point above the dance floor Stoker watched Philip move into the throng and take up a spot between two of the most exposed women. Stoker had earned his father's respect by the time of his death. Both parents would look at the wealth, hear of work offers too numerous for one man, see the circles their son moved in, and see only success, a secure future. Nothing would honour the old man's memory like his son prospering in this same line of work for the rest of his days. The bodyguard rubbed at eyes that had begun to well. He needed to banish thoughts of his dad if he didn't want the floodwaters to breach that mental dam he'd erected. Before Stoker the rap star began to dry hump a blonde in time to the music, the woman in heels that made her at least six inches taller than Philip. His ridiculous movement encapsulated the problem Stoker had with the destiny wished upon him. The vast majority of his charges were worthless, utterly inadequate human beings. From the racist diplomat to the tantrum-throwing diva, movie stars who played sadistic mind-games for their own amusement to that idiot who looked like he had misunderstood sex education and was trying to achieve satisfaction *through* the bimbo's minidress, Stoker wasn't willing to take a bullet or a knife, or even a raw egg, for any of them. This refusal flew in the face of the industry's credo, to protect a client at all costs, but the bodyguard simply didn't care any more.

These thoughts continued buzzing around Stoker's head as Jones arrived at the bar, shook the younger man by the hand and ordered a beer with vodka chaser.

"So, you hit the big time then didya?"

"I guess so."

"'Ere, what's that Tiger bloke like in real life?"

"He's a cunt. His real name's Philip."

Jones laughed uproariously. "Sure looks like a pillock."

"They all are, you're well out of it mate." Stoker went on to list some of the character traits he'd been forced to deal with for the entertainment of his acquaintance. Descriptions of the actress who refused to *do* stairs, the presenter leaving his entourage while frequenting a West London whorehouse, the singer whose arse-cheeks were insured because that was where her talent truly lay. The doorman was greatly amused; laughing loudly as he supped at the beer. When Stoker inquired after him in return he learned Jones had been "headhunted" from a rival club thanks to his proficiency tackling their drug problems. Jones mercilessly ousted anyone caught dealing inside. It was his responsibility to ensure the only pills consumed on the premises were sold by security staff for the profit of management.

"Listen Stoker, you want anything you only have to ask. First sample's free to my mates."

"Better not." The minder kept his distrust of chemicals to himself and pointed at his charge. "I'm working."

"Yeah right, better get back myself." Jones drained his pint before collecting a napkin and pen from the bar. "Listen mate, you don't sound too chuffed with the present line of work if you don't mind me sayin'. Write us yer phone number on that and anything comes up I'll give you a call, alright?"

While Stoker didn't fancy employment that involved kicking the crap out of drug dealers, he didn't wish to be impolite and scribbled down a contact number. Jones finished his short, shook the younger man's hand and left, promising to be in touch.

Stoker thought nothing of the incident for weeks, time when he steadily grew even wearier of the work. The gaps between his acceptance of assignments became longer and longer, Stoker choosing to live off savings and what money his father had bequeathed. When the phone rang one Friday morning Stoker assumed it was the agency, after him for another few days nursemaiding. Instead he heard Jones' unmistakable tones at the other end of the line.

"'Ello mate, got a job lined up if yer interested."

Stoker turned the volume down on his TV and spoke tiredly. "It's not door work is it?"

"Nah, I've packed all that in. Old mate of mine needs two blokes to live and work on his farm for a bit. All sorts of different stuff, no animals or shit-spreading."

Jones informed his acquaintance of the pay-rate on offer and Stoker told Glenn he was interested. Within an hour a tattooed figure in an old Volvo swung into the car park of Stoker's apartment block to collect him.

What struck Stoker about Douglas Elliott on arrival in Cornwall was the similarity in appearance to those forty-something Hollywood actors he had protected and deferred to over the last six years. But unlike those stars, who were invariably short-tempered and egotistical, this man welcomed people to his estate with hospitality and good cheer, showing the pair around his house with a proprietorial burst of pride. On their lengthy journey to the farm Jones had alluded to Elliott's role as a commanding officer in the Falklands war, the men having served time on the islands together. Stoker considered this shared history as he slackened into one of the sofas in the farm's lounge. There was definitely something about Douglas that evoked the rigidity of the military, a comradeship and decisive quality that had undoubtedly served him well in the field. Elliott treated his new recruits on this project with respect then outlined the world they would be creating.

First Douglas explained his faith, how he had found a purpose during the nineties by devoting himself to the word. Now they had the Goddess, there was no looking back. She had foretold Newtopia, seen it would become a thriving outpost, one unique community for those who lived by her visions. The exceptions would be Stoker and Jones who weren't expected to find belief, that

183

wasn't their priority. But for as long as the pair worked in the farm they would have to abide by its rules. In addition to the laws outlined by *The Spirit Of Nagasaki* booklets he gave them, the men wouldn't be allowed to speak of their work with followers, nor would they have the freedom to exploit devotees sexually, no matter how alluring some of the women may prove. Douglas made it clear that a failure to comply with these dictates would result in the instant cessation of their employment. Skimming the leaflet quickly, Stoker found the rules of the compound straightforward enough. He could certainly handle the lack of drink or drugs on-site, and the man wasn't averse to leaving every kind of media behind. He nodded to Jones who signalled their agreement to this new employer.

Pleased with the concurrence, Douglas shook their hands and served afternoon tea, the trio toasting their future in S.O.N. with Earl Grey and Battenberg. Elliott spoke of the people to be rescued from unfortunate lives as well as their own projected spiritual and fiscal gains before leading the pair upstairs for a brief introduction to the Goddess.

Rebecka received them in her quarters, reclining in an antique oak chair with a trace of amusement playing on her symmetrical features. Stoker took the slender hand he was offered and attempted to greet the woman in a relaxed way, the pitch of his voice going awry for the first time since his teenage years, an unsteadiness that betrayed the attraction. The man found her exquisitely beautiful. More than that, Rebecka's knowing presence seemed to bathe the whole room in voluptuous promise. Simply from the way this Goddess held herself Stoker understood the woman to be a dominant and rewarding sexual partner. He had spent hours pouring over lad mag polls on the most desirable females in the world, yet none of those tanned beauties cast this kind of spell. The Goddess glowed with the potency of her fiefdom, empowered by possibility, her enlightened home of Newtopia coming for them all.

Thinking about her later that day as he prepared for bed on what would prove his final night in the East End, Stoker struggled to pinpoint what it was about the woman that caused such a passionate response. Rebecka had reversed the romantic trend of his life whereby the further into his twenties Stoker progressed, the younger his sexual partners became. Teenagers were more easily won over than girls his age, could be taught about masculine priorities and manipulated into behaving in what Stoker considered the correct manner. They weren't hung up on engagement rings or mortgages or meeting the family. But his feelings for this woman were completely different. She might have been ten or even twenty years older than Stoker, but he was still drawn to her like a vulture to carrion. As his life on the farm progressed, the ex-bodyguard came to believe he was getting closer to the Goddess. Yet he would only ever know her platonically, and perhaps this was what kept him under her control until the end. Maybe the fracturing of illusions that comes with requited love would have rendered the feeling weaker than its unrequited counterpart. Whatever the case, in those first minutes when Stoker met Rebecka any doubts he might have harboured about his change in lifestyle disappeared under an avalanche of longing, the need for a role in her life.

After a restless night Stoker packed his belongings, arranged for the flat's contents to be put into storage and phoned his mother, informing her answerphone that she might not hear from him for a while but there was no need to worry. Then he and Jones were back on the road, anticipating the clean air and peaceful way of life awaiting them in deepest Cornwall, Glenn singing along to mindless radio tunes in that working class brogue of his, sounding as if he was deliberately parodying the adolescent vocalists.

At Newtopia the pair were shown to their room, located opposite the quarters Douglas shared with Rebecka, and given new mobile phones, specifically deployed to receive instructions from the leaders, folding away to black rectangles three inches across. The following morning it became clear Jones would be at the beck and call of the Goddess while Douglas made use of his other employee. Stoker envied both men at first, painfully jealous of the time they got to spend in Rebecka's presence, but the feeling passed as he became absorbed by his tasks. The man got over his frustration in time and came to perceive the Goddess as a kind of elemental force. She belonged to no one, and all the men of this movement trailed in her wake equally.

Besides, it was impossible to be angry with Elliott, the man was too courteous and civil, meeting with Stoker on equal terms that morning of his second day to discuss their plan of action. Douglas explained that Stoker had been selected to assist in the more intellectually rigorous assignments since it was immediately obvious he was the more mentally gifted of the two workers. Flattered, Stoker listened carefully as Elliott described the process by which personal testaments and handwritten studies of the Bible came in from Jon Foulkes, the head of the major filtration base in London. To ascertain whether the devotees who composed these works might fit in with Newtopian society, it was necessary to make two separate studies of their pieces. The first involved a psychological interpretation of its content that would be conducted by Douglas himself, but it was the second phase Stoker was being asked to undertake. His work involved an analysis of their handwriting, seeking out positive personality traits and potential warning signs. When the employee agreed, Elliott gathered together a pile of books on the science of graphology and asked Stoker to study them carefully before he began.

Over the following weeks, as Jones supervised the construction of two opaque greenhouses on the farmland, Stoker made copious notes, coming to be confident in his cross-referencing of scribbled summations against the work of London-based followers. In time he grasped the subtleties of the formulae and, with the help of Elliott's guidelines on what makes a disciple, Stoker began constructing profiles of people who were suited to Newtopia.

He checked for flying high-strokes that indicated spirituality and idealism, the lines implying aspiration toward a higher power and a desire to change the world. Stoker looked for right-pulled underloops and a left slant to the script, recognizing that the smaller the text, the better suited its author would be for the devout life, tiny but legible words pointing to an underdeveloped ego and the concentration span necessary for repetitive tasks. Marking out examples in red for future reference, Stoker soon became proficient enough to spot negative inflections at a glance. He noted the vanity and self-interest suggested by sudden flourishes or over-exaggerated capitals, rejected the diminished middle zone of independent thinkers, became wary of writing in the angular style and felt alarm bells go off in his head at the sight of a random slope. Douglas didn't want self-centred, uncooperative, or emotionally unstable acolytes on his farm, no matter how fervent their belief in *The Spirit Of Nagasaki*, and it was up to Stoker to weed these types out through analysis of their unofficial applications.

When the three studies merged into an overwhelmingly positive picture; where Jon's personal observations, Stoker's graphological profile, and Elliott's combination of psychiatric insight and gut feeling suggested a candidate should be brought to the next level, Foulkes was contacted with the good news. This new disciple then found themself closer to the Goddess, allocated a living space of their own inside Newtopia. By this process the rooms of the farmhouse soon filled with delighted men and women, the ideals of the faith realized in this place of farming and prayer. They worked every day tilling the fields and planting seeds, strangers who formed a family while the two employees maintained the hemp crop and, back East, more buildings were leased to cope with the rising influx.

Every few weeks Jones and Stoker travelled to the capital to assist Douglas in the shows he gave to convince the unsure or curious. Along with predictable requirements such as the operation of lights and supplying props, the pair had to remove those who were most touched by the display, clear up afterwards and help with a more covert design. Each member who paid a subscription for the S.O.N. prayer sessions had their data run through Jon's PC for a personal and financial check. This process provided background information for the shows, and an indication of potential targets for the next level. If the figures gleaned from restricted access databases and company web sites interested the faith, they would make a priority of pursuing the individual behind them. This casual follower might work a lucrative job, possess a tendency for high expenditure, or inhabit one of the city's most desirable areas. Any combination of affluent details could single a subscriber out for special attention.

The evening before a show these two thickset men, their sturdy frames ameliorated by expensive suits and the angelic little boy who accompanied them, would appear at the door of the single men or women the research threw back as prosperous. Stoker spoke first, explained they were visiting every registered follower to ensure these casuals attended the following night, although in truth the trio only ever visited the elite few. Those at home expressed joy at being thought of by the Goddess personally, and invariably her representatives were invited inside. Within a few seconds Stoker had a mental evaluation of the home, its decor, furnishings, antiques and general style. If their previous research matched his appraisal, the host living a high life in this home redolent of expensive tastes and personal wealth, they would cast out the net.

As the visitors took tea Stoker would dominate their conversation, limiting the subject matter to tomorrow's performance, sometimes giving a brief and mendacious description of his own "*induction*" into the faith if the homeowner was particularly exhortative. While they talked the boy would ask if he could use the toilet and after receiving directions this fourteen-year-old nephew of Elliott's went through the bathroom cabinets and scribbled down the names of whatever prescription drugs he found there. Upon the boy's return this group would quickly excuse themselves, request their host say hello once in the auditorium tomorrow and leave for another port of call.

Come the following evening Stoker and Jones wandered the hall's assembled crowd, memorizing the seats of those they visited the day before in order to direct Douglas, the Reverend having been briefed on the ailments and interests of these medicated attendees. In the midst of his oration Elliott would point out the targeted individuals, call them up on the stage and reveal an uncanny knowledge of their lives. Sufferings and passions, past failures and current hopes, his mixture of deduction and educated guesswork was followed by Douglas jamming his fingers into the optic nerve of a volunteer to register "divine light" or pressing both hands against their ears, bringing about a buzz he called "the hum of God". By the end of these theatrics the prosperous floaters were convinced of the Reverend's divinity, eager to donate everything they owned in return for a place on one of those bases and the everlasting love of the Goddess.

Stoker understood the success of this elaborate confidence trick although he disliked the preparatory work, research that often involved a hard slog through unsavoury conditions. Trawling the rubbish of casuals to learn of their background and habits was an unpleasant business, while the paper-based waste they had to sift through after it was removed from *The Daily Class* that time proved interminable. In this particular instance they collected documents from the tabloid offices as a precaution after Foulkes had his attention drawn to derogatory remarks about the cult in the newspaper's editorial. From these published remarks Jon deduced that someone at the rag was investigating the church so Stoker and Jones were ordered to spend long hours sifting through stolen reports until they came across a document bearing the phrase "The Spirit

Of Nagasaki". A female reporter on the *Class* was named in connection with this piece and Douglas congratulated them on the result, encouragement that almost made up for the endless hours Stoker spent studying pages whose illicit nature didn't meliorate their dullness. The Reverend Elliott believed that file to be an important find, something the church could use to beat a journalist at her own game and simultaneously counteract negative press. Not only that, the Schwitz woman proved to be so choked up by her subsequent evisceration at the hands of the Reverend, she shocked everyone in the faith by *demanding* they let her inside. Stoker found this outcome rather funny, Elliott remarking on it more than once during the journey back to Newtopia as Jones looked on silently. Who could have predicted the show would end like that?

Back at the farm converts continued to arrive as the six-month gestation period elapsed and the crops grew ready. Stoker went on decoding the scrawled life stories and religious experiences of new recruits in a hundred different styles of handwriting, and despite the employee trying to limit his attention, simply deconstructing the shape and flow, he couldn't help some of the most powerful testaments permeating his skull. What the essays had in common, along with a delight at how the households were run and sycophantic compliments for individual Shepherds, was an overpowering sense of the Goddess. These writers were moved ontologically by her message; the devotees suffered a primitive craving for Rebecka's way of life, hearts crying out to be enlightened. These poetic declarations of a total willingness to follow this woman they might never have met inspired Stoker to seek out the power of her manifesto himself, to see what all the fuss was about. Within her doctrines he found an unerring enunciation of his own instincts, disgust for the world of ostentation that had employed him for so long, a desire for some greater satisfaction than observing your elders' wishes until the dying day. Rebecka's alternative made sense to Stoker, he felt foolish at not finding this way sooner. Her texts filled him with a sense of loss at the years of ungodly priorities, time wasted protecting the contemptible.

Stoker rang Rebecka to request an audience and was immense in his gratitude when she granted him an hour in her presence. The man went to that upper room and poured out his remorse to a listening Goddess, asking if he was hell-bound for failing to find Jesus earlier. Rebecka smiled down at his fretful face, moved onto her knees and laid a hand on his moist forehead. Stoker was healed by her touch, the man awash with love and purity, so gratified he could have remained in that position for hours, this connection calming his soul while a gentle whisper reached his ears. There were reassurances from the Goddess, how the mercy of our Lord was for everyone, forgiveness allowed His children to make their mistakes and be redeemed. The important step had been Stoker's renouncement of his past when he came to work at Newtopia. Rebecka condemned that public life he left behind in the Biblical terms she would later revisit for the benefit of Trina Callow. The Goddess depicted the existences of the famous as utter darkness, said when they fell, for fall they must, ignorance and vanity would not let them realise what had caused the stumble, the lessons of Christ squandered on every one. Stoker could hardly breath, such was the accumulated wave of sensation that washed over him; relief and hope, happiness and a rising desire, the need for the warmth of this nearby form.

"It is the way of all those who live apart from *The Spirit Of Nagasaki*." Rebecka looked up at the young man, her hands remaining on his face. "They have failed to acknowledge God so He has given them up to their way of thinking. They are filled with every kind of wickedness and villainy, living out days of greed and malice." She rose to face Stoker, the tips of their noses almost touching as Rebecka spoke under her breath. "But you are no longer in their midst my brother. Instead you are here, where His children belong. Within the love of the Goddess, a love from which no man may cleave."

Stoker returned twice after that, his heart pounding furiously for hours before each session, Rebecka enrapturing him like a natural phenomenon. She expounded on her people and their role in the church, how they would all soon be called to Jesus, set apart from that corrupt world outside, a place that was about to end in God-given catastrophe. The Goddess had foreseen the fires of damnation, illustrating her point by recounting Bible stories from memory. Stoker found himself hypnotized by her forcefulness and command of the good book. Whatever parable Rebecka related as proof of her contentions; the tales of Abraham and Noah, from Moses to Jesus Himself, she could bring to life every expression and emotion, describe the motivations and morality of each figure. To Stoker it seemed as if she had witnessed the events of the Bible first-hand, playing out before her eyes, like the woman was close enough to God to make His word flesh. The uncontrived ease as Rebecka assumed the mantle of interpreter for this ancient text astonished Stoker, made him feel ridiculous at focussing on her beauty when they had first met. He couldn't imagine how the sageness of this Goddess would fail to win anyone over.

The game of soccer drifted to its end, legs growing tired under a sky that promised rain. Stoker watched the six men saunter off to the farmhouse, joining those who awaited their lunch. He felt no hunger. If Stoker wanted to eat he could take the truck to a nearby village, visit a cashpoint and collect provisions for one. Unfortunately the disciples they weren't privy to his advantages. Since Newtopia's population virtually doubled overnight the stored supplies had proven woefully inadequate. Yesterday's lunch consisted of some weak vegetable soup and a hunk of stale crust, latecomers finding even the bread had run out. This paucity of rations was a consequence of the summons, a ruling that came immediately after Rebecka appeared from her quarters for the first time in weeks, leaving the grounds to join Douglas on some kind of trip. On their return the Reverend came directly to Stoker and Jones, telling the employees that the London end of S.O.N. would be shutting down within days.

Douglas wasn't wholly convinced by this resolution and the man shared some of his misgivings with Stoker. The Reverend Elliott feared his farm would be overrun by converts who could contribute little to the operation, the failure of the vetting process worried him. The Reverend thought Rebecka relied too heavily on the snap judgements of filtration base leaders in taking vital decisions about who should make the trip. Nodding silently, Stoker understood Elliott's unease, but found himself siding with the other acolytes in his belief that any ruling from the Goddess should be obeyed unquestioningly, her orders could only be for their ultimate good. In truth Douglas had become gradually more disgruntled and touchy since the wedding ceremony, that night when he was forced into the bedroom of Jones and Stoker, the latter suspecting his employer's worsening crankiness was as much about personal issues as the good of the church. Everyone could see the Goddess had withdrawn her affections from the Reverend, while the unpleasant atmosphere of rivalry and distaste that arose whenever Douglas and the recently arrived Jon Foulkes were in the same room was another source of needless tension for their church.

191

Firing up another cigarette, Stoker watched Jones and the grey-haired Nolan approach from the main building. These ruptures in leadership bothered Stoker, particularly after the industrious harmony by which Newtopia had been run so far, but he believed the movement would continue to thrive as long as Rebecka remained in control. Nolan reached the seated Stoker and spoke cheerily about the tannoy system they had rigged up, describing the specifications of those speakers which were fitted on every building and inside most rooms. The set-up gave audibility to a voice throughout the compound, and the older man was clearly proud of his achievement. Stoker listened politely and offered Jones a smoke as the tattooed man sat against the barn without a word, lighting his cigarette and failing to respond to Nolan's remarks. His fellow employee hadn't heard Jonesy speak for over a month now, although he still made plenty of noise in bed at night, kept his fellow worker awake with the snortings and eructations of his body. Lying there at night, Stoker often wondered about the monkish quiet in which Glenn spent his days now, a silence that had begun shortly after their last trip to a Cornish club for recreational purposes and which stretched on through the whole of November. This development was a strange one for a man who had always enjoyed jabbering at others in his mutated cockney argot, but if Jones wanted to let his vocal cords atrophy that was up to him. Stoker just hoped he would be more forthcoming whenever they managed another social trip. He wasn't about to let some weird vow curtail these increasingly irregular nights out.

A brusque Elliott strolled over to the three men, requested Nolan's assistance to test the new technology from Rebecka's quarters. Ordering Stoker to alert them by phone if the sound quality failed, the Reverend set off toward the farmhouse with the older man in tow. The two figures that remained seated continued to sit in silence until a crackle from the other side of the structure drew them up, Stoker and Jones walking to the corner where a plastic-covered speaker had been fitted earlier in the day. They stood under the box, staring down at the ground as the voice of Douglas reached their ears, *testing, testing*. A few seconds later he was replaced by the Goddess, her words strong and sure in the chilly air, an intonation that contained the musical lilt which slipped into her voice when she orated to disciples.

"Hello loved ones, what you hear is an inaugural address from my chambers at the very height of Newtopia. From this moment on you will be hearing from me regularly. There are many announcements coming over the next few weeks."

In the doorway of the farmhouse kitchen Jim and Joan shushed their children. The boys ceased their chasing game while Trina gathered Chastity and Niagara to the benches, embracing both girls against the burgeoning evidence of their unborn sibling.

"To all of you who undertook the most important decision in your life and decided to move here from the perdition of London, let me reassure you; you have made the right choice. I know *The Spirit Of Nagasaki* is strong in every one of us, and believe me when I say your reward is imminent. I have seen our ascension and it is coming sooner than I could have dared hope."

In her top floor quarters the dark-eyed woman spoke into the microphone that was set upon her table. Nolan and Douglas stood over her with serious faces, the older man monitoring the system for blips with the Reverend seemed more concerned by the course this speech was taking. Behind them Gareth reclined on Rebecka's double bed, oblivious to everything save the way light played on the ceiling.

"Each of you knows the story of our faith by heart, how the blessed virgin came to me on the beach and showed us the consecrated path. A few days ago I returned to that bay where enlightenment was first found, hoping to discover the Lord's opinion on our progress. Once more I was subjected to that most holy of visitations, the mother Mary assuring me our work here was righteous. She blessed our achievements, calling this family of faith more important than ever, now the day of reckoning approaches."

Queuing for his midday meal, Pete felt the arm of Simon rest upon his shoulder. The man had grown weaker since they journeyed here, was unable to stand unsupported for long periods now. Pete took the weight on his back as, further down the line, Ruth and Nicky locked hands impulsively, the women shutting their eyes and letting their souls be sought out, cleansed by the words.

"She told me the Lord would pass judgement on our race as He did before. The Virgin said I must prepare my flock and gather them to me in readiness. For it is *The Spirit Of Nagasaki* who must lead the new society that emerges from the wrath of God. Only those who follow the way of the S.O.N.

193

will be equipped for this dawning of a new civilization from the ashes of the old. We alone shall be called upon to rebuild our shattered earth for future generations."

Naked under the blanket of a single bed, supine in this dormitory that no longer felt welcoming, Jon experienced a rush of blood to his loins as that feminine voice rang in his ears. Foulkes watched Jane wander across the room and his tumescence faded. Since returning to the domain of the Goddess, Jon's ability to satisfy this girl had evaporated, disappeared along with the man's self-belief.

"Outside our peaceful sanctuary forces are massing against one another. Entire races rush to destruction, forgetting the lesson God gave the warlike, those words of Isaiah: *Nation shall not lift up sword against nation, neither shall they learn war any more.*"

A hiss of interference, like far-off gunfire, before Rebecka's voice returned. "I was granted a vision of the coming rain my brothers and sisters. This apocalypse will be horrendous for unbelievers. We alone shall prevail. We, the chosen ones. The pioneers of Jesus."

Greg stirred the steaming cauldron of broth while Josh stood behind a table filled with bowls and cutlery. Before them Bree waited with Beth, the girls unwilling to receive their meagre portions until the Goddess had finished her benediction.

"One month from today the path we have struggled to cultivate will finally lead us to fulfillment. As the world moves into its new year every force which would denounce or oppose our rule shall be wiped from the face of God's earth. All those sinners who laughed at our way or feared this union will be no more. Those who were taught to hate *The Spirit Of Nagasaki*, just as before us they learned other hatreds, will disintegrate into the annals of history. I have witnessed the clean slate on which we mark our claim my loved ones, seen it as clearly as I see the garden of Newtopia from my window." The woman drew a breath, upping the volume of her voice a notch.

"LET US NOT GIVE UP THE HABIT OF MEETING EACH OTHER MY CHILDREN. INSTEAD, LET US ENCOURAGE ONE ANOTHER ALL THE MORE. FOR YOU SEE, THE DAY OF THE LORD IS COMING NEARER."

Rain was falling on the two men who sat against the barn, stringy locks of hair sticking to Stoker's face as his skin grew damp. Jones rose and extended a hand to his colleague who accepted the gesture, letting his body be pulled up by the arm. Then the pair turned and left to find cover.

Chapter Eight

Someone else was working the inquiry desk today, a sinewy man with wire-rimmed glasses and the outsize head of the encephalitic. He didn't look the type to grant unlimited credit on library services, and Joe didn't have the energy to explain his situation again so he paid for the printouts up front. Drafting the report had taken much of the previous afternoon and on into the night, but it was worth the effort, officializing Stoker's statement to rid himself of the facts. Upon leaving the station Sweeney had collected his laptop from the boot of the Carlton and set to work, feeling relief as he read the text back late yesterday evening. He'd achieved what they sent him out here to do, got the blunt facts of this cult's spiral into eschatology and mass death set out comprehensively and in plain English. His prose was starkly brutal in places and that couldn't be helped. The facts Joe worked from were too important to be adulterated.

Inserting silver coins into the machine's slot, Sweeney took a copy of the six-page document before faxing the original to the Critical Incident Division, for the attention of Assistant Commissioner Brett Thomson of the Specialist Operations Department. From there Thomson's secretary would send the report to Sweeney's other superiors, the heads of the serious crime division. These men would then have until late afternoon to study the text, by which time Sweeney aimed to be back at New Scotland Yard. Of course he could have e-mailed the transcript directly, but the likelihood his missive would have remained unseen by men away from their computer screens was too high. Even in the branches of police that were spearheading the force into the twenty-first century old habits died hard, procedure remaining much the same as it always had, despite the evolution of technology. Where documentation was concerned a hard copy went to the boss in question on the date requested, a paper trail whereby pages could be studied without the need for a screen, read on the way to meetings or conferences if time was at a premium.

Sweeney went over his words one last time before taking his leave of the public library. Once he started to talk Stoker had been unable to stop. It was as if, after uncorking, months of these fermenting observations could only foam out of his mouth, an unstoppable flow. The entire personal history of the witness spilled out over two hours and twenty minutes, Joe having to excuse himself twice when the tape in his Dictaphone was about to run out. Stoker hadn't suspected he was being recorded, despite the faint click when Sweeney failed to catch the end in time, so absorbed was the captive in his story's cathartic surge. The Investigator found no reason to disbelieve this man's confession. Joe had taken hundreds of statements down the years and he knew how to recognise when a witness was withholding information or glossing a story to present himself favourably. This man behaved in too defeated a way to be lying. In his version of events, Stoker came out as badly as anyone.

The fax machine beeped once to indicate a successful transmission and Joe placed the document back in his file. This account was one preliminary overview, an essay that would form the basis of future investigation, both local and national, as well as documentary evidence against the unwitting prisoner. Stoker was an accessory to murder at the very least, but Sweeney was careful to recommend a full psychiatric evaluation before he was forced to answer any charges. Merely absorbing the man's story had an anaesthetising effect on Joe, and afterwards he felt numbed through to the inside, hardly aware of his ongoing aches and pains. If the simple act of hearing what happened had an effect like this on the interrogator, he hated to think what Stoker was going through, that man who had actually lived out the story he described, actively contributing to the horror.

Joe collected his papers and walked out into the frosty day, the beginnings of what forecasters promised to be the coldest February in years. He crossed the high street and threw the files into his car, the work landing on the back seat beside those belongings he had assembled that morning. After hurriedly packing Sweeney had stumbled down to discover more statements awaiting him. Four of the interred corpses were found to be in the early stages of malnutrition, while another dead man was H.I.V. positive. The pathologist noted that this man, who had suffered previous convictions for child sex offences, would have died from Kaposi's Sarcoma within weeks had the cult not intervened. That none of the other victims suffered from this virus supported Stoker's contention regarding promiscuity in the faith. Although Yately the pathologist noted that two females tested positive for chlamydia while three more were hypertrophic, spontaneously aborting at the moment of death.

In relation to the leaders, further information was starting to filter through about the deceased men. Jon Foulkes had once run a logistics company and continued to be retained by the corporation in an 'advisory capacity' until his move to Cornwall. There was little of interest in his personal life beyond an estranged wife who refused to talk with frustrated policemen. More intriguing was the flamboyant individual who owned the farm. Douglas Elliott had spent much of the eighties in the army, ultimately rising to the rank of major as a result of several heroic acts during the Falklands conflict. By the end of the decade Elliott had left the forces and was beginning to dabble in religion-themed trickery; promising heaven by mail order, spending time with American evangelists and booking small venues around the West Country, events that now looked like dry runs for his role in the cult.

While absorbing this information Joe forced down the grease of the guest house breakfast and reflected on the state of play as he saw it. There were five obvious culprits. Two were dead at the hands of the beast they had created, one safely under lock and key, and a final pair still out there. Yet the deeper Sweeney looked, the more this blame extended, until everyone mentioned by the witnesses came away with dirt on their hands. Without people who were willing to be led, or the unquestioning support of men who could have put a stop to it, this religion might never have grown into its final horror, the climactic engulfing.

Sweeney moved into the police station and shook Dickson's hand, clearing his temporary office of ashtrays and stained mugs so that the Devon and Cornwall Police could appropriate this space. He left in a surfeit of courtesy, thank yous for officers on the front desk and a promise for the Inspector that he would receive a copy of the report as soon as Sweeney's bosses gave their approval.

Outside Joe lit a cigarette and watched a black Labrador halt its owner at the kerbside. The dog waited for a milk float to pass before leading the blind man across the road. The sight stirred an old memory in Sweeney, taking the Investigator back to a situation he had dreamt about several times since it happened, waking up afterwards each time agitated and downhearted.

A couple of years after Joe moved to London he found himself growing painfully disillusioned, both by the city and his role there, a failure to plug the tide of scum that rose up to devour good people, no matter how much effort the police departments put into stemming it. Sweeney had taken to leaving his office for lunch in St. James' Park, finding relief in the innocent wonder of visitors and those immaculately kept gardens where a man might forget the corruption of the city. On this particular afternoon Joe begrudgingly left his spot before the waterfowl when his hour had elapsed and fought back to that glistening building against the race and clutter of London. Once away from the park, Sweeney was stopped in his tracks all of a sudden, stilled by a hopeless sight across the stream of vehicles that thundered along the major thoroughfare. Before Joe a guide dog sat beside its sightless master, men in suits hurrying around them and lorries rushing inches from the creature's nose. The pair waited for a gap in traffic that didn't come, hard enough as it was for a pedestrian to cross there, this street with its kamikaze motorists running red lights and the sirens of approaching emergency vehicles. Hundreds of people were knocked over in London every year, simply because they got fed up waiting for spaces that didn't appear. Here was a single hound, lingering in the vain hope the road would clear while safeguarding its blind master. Joe watched them stuck there for several minutes, the nearest pedestrian crossing a quarter of a mile away and no let up in the onrush of cars that might allow the pair a window across. After what seemed like an eternity Sweeney became thoroughly depressed by the dog's impossible task, so many sights and sounds assailing that canine from every direction, he turned to force an escape route through the throng. Racing off to his workplace, Joe tried to cast out the futility of that scene he'd escaped as grit and smoke stung at his eyes.

The driver's side of Sweeney's black Carlton unlocked automatically in response to the electronic signal from his key fob. That desperate sleaze-ridden hole of a city, a place that paused in its misguided purpose for no one, was where Joe had to return this January afternoon. London, a town where he lived and worked and rarely found respite from the mad scramble to exist, every day assaulted by the madness to some degree, like that poor dog charged with the unachievable. Only when he travelled somewhere like Shelton did it become clear to Joe Sweeney that a man should not live that way. Sweeney turned his key and listened to the engine purr into life. He would delay the journey for half an hour, they would have to wait. Turning the Carlton away from the eastbound road, the Investigator drove out of Shelton.

The distant farm gave out vibrations of the atrocity, a radiation tragic places pass to those who know of the inhuman events they've seen. Joe left his car before the swinging gate and moved along the pathway on foot, nodding to Wilson who neared the end of his daily shift blocking the way to this compound. To the unaware it could have been any dilapidated property, farmland abandoned due to penury or failing health. The main house was securely locked while that great barn dominated the skyline, like a gutted abattoir or burnt-out workhouse.

Joe closed his eyes, the restless dead coming into his mind. When he looked again apparitions lingered between the buildings. Smock-clad men worked the fields as ill-defined children played in the shadows of crumbling outhouses. Women laid out benches for lunch, their faces fluid and indistinct. Sweeney observed this activity, feeling removed from the industry before him. From one of the greenhouses a shimmering figure emerged, this shape moving across mounds of earth, soil piled high from recent exhumations. The Investigator felt his heart rate increase as the individual came towards him, this thing not so much ghostly as pronounced and purposeful, its frame becoming clear as the figure grew near. Joe recognized that face, the square jaw and intent expression he had seen the photographs, Douglas moving inexorably closer. This phantom held its pace even within feet of Sweeney. The Investigator didn't breathe, his insides reverberating as dozens of transparent disciples went about their business obliviously. The lips of Elliott contorted and Joe tried to hear what the wraith was saying. In a matter of seconds the apparition would be upon him. Terror surged through Sweeney. What horrendous effect would contact with this wan likeness have on his trembling body? Joe closed his eyes just as Douglas Elliott made impact. There was nothing. Nothing followed the collision but a detached horror, like that of a sleeper woken from life-threatening nightmares.

The silence of the day was broken by the squawking of heavy black birds in far off branches. His eyes flicked open and Joe thrust both hands into his coat pockets. All he saw now was a deserted group of ramshackle structures, isolated acres of nothing. Sweeney fumbled to unscrew the lid the bottle he carried and swallowed two pills down, almost choking as the lack of saliva caused one of the capsules to stick in his throat.

Smoke floated from Wilson's mouth and his gloved hands made flumping noises, smacked together against the cold. The officer heard Joe approach and held up his packet of cigarettes.

"Thank you sergeant." Joe returned the carton and lit his smoke. "How are things going?"

"Not so bad in the daytime." Wilson jerked a thumb toward the farm at his back. "Don't like going up there much after dark. It's bad enough down here at night. You hear things sometimes." His eyes stared off down the track. "What brings you back to this Godforsaken place Joe? There's nothing here now."

"I know." Joe took a long drag. "But I've got what I came for so I'm off to London."

"That's good."

"I just needed to see the place once more, thought it might set something in me at rest." A beetle crawled over Joe's shoe. "Didn't really work, but I needed to come."

Wilson nodded and dropped the butt of his cigarette, it was difficult to tell how many of these words penetrated the policeman's stone-faced exterior. Joe wasn't sure either of them understood what he was trying to say.

"I'm don't know if I'll ever get over this." The sergeant looked to the surrounding countryside. "My wife won't leave me alone about it, says I'm bottling things up like I never have before. I tell her I'm not allowed to talk about the things I've seen but she doesn't believe me. Eileen can't see how my job can be as valuable as our marriage."

"You won't have to keep this hidden much longer, they'll break the news soon. We might even ask the public for help. Two fugitives are on the loose." Sweeney formed a mental picture of his urbane bosses, how they would strive to capture the remaining ringleaders at all costs. Only this result would end the case, provide justice for all. But those ghosts out there would never rest easily, no matter who the courts imprisoned.

"What do you think happened to the souls lost here sergeant? As a religious man yourself?"

"Poor sods." Wilson glanced at Sweeney. "The Lord will see fit to bring them in Joe. I know it sometimes feels like God despises his creations, but we need our faith to be strong, particularly after something like this."

"That's admirable, yes."

"It's a comfort to me and to their relatives, thinking of them waiting for us up in heaven. I'll admit, I've suffered my doubts in the past." Removing his helmet, Wilson smoothed down thinning hair. "But we have to go on trusting in His work, otherwise there's nothing."

"I understand sergeant, goodbye."

They shook hands loosely and Joe made his way back to the car, past hedgerows still white from the recent frosts. In a way Sweeney envied Wilson's pure-hearted belief, Joe's opinions of religious faiths had been devolving for years, the past few days triggering a rush of atheistic sentiment. Now Joe saw religion as a malignant cloud, the driving force and obscuring factor for every act of barbarity humankind conspired to perpetrate. Belief fuelled hatred in those wronged by opposing creeds, murderous insurgents creating a need for vengeance in their surviving children, sons going on to perpetuate the whole sorry mess. A snake of piety writhed in the hearts of men. The human race wasn't warlike from birth but fell victim to a serpent that grew and grew, struck at violent enemies years after their deeds, continued the vicious cycle of sectarianism and intolerance, an ever-spiralling rule of bloodthirsty retribution.

Joe kicked a rock away from the tyre of the Carlton and opened its door. He would have liked to be the sort of person who could swallow what the police forces around the country were feeding bereaved families. Justice was on its way. The guilty parties would be caught, punished in a way that gave loved ones release from the grief. The day of atonement was coming, when Rebecka would stand before them all and be made to answer for what she'd done. Sweeney wanted this scene as much as anyone, but that didn't mean he thought it could happen. With age came a resigned purview of humanity, and Joe had learnt to trust in history rather than the law. The passage of time levelled out polarized sides of this planet, annals restoring equanimity to a system that won a million unrecorded victories every day. And above this success that black fog was always present, lurking at the edge of possibility, ready to engulf people without regard for their everyday hopes or modest triumphs. This cloud would call itself holy war or collateral damage, natural disaster or *The Spirit Of Nagasaki*. And the cloud brought with it a rain of grief and anger, a destructive pattern that residents of this world were powerless to escape.

Accelerating down the empty lane, Joe checked his watch and headed for the carriageway, that direct route to his city of the privileged and unkind, the way home.

Douglas

"For whoever wants to save his life will lose it, but whoever loses his life for me will save it. What good is it for a man to gain the whole world, and yet lose or forfeit his very self?"

- Luke, 9:23

Turning repeatedly in bed, the Reverend wished his body would doze. He was peacefully alone in this room for once but Elliott's mind raced too quickly for sleep. Douglas lay on his back and pulled up the scratchy blankets, wondering if he'd gone too far. Not that it wasn't time someone told Rebecka a few home truths. Foulkes would never say anything, he remained too in thrall to the force of the woman, while those below her in the hierarchy didn't dare question their Goddess. The way Douglas saw it, restoring a little common sense to this set-up fell to him, particularly after today's announcement. It was the latest in a long line of edicts from Rebecka that showed a growing distance from the lives of her people. Since that first speech across the new PA, when her most recent coastal trance led to predictions of the world ending, the Goddess had gone on to issue increasingly arbitrary and wearisome orders, culminating in today's command. All male residents were told to collect spades and dig two parallel pits in a section of land behind the first greenhouse. The purpose of these holes, as clarified in the broadcast, was "to allow God to breathe". It didn't seem to matter that the frost-hardened January ground was all but immovable. Nor did Rebecka care several of the males weren't strong enough to force their shovels into the soil. The Goddess needed these excavations undertaken, holes six feet long and several metres in depth, so undertaken they would be, even at the risk of pneumonia, exhaustion and the exacerbation of existing illnesses.

On hearing this dictate Douglas immediately requested an audience with Rebecka, but by the time she deigned to receive him it was early evening and the pits were finished, one man having to be revived after he collapsed midway through the excavation while others bandaged frostbitten fingers. When confronted with the Reverend's anger at such consequences the Goddess hid behind summations from the good book, fingering that heavy crucifix she had taken to wearing around her neck.

"Good soldiers of Christ Jesus must endure their share of suffering Douglas, you know this as well as I."

"Their share, yes." Elliot was ready for her tactics. He wasn't about to be outdone when it came to knowledge of the Bible. "But this was too much for many of our brothers. Does it not state in Corinthians that the body is made up, not of one part but many? The eye cannot say to the hand: *I don't need you!* And the head cannot say to the feet: *I don't need you!* If one part suffers, then every part suffers with it."

Rebecka sighed, still a striking woman with that taut body and dermal lustre, even if the lines on her face had deepened in degree and those dark patches under her obsidian eyes were several shades blacker since the first prediction. Standing to the right Jon watched proceedings with a studied indifference while behind him the boy called Gareth lay on Rebecka's bed with both feet in the air, flicking through the pages of a magazine. The teenager looked well-fed and unconcerned, dressed in a secular garb of polo shirt and slacks, his demeanour a flagrant breach of several church rules.

"That section of which you speak deals with *Christianity* my Reverend." The Goddess addressed a section of wall behind Elliott's person. "Ours is a new way, as you well know. We are not beholden to those traditions of which you speak."

"The intricacies of the point matter little, my point is this: If we continue to push devotees then more of them will require medical attention. This means bringing outsiders in."

"That is not something you need concern yourself with."

A period of silence gripped the room, broken only by the rustle of pages from the boy on the double bed. Annoyed at the dismissive treatment he was receiving at the hands of Rebecka and frustrated by the life he had come to lead, Douglas looked to Jon for some kind of reaction. From within his greying smock Foulkes stared at them with what Douglas perceived as a trace of mockery in his cerulean eyes.

"Perhaps it is not my place, I have plenty of other worries to contend with." Elliott addressed the implacable Foulkes now. "I take it you are aware we almost lost your girlfriend to forces beyond our control."

Jon grunted under his breath. "She doesn't mean anything to me."

"What Jane does or does not mean to you is beside the point Jon. She was almost kidnapped. Had it not been for Stoker's prompt action in removing the intruders before they reached their hostage she would have been lost. I hate to think what might have happened had those trespassers entered the building." Douglas turned his attention to Rebecka. "Those men knew exactly what they were doing, coming here to abduct the girl and warp her mind against us. We have to ask ourselves how they traced her to Newtopia. I can only assume her *Shepherd* wasn't careful enough." He shot a meaningful glance at Jon who experienced a sudden urge to argue with this embodiment of superior. One look from Rebecka dissuaded him.

"I will investigate your concerns Reverend, you can be sure of that." She touched the glinting metal of her cross. "In the meantime, we must remain on high alert. It is our responsibility to project the appropriate level of vigilance onto our flock."

"So be it. We shall leave the next move of those who would come against us up to speculation." Elliott leaned forward to emphasize his views. "This is not our only worry my Goddess. Each day brings news of other antagonists, be they the Inland Revenue, local authorities, or the continuing threat from the media. Many would make incursions for the purpose of undermining our stronghold. While I field the problems as best I can, these men will not be turned away forever."

The fingers of this woman clawed at her lengthy black hair. "Did the lessons of Christ teach you nothing my Reverend? The fate of God's emissaries will always be martyrdom in their own time. These adversaries of which you speak are a necessary evil. They help us live on in the hearts of future generations." Rebecka stroked her mouth. "I expected this opposition. Your words only serve to reassure me we are on the correct path."

The man and woman faced each other in their unique robes of office, flowing blacks and reds that were very different from the coarse coverall Jon wore as he listened to this talk and felt nothing. Foulkes had increasingly come to experience the sensation of indifference through recent days, as if he were hovering above the events of Newtopia, without a role to play but too full of residual loyalty and love for the Goddess to walk away. Across from Jon the boy stared at black and white photos in the publications scattered around him,

Gareth wasn't even listening.

Douglas rose up from his chair, as if to leave. "I believed it was my place to warn you Goddess, that's all. Never once would it cross my mind to show disrespect. Perhaps you cannot see clearly, shut away up here. But unless the way of S.O.N. is changed we stand to lose more than just the occasional disciple. Who can tell what lies will be spread in the world of sinners by those who abscond?"

Standing to meet him, Rebecka laid a hand on Elliott's forehead. "The laws of the lost are not our laws my brother." Her touch was like long-forgotten silk. "Our time is coming, of this I am certain. Once we are victorious all the adversity you speak of will prove worthwhile. Recall the lesson of our Lord Reverend: *We are subjected to every kind of hardship, but never distressed. We see no way out, but we never despair. We are pursued, but never cut off; knocked down, but still have life in us.*"

Douglas infused his smile with warmth he did not feel and soundlessly left the room. Once again the psychological and somatic realities of her followers were disregarded, forcing Elliott to assist these struggling devotees as he attempted to retain control over the compound. This pressure had grown since the whole faith moved out to Newtopia, but Douglas knew he couldn't abandon his property or gift for leadership. He'd given up for a while once, when the world didn't end as she said it would, but Elliott was soon back. But then the Reverend shut himself away for several days, unwilling to face people who were let down by the lapse in Rebecka's foresight, her first moment of fallibility. About this same time the redhead called Joanne skipped out of the compound, the disillusionment and misery of her life evidently overpowering any devotion to *The Spirit Of Nagasaki*. Stoker relayed the fall out from her dorm, investigated Joanne's behaviour and discovered the girl had been finding it difficult after so long in the sequestration of Cornwall. Yet her room-mates never suspected the redhead would take herself away in the middle of the night, presumably hitching a lift from somewhere near the farm back into the secular world. It was a bad omen, Joanne had been a part of this church from the start, but Elliott wasn't surprised at her departure. The only shock for him was that more followers didn't abandon S.O.N. after Rebecka failed them. He wished the other leaders shared his knowledge of anthropology. Then one of the Shepherds might have spotted the girl's unhappiness and nipped it in the bud. Sadly, only he was gifted enough to see the warning signs. From the moment when he heard of this disappearance, Douglas vowed to go back among his people, spending the days where he might be aware of their dissatisfactions.

In fact there was surprisingly little discontent, the devotees were making the best of their situation. Elliott eased problems where he could, ordering Stoker to bring in bedding and foodstuffs from outside the compound. These followers accepted Rebecka's convoluted reasoning, saw her failure as a mere blip in their collective destiny. The flock fell for the story wholesale, living for the time that would remain forever imminent, allowing the Goddess to go on without admitting her mistake.

That misjudgement came towards the end of December, a time when it seemed like Douglas was the only inhabitant of Newtopia who didn't believe in the final days. For everyone else the predicted cataclysms of the New Year were real and nigh, the culmination of a difficult and testing month for them. Twelve days after that first prediction another edict came across the speakers. Rebecka called upon all of S.O.N. to observe a fortnight's celibacy in the lead up to Christmas, honouring the infinite mercy of our Lord with the abstention and building up energy levels in preparation for the imminent rule of the church. Elliott was forced to give up his nights in the dormitory beside Beth's tender flesh, lest prying eyes witness her breaking the sexual moratorium. Douglas did not wish to risk banishment for this teenager whose healing caresses and sympathetic ear had become such a tonic since he was ousted from the chambers of the Goddess.

What rankled with the Reverend most, as he left Beth's bed and returned to that room where his employees slept, wasn't so much the randomness of this new law, Douglas had enough self-control to go for a couple of weeks without intercourse, but Rebecka's failure to observe it. The sounds that emanated from the opposite bedroom every morning and at night indicated she was still unlocking that boy's physical potential and their intercourse would continue all through the fortnight of carnal prohibition. In jealousy and frustration the Reverend sought out allies, striking up a conversation with Foulkes at last. Jon had taken himself away from human contact since the relocation, sleeping in a cot at the edge of the downstairs meeting room, and one December afternoon Douglas happened upon him in the kitchen, inviting Jon to the privacy of the top floor and attempting to garner his opinion.

In the bedroom Elliott handed over a mug of tea and asked Foulkes what he thought of the relations between Gareth and Rebecka.

"To begin with, his name's not really Gareth." There was a general hostility to Jon's voice. "I think we all know that young man's real identity. You'd have to be blind not to figure it out."

Holding his brew with both hands for the heat, Douglas looked the man up and down. The truculence in Jon's gimlet eyes seemed directed at him, but the Reverend had no idea what he could have done to provoke such rancour. Surely they were both comrades? Believers in the organization and fellow cuckolds at the hands of the Goddess. If Jon's previous responsibilities had vanished it was no fault of the Reverend Elliott's. There remained plenty to occupy him around the farm, had Foulkes only taken time to seek out the tasks. If Jon's obstreperousness came from spending day after day achieving nothing more than inert brooding there was nobody to blame but himself. Douglas couldn't understand how their personalities set them at unavoidable odds. They were adversaries because Jon had been raised to trust few men but himself, while decades in business trained his eye for chicanery or fakes. This man before Foulkes personified these hated traits and so Jon's revulsion for the evangelist was instinctual and unaffected, it couldn't be undermined by congeniality or sincere proclamations. Both men had reached the peak of their respective professions unable to defer or follow orders, and while the pair made an exception for the other-worldly status of Rebecka, this struggle of masculine dominance leant a fraught edge to contact between the pair.

Unable to pinpoint the cause of Foulkes' dislike, and without sufficient self-awareness to suspect flaws in his own character, Douglas ploughed on with the questions, his patina of good humour failing to bridge the gulf between them.

"Are you sure Gareth can be him?" Credulity in the query. "I find it difficult to believe the presence of a heir to the British throne wouldn't make the papers."

"You're being naive." Jon set down his tea, spoke now in with calm. "The facts of this boy can be easily hushed up. They keep quiet the proclivities of youngsters in the family all the time. Suppose our *Gareth* is taking a year out from his university course? What if the man ends up here instead of travelling around Europe like he said he would?" Foulkes stood. "Legally he's an adult and entitled to certain freedoms. It doesn't matter how many peasants worship the ground he walks on or what his future holds. As long as he phones home now and again with a convincing story I'm sure his father would be willing to let the boy have a few adventures before he becomes a full-time ambassador for the state." Jon turned his back on Elliott and made for the doorway. "Now, if you'll excuse me, this room is beginning to make me feel sick."

That was all Douglas could get out of him, not that he tried again after that. Instead the Reverend attended to business and waited for the ban on sexual contact to be lifted, hurrying from Rebecka's door when indecorous teenage groans reached his ears. Elliott managed to shut out these sounds for the most part, but when the implications of the noises caught his imagination Douglas was immediately transported back to the times he clashed with her voracious appetite. His tussles with the Goddess must have looked like the fights of ornery dogs, neither creature willing to give up the principal role without a struggle, carnal altercations that continued for much of the night. To a voyeur these couplings might have seemed devoid of pleasure, yet the length and breadth of the unions spoke of a different truth. Rebecka's complete command of her body was combined with an almost preternatural ability to locate erogenous zones, inflicting pressure at exact moments to delay the climax of her partner; bringing every male she slept with back for more. For his part Douglas was more than equal to the challenge, possessing a capacity to continue when he should have been sated that was almost tantric, refusing to stop until his mouth and loins brought an arch to the back and gasps from the throat of this female who never let herself go otherwise. Thinking about it, there was no way the kid could make Rebecka's body sing with pleasure the way he did. But Gareth got to be with her thanks to an accident of birth, the desirability of his blue blood, inadequacies as a lover apparently mattering little to the Goddess these days. The times he overheard their lovemaking, Douglas failed to keep his jealousy at bay. Without Beth's tiny hands and grateful smile to relieve the pressure, his contempt only grew.

During this sexless period the weather turned icy, a cold snap that left many Newtopians more interested in huddling together to raise body temperatures than copulation. The main building had always been difficult to keep warm, but it was a sauna compared with those outhouses where a lack of space forced many of the recently arrived men to bed down. Once the hemp had been harvested Douglas did what he could, arranging for heaters to be moved into the animal sheds and sending Stoker out to purchase gas canisters and sheets of corrugated iron. Nolan and Jones used the metal to seal up three sides of each structure, but they had to leave a space for entry so the warmth continued to leak away. Those men living there stayed inside several layers of clothing at all times, wore hats and gloves and many sets of underclothes along with their heavy smocks, extremities protected as best they could. Many were hardy enough to remain strong, and there were plenty of men to replace those left weak by chills or hypothermia, but the compound's sickly were taking far too long to recover. Douglas came to realise this increased physical decrepitude was linked to the lack of nutrition, but he was unwilling to bring in supplies without word from the Goddess. Everything bought recently had been paid for with his personal funds and Elliott wasn't happy about the way S.O.N. was progressing financially. The cult's bank accounts remaining untouched and abundant as if fell to him to keep Newtopia ticking over.

Finally it took the sight of a pregnant Trina Callow to force the Reverend into action, the former celebrity giving up much of her dinner so Chastity and Niagara could eat. Stunned by this sight, the humble manner with which this expecting woman gave away the most basic of meals so her two girls could fill their bellies, Douglas resolved to stop his farm from resembling a third world country. As Rebecka seemed unconcerned by the people around her, rarely receiving visitors as she refined her speeches or continued working on Gareth, Douglas was left to take the initiative. He placed a call to a Cornish warehouse and the next day heralded both milder weather and rejoicing throughout the faith as a lorry pulled up to their gate. The followers assisted Douglas, unloading provisions or carrying the lighter goods to the farmhouse, and that evening the people he had come to think of as his foot soldiers ate well for the first time in weeks. The Reverend joined them on the ground, feeling loved and welcome as he tucked in, wincing when the cost of this food appeared unbidden in his head.

Wide awake now, Douglas rested on his side, eyes staring into the darkness. The assumption he would personally fund the survival of these enervated men and women rankled. He felt like the sponsor of some disaster-struck Asian village. The Reverend always saw *The Spirit Of Nagasaki* as a profitable enterprise, with three executives at the top, salaried employees below them on the ladder, and acolytes occupying the lower rungs. These last individuals received no actual capital, relying instead on Rebecka to provide them with the essentials. Not only had the Goddess ignored her people for the past six weeks or more, she was indifferent to the financial circumstances of her fellow leaders. Douglas had no problem passing a third of the profits onto Foulkes. Despite his current inertia the man had expended much in getting the movement started, but at the moment Rebecka was appropriating all of his money. Elliott was damned if he was going to stand by and let her keep everything.

The man cast uncomfortable blankets to the floor and rose from his bed. Stoker and Jones were nowhere to be seen and that felt strange. The pair tended to retire early and sleep through the night, Douglas left restless thanks to rogue thoughts and ongoing worries, not to mention the slumbering grunts nearby. Tonight they had been snoring by the time Elliott retired but the Reverend heard them rise again several hours after midnight. Moving swiftly, the two men dressed and left, Douglas believing at first they were off to some all-night rave or party, Stoker having mentioned more than once how tired he was of all work and no play. After dwelling on the disappearances Elliott had gradually changed his mind about them, wondering now if the pair weren't engaged in actions they didn't want him to know about.

He stood and approached the bedroom window. Through the dirty glass vehicles belonging to the organization were parked before those outbuildings where disciples slept. The Reverend shivered and climbed into the clothes he usually wore around Newtopia, seeing his best suit at the back of the wardrobe as he extracted the dark sweater and trousers. The last time Douglas had dug that suit out was New Year's Eve, although he couldn't help wondering why he had bothered on the morning of December 31st, even as he brushed fluff off the material. The way a few weeks ago everybody believed the end of the world would come inside twelve hours had seemed phenomenal to him, but the Reverend was isolated in his scepticism and that meant he had to hide his doubts from the troops. Rebecka wandered the compound that afternoon, becoming ubiquitous for a day as she assuaged fears in person, staring Douglas down with unquenchable ferocity as he privately asked her what would happen if she was wrong.

Beth had regarded her lover with a kind of indulgent ridicule for planning beyond the coming night and even Stoker seemed convinced, packing his belongings in readiness and walking around with a hangdog expression on that wintry Tuesday, like the Saint Bernard whose rescue attempt has failed. The pleasures of Christmas week were long gone for these people. There would be no more dancing to celebrate the legacy of Jesus or calls for collective prayer, sexuality forgotten as souls were readied for ascension. On the twenty-fifth Rebecka's carnal sanction had been lifted, men and women of the movement coming together repeatedly, energized by desire and seeing each other afresh after two weeks of abstinence. Even as he thrilled at the return to Beth's bed, Douglas grimly speculated how many female followers would be impregnated during that week, more mouths to feed in nine months time. By New Year's Eve all were gratified. This sudden mating season was over and devotees began preparing themselves for the apocalypse. Elliott rose late that day, dragged himself around a compound lost to anticipation. Possessions were collected in neat bundles, put away ready to accompany their owners on the *next phase* their Goddess told them to expect. Inside shared rooms brothers and sisters spent the afternoon sat in circles, attempting to purge their minds of the world they remembered, obeying the words that came over the public address system. Rebecka extolled her people to "forget the past" and "pinpoint the holy light inside". Ignoring these commands, Douglas withdrew to the kitchen, escaping the sense of impending elevation by cooking a meal for one. He was left alone in these toils, each other individual rejecting food on this landmark day. Their concentration was set on the most pressing issue, spiritual readiness for their role as God's survivors.

When darkness fell the men and women gathered outside to sit at the feet of the Goddess who paced the yard, giving out a final briefing on the imminent salvation. Elliott ate his casserole and watched her theatrics from a doorway, one hundred eyes transfixed by the motion as Rebecka cast hands to heaven, called out to Jesus, flung back her finely proportioned head and let the spirit move her once more. Stabbing the last pieces of meat with a fork, Douglas finished his food and went inside to wash up. By the time he returned the Goddess had retired for meditation and to await her summons from the Lord. Candles flickered between those people who remained, Elliott taking a seat next to Beth, pulling her close to him on the bench. The girl resisted, keeping her gaze fixed on the promise of that night sky. Every acolyte looked upwards, like astronomers waiting for a comet. The expectation grated on Douglas. He imagined standing before the crowd and making an announcement of his own. How there would be no blaze from the heavens, no pellucid signal in the darkness above, no deliverance this night or any other. Instead they should go inside and get some rest, forget about tonight and look to the New Year.

He said nothing. Rebecka didn't require him to undermine her words, they would be discredited instantly when the next day dawned. Tired by the expectant hush and driven to a sulk by Beth's resistance, the Reverend took himself off to sleep alone. If this really was to be their last night on earth let the end come to him in a warm bed, not outdoors numbed by chill air and boredom. Douglas slept soundly and forgot all about the prediction as his people instinctively found their way inside during the night, fell to rest upon carpets and floors.

Come his habitual eight o'clock rise Douglas opened the curtains to a bright dawn and a fresh start. Something nagged at the back of his mind, but such was Elliott's inability to process his thoughts of a morning the worry remained an indefinite pulse as he went downstairs to freshen up. Only when a miniature speaker above the bathroom sink fizzed to life did Douglas remember that there wasn't meant to be a landscape outside his window, or a morning like any other.

"My children, I bring bad news on this day of days." The tones of Rebecka crackling through the air were remarkably calm for someone whose plausibility had been shattered. Elliott began his daily shave with a feeling of satisfaction. He had been right all along.

"Our ascendancy was thwarted last night, defeated by Satan. The devil seeks to prevent this new world our Lord has planned. Lucifer wishes the sin he craves to go on thriving through this debased world. He shall not succeed." In rooms and outbuildings converts awoke to this determined voice. "Our enemies can never win while Christ is strong. The profane actions of the Godless shall destroy them yet." The razor Douglas nicked Douglas on the cheek. "Yesterday saw Satan use his power to achieve an interruption to our coming life of purity and holiness. Yet this delay is only temporary." Swearing to himself, Elliott watched red fluid appear in his reflection. "From now on Newtopia must be considered a battleground in the fight between Jesus and the forces that would stand against Him. To defeat the devil we must remain on our guard from this moment forth. Only with eternal vigilance can the world be created anew." Upon finishing his ablutions the Reverend brought a handkerchief to his cheek and stemmed the flow of blood. The announcement continued.

"Today has been designated a day of silence by our Lord. Instead of communicating through speech, the church will spend these hours reflecting on the demons massed against us. Let me tell you this my people; our destiny remains achievable. Still we must redouble our efforts, strive twice as hard to be forever good and pious. Last night I was blessed with a vision from God and I shall tell you now what I saw. He remains in control, but the Lord cannot create a new kingdom without perfection in all those who follow the way of the S.O.N. I saw Satan rise through our failure, his strength coming from our mistakes and weaknesses. If this imperfection is allowed to continue, we shall never receive our reward. Neither shall we deserve it. I realise your lives have been difficult these past weeks, but that is as nothing to what must be endured if the church is to succeed. That is all. Go with love my children."

Rebecka was as good as her word. Throughout January the edicts grew more frequent and strenuous, devotees ordered to remain mute at least one day every week, these dates selected without warning and apparently at random. The morning after Joanne was confirmed missing an angry Goddess brought in a twenty-four hour fast that Douglas alone pointedly refused to observe. Stoker and Jones were called in to monitor those Rebecka suspected of breaking her moratoria, the duo ensuring weak-minded disciples respected her decrees, did not speak or eat at the prohibited times. Rebecka's instructions culminated in all-night prayer sessions during the middle of January and finally that call to dig. A pointless proclamation designed to further weaken run-down followers in Douglas' mind. It wasn't as if those great holes really could release the pressure of Christ, relax the hold of our Lord over a people cowed into submission, devotees who spent every conscious moment bringing Him to mind in an atmosphere of ongoing postponement. While men struggled to shift the frozen soil Elliott circuited Newtopia to see if he could offer assistance, a practical distraction that might cast the nebulous worries from his mind.

The Reverend wasn't encouraged by what he saw around the compound. His domain was like a depleted aid station in the centre of a conflict. No medicine or doctors could be found in this war zone, only sickness and the uncertainty of a lost populace. In one of the dormitories Joan Saxon stroked the face of her eldest son, the child shaking as he lay in bed, laid low by what looked like a particularly virulent strain of flu. At the first outhouse a half-caste man with a broken front tooth mumbled something to Elliott, the condition of his former Shepherd apparently causing the concern. Douglas remembered when Simon Thistlewood had been fat and jolly. Now the man was wasting away to nothing from some undiagnosed disease, brown and purple spots dotting his filmy skin.

Even when Elliott saw no specific illnesses there always existed the more general afflictions of exhaustion and listlessness, as though the threat of evil and Rebecka's demands could twist bodies into unnatural shapes. If the brothers and sisters were contorted physically, Douglas hated to speculate on their collective mental state. Beth was one unfortunate example. Ever since that prophecy went unfulfilled she had exhibited signs of strain, separating herself from him and the group to live for Rebecka's announcements. The girl ignored all other disciples and rarely even acknowledged her lover, no longer permitting the intimacy Douglas craved. The man was pained by this loss, that sweet girl-child had been Elliott's steadying influence, a ship in harbour amid the unpredictable seas of Newtopia. Yet Beth had become unmoored of late, would scream at Douglas to leave or freeze like a statue at his unwanted touch, and the Reverend didn't know how to get their relations back on track. Just as his efforts for the faith as a whole were brief fixes to an irresolvable problem, so the fragmenting sanity of a partner was something he'd never coped with before. Laying awake at night and turning possible solutions over in his head, Douglas would consider flawed courses of action until daybreak, tying his mind in knots.

A stocky figure led a second shape out of the farmhouse and across the compound. Something was happening outside the window, unspoken developments taking place on his property, events that Douglas had a right to know about. Slipping on his shoes and long black coat Elliott left his room, pausing across the corridor to listen at her door. No noises came to his ears so he turned the handle and entered. Inside Gareth lay alone in Rebecka's bed, asleep with his hands between his knees. Elliott scanned the rest of the room, failing to distinguish other presences. He left the boy to slumber and crept down the stairs, gripping the handrail tightly through this darkened descent. The slightness of the Reverend's movement, his soft tread and ability to sink into shadowed camouflage at a moment's notice, testified to that army instruction. Months of combat preparation that had once provided Elliott with the structure his younger days required.

For years after the young soldier completed his training it seemed he would never see action. Throughout those officer examinations Douglas took to kill time and passed without breaking sweat, after all manner of courses, from man-management to foreign cultures, the biggest threat to a military man's well-being was a posting in Ulster, something that never came his way. Then the incumbent Prime Minister hit upon an unlikely method of turning a general election she was destined to lose, and so the Falklands conflict began, hundreds of young lives jeopardized over a smattering of tiny islands containing two-thousand sheep farmers. This war made Elliott a commanding officer, his effective deployment of men in the battle for Port Stanley and ability to make snap judgements raising him from Captain to Major by the time occupying Argentines turned on their heels and the invasion was finally repelled. Douglas spent those jubilant last days of the war, not amongst the many celebrations, but quietly taking stock in an East Falkland hotel, pondering the future paths he might take now that victory had been achieved. Soon Elliott and his men, soldiers who had learned how to be British winners, would return to their home country and a rapturous welcome, but Douglas wasn't the same man he'd been before the enemy landed on South Georgia. Landmark conflicts brought with them many threats, risks to the individual Elliott didn't relish gambling on any more. He understood now that one misguided order from those above him in the chain of command could lead troops into an impossible skirmish from which no men emerged alive. The major found himself ready to enjoy life upon that return to England, back into a life he might easily have lost. Douglas felt his aspirations changing even as he relaxed for the first time in months, moving away from the services with every day of leave that passed. Perhaps the man would turn his energies towards earning that fortune the army could never offer.

Bored by the desolate greenery that made up the view, Douglas explored the contents of his hotel room before his evening meal. The furnishings of this East coast guest house were basic in the extreme, and there was little of interest here except a claret-coloured Bible in one of the bedside drawers. *Left by Gideons* said the inside cover of this book Elliott leafed through. They were certainly thorough in their philanthropic service thought Douglas, guessing some lonely people here in the Falklands appreciated this donation. Many looked for guidance in these parables and stories sooner or later, and Major Elliott's most vivid recollections of Christianity went back to his time in primary school. His class had been visited by a God-fearing man, with them briefly to spread the word of Jesus. This adult described Christ's message as so powerful it could inspire a man to memorize the New Testament in its entirety.

In order to test the veracity of this claim, astonishing to a group of nine year olds who forgot their times tables every weekend, the teacher handed a copy of the text to that pupil with the highest reading age. Each time a chosen schoolmate cried; "STOP!", Douglas would cease flicking through the pages and pick a line at random to quote. After a few sentences the Christian took up his enunciation from memory, talking over the child until the end of the paragraph, whereupon Douglas was required to confirm that this man had indeed been correct, his words identical to those on the Bible's pages. The class repeatedly gasped at the boy's agreement, less enraptured by the power of faith than the sheer cabaret in this demonstration. Only Douglas knew how little resemblance these orations bore to the page, the boy failing to correct the Christian man after the first couple of instances. Elliott soon realized it was easier for him to agree rather than point out the man's errors and spoil the trick. The young Douglas chose instead to say *yes, that's completely right*, again and again, avoiding harsh looks from his teacher or accusations of nit-picking from the assembled class.

Thinking back to that afternoon from his rented room, Douglas realized how likely it was that Christian pulled the same trick all around the country, a mnemonic swindle to wow impressionable minds. The bluffer gambled on that child selected to read, that they would be too intimidated or apathetic to speak of his mistakes. How many kids around the nation had their nascent faith reaffirmed by his faulty showmanship? Elliott wondered about it as he sat there, staring at the words of that complimentary hotel Bible.

From that day on further understanding came to Douglas. He deduced that religion was magic, a spell cast by the church over its congregation. Attendees needed the love of God to be powerful, faith overcoming the harsh realities of their world. Soon Elliott would habitually carry a copy of the scriptures, get through hours of Bible study every day, fascinated by the possibilities. Clearly people needed relief from the unspoken pivot of their existence, the knowledge that *life equals suffering*. The form that reassurance took mattered little, as long as it convinced the pious and brought success for the leaders. Here was a comfort everyday folk would pay good money for, just as they did for the distractions of entertainment and the solace of material things. The potential profit margins were enormous.

Douglas edged into the first dormitory and glanced over the living space. A dozen or more sections made up this room, followers arrayed on beds or those mattresses between them, wheezing as they slept. He made out a few empty areas in the cramped space and backed out, sidling down the second set of steps. The route by which Elliott had found his destiny here, running this Cornish commune, was a strange and convoluted one. His first act after hitting on that idea was to use the pay he'd accumulated during the Falklands conflict to take a trip across the Atlantic. This journey was the beginning of his quest, a mission to discover how a man, skilled in diplomacy and possessing both intelligence and ambition, could profit from the religious need.

A brief journey into this potential gold mine became a three-year residency in the American heartland as Douglas developed a taste for theatrics, touring the mid-west with a family of evangelists and making guest appearances on cable TV channels to support the *Cash For Christ* plea. While on-screen Elliott adopted the Texan accent he had been perfecting but reverted to an English lilt off-camera for those many women seduced by his stately charms. The Reverend moved from church to church, earning only scraps from this supporting role in the faiths, but the money proved enough to sustain his studies. Douglas was keen to observe the techniques of Jerry Falwell and Oral Roberts and develop his own brand of showmanship before modest crowds in places like Nebraska and Kentucky. A good preacher brought light into the eyes of a salvation-seeking believer and, more salutary than this metaphysical reward, were the figures. A man could live for months on the donations collected during a successful hour of brimstone and healing.

Douglas took lessons from the Americans he would never have absorbed within the modesty and withdrawal fostered by English faiths. Experienced men with fake tans taught Elliott how to give people a release from their fears, take the congregation to that heavenly fulfilment they craved through dancing here on earth. He became proficient at spotting personal quirks within seconds and discovered how to exploit individuality to lucrative effect. Those were heady times, but Douglas always knew he would return to his home country eventually, and when his knowledge gleaned from the U.S. felt unsurpassable Elliott took a flight back to London. He disembarked at Heathrow three years after his departure, still carrying his single suitcase but now with a head full of great notions.

Back in the city word reached Douglas his father had died. The man was gone, that one who had instilled the knowledge into his son from an early age; that wealth is the only sure route to happiness. The parent left Elliott with a substantial inheritance and one sprawling property, situated deep in the Cornish countryside. Throughout the nineties he could afford to live a leisurely existence, experimenting with schemes and proposals while the money was gradually frittered away. Douglas studied theologies and planned his routines until that wondrous Goddess appeared on the local news, speaking of her visions so plausibly. Now he had discovered his muse, here was a kindred spirit who could utilise Douglas' skills, mould him into a vital part of the machinery that powered her new church.

Down at ground level the third piece of the human puzzle dozed within his cot, curled up alone in what used to be the lounge. Whatever was happening outside this building tonight Foulkes wasn't a part of it. Douglas passed his sleeping form and moved into the kitchen, almost stumbling over a chair as he negotiated the darkness. Chill air rushed through the gap and bit into the man as he unlatched the front door, Elliott had to gird himself as he stepped out into the freezing night. How long ago those first months seemed to Douglas now, all the satisfying times as *The Spirit Of Nagasaki* came into being. The creation of a manifesto for his budding faith, a labour of love that left the recently christened Reverend feeling purposeful and rewarded, like a childless couple who are finally given permission to adopt.

From there his confidence and power could only grow. Elliott refined his evangelism during rabble-rousing shows of recruitment, watched profit margins rise as scores of followers craved his presence, hanging on the Reverend's every word. All the time a concurrent stream of pleasure powered his unseen life. Time spent with the Goddess was the most gratifying Douglas had ever experienced, working closely with the leader every day, amazed at Rebecka's empathy and the accuracy of her intuition. Then those nights of sexual union, a sateless need in her body, the stamina to make love again and again.

So where did it all go wrong? That was what Elliott asked himself now, standing there before the entrance to the farmhouse, looking for some human sign to guide his next move. How had they managed to undermine such a remunerative set-up? Why had this thriving faith degenerated into the squalor of recent days? Douglas listened to the night around him as if it could provide answers. A far-off drift of voices came from somewhere across the compound as clouds passed over the moon. The satellite lit up Elliott's progress as he walked beyond the yard, quickly coming to be obscured once again.

From the edge of the barn Douglas could see three people at the end of the first greenhouse. His breath was harsh and rapid as the man watched these individuals. Two thick-bodied figures stood over what looked like a person on the ground, while the female lurking nearby was unmistakably Rebecka. That man he identified as Jones bent down to the prone form and heaved it away, moving briefly out of Elliott's vision before returning with a spade to shift some of the piled earth onto what Douglas now realized was a body. Glenn shovelled dirt for a couple of minutes until Rebecka signalled for him to stop, speaking at length with this pair of men, words Elliott couldn't make out. The duo strode away from her at speed, heading straight for the Reverend. Seeing their approach, Douglas turned and ran, praying the crunch of his feet on earth wouldn't carry to their ears.

When he reached the far side of the barn Elliott stopped in his tracks, waiting long seconds before he peered back at the area from where he'd come. Those two workers were heading toward the farmhouse, their backs safely towards him. Douglas kept to the wall as he stepped back against the width of the barn. He could see Rebecka beside the pits, facing away from him with her hands in the air, crucifix hanging from her right arm, fingers bent above as though poised to catch some falling object from the sky.

Now might be his only chance to get within earshot and Elliott decided to take it. A quick check over the surroundings before he covered those forty yards separating barn and greenhouse in a diagonal dash. Douglas kept his head down all the while and hoped that woman was too caught up in her reverie to notice.

He made it to the glass structure, hidden from the view of Rebecka by tinted panes now. Douglas couldn't afford to rest. He didn't know how long it would be before the men re-emerged. Only when he made it to a position that was covered on the two dangerous sides did the Reverend allow himself a measure of relief, fighting both the urge to cough and a rising nausea as he gulped in air.

When Douglas had recovered from his exertion the man inched his head round the corner of the darkened greenhouse. Rebecka was no more than ten metres away, apparently caught up in another of her visions. The woman made a low noise as she stood there in the darkness, the soil heaped beside her. Then the Goddess grew silent, the cross sliding down her forearm to rest in the grip of a hand as she allowed her arms to drop. The figure turned away from Douglas and spoke to an unseen party that had arrived behind her.

"Bring them over here."

Douglas pulled back the exposed part of his face as more individuals moved into view.

"The older one must come to me first."

Millimetre by millimetre, Elliott extended the side of his head past the corner of the greenhouse until his left eye protruded far enough to see. Seven shapes took part in the unfolding scene, each too preoccupied to notice the sliver of Douglas watching from the side. Rebecka was knelt on the ground, her hands on the shoulders of the taller Saxon child who sniffled with the ongoing effects of influenza. Behind this boy his mother was restrained, Stoker forcing Joan's hands together behind her back. Next to this pair Jim Saxon clutched his younger son, the boy facing his father's chest as Jones loomed close by.

"Be beautiful in your heart by being gentle and quiet my child." Rebecka placed the thick metal chain of her crucifix over the boy's head. "This kind of beauty will last, God considers it to be special." She twisted the chain. "Do not struggle against the will of our Lord, the time has come for you to enter His kingdom."

Stoker clamped a hand over the mother's mouth as painful gurgling noises came from the small boy. Jones moved closer to the father but Jim made no effort to save his oldest son, that narrow-eyed man trembling in the night air. The child stiffened and Rebecka released her hold, allowing the boy to fall to the ground, a bluish tinge to his face. The woman replaced the cross around her neck and gathered the corpse to her, carrying the dead child to the nearest pit. Once there Rebecka dropped this body, a cadaver that landed in the hole with a thud.

She returned to her original position.

"May the other be brought to me."

Unable to watch, Douglas withdrew, leaning back against the glass. His brain felt like it was expanding, would burst from his head, grey matter pummelling the inside of Elliott's skull like a hatching reptile while the thump in his ears was a pounding of hooves on turf, noise all merging in a locomotive rush. The other boy was dying nearby and Elliott didn't know what to do. His limbs felt immovably leaden and it took all of the man's resources to fight the urge to collapse. Unable to accept what he'd seen, Elliott forced his gaze back around the corner, hoping it had been some hallucination that would fade like a mirage.

Stoker directed Joan forward with one hand, keeping the other firmly clamped over her mouth. There was something primal and anguished in the fluid eyes of the Saxon woman.

"It is alright my friend, she will not make a sound, will you sister?" The worker released his grip and Joan sank to her knees before Rebecka, crying softly. "Enough my child, do not grieve. We shall be joined with our loved ones soon enough." She lifted the chain from her throat and brought it down over Joan's head. "I only wish I could join you my sister. Alas, my work in this world is not yet complete."

Rebecka pulled the metal strap taught and resistance quickly left her victim, Joan's life extinguished within seconds. Thirty feet away Douglas couldn't shift his eyes from these events, how terribly he was entranced. Stoker hefted Joan over his shoulder and took her to the far pit, shovelling earth onto this pale corpse once it had disappeared into the void.

The voice of the Goddess was dulcet and inviting. "Approach my altar won't you James?"

Head bowed, body as limp as a rag doll, Jim Saxon stumbled forward without the need for further prompts. Rebecka throttled him with little ceremony, her chain digging into his whitened skin, the woman using all the force of her body to dispatch this disciple. When it was over Jones and Stoker carried the man to his grave while Rebecka remained in the same position with closed eyes, her ligature raised heavenwards.

Released from this mesmeric moment, Douglas staggered backwards and dropped to the ground. Too late Elliott realized he was making noise as his hands broke the fall. No one came to investigate the sound. A January breeze whipped at his face as Douglas listened to the earth being shifted onto that murdered family a short distance away. The burial was followed by some kind of instruction from Rebecka then the heavy tread of feet growing slowly fainter. Under his fingers the ground felt lunar and wrong. Somewhere in the distance a bird cried once. Douglas crawled to the glass frame as though sheltering from sniper fire. In the distance one of the henchmen entered the farmhouse. The shock was wearing off and Elliott's mind had begun to process the facts. Clearly the Goddess was discarding those she no longer needed, cutting her losses and escaping while she still could. The earth wasn't about to plunge into Armageddon, nuclear or otherwise. Rebecka had to bring about the end of existence herself, for those who lived by her visions. The woman must have wearied of playing for time. There was only so much talk of satanic bogeymen even the most gullible devotee would take. Murder was a last roll of the dice for Rebecka. She was tying up loose ends and getting out, leaving her waste behind on the farm. These pieces of evidence would remain on Elliott's property and link the crimes to him. A visceral quake ran through the Reverend's body and he nearly keeled over again. It took a few seconds for the man to recover and rise to his feet, desperately searching for a way to turn this around.

Footsteps on the other side of the greenhouse told him of further movement. Douglas side-stepped away from the edge feeling drained of all purpose, outnumbered and unable to get away. A lone girl was brought before Rebecka this time. Stoker relinquished his grip on her hand as he nudged the female towards her Goddess. This was a young brunette, androgynous in the boyish cut to her sleep-mussed hair and the unflattering smock. A sudden concretion came to his gut. Elliott recognized this disciple.

Beth.

The Goddess beckoned the girl closer and motioned for her to kneel. Something uncontrollable coursed through the watching man's nervous system, right down into his soul. Rebecka placed the crucifix around Beth's neck. Ten metres to her right Douglas emerged from his hiding place.

"Enough." Four pairs of eyes turned to him. "Leave her alone Rebecka."

"It isn't your place to interfere."

Douglas moved toward the women. "I've seen enough, this stops right now."

"As you wish." Her face angled toward the tattooed figure. "Glenn, please."

Jones stepped between Beth and Elliott. The Reverend tried to shove him aside but Jones responded by grabbing Douglas' arm. Elliott managed to wrench free and retreated a few paces. To the right Stoker watched proceedings with growing agitation, waiting for some kind of order to be restored. Angered by the resistance, Jones came at Douglas guilelessly and received a right hook for his trouble, Elliott connecting with all he had. The blow put Jones off-balance and he staggered back. Another punch would have sent Glenn to the ground, but rather than follow up Douglas lunged for Beth. The girl shied away from his grasp, moving closer to Rebecka. For a moment the Reverend was bewildered, Beth's evasion suggested he was the threat and this murderous woman her protector. During these seconds Douglas forgot about the man behind him. With all his might Jones landed an uppercut to his kidneys, taking the breath from Douglas who lost his footing. Glenn caught Elliott's chin with his knee as the man went down. There was the crack of teeth and blood oozed from the Reverend's mouth. When Douglas hit the floor Jones landed a powerful kick to his stomach.

From somewhere far away Elliott heard Rebecka speak.

"Get him up."

Then Douglas was being raised, the bear hug around his chest inhibiting his respiration. The man coughed and gasped, breath coming in short hacking noises. Jones loosened the grip enough for his captive's lungs to take in air.

Spitting liquid from the mess of red that was once his mouth, Elliott tried to speak with authority. "Get her Stoker." Douglas looked into the unsure eyes of his employee. "This can stop right now if you take hold of Rebecka."

Jones tightened the clinch to silence his captive. Stoker glanced from Douglas to the Goddess, unable to make a decision.

"Do not listen to him my brother." Rebecka's black eyes were ablaze, her commands sharp and clear. "He would threaten the work of Christ. You know what must be done."

There were stars before Elliott's vision and he could feel his body wanting to pass out. Douglas gathered his remaining strength, all the massed power of desperation in him, and wielded it against the man around him. In one motion Douglas kicked his heel against Glenn's shin, pulled an arm free from the weakened grasp and brought his elbow back at speed. He connected with the throat of Jones who stumbled back, clutching at his neck.

"You think this is what Jesus would want?" Freed now, Elliott steadied himself, wiping spittle and blood from his lips. "This farm is my property and you have my girl, stop this and let her go."

The woman smiled as an unrestrained Beth stayed before her Goddess. "She doesn't seem to want you Reverend." Rebecka addressed Stoker. "Restrain him now!"

Roused from his vacillation by the unchallengeably harsh voice, the lank-haired man came at Douglas.

"Don't Stoker, you're making a mistake." He raised both hands to placate the younger man. Stoker forced them behind Elliott's back. "You work for me for God's sake! She'll betray you in the end, just like she betrays everyone."

"Quiet!" Rebecka looked to Jones who was holding his throat, approaching the two men with a furious expression on his face.

"Glenn!"

Jones reached the pair and lifted his arms above Douglas, balling both sets of fingers together as he prepared to bring his weight down.

"GLENN!"

The virulence of Rebecka's voice penetrated his male instincts once more. Instead of caving in the Reverend's skull, Jones dropped his hands and looked to the Goddess.

"Come over here; we want him to see this." The tattooed man stared at Douglas hatefully before joining Rebecka, fingertips touching the tender swelling on his chin. The Goddess returned her attention to the girl before her who had remained calm throughout this altercation. In the background Stoker kept the pressure on Elliott.

"As Christ surrendered his life for us, so we must surrender our lives for him." The woman gripped that chain adorning Beth's neck. "The precious gift of life was granted to you, now this gift must be returned."

Rebecka tightened this makeshift noose, turning her face to Douglas as she did so, sleek hair shining brilliantly in the moonlight. At her hands the girl convulsed through her death throes, Beth's tongue lolling over her lower lip as she expired.

"I fail to understand why you must be sentimental for any single part of this whole my Reverend. They are cattle, nothing more." The spasms ceased and the girl slumped away. Elliott tried to scream his frustration but all that came out was a low grunt of pain, the man's head drooping in capitulation.

"Come and see the works of God my people. He is terrible in His doing toward the children of men." Rebecka relinquished her hold and took the cross off the corpse. "You may remove it now Glenn." Jones dragged Beth's body towards a burial pit by her feet, his powerful torso inclined forwards. With the index finger of her right hand Rebecka motioned for Douglas to be brought before her.

"I wish it had not come to this my Reverend." Stoker pushed Elliott down by the shoulders. "Yet I suppose I always knew it would."

"What is the point of all this?" On his knees in front of her, painful impulses coming at his brain from what seemed like every part of his body, Elliott spat out his defiant last words. "Tell me woman, what's the bloody point?"

"Tonight we send those who might go against us to meet their maker." Behind his crouched figure Stoker and Jones held an arm each, forcing Douglas to look into Rebecka's eyes. Those blackened orbs were as alluring as ever, but there was something callous in them now. The woman lifted her metal chain over his head, brushing his split lip with the crucifix as it came down.

"No one can remain who might wish to prevent the coming holocaust." A thoughtful note, both intimate and deathly, had entered the woman's whisper. She tensed the silver cord. "Your girl could not be trusted to respond correctly on the morrow. She was irrational and may have fled." The chain cut off Elliott's air supply, his throat making the involuntary noises that come with asphyxiation. "As for you my brother, I cannot help but feel disappointment at your lack of understanding. The Lord didn't tell me you would turn against us, but if He had I would not have believed." Both eyeballs bulged in their sockets as the tremendous strength of this woman was brought to bear. There was impotent panic alongside the pain now. In some objective recess of his mind Douglas knew he was on the cusp of consciousness.

"I waited to see how you would respond. That waiting is over."

With an abrupt lurch the man blacked out.

Shafts of light cast themselves down through the darkness. A sensation of immobility as thousands of tiny clods landed on his body. Douglas opened his eyes a crack and squinted. Far above two shapes were illuminated by the moon's celestial lustre. They shovelled at earth, dirt landing on his face and filling both nostrils. Some urgency came to Elliott's mind but his body was too weak to rise, the weight of soil keeping him inert. Lumps landed with rhythmic crashes, a measured thump as earth rejoined earth. Over this uniform noise Douglas made out a forceful voice, that of a woman uttering some kind of valediction, or perhaps a prayer.

"*Like sheep they are laid in the grave. Death shall feed on them, and the upright shall have dominion over them in the morning. But God will redeem my soul from the power of the grave, for he shall receive me.*"

The sound of someone hawking up spit, then nothing.

Chapter Nine

The shambling man in the raincoat didn't look up as he passed the security desk, moving onward to the exit doors instead. Outside this aluminium-coated building the city was lit up like a space station, that sodium-vapour gleam conveying central London's cocksure importance. The figure failed to notice these lights. Nor did he consider the bucolic wonderland of St. James Park nearby, a darkened outpost of well-tended garden in the metropolitan dirt. Rather the man turned away, firing up a cigarette as he shuffled down Broadway.

Joe Sweeney's mind was a good way apart from the bustle of the weekday evening. The previous hour of his life was occupying Joe's thoughts completely. Every time Sweeney went over what had happened in Thomson's office his conclusions grew more discouraging, Joe beginning to feel disgusted by his easy quiescence. The Investigator had reached Surbiton around twilight, leaving the Carlton in a street by his house and rushing to catch the train, transport that would avoid the gridlock of workday's end. By the time he reached New Scotland Yard the clocks had passed six and many of the departmental heads were gone for the evening. Only the Assistant Commissioner remained to debrief his Special Investigator, Brett Thomson calling Sweeney in to summarize the division's opinion of his report and those decisions made to take this case forward. Immediately Sweeney recognized the response as guarded, a less than positive reaction to his preliminary brief. Joe got the feeling that Thomson didn't want to be speaking with him. The boss avoided Sweeney's eyes from behind his desk, complained to himself of petty matters.

"Damn biros, always running out. She was supposed to order more in." He threw away the empty pen and motioned to the chair before Joe. "Do have a seat Investigator Sweeney, I'll be with you in a minute."

Brett Thomson was in his fifties, slightly younger than Joe but never uncomfortable treating him like a junior. The Assistant Commissioner came from a long line of successful policemen, instilled with an emotionless approach and equanimity of judgement from an early age. This wasn't the sort of man you found likeable or otherwise thought Joe, considering that head of striking white hair above the man's podgy face. It was a mystery to Sweeney how loved ones or antagonists nurtured strong feelings for his boss either way. Nobody Joe knew had ever reacted in an extreme way towards him.

"Here it is." Thomson extracted a copy of the report and studied it with heavy-lidded eyes. From where he sat Sweeney could see that large sections of the paperwork had been blotted out while crudely drawn asterisks filled the margins. Making self-consciously reflective noises, the Commissioner skimmed half a dozen sheets and looked Joe squarely in the face.

"Thank you for the work you did on this Joe, I know writing it can't have been easy."

"That's my job."

"And you do it very well." The man returned his attention to the document. "However we will have to make some changes before this report can be cascaded down the line."

"Yes?"

"Yes, we will exorcise some parts of Stoker's statement. Those sections that relate to drugs in the main." Something negative flitted across Sweeney's face. Thomson was not slow in spotting it. "Don't worry Joe, we won't require any more input from you at this stage. My secretary is on hand to make the alterations first thing in the morning."

"What will you be leaving out sir, if I might ask."

"Well, with two of the culprits still at large, the division feels any divergence in focus would be counterproductive." Sweeney nodded. He knew what was at the source of this doublespeak. "Unfounded allegations would reflect badly on certain individuals. They have no place in the investigation as it stands."

Around them gaudy signs advised visitors not to smoke, an order displayed on doors and windows, making Joe wonder how much longer he would be trapped in this office. Within that five thousand-word document Sweeney had endeavoured to give a complete picture of the events leading up to this tragedy. His overview could never have been achieved without reference to the government's collusion, how the leaders of the cult paid off local authorities and officials. Sweeney caught the glare opposite with a knowing look. He supposed part of him had always known these assertions wouldn't go down well, but he had included every fact at his disposal just the same.

"Have you contacted the Home Office?" Joe asked.

"You mean about this *Alderon* character the witness identified?" Thomson leafed through his papers, fruitlessly searching for a mention of the name. "The head of our major enquiry team has spoken with the department in question and the relevant figures will be alerted to the matter. I'm confident it can be dealt with internally." Of course it can, thought Joe. "Is there anything else?"

Keeping his cynicism to himself, Sweeney spoke warily. "The implications are enormous."

"Yes Joe, but there remains a time and a place for everything." Weariness underpinned Thomson's voice. Although he hid it well, Sweeney knew this man was finding their conversation tiresome. "Questions must have been raised by your investigation will be answered at the enquiry. First of all there are guilty parties to locate and detain."

Over his long years of experience Sweeney had come to understand the ways by which enquiries whitewashed public servants. This case was no different. The commissioner's evasive manner told Joe that the truth would never come out. Another cover-up consigned to the history of this desiccated nation, more stonewalling for families of the restless dead. The highest authority in the room deflecting talk away from the ramifications of corruption.

"We located the girl who escaped the cult earlier today. Joanne Greening is in custody as we speak. Initial questioning of the witness supports your report, except where I've indicated. The girl saw no evidence of drug consumption or cultivation on the farm." No, thought Sweeney, she wouldn't have. "So far Joanne has been unable to give us any clues as to the whereabouts of the remaining fugitives, but we are satisfied she will cooperate fully. Her deposition is likely to be vital in our case against this Stoker fellow."

"You noted my recommendations?"

"Our doctors will give Stoker a comprehensive series of tests this week after we bring him to London. I doubt very much they will find psychological abnormalities in what is, by all accounts, an exceptionally lucid individual. Still, he shall run the gamut just the same." Joe tried to interject but the commissioner spoke over him. "Listen Sweeney, we're going public with this incident tomorrow afternoon and you know as well as I what could happen if we fail to pull in Rebecka Marsden or Glenn Jones. Having someone in reserve is always necessary for cases like this." Thomson ran a hand through his white hair. "The public requires justice. Unfortunately we don't have a choice but to throw the book at Stoker."

Sweeney could feel frustration rising in his blood. If he wasn't careful the sensation would snowball into something beyond his control. "I still believe the scapegoating of a single man will backfire."

"You can't scapegoat someone if they're guilty." An undertow of irritation from the man. "Quite frankly Joe I was disappointed with much of what you wrote. We can salvage the basic facts of your report, but I'd hoped you of all people would understand what is required of a Special Investigator in times such as these. Circumlocutory attacks on government departments help no one, and what did you hope to achieve with all that blather at the end?" Thomson brought out the final page and read from the text. "*The only way to prevent such a catastrophe from occurring again is to change society in such a way citizens no longer seek a solution for their unhappiness through the messages of extreme religions. As for how we can go about this, I must admit, I have no idea at present.*"

"I ask you to accept my apologies sir." At that moment all Sweeney wanted was to get outside for a smoke. His true feelings were buried under professional formality. "There's been a great deal of strain in my life lately."

"No matter, no matter. Don't think we're not grateful for the hours you have invested in what was by no means an easy situation." The Commissioner tidied away his papers. "To express our gratitude for your efforts I've agreed to a month's paid release." Thompson rose and extended a hand that Sweeney shook. "Use this time wisely Joe. Relax for a while, forget about the case, it's someone else's problem now. Go and spend time with your family, I'm sure they'll appreciate it."

The Investigator lit a cigarette from the gleaming dog-end of the previous one. Before him the newspaper sellers of Victoria Street yelled 'FINAL!', folding copies of the Standard for paying commuters, the posters on their stalls announcing suicide bombs and terrorist activity, celebrity engagements or the premature death of famous men. Up ahead the pavement was filled by a crush of commuters, men and women scampering to reach coach or train stations, hoping to complete journeys before this evening turned to night. Avoiding these desperate masses, Joe turned right, waiting for a green man to light his way through traffic. In some ways Sweeney wished he had used up his remaining courage against Thomson, taking the superior to task for his attitude, puncturing Brett's complacency with a stand on behalf of the dead. Unfortunately the Assistant Commissioner was only one man, and self-righteousness was worthless against the political manoeuvring of bosses who could relieve Joe of his role immediately. Besides, Sweeney wasn't up to a full-blown argument. He felt light-headed and drowsy this cloudy evening, tired of work and its web of interlaced conspiracies. The plots grew exponentially with each piece of uncovered evidence, until all hope of assembling the story into some kind of coherent whole was lost, dissipating like his motivation.

The next day's press conference would be another masterpiece of partial revelation, the Chief Commissioner withholding vital facts in favour of simpler admissions, an explanation that contained enough detail for the papers to construct a neat story of connivance and intrigue. Underneath the initial shock pressmen would be reassured, journalists knowing the police were pursuing their many lines of inquiry. What the reporters didn't realise was that none of these leads were promising. The investigative team had no direct links to that woman responsible for the massacre and few pointers at her current location. The Met was left to work from second-hand rumour and flawed guesswork.

In a world of his own Sweeney walked the kerb, passing banks and discount clothing stores. He looked to the other side of a junction and saw scaffold encasing an enormous office block. Hundreds of connected poles fitted together reaching up thirty floors, maybe more. Joe stopped before this sight, those trailing in his wake having to dodge the man staring up at the building's summit. Craning his neck, Sweeney found himself entranced by this construction for reasons he couldn't pinpoint, caught by an unsteadiness rising from his feet as Joe blankly absorbed the sight. Despite being at ground level vertigo overwhelmed him, catching the man in its dizzying stupor. Sweeney felt as if he were up there on that lonely metal, clinging desperately to its temporary cage. He experienced a quaking in the knees and a wave of giddiness, as if he were about to keel over, there on a busy London street. Joe let his cigarette fall to the ground and struggled across the pavement, swaying like the victim of some centrifugal force. After several seconds of struggle Sweeney came to an enclosed doorway, three steps serving as an impromptu resting place. The man crumpled downwards, hoping to ride out these feelings of faintness.

Minutes passed and his eyesight cleared. Joe saw clearly again now, life carrying on as normal away from the alcove, hundreds of rushing bodies paying no attention to the well-being of this man a few feet away. Sweeney took gulps of the polluted air, wondering whether another pill would serve to ease or exacerbate his condition. He was certain this wasn't a sickness brought about by the medication, not the result of gloominess or fatigue. No, a Special Investigator had to immerse himself in his work to the detriment of other concerns, become utterly enclosed until his efforts were no longer required. Whereupon he would be expected to cast off a case and its hold over him in an instant.

Take a break Thomson said, go on holiday, rest up, forget about it. Minutes later here Joe was, disabled in a filthy niche, the stink of urine and rotting rubbish around him, haunted by visions that wouldn't go away. On Victoria Street every woman had Rebecka's face. All of them resembled the photographs, those pictures of an ex-prostitute who disposed of people like unwanted insects in the garden. Marsden was out there somewhere. She could be any of these dashing females, unnoticed and disguised at dusk, preparing her next move. Ready for more amoral manipulation and her second kingdom, a sequel to that hell on earth.

Joe lit another smoke, each drag restoring a little of his sanity. By the time his cigarette was dead Joe Sweeney had regained his composure. He brought out his mobile and turned on the device. It displayed the voicemail symbol. Having a message wasn't surprising, Joe had failed to check his phone for days. Rather than listen to it, Sweeney raised himself slowly, level-headed now as he rejoined the throng, breaking off after a few paces for the colour and light of MacDonald's.

Long queues extended from the cashiers but Joe wasn't interested in fast food. Instead he walked on, across the disinfected smoothness of the restaurant's lavatory, punching several buttons into his phone as he walked. The wavering voice of a middle-aged woman came on the line.

"Hello?"

"Lil? It's me."

"Joe, oh Joe! Where have you been? You'll never guess what's happened!"

Lillian Sweeney had been planning to admonish her husband for his self-imposed isolation this week, reprimands after which Joe would regret his inconsideration, think twice about being mean to her again. This less than conciliatory intention was at the forefront of Lillian's mind all the way up until mid-morning of that day, a time when the thrill of big news washed all negativity away.

"I'm coming home Lil, it's over." Joe's voice was strained and emotional. "I'll explain more later but I, I want to apologize."

"It doesn't matter love, I don't mind." What was the matter with his wife of thirty years? She sounded for all the world like a breathless schoolgirl, not the outraged harpy he had been expecting.

"Sarah got the results of her CAT scan today."

"I'd forgotten all about that."

"We're going to have a granddaughter Joe, isn't that something? Everything's normal, Sarah and Clark are awfully excited. Isn't it something, a beautiful little girl." Lillian waited for a response. Inside that lavatory Sweeney leant against a cubicle and waited to experience an emotion, some feeling to compliment the delight of his wife. Nothing came to him.

"Are you there Joe? Say something for God's sake."

Sweeney looked around him. This washroom was identical to thousands of others around the world. Threads of soap the colour of blancmange lay across sinks. Torn paper towels spilled from wastebaskets.

"I'm coming home now love." Joe said. Then he switched off the phone.

Rebecka & Gareth

"There is nothing going on in the world at the moment I find distressing or have a view on."

- Michael Owen, *England Footballer*

The white minibus drew up to the waiting zone in front of the provincial airport. A square-shouldered young man jumped from the rear, lifting two suitcases out after him. In the front seat an older woman paused to thank her male driver, the patches of bruising to his jaw and neck dark and painful in the daylight.

Jones remained silent, watching Rebecka hold her zippered bag against the cotton of that ankle-length black dress as she stepped from the vehicle. Wrenching at the gearstick, the driver accelerated away to begin his extended journey across the country, a trip that would be punctuated by several rest stops when Glenn attempted to gather sleep-deprived resources. This endless travelling was difficult but unavoidable, despite its inconspicuous appearance this van needed to be destroyed. Jones knew a man in the North who could strip and dispose of the vehicle in hours. The tattooed driver indicated right and headed for the motorway, his share of the S.O.N. spoils safely tucked away in the glove compartment, new starts and the future on his mind.

From the entrance Gareth waved happily at the departing minibus, like a cub scout sending out his goodbyes before camp. Then the teenager picked up their hefty luggage and led the way through the automatic doors, playing the role of alpha male for Rebecka's benefit. Once they were inside the boy took a seat while his companion approached the administration desk, collected tickets they had booked two weeks earlier under the name Anna Michaels. Gareth pulled a magazine from the pocket of his coat and struggled to read through his sunglasses. The wraparound shades had to remain on his face until they were out of the country, a strict order from his travelling companion who now received their passes and purchased a newspaper before rejoining the young man.

Their flight would board in thirty minutes so there was plenty of time to waste. Refusing to let herself think of the place they'd left, Rebecka glanced over the headlines in today's *Class*. House prices were rising at their highest rate ever. The Queen continued her tour of Britain. Several countries on the Indian subcontinent prepared for nuclear strikes against their neighbours. The world bored Rebecka and the woman looked over to Gareth instead. His golden-brown hair had filled out pleasingly since agreeing to her wish that he grow it; the locks almost reaching his shoulders now, those sunglasses covering his uniquely emerald eyes. Few would have guessed Gareth's true heritage from the way he appeared, exposed features giving little away, just those petite ears inherited from his mother and the paternal side's flattened bridge of the nose. The teenager was too absorbed in tales of superannuated celebrity to notice her attention, scuttlebutt filling the pages of retrospective Hollywood publications he read habitually. The current periodical was one of many Gareth cherished, stories pieced together by hacks in decades gone by. Set against monochrome images of the stars were outdated gossip columns to hold the young man enrapt. From the heroically priapic exploits of Errol Flynn, to Ava Gardner's bad luck in love, Gareth accepted these confabulations as gospel. Many times over her weeks with him Rebecka had to force herself to be attentive as the boy explained his fascination with these lost days. How the gossamer stars of yesteryear shone more brightly than contemporary media types. This youngster would take the real-life soap opera of Burton and Taylor over the brainless contentment of iconic footballers and their wives every time.

When Gareth spoke of his childhood he always lingered on those times he'd spent alone, hours when he found comfort in the personal history of idols or descriptions of the glamorous L.A. life. His parents were away frequently, enduring state visits or holidaying apart, and through those long weeks the boy found himself in the care of nannies and courtiers, servants who didn't genuinely care about him and so failed to assuage his loneliness. His heart would be calmed by accounts of other generations and their fame, Gareth reading favoured tales to the dozens of toys that littered his room, pretending these stuffed animals were other princes and princesses. Soon the boy no longer felt discarded or sad, more like a 1950s confidant, regaling his new friends with big screen anecdotes and entrancing hearsay.

While this habit of reading aloud to the inanimate dissipated with maturity, his enthusiasm for lost celebrity continued. Rebecka was unable to sway this young man from the branch of history that fascinated him so, although it was easy to distract him from this hobby when she took him to her bed. The leader let Gareth's obsession pass. She knew every child needed people to admire during the confusion of puberty, and Gareth's adolescence had been more publicly agonizing than most. When blue blood makes someone immediately adored for no reason of merit, their face ubiquitous thanks to a celestial quirk, comrades in fame and renown were of little interest, would only look up to you with deference in spite of their status, marvel meaninglessly. Rebecka understood Gareth's retreat into an imaginary past and she nurtured the boy without rebukes, seeing this endless support for his feelings as a vital part in the exploitation.

That morning she kept Gareth far from the action, instilling into him how important it was to be up and inside the S.O.N. bus by nine, ignoring any announcements as they followed this pre-planned schedule. Upon waking the teenager climbed into his everyday clothes while Rebecka sat at her table and woke her disciples through the P.A., directing all followers to gather at the back of the main building within five minutes. In dormitories and outbuildings devotees groggily pulled on their smocks and obeyed her crisp command.

Stoker and Jones guided the crowd across the compound, individuals too confused by the suddenness of this order to notice how many brothers and sisters were missing from their congregation. Thirty acolytes were ushered into the lightless barn and told to sit on that thick carpet of straw covering the ground. Once they were settled, faces looking up blearily, the Goddess appeared in the entrance, backlit by the morning sky.

"The time is finally here, we have entered these last days of the prophecy. The Lord has brought my children into the light. He keeps them away from lovers of their own selves; the covetous, the boastful, the proud and the blasphemous. Sinners who, even now, perish for their impure lives."

Away from the doorway Stoker and Jones jogged between truck and building carrying plastic containers of dark liquid, the men placing these weighty receptacles at the side of the great barn.

"I am filled with immense joy. We have pleased Him with our devotion brothers and sisters. Together we created Newtopia, a truly revolutionary place of worship, isolated from the wickedness God sees across our planet. That continuous evil in the hearts of men who will never be saved."

Jones passed tools from the vehicle's front seat to his co-worker before hurrying off towards Gareth. The tattooed man helped this teenager as he struggled to carry bulging suitcases from the farmhouse.

Rebecka closed her eyes. "Oh my Jesus! I am no longer of this world! Hear my voice as they come to you!" She raised shaking arms heavenwards. "They are coming Holy Father. May the people rise again in your name!"

Ensuring the young man was safely in the back of the van, unaware of other activities as he settled down to read, Jones ran across to where Stoker crouched beside the containers and helped him unscrew the caps. On the other side of the barn Rebecka lowered her hands and studied *The Spirit Of Nagasaki* one final time.

"We treated each of you just as a father treats his own children. We encouraged you, we comforted you, and we kept urging you to live the life that pleases God. Well brothers and sisters, the time is here. Now comes the moment of discovery. I hope you have pleased Jesus with your ways."

The men returned to the doorway, Stoker and Jones flanking the Goddess in a square of light before the murky interior. The employees stared ahead, above those cross-legged followers, a hammer in each of their right hands.

"Remain peaceful and quiet, for the time of your Lord is here. Though I must leave you in the hands of destiny, do not forget; I am with you always. Even to the end of the world. Each of you is blessed, and my heart fills with love for all my children."

She took a step back, allowing the men to shut the barn door, gradually blocking out the light. Stoker pulled a handful of nails from his pocket and banged them into the upper sections of wood, Jones doing the same below. Rebecka strode to the van and opened the passenger door, talking in her normal voice with Gareth as she joined him inside. Dashing to the rear of the barn, Stoker picked up one of the containers and began drenching its exterior in petrol. Jones finished sealing the door and came over, clapping Stoker on the back before speaking. The younger employee revived briefly from his trance, aware enough now to be shocked by Glenn breaking his vow of silence after all this time.

"Good luck mate, alright? Get rid of the truck and phone us if you 'ave any trouble. I'll see you around."

Then he was gone and Stoker was the silent one now, refusing to be distracted from the task at hand, this final mission of the S.O.N. enterprise. Stoker pushed stray hair from his eyes and picked up two of the containers, running with them as fuel sloshed to the earth, spilling beside his shoes.

He was emptying the final litres onto more wooden sections of the barn when an engine sprang to life behind him, Jones launching the minibus back into the secular world. Kicking the receptacles against the sodden side of the barn, Stoker threw the black square of his mobile down there after them. Noises could be heard from within the structure now, yells and cursing. Stoker moved a few yards from the wall and lit a match. He watched the head burn for a few seconds before dropping it onto one of the accumulated pools of gasoline. Then Stoker turned, walking from the scene at an unhurried pace, the barn catching light then bursting into flames behind him.

The next step they had agreed was for him to get in the truck and drive off, motor far from this site. Instead Stoker chose to wander away from the vehicle, across ploughed fields and grassy plains. The brown eyes of this man were gigantic and blank in the winter sunlight, rivulets of sweat running down his face and back. Overhead a crow circled the farm, cawing shrilly as Stoker walked on, choosing a direction that led nowhere in particular, dazed and insensible as an amnesiac. As smoke billowed from the pyre blazing in his wake the man left the compound.

A first flight call could be heard through the airport. Rebecka sent Gareth to check in their suitcases while she joined the passenger queue. Her hand luggage was passed through the electronic checks before the teenager met up again with this woman, the pair called upon to show their passports. 'Anna Michaels' and 'Gareth Smale' gained admittance to the waiting area with barely a second glance. These were false names that had originally belonged to untraceable Liverpool babies, infants who each expired around the same time Rebecka and Gareth were born. Over the months Marsden had accumulated the paperwork to support these identities, beginning with birth certificates replacing those supposedly lost, then National Insurance numbers. She created bank accounts using nominal sums and finally received two passports in the middle of December. Worryingly, the photograph of Gareth depicted his former incarnation; short hair and a too-familiar face, but the tight-lipped official on duty barely registered the image of that innocent-looking lad, a naive boy who might have been the woman's nephew.

In the departure lounge Rebecka ignored her fellow travellers and eased into one of the foamy seats. Windows made up three vitreous walls surrounding them, Gareth stood opposite to observe the flights, his frame pushed close to the glass. The teenager was the only source of excitement in this place. Everyone else gave out a tangible air of weary anticipation, the sense those waiting to board had seen too many airports in their lifetimes. Rebecka flipped through *The Daily Class*, pausing over sections entitled *Woman* and *Style*, fashion spreads for the underweight and another gamine pop star confirming her bulimic tendencies. The tabloid reported this girl's "brave battle" with optimism, her family hopeful she would prevail, overcome this debilitating condition and regain her health. Rebecka sighed and turned the page. She had seen them all down the years, every kind of screwed up female, victims of that pervasive perfection on TV shows and billboards. They had all suffered, from the working girl who deliberately maintained her hunger because everything else was out of control, to the weight-conscious young mother who didn't feed her female baby well enough. From the failed student taking two-dozen laxatives a day so she would die thin, to the slimmers of the month who embraced the one-stone solution until their weight halved. The way of the S.O.N. helped some of these lost females for a while, but there was no real cure for that way of thinking. The girls she had known were better off with the quick death Rebecka's alter ego had granted them. The Goddess had been forced into playing Abraham, offering up a supreme sacrifice in return for divine asylum. Her children were fulsomely prepared for the next world, living their last months as earthly tourists awaiting permanent transcendence. That was the way it had to be. The transitory sadness of human life, its alienation and restraint, would always prove too much for such simple creatures

Airport workers stood aside, allowing the travellers to pass. Gareth's desired place first aboard was compromised as he paused beside these uniformed men, urging Rebecka to hurry up. She rose from her comfy chair and walked at a leisurely pace, unwilling to kowtow to the impatient eagerness of a silly boy. Together they descended onto the tarmac where the plane waited, one giant white arrow gleaming with potential.

When the barn door closed many of the followers rose and began to spread out, exploring the extremes of this sudden darkness. Jon got to his feet, eyesight adjusting to an interior only lit by two window-slits high on each side. Today's words from the Goddess bypassed Foulkes for the most part; he usually switched off whenever the Biblical talk started up. But Jon understood enough of the tone in her voice and the current situation to know why an alien entity was growing in his gut, pulsating with panic as it passed foreboding through his body. He watched the crowd disseminate, disciples making for the far reaches or converging in groups, a few snatches of conversation all but drowned out by banging from outside.

"...not up to us, I saw the..."

"..what do we do now?"

"She meant all this to happen, why we don't trust...."

"...can't stay here forever, where is..."

Foulkes tuned out this babble, wondering where Rebecka would go now, what had happened to Elliott, whether the past would flash before his eyes soon. Jon knew he should have been more suspicious, particularly during these last few days, all that running around after Rebecka in a manner similar to his efforts when S.O.N. began. The man had been asked to create investment accounts through his laptop, transfer the faith's offshore funds into an unfamiliar name, arrange for a sizeable cash sum to be available at Torminster bank for Jones and *Anna* to collect. At the time these developments were more a source of amusement than concern. Switching money away from the unsuspecting grasp of Douglas reminded Jon of old times, that conspiracy between him and the Goddess where Elliott played no part, was left the hapless victim. The cycle of this religion was approaching its end that much was clear. Rebecka was wise to have plenty of cash on standby for such a time as the base was abandoned. What Jon hadn't realized until this moment of entrapment was how he wasn't included in the getaway plans. Where once Foulkes might have felt betrayed and infuriated, distraught at ending this carefully prepared space with no way out, today it struck him as nothing more than absurd. For weeks he had been empty of all human emotion, and now Jon finally felt something he wasn't surprised to recognize it as mirth. Shock waves of hilarity doubled him up, laughter at the ridiculousness of it all, his surprise ending surrounded by perplexed devotees.

A rich odour filled the barn, liquid oozing through the gaps to darken straw lining the walls. Shivers of alarm cut through the confined space and several men tried to barge the door down. Nolan was one of them, kicking hay away as the group struggled to force their way out.

Near the back this insulation was arranged in heaps, dry material piled to a height of several feet. Pete helped Simon down and he rested in the soft substance. Thistlewood was pockmarked and weak, oblivious to everything but his own suffering. When the man flopped into the straw additional pain registered on his face, Simon's body jerking sideways. Pete moved him aside to see what was concealed beneath these dirty-yellow heaps, sucking at his broken tooth as he revealed a row of fuel cans.

The barricaded wood of the entrance was pummelled with fists and feet but Josh couldn't feel any progress. He abandoned these efforts and returned to the centre of the barn where Bree waited for him, the girl tiny and still amid this despairing effort, an expression of utter bewilderment on her face.

Apart from this throng Ruth stood with her arms outstretched, letting every language flow through her body. Schwitz welcomed Jesus with the sound of her voice, exultant cries from the depths of her trance mixing with the terrified hollers and screams for help.

Trina raced from her family to the door, the pregnant woman smashing at wood as Keith shouted for her. His grip on the cowering forms of Chastity and Niagara remained tight as the man called for his wife to come back.

The fuel was ignited from outside, creating a heat that burned through the straw, fire igniting the store of petroleum.

Most of those trapped inside were killed immediately. A fireball sent charred bodies to the burning floor.

The great orb of flame shot forward and up, unstoppable in its force. Nolan had enough time to recognize a familiar smell before he was reduced to meat, that acrid stench of burning flesh Charlie had endured once before.

Jon grabbed the arm of the woman beside him and flung Trina to a section of floor. He dived on her as the ball of fire hit them, shielding her pregnant body from the sudden force.

Flames raced up the walls and across the ceiling, smoke rushing out of the window-slits, a surge forming an enormous cloud to block out the sky.

Jon could feel the back of his body burning, this pain beyond excruciating. Underneath his peeling flesh Trina whimpered and sobbed, trying to keep herself small even as she recognized that everything was lost. Somewhere beyond this unimaginable agony, Jon asked why his last act should be a stab at heroism after a lifetime of such cowardice and lies. He wondered if the instinct was to protect the woman or her unborn child. Then the agony of his wounds became too much and Jon Foulkes lost consciousness.

Seconds passed, maybe minutes. The structure continued to incandesce, immolated corpses smouldering where they fell. Hay turned to ash in the heat that warped the wood of the barn, weakening man-made barriers.

Her hair was singed and some of Trina's extremities had been scorched by the flames, but her pain was bearable. This man on top of her wasn't about to move so she shifted Jon's weight, choking on the fumes that surrounded them. Trina's lungs demanded oxygen and the woman knew she was facing suffocation as harsh sounds began coming from somewhere above her head. The woman strained to listen. These noises were definitely outside. That could only mean someone was here to rescue her. Easing Jon off her torso, Trina moved up onto her knees and coughed out smoke. They were coming. She was going to make it. The Lord had saved them. Her baby would survive. How wondrous were His ways!

Trina's movement woke Jon from his blackout. Much to his surprise Foulkes wasn't dead, but the man could feel the reaper hovering over him. Every inch of skin was fire-blackened. No grafts would make him well now.

His blue eyes followed the action of the woman as she struggled to get up. With a crash of splinters the barn door flew inwards, releasing a cloud of smoke out into the world. Trina ran the few yards to the gap, thinking only of this imminent reprieve. In her relief the woman failed to hear Jon's garbled warning, neglecting to watch her step in her headlong dash. While the woman was trapped on the floor her clothing had absorbed some of the fuel, left the grey material horribly flammable. A few feet before the exit a patch of straw was still burning. When Trina trod on the flame it licked at her ankle, set fire to the bottom of her smock. Trina screamed and bolted for salvation, her whole body enveloped by the living glow of flame. Behind her the terribly burnt man inched forward, the fire in his path going unnoticed as it licked at his failing body.

Rebecka fingered the zipper of her valise, resisting a childish urge to unclasp the case and touch the bundles of banknotes inside, hidden there amongst underwear and toiletries. Next to her Gareth locked and unlocked his seat belt several times before skimming the in-flight magazines, the teenager quickly rejecting these glossies for a periodical of his own.

A stewardess appeared from the cabin and drew their attention to the airline's emergency procedures. She was a young girl, heavily made-up and not much more than Gareth's age. At a glance Rebecka would have concluded her to be exceptionally pretty, but what the girl actually looked like under all that eyeliner, lipstick, blusher and mascara was anybody's guess. Gareth was soon bewitched by her, removing his sunglasses to get a better look, so Rebecka reached across then and tapped him on the wrist. This movement, at once admonishing and intimate, made the boy replace his shades and move lower into his window seat. The woman beside him smiled with satisfaction. This evidence of her hold over him was explicit and gratifying.

She had learned that sex equalled power early on, having been awakened to her body at a young age. After the pain of that initial encounter subsided Rebecka Marsden took several lessons from it, realizing she ought to be the one to distribute or withhold favours, wresting control from those males in the battlefield of sexuality, her body wielded as both weapon and reward. Beyond the superficiality of technique and expertise, the secret to desirability lay not in what you had but how it was used. An old story perhaps, but this cliché wouldn't have stuck around were it not based on a truth. Every girl could become seductive when clad in finery and painted as a canvas. Even the personally contemptible or physically plain had the potential to be reconstructed from scratch, taught to magnetize the male libido through the dramatics of flirtation. Soon the men this creation turned on would fall for her charms. They were all clones of masculinity, each propelled by a single urge. Rebecka's business instincts enabled her to run the most popular whorehouse on the Mersey, and she knew this world was a woman's for the taking. Yet her attempts to convince the other girls only led to failure. Too many of the hookers were afflicted by some imposed morality or the spinelessness of *conscience* and *sensitivity*. None of them seemed able to use their God-given qualities, that raw sexuality and low cunning, and certainly not in the same ruthless manner as the males exercised their strengths. This timidity kept females in a state of dependency, she saw that. Rebecka vowed to level out this imbalance wherever she could. The woman grasped every opportunity that came her way without pusillanimity, her creed taking Marsden from her humble beginnings to mountainous riches, leaving nothing to regret. She had always expected her philosophy to leave casualties, of one kind or another.

The pilot announced their impending take-off, this man's voice giving a brief description of the weather into which they would be flying. Rebecka looked to her right, her teenage companion engrossed in an interview with Bogart and Bacall where the stars described their idyllic home life and generation spanning romance. Gareth was all hers now, an enamoured teenager and bargaining chip, a lover, hostage, pupil and surrogate son, her meal ticket if the money ran out. His family would be on hand to wire the youngster an allowance whenever he requested funds.

Rebecka Marsden studied his handsome features. Here was a fascinating example of youth's lack of reflection. Gareth rarely considering tomorrow, let alone the future. Her lover appeared unconcerned by the dissolution of his recent circumstances, untroubled at the prospect of a flight into the unknown. Such was the security of privilege she supposed. A result of growing up in the ancient system that operated to honour birthrights and keep royalty apart from the world. It wasn't much of a step for this prospective monarch to assume a false name and travel incognito. He was self-assured enough to believe the decisions of a prince could only be for the best. Yet for all this inherent superiority, Gareth had come to Rebecka a virgin. His confidence had failed to encompass things that were never mentioned by well-bred elders. The boy soon received a tutoring in the sexual, his teacher devoid of the expectancy shown by those star-struck young girls who threw themselves at some image of him. Rebecka mentored Gareth in the tinctures of eroticism, improved his performance without remonstration or harsh words, put no pressure on him to prove anything. Newtopia was the perfect backdrop to his initiation, the pair entwined where no servile staff could interrupt, a palace without the clicking of a telephoto lens. She made him a man and reaped her reward. The benefits of deference to royalty awaited this female fugitive, protection against her past, taxpayer money to replace the currency in her lap if she required it. There was no limit to the opulence of this life she would lead. Rebecka intended to indulge every fantasy, create dreams on earth, even build another Elysium if such an opportunity arose. All the possibilities of wealth were open to her.

Noises from the engine floated across the runway as their pilot began his final preparations. The pretty stewardess worked the aisle with a tray of complimentary drinks. Rebecka refused the offer of wine with a slight shake of the head while the boy made indecisive noises. Gareth touched his face nervously, hands pulling the sunglasses off, placing them on top of his head as the teenager looked over the refreshments this young lady offered. For an instant, as he removed the disguise, Rebecka thought she caught a flash of recognition in the hazel eyes of the stewardess. The moment left her heartbeat irregular, fear the overriding sensation for the first time Rebecka Marsden could remember.

Just as quickly the flicker of realization left the airline worker's face. Passing the requested cup of fruit drink to her attractive male passenger, the stewardess put unprofessional thoughts from her mind until her shift's end and moved on to the next row.